The Story of Charles Strange by Mrs Henry Wood

COMPLETE IN THREE VOLUMES

Ellen Price was born on 17th January 1814 in Worcester.

In 1836 she married Henry Wood, whose career in banking and shipping meant living in Dauphiné, in the South of France, for two decades. During their time there they had four children.

Henry's business collapsed and he and Ellen together with their four children returned to England and settled in Upper Norwood near London.

Ellen now turned to writing and with her second book 'East Lynne' enjoyed remarkable popularity. This enabled her to support her family and to maintain a literary career.

It was a career in which she would write over 30 novels including 'Danesbury House', 'Oswald Cray', 'Mrs. Halliburton's Troubles', 'The Channings' and 'The Shadow of Ashlydyat'.

Sadly, her husband, Henry died in 1866.

Ellen though continued to strive on. In 1867, she purchased the magazine 'Argosy', founded two years previously by Alexander Strahan. She was a prolific writer and wrote much of the magazine herself although she had some very respected contributors, amongst them Hesba Stretton and Christina Rossetti. Although she would gradually pare down writing for the magazine she continued to write novel after novel. Such was her talent that for a time she was, in Australia, more popular than Charles Dickens.

Apart from novels she was an excellent translator and a writer of short stories. 'Reality or Delusion?' is a staple of supernatural anthologies to this day.

Ellen Wood died of bronchitis on 10th February 1887. He estate was valued at a very considerable £36,000.

She is buried in Highgate Cemetery, London.

A monument to her in Worcester Cathedral was unveiled in 1916.

Index of Contents

VOLUME I

CHAPTER I

EARLY DAYS

I, Charles Strange, have called this my own story, and shall myself tell a portion of it to the reader; not all.

May was quickly passing. The drawing-room window of White Littleham Rectory stood open to the sunshine and the summer air: for the years of warm springs and long summers had not then left the land. The incumbent of the parish of White Littleham, in Hampshire, was the Reverend Eustace Strange. On a sofa, near the window, lay his wife, in her white dress and yellow silk shawl. A young and lovely lady, with a sweet countenance; her eyes the colour of blue-bells, her face growing more transparent day by day, her cheeks too often a fatal hectic; altogether looking so delicately fragile that the Rector must surely be blind not to suspect the truth. She suspected it. Nay, she no longer suspected; she knew. Perhaps it was that he would not do so.

"Charley!"

I sat at the end of the room in my little state chair, reading a new book of fairy tales that papa had given me that morning. He was as orthodox a divine as ever lived, but not strait-laced, and he liked children to read fairy tales. At the moment I was deep in a tale called "Finetta," about a young princess shut up in a high tower. To me it was enchanting.

"Yes, mamma."

"Come to me, dear."

Leaving the precious book behind me, I crossed the room to the sofa. My mother raised herself. Holding me to her with one hand, she pushed with the other the hair from my face and gazed into it. That my face was very much like hers, I knew. It had been said a hundred times in my hearing that I had her dark-blue eyes and her soft brown hair and her well-carved features.

"My pretty boy," she said caressingly, "I am so sorry! I fear you are disappointed. I think we might have had them. You were always promised a birthday party, you know, when you should be seven years old."

There had been some discussion about it. My mother thought the little boys and girls might come; but papa and Leah said, "No—it would fatigue her."

"I don't mind a bit, mamma," I answered. "I have my book, and it is so pretty. They can come next year, you know, when you are well again."

She sighed deeply. Getting up from the sofa, she took up two books that were on the stand behind her, and sat down again. Early in the spring some illness had seized her that I did not understand. She ought to have been well again by this time, but was not so. She left her room and came downstairs, and saw friends when they called: but instead of growing stronger she grew weaker.

"She was never robust, and it has been too much for her," I overheard Leah say to one of the other servants, in allusion to the illness.

"What if I should not be here at your next birthday, Charley?" she asked sadly, holding me to her side as she sat.

"But where should you be, mamma?"

"Well, my child, I think—sometimes I think—that by that time I may be in heaven."

I felt suddenly seized with a sort of shivering. I neither spoke nor cried; at seven years old many a child only imperfectly realizes the full meaning of anything like this. My eyes became misty.

"Don't cry, Charley. All that God does must be for the best, you know: and heaven is a better world than this."

"Oh, mamma, you must get well; you must!" I cried, words and tears bursting forth together. "Won't you come out, and grow strong in the sunshine? See how warm and bright it is! Look at the flowers in the grass!"

"Ay, dear; it is all very bright and warm and beautiful," she said, looking across the garden to the field beyond it. "The grass is growing long, and the buttercups and cowslips and blue-bells are all there. Soon they will be cut down and the field will be bare. Next year the grass and the flowers will spring up again, Charlie: but we, once we are taken, will spring up no more in this world: only in heaven."

"But don't you think you will get well, mamma? Can't you try to?"

"Well, dear—yes, I will try to do so. I have tried. I am trying every day, Charley, for I should not like to go away and leave my little boy."

With a long sigh, that it seemed to me I often heard from her now, she lay for a moment with her head on the back of the sofa and closed her eyes. Then she sat forward again, and took up one of the books.

"I meant to give you a little book to-day, Charley, as well as papa. Look, it is called 'Sintram.' A lady gave it me when I was twelve years old; and I have always liked it. You are too young to understand it yet, but you will do so later."

"Here's some poetry!" I cried, turning the leaves over. The pleasure of the gift had chased away my tears. Young minds are impressionable—and had she not just said she would try to get well?

"I will repeat it to you, Charley," she answered. "Listen."

"Repeat it?" I interrupted. "Do you know it by heart?—all?"

"Yes, all; every line of it.

"'When death is drawing near,
And thy heart sinks with fear,
And thy limbs fail,
Then raise thy hands and pray
To Him who cheers the way,
Through the dark vale.

"'See'st thou the eastern dawn?
Hear'st thou, in the red morn,
The angels' song?
Oh! lift thy drooping head,
Thou who in gloom and dread

Hast lain so long.

"'Death comes to set thee free;
Oh! meet him cheerily,
As thy true friend;
And all thy fears shall cease,
And in eternal peace
Thy penance end.'

You see, Charley, death comes not as a foe, but as a friend to those who have learnt to look for him, for he is sent by God," she continued in a loving voice as she smoothed back my hair with her gentle hand. "I want you to learn this bit of poetry by heart, and to say it sometimes to yourself in future years. And—and—should mamma have gone away, then it will be pleasant to you to remember that the angels' song came to cheer her—as I know it will come—when she was setting out on her journey. Oh! very pleasant! and the same song and the same angel will cheer your departure, my darling child, when the appointed hour for it shall come to you."

"Shall we see the angel?"

"Well—yes—with the eye of faith. And it is said that some good people have really seen him; have seen the radiant messenger who has come to take them to the eternal shores. You will learn it, Charley, won't you—and never forget it?"

"I'll learn it all, every verse; and I will never forget it, mamma."

"I am going to give you this book, also, Charley," she went on, bringing forward the other. "You—"

"Why, that's your Bible, mamma!"

"Yes, dear, it is my Bible; but I should like it to be yours. And I hope it will be as good a friend to you as it is now to me. I shall still use it myself, Charley, for a little while. You will lend it me, won't you? and later, it will be all your own."

"Shall you buy another for yourself, then?"

She did not answer. Her face was turned to the window; her yearning eyes were fixed in thought upon the blue sky; her hot hands were holding mine. In a moment, to my consternation, she bent her face upon mine and burst into a flood of tears. What I should have said or done, I know not; but at that moment my father came swiftly out of his study, into the room. He was a rather tall man with a pale, grave face, very much older than his wife.

"Do you chance to remember, Lucy, where that catalogue of books was put that came last week? I want—"

Thus far had he spoken, when he saw the state of things; both crying together. He broke off in vexation.

"How can you be so silly, Lucy—so imprudent! I will not have it. You don't allow yourself a chance to get well—giving way to these low spirits! What is the matter?"

"It is nothing," she replied, with another of those long sighs. "I was talking a little to Charley, and a fit of crying came on. It has not harmed me, Eustace."

"Charley, boy, I saw some fresh sweet violets down in the dingle this morning. Go you and pick some for mamma," he said. "Never mind your hat: it is as warm as midsummer."

I was ready for the dingle, which was only across the field, and to pick violets at any time, and I ran out. Leah Williams was coming in at the garden gate.

"Now, Master Charles! Where are you off to? And without your hat!"

"I'm going to the dingle, to get some fresh violets for mamma. Papa said my hat did not matter."

"Oh," said Leah, glancing doubtfully at the window. I glanced too. He had sat down on the sofa by mamma then, and was talking to her earnestly, his head bent. She had her handkerchief up to her face. Leah attacked me again.

"You've been crying, you naughty boy! Your eyes are wet still. What was that for?"

I did not say what: though I had much ado to keep the tears from falling. "Leah," I whispered, "do you think mamma will get well?"

"Bless the child!" she exclaimed, after a pause, during which she had looked again at the window and back at me. "Why, what's to hinder it?—with all this fine, beautiful warm weather! Don't you turn fanciful, Master Charley, there's a darling! And when you've picked the violets, you come to me; I'll find a slice of cake for you."

Leah had been with us about two years, as upper servant, attending upon mamma and me, and doing the sewing. She was between twenty and thirty then, an upright, superior young woman, kind in the main, though with rather a hard face, and faithful as the day. The other servants called her Mrs. Williams, for she had been married and was a widow. Not tall, she yet looked so, she was so remarkably thin. Her gray eyes were deep-set, her curls were black, and she had a high, fresh colour. Everyone, gentle and simple, wore curls at that time.

The violets were there in the dingle, sure enough; both blue and white. I picked a handful, ran in with them, and put them on my mother's lap. The Rector was sitting by her still, but he got up then.

"Oh, Charley, they are very sweet," she said with a smile—"very sweet and lovely. Thank you, my precious boy, my darling."

She kissed me a hundred times. She might have kissed me a hundred more, but papa drew me away.

"Do not tire yourself any more to-day, Lucy; it is not good for you. Charley, boy, you can take your fairy tales and show them to Leah."

The day of the funeral will never fade from my memory; and yet I can only recall some of its incidents. What impressed me most was that papa did not stand at the grave in his surplice reading the service, as I had seen him do at other funerals. Another clergyman was in his place, and he stood by me in silence, holding my hand. And he told me, after we returned home, that mamma was not herself in the cold dark grave, but a happy angel in heaven looking down upon me.

And so the time went on. Papa was more grave than of yore, and taught me my lessons daily. Leah indulged and scolded me alternately, often sang to me, for she had a clear voice, and when she was in a good humour would let me read "Sintram" and the fairy tales to her.

The interest of mamma's money—which was now mine—brought in three hundred a year. She had enjoyed it all; I was to have (or, rather, my father for me) just as much of it as the two trustees chose to allow, for it was strictly tied up in their hands. When I was twenty-four years of age—not before—the duties of the trustees would cease, and the whole sum, six thousand pounds, would come into my uncontrolled possession. One of the trustees was my mother's uncle, Mr. Serjeant Stillingfar; the other I did not know. Of course the reader will understand that I do not explain these matters from my knowledge at that time; but from what I learnt when I was older.

Nearly a year had gone by, and it was warm spring weather again. I sat in my brown-holland dress in the dingle amidst the wild flowers. A lot of cowslips lay about me; I had been picking the flowers from the stalks to make into a ball. The sunlight flickered through the trees, still in their tender green; the sky was blue and cloudless. My straw hat, with broad black ribbons, had fallen off; my white socks and shoes were stretched out before me. Fashion is always in extremes. Then it was the custom to dress a child simply up to quite an advanced age.

Why it should have been so, I know not; but while I sat, there came over me a sudden remembrance of the day when I had come to the dingle to pick those violets for mamma, and a rush of tears came on. Leah took good care of me, but she was not my mother. My father was good, and grave, and kind, but he did not give me the love that she had given. A mother's love would never be mine again, and I knew it; and in that moment was bitterly feeling it.

One end of the string was held between my teeth, the other end in my left hand, and my eyes were wet with tears. I strung the cowslips as well as I could. But it was not easy, and I made little progress.

"S'all I hold it for oo?"

Lifting my eyes in surprise—for I had thought the movement in the dingle was only Leah, coming to see after me—there stood the sweetest fairy of a child before me. The sleeves of her cotton frock and white pinafore were tied up with black ribbons; her face was delicately fair, her eyes were blue as the sky, and her light curls fell low on her pretty neck. My child heart went out to her with a bound, then and there.

"What oo trying for, 'ittle boy?"

"I was crying for mamma. She's gone away from me to heaven."

"S'all I tiss oo?"

And she put her little arms round my neck, without waiting for permission, and gave me a dozen kisses.

"Now we make the ball, 'ittle boy. S'all oo dive it to me?"

"Yes, I will give it to you. What is your name?"

"Baby. What is oors?"

"Charles. Do you—"

"You little toad of a monkey!—giving me this hunt! How came you to run away?"

The words were spoken by a tall, handsome boy, quite old compared with me, who had come dashing through the dingle. He caught up the child and began kissing her fondly. So the words were not meant to hurt her.

"It was oo ran away, Tom."

"But I ordered you to stop where I left you—and to sit still till I came back again. If you run away by yourself in the wood, you'll meet a great bear some day and he'll eat you up. Mind that, Miss Blanche. The mamsie is in a fine way; thinks you're lost, you silly little thing."

"Dat 'towslip ball for me, Tom."

Master Tom condescended to turn his attention upon me and the ball. I guessed now who they were: a family named Heriot, who had recently come to live at the pretty white cottage on the other side the copse. Tom was looking at me with his fine dark eyes.

"You are the parson's son, I take it, youngster. I saw you in the parson's pew on Sunday with an old woman."

"She is not an old woman," I said, jealous for Leah.

"A young one, then. What's your name?"

"Charles Strange."

"He dot no mamma, he try for her," put in the child. "Oo come to my mamma, ittle boy; she love oo and tiss oo."

"When I have made your ball."

"Oh, bother the ball!" put in Tom. "We can't wait for that: the mamsie's in a rare way already. You can come home with us if you like, youngster, and finish your ball afterwards."

Leaving the cowslips, I caught up my hat and we started, Tom carrying the child. I was a timid, sensitive little fellow, but took courage to ask him a question.

"Is your name Tom Heriot?"

"Well, yes, it is Tom Heriot—if it does you any good to know it. And this is Miss Blanche Heriot. And I wish you were a bit bigger and older; I'd make you my playfellow."

We were through the copse in a minute or two and in sight of the white cottage, over the field beyond it. Mrs. Heriot stood at the garden gate, looking out. She was a pretty little plump woman, with a soft voice, and wore a widow's cap. A servant in a check apron was with her, and knew me. Mrs. Heriot scolded Blanche for running away from Tom while she caressed her, and turned to smile at me.

"It is little Master Strange," I heard the maid say to her. "He lost his mother a year ago."

"Oh, poor little fellow!" sighed Mrs. Heriot, as she held me before her and kissed me twice. "What a nice little lad it is!—what lovely eyes! My dear, you can come here whenever you like, and play with Tom and Blanche."

Some few years before, this lady had married Colonel Heriot, a widower with one little boy—Thomas. After that, Blanche was born: so that she and Tom were, you see, only half-brother-and sister. When Blanche was two years old—she was three now—Colonel Heriot died, and Mrs. Heriot had come into the country to economize. She was not at all well off; had, indeed, little beyond what was allowed her with the two children: all their father's fortune had lapsed to them, and she had no control over it. Tom had more than Blanche, and was to be brought up for a soldier.

As we stood in a group outside the gate, papa came by. Seeing me, he naturally stopped, took off his hat to Mrs. Heriot, and spoke. That is how the acquaintanceship began, without formal introduction on either side. Taking the pretty little girl in his arms, he began talking to her: for he was very fond of children. Mrs. Heriot said something to him in a low, feeling tone about his wife's death.

"Yes," he sighed in answer, as he put down the child: "I shall never recover her loss. I live only in the hope of rejoining her THERE."

He glanced up at the blue sky: the pure, calm, peaceful canopy of heaven.

CHAPTER II

CHANGES

"I shall never recover her loss. I live only in the hope of rejoining her THERE."

It has been said that the vows of lovers are ephemeral as characters written on the sand of the sea-shore. Surely may this also be said of the regrets mourners give to the departed! For time has a habit of soothing the deepest sorrow; and the remembrance which is piercing our hearts so poignantly to-day in a few short months will have lost its sting.

My father was quite sincere when speaking the above words: meant and believed them to the very letter. Yet before the spring and summer flowers had given place to those of autumn, he had taken unto himself another wife: Mrs. Heriot.

The first intimation of what was in contemplation came to me from Leah. I had offended her one day; done something wrong, or not done something right; and she fell upon me with a stern reproach, especially accusing me of ingratitude.

"After all my care of you, Master Charles—my anxiety and trouble to keep your clothes nice and make you good! What shall you do when I have gone away?"

"But you are not going away, Leah."

"I don't know that. We are to have changes here, it seems, and I'm not sure that they will suit me."

"What changes?" I asked.

She sat at the nursery window, which had the same aspect as the drawing-room below, darning my socks; I knelt on a chair, looking out. It was a rainy day, and the drops pattered thickly against the panes.

"Well, there's going to be—some company in the house," said Leah, taking her own time to answer me. "A lot of them. And I think perhaps there'll be no room for me."

"Oh, yes there will. Who is it, Leah?"

"I shouldn't wonder but it's those people over yonder," pointing her long darning-needle in the direction of the dingle.

"There's nothing there but mosses and trees, Leah. No people."

"There is a little farther off," nodded Leah. "There's Mrs. Heriot and her two children."

"Oh, do you say they are coming here!—do you mean it?" I cried in ecstasy. "Are they coming for a long visit, Leah?—to have breakfast here, and dine and sleep? Oh, how glad I am!"

"Ah!" groaned Leah; "perhaps you may be glad just at first; you are but a little shallow-sensed boy, Charley: but it may turn out for better, or it may turn out for worse."

To my intense astonishment, she dropped her work, burst into tears, and threw her hands up to her face. I felt very uncomfortable.

"What is it, Leah?"

"Well, it is that I'm a silly," she answered, looking up and drying her eyes. "I got thinking of the past, Master Charley, of your dear mamma, and all that. It is solitary for you here, and perhaps you'll be happier with some playfellows."

I went on staring at her.

"And look here, Master Charles, don't repeat what I've said; not to anybody, mind; or perhaps they won't come at all," concluded Leah, administering a slight shaking by way of enforcing her command.

There came a day—it was in that same week—when everything seemed to go wrong, as far as I was concerned. I had been at warfare with Leah in the morning, and was so inattentive (I suppose) at lessons in the afternoon that papa scolded me, and gave me an extra Latin exercise to do when they were over, and shut me up in the study until it was done. Then Leah refused jam for tea, which I wanted; saying that jam was meant for good boys, not for naughty ones. Altogether I was in anything but an enviable mood when I went out later into the garden. The most cruel item in the whole was that I could not see I had been to blame, but thought everyone else was. The sun had set behind the trees of the dingle in a red ball of fire as I climbed into my favourite seat—the fork of the pear-tree. Papa had gone to attend a vestry meeting; the little bell of the church was tinkling out, giving notice of the meeting to the parish.

Presently the bell ceased; solitary silence ensued both to eye and ear. The brightness of the atmosphere was giving place to the shades of approaching evening; the trees were putting on their melancholy. I have always thought—I always shall think—that nothing can be more depressing than the indescribable melancholy which trees in a solitary spot seem to put on after sunset. All people do not feel this; but to those who, like myself, see it, it brings a sensation of loneliness, nay, of awe, that is strangely painful.

"Ho-ho! So you are up there again, young Charley!"

The garden-gate had swung back to admit Tom Heriot. In hastening down from the tree—for he had a way of tormenting me when in it—I somehow lost my balance and fell on to the grass. Tom shrieked out with laughter, and made off again.

The fall was nothing—though my ankle ached; but at these untoward moments a little smart causes a great pain. It seemed to me that I was smarting all over, inside and out, mentally and bodily; and I sat down on the bench near the bed of shrubs, and burst into tears.

Sweet shrubs were they. Lavender and rosemary, old-man and sweet-briar, marjoram and lemon-thyme, musk and verbena; and others, no doubt. Mamma had had them all planted there. She would sit with me where I was now sitting alone, under the syringa trees, and revel in the perfume. In spring-time those sweet syringa blossoms would surround us; she loved their scent better than any other. Bitterly I cried, thinking of all this, and of her.

Again the gate opened, more gently this time, and Mrs. Heriot came in looking round. "Thomas," she called out—and then she saw me. "Charley, dear, has Tom been here? He ran away from me.—Why, my dear little boy, what is the matter?" For she had seen the tears falling.

They fell faster than ever at the question. She came up, sat down on the bench, and drew my face lovingly to her. I thought then—I think still—that Mrs. Heriot was one of the kindest, gentlest women that ever breathed. I don't believe she ever in her whole life said a sharp word to anyone.

Not liking to tell of my naughtiness—which I still attributed to others—or of the ignominious fall from the pear-tree, I sobbed forth something about mamma.

"If she had not gone away and left me alone," I said, "I should never have been unhappy, or—or cried. People were not cross with me when she was here."

"My darling, I know how lonely it is for you. Would you like me to come here and be your mamma?" she caressingly whispered.

"You could not be that," I dissented. "Mamma's up there."

Mrs. Heriot glanced up at the evening sky. "Yes, Charley, she is up there, with God; and she looks down, I feel sure, at you, and at what is being done for you. If I came home here I should try to take care of you as she would have done. And oh, my child, I should love you dearly."

"In her place?" I asked, feeling puzzled.

"In her place, Charley. For her."

Tom burst in at the gate again. He began telling his stepmother of my fall as he danced a war-dance on the grass, and asked me how many of my legs and wings were broken.

They came to the Rectory: Mrs. Heriot—she was Mrs. Strange then—and Tom and Baby. After all, Leah did not leave. She grew reconciled to the new state of things in no time, and became as fond of the children as she was of me. As fond, at least, of Tom. I don't know that she ever cared heartily for Blanche: the little lady had a haughty face, and sometimes a haughty way with her.

We were all as happy as the day was long. Mrs. Strange indulged us all. Tom was a dreadful pickle—it was what the servants called him; but they all adored him. He was a handsome, generous, reckless boy, two years older than myself in years, twice two in height and advancement. He teased Leah's life out of her; but the more he teased, the better she liked him. He teased Blanche, he teased me; though he would have gone through fire and water for either of us, ay, and laid down his life any moment to save ours. He was everlastingly in mischief indoors or out. He called papa "sir" to his face, "the parson" or "his reverence" behind his back. There was no taming Tom Heriot.

For a short time papa took Tom's lessons with mine. But he found it would not answer. Tom's guardians wrote to beg of the Rector to continue to undertake him for a year or two, offering a handsome recompense in return. But my father wrote word back that the lad needed the discipline of school and must have it. So to school Tom was sent. He came home in the holidays, reckless and random, generous and loving as ever, and we had fine times together, the three of us growing up like brothers and sister. Of course, I was not related to them at all: and they were only half related to each other.

Rather singularly, Thomas Heriot's fortune was just as much as mine: six thousand pounds: and left in very much the same way. The interest, three hundred a year, was to maintain and educate him for the army; and he would come into the whole when he was twenty-one. Blanche had less: four thousand pounds only, and it was secured in the same way as Tom's was until she should be twenty-one, or until she married.

And thus about a couple of years went on.

No household was ever less given to superstition than ours at White Littleham Rectory. It never as much as entered the mind of any of its inmates, from its master downwards. And perhaps it was this complete indifference to and disbelief in the supernatural that caused the matter to be openly spoken of by the Rector. I have since thought so.

It was Christmas-tide, and Christmas weather. Frost and snow covered the ground. Icicles on the branches glittered in the sunshine like diamonds.

"It is the jolliest day!" exclaimed Tom, dashing into the breakfast-room from an early morning run half over the parish. "People are slipping about like mad, and the ice is inches thick on the ponds. Old Joe Styles went right down on his back."

"I hope he was not hurt, Tom," remarked papa, coming down from his chamber into the room in time to hear the last sentence. "Good-morning, my boys."

"Oh, it was only a Christmas gambol, sir," said Tom carelessly.

We sat down to breakfast. Leah came in to see to me and Tom. The Rector might be—and was—efficient in his parish and pulpit, but a more hopelessly incapable man in a domestic point of view the world never saw. Tom and I should have come badly off had we relied upon him to help us, and we might have gobbled up every earthly thing on the table without his saying yea or nay. Leah, knowing this, stood to pour out the coffee. Mrs. Strange had gone away to London on Wednesday (the day after Christmas Day) to see an old aunt who was ill, and had taken Blanche with her. This was Friday, and they were expected home again on the morrow.

Presently Tom, who was observant in his way, remarked that papa was taking nothing. His coffee stood before him untouched; some bacon lay neglected on his plate.

"Shall I cut you some thin bread and butter, sir?" asked Leah.

"Presently," said he, and went on doing nothing as before.

"What are you thinking of, papa?"

"Well, Charley, I—I was thinking of my dream," he answered. "I suppose it was a dream," he went on, as if to himself. "But it was a curious one."

"Oh, please tell it us!" I cried. "I dreamt on Christmas night that I had a splendid plum-cake, and was cutting it up into slices."

"Well—it was towards morning," he said, still speaking in a dreamy sort of way, his eyes looking straight out before him as if he were recalling it, yet evidently seeing nothing. "I awoke suddenly with the sound of a voice in my ear. It was your mamma's voice, Charley; your own mother's; and she seemed to be standing at my bedside. 'I am coming for you,' she said to me—or seemed to say. I was wide awake in a moment, and knew her voice perfectly. Curious, was it not, Leah?"

Leah, cutting bread and butter for Tom, had halted, loaf in one hand, knife in the other.

"Yes, sir," she answered, gazing at the Rector. "Did you see anything, sir?"

"No; not exactly," he returned. "I was conscious that whoever spoke to me, stood close to my bedside; and I was also conscious that the figure retreated across the room towards the window. I cannot say that I absolutely saw the movement; it was more like some unseen presence in the room. It was very odd. Somehow I can't get it out of my head— Why, here's Mr. Penthorn!" he broke off to say.

Mr. Penthorn had opened the gate, and was walking briskly up the path. He was our doctor; a gray-haired man, active and lively, and very friendly with us all. He had looked in, in passing back to the village, to tell the Rector that a parishioner, to whom he had been called up in the night, was in danger.

"I'll go and see her," said papa. "You'd be none the worse for a cup of coffee, Penthorn. It is sharp weather."

"Well, perhaps I shouldn't," said he, sitting down by me, while Tom went off to the kitchen for a cup and saucer. "Sharp enough—but seasonable. Is anything amiss with you, Leah? Indigestion again?"

This caused us to look at Leah. She was whiter than the table-cloth.

"No, sir; I'm all right," answered Leah, as she took the cup from Tom's hand and began to fill it with coffee and hot milk. "Something that the master has been telling us scared me a bit at the moment, that's all."

"And what was that?" asked the Doctor lightly.

So the story had to be gone over again, papa repeating it rather more elaborately. Mr. Penthorn was sceptical, and said it was a dream.

"I have just called it a dream," assented my father. "But, in one sense, it was certainly not a dream. I had not been dreaming at all, to my knowledge; have not the least recollection of doing so. I woke up fully in a moment, with the voice ringing in my ears."

"The voice must have been pure fancy," declared Mr. Penthorn.

"That it certainly was not," said the Rector. "I never heard a voice more plainly in my life; every tone, every word was distinct and clear. No, Penthorn; that someone spoke to me is certain; the puzzle is— who was it?"

"Someone must have got into your room, then," said the Doctor, throwing his eyes suspiciously across the table at Tom.

Leah turned sharply round to face Tom. "Master Tom, if you played this trick, say so," she cried, her voice trembling.

"I! that's good!" retorted Tom, as earnestly as he could speak. "I never got out of bed from the time I got into it. Wasn't likely to. I never woke up at all."

"It was not Tom," interposed papa. "How could Tom assume my late wife's voice? It was her voice, Penthorn. I had never heard it since she left us; and it has brought back all its familiar tones to my memory."

The Doctor helped himself to some bread and butter, and gave his head a shake.

"Besides," resumed the Rector, "no one else ever addressed me as she did—'Eustace.' I have not been called Eustace since my mother died, many years ago, except by her. My present wife has never called me by it."

That was true. Mrs. Strange had a pet name for him, and it was "Hubby."

"'I am coming for you, Eustace,' said the voice. It was her voice; her way of speaking. I can't account for it at all, Penthorn. I can't get it out of my head, though it sounds altogether so ridiculous."

"Well, I give it up," said Mr. Penthorn, finishing his coffee. "If you were awake, Strange, someone must have been essaying a little sleight-of-hand upon you. Good-morning, all of you; I must be off to my patients. Tom Heriot, don't you get trying the ponds yet, or maybe I shall have you on my hands as well as other people."

We gave it up also: and nothing more was said or thought of it, as far as I know. We were not, I repeat, a superstitious family. Papa went about his duties as usual, and Leah went about hers. The next day, Saturday, Mrs. Strange and Blanche returned home; and the cold grew sharper and the frozen ponds were lovely.

On Monday afternoon, the last day of the year, the Rector mounted old Dobbin, to ride to the next parish. He had to take a funeral for the incumbent, who was in bed with gout.

"Have his shoes been roughed?" asked Tom, standing at the gate with me to watch the start.

"Yes; and well roughed too, Master Tom," spoke up James, who had lived with us longer than I could remember, as gardener, groom, and general man-of-all-work. "'Tisn't weather, sir, to send him out without being rough-shod."

"You two boys had better get to your Latin for an hour, and prepare it for me for to-morrow; and afterwards you may go to the ponds," said my father, as he rode away. "Good-bye, lads. Take care of yourself, Charley."

"Bother Latin!" said Tom. "I'm going off now. Will you come, youngster?"

"Not till I've done my Latin."

"You senseless young donkey! Stay, though; I must tell the mamsie something."

He made for the dining-room, where Mrs. Strange sat with Blanche. "Look here, mamsie," said he; "let us have a bit of a party to-night."

"A party, Tom!" she returned.

"Just the young Penthorns and the Clints."

"Oh, do, mamma!" I cried, for I was uncommonly fond of parties. And "Do, mamma!" struck in little Blanche.

My new mother rarely denied us anything; but she hesitated now.

"I think not to-night, dears. You know we are going to have the school-treat tomorrow evening, and the servants are busy with the cakes and things. They shall come on Wednesday instead, Tom."

Tom laughed. "They must come to-night, mamsie. They are coming. I have asked them."

"What—the young Penthorns?"

"And the young Clints," said Tom, clasping his stepmother, and kissing her. "They'll be here on the stroke of five. Mind you treat us to plenty of tarts and cakes, there's a good mamsie!"

Tom went off with his skates. I got to my books. After that, some friends came to call, and the afternoon seemed to pass in no time.

"It is hardly worth while your going to the ponds now, Master Charles," said Leah, meeting me in the passage, when I was at last at liberty.

In looking back I think that I must have had a very obedient nature, for I was ever willing to listen to orders or suggestions, however unpalatable they might be. Passing through the back-door, the nearest way to the square pond, to which Tom had gone, I looked out. Twilight was already setting in. The evening star twinkled in a clear, frosty sky. The moon shone like a silver shield.

"Before you could get to the square pond, Master Charley, it would be dark," said Leah, as she stood beside me.

"So it would," I assented. "I think I'll not go, Leah."

"And I'm sure you don't need to tire yourself for to-night," went on Leah. "There'll be romping enough and to spare if those boys and girls come."

I went back to the parlour. Leah walked to the side gate, wondering (as she said afterwards) what had come to the milkman, for he was generally much earlier. As she stood looking down the lane, she saw Tom stealing up.

"He has been in some mischief," decided Leah. "It's not like him to creep up in that timorous fashion. Good patience! Why, the lad must have had a fright; his face is white as death."

"Leah!" said the boy, shrinking as he glanced over his shoulder. "Leah!"

"Well, what on earth is it?" asked Leah, feeling a little dread herself. "What have you been up to at that pond? You've not been in it yourself, I suppose!"

"Papa—the parson—is lying in the road by the triangle, all pale and still. He does not move."

Whenever Master Tom Heriot saw a chance of scaring the kitchen with a fable, he plunged into one. Leah peered at him doubtfully in the fading light.

"I think he is dead. I'm sure he is," continued Tom, bursting into tears.

This convinced Leah. She uttered a faint cry.

"We took that way back from the square pond; I, and Joe and Bertie Penthorn. They were going home to get ready to come here. Then we saw something lying near the triangle, close to that heap of flint-stones. It was him, Leah. Oh! what is to be done? I can't tell mamma, or poor Charley."

James ran up, all scared, as Tom finished speaking. He had found Dobbin at the stable-door, without sign or token of his master.

Even yet I cannot bear to think of that dreadful night. We had to be told, you see; and Leah lost no time over it. While Tom came home with the news, Joe Penthorn had run for his father, and Bertie called to some labourers who were passing on the other side of the triangle.

He was brought home on a litter, the men carrying it, Mr. Penthorn walking by its side. He was not dead, but quite unconscious. They put a mattress on the study-table, and laid him on it.

He had been riding home from the funeral. Whether Dobbin, usually so sure-footed and steady, had plunged his foot into a rut, just glazed over by the ice, and so had stumbled; or whether something had startled him and caused him to swerve, we never knew. The Rector had been thrown violently, his head striking the stones.

Mr. Penthorn did not leave the study. Two other surgeons, summoned in haste from the neighbouring town, joined him. They could do nothing for papa—nothing. He never recovered consciousness, and died during the night—about a quarter before three o'clock.

"I knew he would go just at this time, sir," whispered Leah to Mr. Penthorn as he was leaving the house and she opened the front-door for him. "I felt sure of it when the doctors said he would not see morning light. It was just at the same hour that he had his call, sir, three nights ago. As sure as that he is now lying there dead, as sure as that those stars are shining in the heavens above us, that was his warning."

"Nonsense, Leah!" reproved Mr. Penthorn sharply.

Chances and changes. The world is full of them. A short time and White Littleham Rectory knew us no more. The Reverend Eustace Strange was sleeping his last sleep in the churchyard by his wife's side, and the Reverend John Ravensworth was the new Rector.

Tom Heriot went back to school. I was placed at one chosen for me by my great-uncle, Mr. Serjeant Stillingfar. Leah Williams left us to take service in another family, who were about to settle somewhere on the Continent. She could not speak for emotion when she said good-bye to me.

"It must be for years, Master Charles, and it may be for ever," she said, taking, I fancy, the words from one of the many favourite ditties, martial or love-lorn, she treated us to in the nursery. "No, we may never meet again in this life, Master Charles. All the same, I hope we shall."

And meet we did, though not for years and years. And it would no doubt have called forth indignation from Leah had I been able to foretell how, when that meeting came in after-life, she would purposely withhold her identity from me and pass herself off as a stranger.

Mrs. Strange went to London, Blanche with her, to take up for the present her abode with her old aunt, who had invited her to do so. She was little, if any, better off in this second widowhood than she had been as the widow of Colonel Heriot. What papa had to leave he left to her; but it was not much. I had my own mother's money. And so we were all separated again; all divided: one here, another there, a third elsewhere. It is the way of the world. Change and chance! chance and change!

CHAPTER III

MR SERJEANT STILLINGFAR

Gloucester Place, Portman Square. In one of its handsome houses—as they are considered to be by persons of moderate desires—dwelt its owner, Major Carlen. Major Carlen was a man of the world; a man of fashion. When the house had fallen to him some years before by the will of a relative, with a substantial sum of money to keep it up, he professed to despise the house to his brother-officers and other acquaintants of the great world. He would have preferred a house in Belgrave Square, or in Grosvenor Place, or in Park Lane. Major Carlen was accustomed to speak largely; it was his way.

Since then, he had retired from the army, and was master of himself, his time and his amusements. Major Carlen was fond of clubs, fond of card-playing, fond of dinners; fond, indeed, of whatever constitutes fast life. His house in Gloucester Place was handsomely furnished, replete with comfort, and possessed every reasonable requisite for social happiness—even to a wife. And Major Carlen's wife was Jessy, once Mrs. Strange, once Mrs. Heriot.

It is quite a problem why some women cannot marry at all, try to do so as they may, whilst others become wives three and four times over, and without much seeking of their own. Mrs. Heriot (to give her her first name) was one of these. In very little more than a year after her first husband died, she married her second; in not any more than a year after her second husband's death, she married her third. Major Carlen must have been captivated by her pretty face and purring manner; whilst she fell prone at the feet of the man of fashion, and perhaps a very little at the prospect of being mistress of the house in Gloucester Place. Anyway, the why and the wherefore lay between themselves. Mrs. Strange became Mrs. Carlen.

Reading over thus far, it has struck me that you may reasonably think the story is to consist chiefly of marrying and dying; for there has been an undue proportion of both events. Not so: as you will find as you go on. Our ancestors do marry and die, you know: and these first three chapters are only a prologue to the story which has to come.

Christmas has come round again. Not the Christmas following that which ended so disastrously for us at White Littleham Rectory, but one five years later. For the stream of time flows on its course, and boys and girls grow insensibly towards men and women.

It had been a green Christmas this year. We were now some days past it. The air was mild, the skies were blue and genial. Newspapers told of violets and other flowers growing in nooks, sheltered and unsheltered. Mrs. Carlen, seated by a well-spread table, half dinner, half tea, in the dining-room at Gloucester Place, declared that the fire made the room too warm. I was reading. Blanche, a very fair and pretty girl, now ten years old, sat on a stool on the hearthrug, her light curls tied back with blue ribbons, her hands lying idly on the lap of her short silk frock. We were awaiting an arrival.

"Listen, Charles!" cried mamma—as I called her still. "I do think a cab is stopping."

I put down my book, and Blanche threw back her head and her blue ribbons in expectation. But the cab went on.

"It is just like Tom!" smiled Mrs. Carlen. "Nothing ever put him out as it does other people. He gives us one hour and means another. He said seven o'clock, so we may expect him at ten. I do wish he could have obtained leave for Christmas Day!"

Major Carlen did not like children, boys especially: yet Tom Heriot and I had been allowed to spend our holidays at his house, summer and winter. Mrs. Carlen stood partly in the light of a mother to us both; and I expect our guardians paid substantially for the privilege. Tom was now nearly eighteen, and had had a commission given him in a crack regiment; partly, it was said, through the interest of Major Carlen. I was between fifteen and sixteen.

"I'm sure you children must be famishing," cried Mrs. Carlen. "It wants five minutes to eight. If Tom is not here as the clock strikes, we will begin tea."

The silvery bell had told its eight strokes and was dying away, when a cab dashing past the door suddenly pulled up. No mistake this time. We heard Tom's voice abusing the driver—or, as he called it, "pitching into him"—for not looking at the numbers.

What a fine, handsome young fellow he had grown! And how joyously he met us all; folding mother, brother and sister in one eager embrace. Tom Heriot was careless and thoughtless as it was possible for anyone to be, but he had a warm and affectionate heart. When trouble, and something worse, fell upon him later, and he became a town's talk, people called him bad-hearted amongst other reproaches; but they were mistaken.

"Why, Charley, how you have shot up!" he cried gaily. "You'll soon overtake me."

I shook my head. "While I am growing, Tom, you will be growing also."

"What was it you said in your last letter?" he went on, as we began tea. "That you were going to leave school?"

"Well, I fancy so, Tom. Uncle Stillingfar gave notice at Michaelmas."

"Thinks you know enough, eh, lad?"

I could not say much about that. That I was unusually well educated for my years there could be no doubt about, especially in the classics and French. My father had laid a good foundation to begin with, and the school chosen for me was a first-rate one. The French resident master had taken a liking to me, and had me much with him. Once during the midsummer holidays he had taken me to stay with his people in France: to Abbeville, with its interesting old church and market-place, its quaint costumes and uncomfortable inns. Altogether, I spoke and wrote French almost as well as he did.

"What are they going to make of you, Charley? Is it as old Stillingfar pleases?"

"I think so. I dare say they'll put me to the law."

"Unfortunate martyr! I'd rather command a pirate-boat on the high seas than stew my brains over dry law-books and musty parchments!"

"Tastes differ," struck in Miss Blanche. "And you are not going to sea at all, Tom."

"Tastes do differ," smiled Mrs. Carlen. "I should think it much nicer to harangue judges and law-courts in a silk gown and wig, Tom, than to put on a red coat and go out to be shot at."

"Hark at the mamsie!" cried Tom, laughing. "Charley, give me some more tongue. Where's the Major to-night?"

The Major was dining out. Tom and I were always best pleased when he did dine out. A pompous, boasting sort of man, I did not like him at all. As Tom put it, we would at any time rather have his room than his company.

The days I am writing of are not these days. Boys left school earlier then than they do now. I suppose education was not so comprehensive as it is now made: but it served us. It was quite a usual thing to place a lad out in the world at fourteen or fifteen, whether to a profession or a trade. Therefore little surprise was caused at home by notice having been given of my removal from school.

At breakfast, next morning, Tom began laying out plans for the day. "I'll take you to this thing, Charley, and I'll take you to that." Major Carlen sat in his usual place at the foot of the table, facing his wife. An imposing-looking man, tall, thin and angular, who must formerly have been handsome. He had a large nose with a curious twist in it; white teeth, which he showed very much; light gray eyes that stared at you, and hair and whiskers of so brilliant a black that a suspicious person might have said they were dyed.

"I thought of taking you boys out myself this afternoon," spoke the Major. "To see that horsemanship which is exhibiting. I hear it's very good. Would you like to go?"

"Oh, and me too!" struck in Blanche. "Take me, papa."

"No," answered the Major, after reflection. "I don't consider it a fit place for little girls. Would you boys like to go?" he asked.

We said we should like it; said it in a sort of surprise, for it was almost the first time he had ever offered to take us anywhere.

"Charles cannot go," hastily interrupted Mrs. Carlen, who had at length opened a letter which had been lying beside her plate. "This is from Mr. Serjeant Stillingfar, Charley. He asks me to send you to his chambers this afternoon. You are to be there at three o'clock."

"Just like old Stillingfar!" cried Tom resentfully. Considering that he did not know much of Serjeant Stillingfar and had very little experience of his ways, the reproach was gratuitous.

Major Carlen laughed at it. "We must put off the horsemanship to another day," said he. "It will come to the same thing. I will take you out somewhere instead, Blanchie."

Taking an omnibus in Oxford Street, when lunch was over, I went down to Holborn, and thence to Lincoln's Inn. The reader may hardly believe that I had never been to my uncle's chambers before, though I had sometimes been to his house. He seemed to have kept me at a distance. His rooms were on the first floor. On the outer door I read "Mr. Serjeant Stillingfar."

"Come in," cried out a voice, in answer to my knock. And I entered a narrow little room.

A pert-looking youth with a quantity of long, light curly hair and an eye-glass, and not much older than myself, sat on a stool at a desk, beside an unoccupied chair. He eyed me from head to foot. I wore an Eton jacket and turn-down collar; he wore a "tail" coat, a stand-up collar, and a stock.

"What do you want?" he demanded.

"I want Mr. Serjeant Stillingfar."

"Not in; not to be seen. You can come another day."

"But I am here by appointment."

The young gentleman caught up his eyeglass, fixed it, and turned it on me. "I don't think you are expected," said he coolly.

Now, though he had been gifted with a stock of native impudence, and a very good stock it was at his time of life, I had been gifted with native modesty. I waited in silence, not knowing what to do. Two or three chairs stood about. He no doubt would have tried them all in succession, had it suited him to do so. I did not like to take one of them.

"Will my uncle be long, do you know?" I asked.

"Who is your uncle?"

"Mr. Serjeant Stillingfar."

He put up his glass again, which had dropped, and stared at me harder than before. At this juncture an inner door was opened, and a middle-aged man in a black coat and white neckcloth came through it.

"Are you Mr. Strange?" he inquired, quietly and courteously.

"Yes. My uncle, Mr. Serjeant Stillingfar, wrote to tell me to be here at three o'clock."

"I know. Will you step in here? The Serjeant is in Court, but will not be long. As to you, young Mr. Lake, if you persist in exercising your impudent tongue upon all comers, I shall request the Serjeant to put a stop to your sitting here at all. How many times have you been told not to take upon yourself to answer callers, but to refer them to me when Michael is out?"

"About a hundred and fifty, I suppose, old Jones. Haven't counted them, though," retorted Mr. Lake.

"Impertinent young rascal!" ejaculated Mr. Jones, as he took me into the next room, and turned to a little desk that stood in a corner. He was the Serjeant's confidential clerk, and had been with him for years. Arthur Lake, beginning to read for the Bar, was allowed by the Serjeant and his clerk to sit in their chambers of a day, to pick up a little experience.

"Sit down by the fire, Mr. Strange," said the clerk. "It is a warm day, though, for the season. I expected the Serjeant in before this. He will not be long now."

Before I had well taken in the bearings of the room, which was the Serjeant's own, and larger and better than the other, he came in, wearing his silk gown and gray wig. He was a little man, growing elderly now, with a round, smooth, fair face, out of which twinkled kindly blue eyes. Mr. Jones got up from his desk at once to divest him of wig and gown, producing at the same time a miniature flaxen wig, which the Serjeant put upon his head.

"So you have come, Charles!" he said, shaking hands with me as he sat down in a large elbow-chair. Mr. Jones went out with his arm full of papers and shut the door upon us.

"Yes, sir," I answered.

"You will be sixteen next May, I believe," he added. He had the mildest voice and manner imaginable; not at all what might be expected in a serjeant-at-law, who was supposed to take the Court by storm on occasion. "And I understand from your late master that in all your studies you are remarkably well advanced."

"Pretty well, I think, sir," I answered modestly.

"Ay. I am glad to hear you speak of it in a diffident, proper sort of way. Always be modest, lad; true merit ever is so. It tells, too, in the long-run. Well, Charles, I think it time that you were placed out in life."

"Yes, sir."

"Is there any calling that you especially fancy? Any one profession you would prefer to embrace above another?"

"No, sir; I don't know that there is. I have always had an idea that it would be the law. I think I should like that."

"Just so," he answered, the faint pink on his smooth cheeks growing deeper with gratification. "It is what I have always intended you to enter—provided you had no insuperable objection to it. But I shall not make a barrister of you, Charles."

"No!" I exclaimed. "What then?"

"An attorney-at-law."

I was too much taken by surprise to answer at once. "Is that—a gentleman's calling, Uncle Charles?" I at length took courage to ask.

"Ay, that it is, lad," he impressively rejoined. "It's true you've no chance of the Woolsack or of a judgeship, or even of becoming a pleader, as I am. If you had a ready-made fortune, Charles, you might eat your dinners, get called, and risk it. But you have not; and I will not be the means of condemning the best years of your life to anxious poverty."

I only looked at him, without speaking. I fancy he must have seen disappointment in my face.

"Look here, Charles," he resumed, bending forward impressively: "I will tell you a little of my past experience. My people thought they were doing a great thing for me when they put me to the Bar. I thought the same. I was called in due course, and donned my stuff gown and wig in glory—the glory cast by the glamour of hope. How long my mind maintained that glamour; how long it was before it began to give place to doubt; how many years it took to merge doubt into despair, I cannot tell you. I think something like fifteen or twenty."

"Fifteen or twenty years, Uncle Stillingfar!"

"Not less. I was steady, persevering, sufficiently clever. Yet practice did not come to me. It is all a lottery. I had no fortune, lad; no one to help me. I was not clever at writing for the newspapers and magazines, as many of my fellows were. And for more years than I care to recall I had a hard struggle for existence. I was engaged to be married. She was a sweet, patient girl, and we waited until we were both bordering upon middle age. Ay, Charles, I was forty years old before practice began to flow in upon me. The long lane had taken a turning at last. It flew in then with a vengeance—more work than I could possibly undertake."

"And did you marry the young lady, Uncle Charles?" I asked In the pause he came to. I had never heard of his having a wife.

"No, child; she was dead. I think she died of waiting."

I drew a long breath, deeply interested.

"There are scores of young fellows starving upon hope now, as I starved then, Charles. The market is terribly overstocked. For ten barristers striving to rush into note in my days, you may count twenty or thirty in these. I will not have you swell the lists. My brother's grandson shall never, with my consent, waste his best years in fighting with poverty, waiting for luck that may never come to him."

"I suppose it is a lottery, as you say, sir."

"A lottery where blanks far outweigh the prizes," he assented. "A lottery into which you shall not enter. No, Charles; you shall be spared that. As a lawyer, I can make your progress tolerably sure. You may be a rich man in time if you will, and an honourable one. I have sounded my old friend, Henry Brightman, and I think he is willing to take you."

"I am afraid I should not make a good pleader, sir," I acknowledged, falling in with his views. "I can't speak a bit. We had a debating-club at school, and in the middle of a speech I always lost myself."

He nodded, and rose. "You shall not try it, my boy. And that's all for to-day, Charles. All I wanted was to sound your views before making arrangements with Brightman."

"Has he a good practice, sir?"

"He has a very large and honourable practice, Charles. He is a good man and a gentleman," concluded the Serjeant emphatically. "All being well, you may become his partner sometime."

"Am I not to go to Oxford, sir?" I asked wistfully.

"If you particularly wish to do so and circumstances permit it, you may perhaps keep a few terms when you are out of your articles," he replied, with hesitation. "We shall see, Charles, when that time comes."

"What a shame!" exclaimed Mrs. Carlen, when I reached home. "Make you a lawyer! That he never shall, Charles. I shall not allow it. I will go down and remonstrate with him."

Major Carlen said it was a shame; said it contemptuously. Tom said it was a double-shame, and threw a host of hard words upon Mr. Serjeant Stillingfar. Blanche began to cry. She had been reading that day about a press-gang, and quite believed my fate would be worse than that of being pressed.

After breakfast, next morning, we hastened to Lincoln's Inn: I and Mrs. Carlen, for she kept her word. I should be a barrister or nothing, she protested. All very fine to say so! She had no power over me whatever. That lay with Mr. Serjeant Stillingfar and the other trustee, and he never interfered. If they chose to article me to a chimneysweep instead of a lawyer, no one could say them nay.

Mr. Jones and young Lake sat side by side at the desk in the first room when we arrived. Mr. Serjeant Stillingfar was in his own room. He received us very kindly, shaking hands with Mrs. Carlen, whom he had seen occasionally. Mrs. Carlen, sitting opposite to him, entered upon her protest, and was meekly listened to by the Serjeant.

"Better be a successful attorney, madam, than a briefless barrister," he observed, when she finished.

"All barristers are not briefless," said Mrs. Carlen.

"A great many of them are," he answered. "Some of them never make their mark at all; they live and die struggling men." And, leaning forward in his chair—as he had leaned towards me yesterday—he repeated a good deal that he had then said of his own history; his long-continued poverty, and his despairing struggles. Mrs. Carlen's heart melted.

"Yes, I know. It is very sad, dear Mr. Serjeant, and I am sure your experience is only that of many others," she sighed. "But, if I understand the matter rightly, the chief trouble of these young barristers is their poverty. Had they means to live, they could wait patiently and comfortably until success came to them."

"Of course," he assented. "It is the want of private means that makes the uphill path so hard."

"Charles has his three hundred a year."

The faint pink in his cheeks, just the hue of a sea-shell, turned to crimson. I was sitting beyond the table, and saw it. He glanced across at me.

"It will take more money to make Charles a lawyer and to ensure him a footing afterwards in a good house than it would to get him called to the Bar," he said with a smile.

"Yes—perhaps so. But that is not quite the argument, Mr. Serjeant," said my stepmother. "Any young man who has three hundred a year may manage to live upon it."

"It is to be hoped so. I know I should have thought three hundred a year a perfect gold-mine."

"Then you see Charles need not starve while waiting for briefs to come in to him. Do you not see that, Mr. Serjeant?"

"I see it very clearly," he mildly said. "Had Charles his three hundred a year to fall back upon, he might have gone to the Bar had he liked, and risked the future."

"But he has it," Mrs. Carlen rejoined, surprise in her tone.

"No, madam, he has it not. Nor two hundred a year, nor one hundred."

They silently looked at one another for a full minute. Mrs. Carlen evidently could not understand his meaning. I am sure I did not.

"Charles's money, I am sorry to say, is lost," he continued.

"Lost! Since when?"

"Since the bank-panic that we had nearly two years ago."

Mrs. Carlen collapsed. "Oh, dear!" she breathed. "Did you—pray forgive the question, Mr. Serjeant—did you lose it? Or—or—the other trustee?"

He shook his head. "No, no. We neither lost it, nor are we responsible for the loss. Charles's grandfather, my brother, invested the money, six thousand pounds, in bank debentures to bring in five per cent. He settled the money upon his daughter, Lucy, and upon her children after her, making myself and our old friend, George Wickham, trustees. In the panic of two years ago this bank went; its shares and its debentures became all but worthless."

"Is the money all gone? quite gone?" gasped Mrs. Carlen. "Will it never be recovered?"

"The debentures are Charles's still, but they are for the present almost worthless," he replied. "The bank went on again, and if it can recover itself and regain prosperity, Charles in the end may not greatly suffer. He may regain his money, or part of it. But it will not be yet awhile. The unused portion of the income had been sunk, year by year, in further debentures, in accordance with the directions of the will. All went."

"But—someone must have paid for Charles all this time—two whole years!" she reiterated, in vexed surprise.

"Yes! it has been managed," he gently said.

"I think you must have paid for him yourself," spoke Mrs. Carlen with impulse. "I think it is you who are intending to pay the premium to Mr. Brightman, and to provide for his future expenses? You are a good man, Mr. Serjeant Stillingfar!"

His face broke into a smile: the rare sweet smile which so seldom crossed it. "I am only lending it to him. Charley will repay me when he is a rich man. But you see now, Mrs. Carlen, why a certainty will be better for him than an uncertainty."

We saw it all too clearly, and there was no more remonstrance to be made. Mrs. Carlen rose to leave, just as Mr. Jones came bustling into the room.

"Time is up, sir," he said to his master. "The Court will be waiting."

"Ah, so: is it? Good-morning, madam," he added, politely dismissing her. "I shall send for you here again in a day or two, Charles."

"Thank you for what you are doing for me, Uncle Charles," I whispered. "It is very kind of you."

He laid his hand upon my shoulder affectionately, keeping it there for a few seconds. And as we went out, the last glimpse I had was of his kind, gentle face, and Mr. Jones standing ready to assist him on with his wig and gown.

And we went back to Gloucester Place aware that my destiny in life was settled.

CHAPTER IV

IN ESSEX STREET

Henry Brightman's offices were in Essex Street, Strand, near the Temple. He rented the whole house: a capital house, towards the bottom of the street on the left-hand side as you go down. His father, who had been head and chief of the firm, had lived in it. But old Mr. Brightman was dead, and his son, now sole master, lived over the water on the Surrey side, in a style his father would never have dreamt of. It was a firm of repute and consideration; and few legal firms, if any, in London were better regarded.

It was to this gentleman my uncle, Mr. Serjeant Stillingfar, articled me: and a gentleman Henry Brightman was in every sense of the term. He was a slender man of middle height, with a bright, pleasant face, quick, dark eyes, and brown hair. Very much to my surprise, I found, when arrangements were being made for me, that I was to live in the house. Serjeant Stillingfar had made it a condition that I should do so. He and the late Mr. Brightman had been firm friends, and his friendship was continued to Henry. An old lady, one Miss Methold, a cousin of the Brightmans, resided in the house, and I was to take up my abode with her. She was a kind old thing, though a little stern and reserved, and she made me very comfortable.

There were several clerks; and one articled pupil, who was leaving the house as I entered it. The head of all was a gentleman named Lennard, who seemed to take all management upon himself, under Mr. Brightman. George Lennard was a tall spare man, with a thin, fair, aristocratic face and well-formed features. He looked about thirty-five years old, and an impression prevailed in the office that he was well-born, well-connected, and had come down in the world through loss of fortune. A man of few words, attentive, and always at his post, Lennard was an excellent superintendent, ruling with a strict yet kindly hand.

One day, some weeks after I had entered, as I was at dinner with Miss Methold in her sitting-room, and the weather was warm enough for all doors to be open, we heard horses and carriage-wheels dash up to the house. The room was at the head of the stairs, leading from the offices to the kitchen: a large, pleasant room with a window looking towards the Temple chambers and the winding river.

"What a commotion!" exclaimed Miss Methold.

I went to the door, and saw an open barouche, with a lady and a little girl inside it, attended by a coachman and footman in livery.

"It is quite a grand carriage, Miss Methold."

"Oh," said she, looking over my shoulder: "it is Mrs. Brightman."

"Very proud and high-and-mighty, is she not?" I rejoined, for the clerks had talked about her.

"She was born proud. Her mother was a nobleman's daughter, and she'll be proud to the end," said the old lady. "Henry keeps up great show and state for her. Of course, that is his affair, not mine."

"I hear he has a charming place at Clapham, Miss Methold?"

"So do I," she answered rather bitterly. "I have never seen it."

"Never seen it?" I echoed in surprise.

"Never," she answered. "I have not even been invited there by her. Never once, Charles. Mrs. Brightman despises her husband's profession in her heart; she despises me as belonging to it, I suppose, and as a poor relation. She has never condescended to get out of her carriage to enter the office here, and has never asked to see me, here or there. Henry has invited me down there once or twice when she was away from home, but I have said, No, thank you."

Mr. Lennard came in. The clerks, one excepted, had gone out to dinner. "Do you know whether it will be long before Mr. Brightman comes in, or where he has gone to?" he said to Miss Methold.

"Indeed, I do not," she answered rather shortly. "I only knew he was out by his not appearing now at luncheon."

"Charles, go to the carriage and tell Mrs. Brightman that we don't know how long it may be before Mr. Brightman comes in," said he.

I rather wondered why he could not go himself as I took out the message to Mrs. Brightman.

She had a fair proud face, and her air was cold and haughty as she listened to me.

"Let this be given to him as soon as he comes in," she said, handing me a sealed note. "Regent Street; Carbonell's," she added to the footman.

As the carriage turned and bowled away, I caught the child's pretty face, a smile on her rosy lips and in her laughing brown eyes.

I may as well say here that young Lake had struck up an acquaintanceship with me. The reader may remember that I saw him at the chambers of Mr. Serjeant Stillingfar. I grew to like him greatly. His faults were all on the surface; his heart was in the right place. Boy though he was, he was thrown upon himself in the world. I don't mean as to money, but as to a home; and he steered his course unscathed through its shoals. The few friends he had lived in the country. He had neither father nor mother. His lodgings were in Norfolk Street, very near to us. Miss Methold would sometimes have him in to spend Sunday with me; and now and then, but very rarely, he and I were invited for that day to dine with Mr. Serjeant Stillingfar.

The Serjeant lived in Russell Square, in one of its handsomest houses. But he kept, so to say, no establishment; just two or three servants and a modest little brougham. He must have been making a great deal of money at that time, and I suppose he put it by.

"Ah! you don't know, Charley," Lake said to me one evening when I was in Norfolk Street, and we began talking of him. "It is said his money went in that same precious bank which devoured yours; and it is thought that he lives in this quiet manner, eschewing pomps and vanities, to be able to help friends who were quite ruined by it. Old Jones knows a little, and I've heard him drop a word or two."

"I am sure my uncle is singularly good and kind. Those simple-minded men generally are."

Lake nodded. "Few men, I should say, come up to Serjeant Stillingfar."

A trouble had come to me in the early spring. I thought it a great one, and grieved over it. Major Carlen gave up his house in Gloucester Place, letting it furnish for a long term, and went abroad with his wife. He might have gone to the end of the world for ever and a day, but she was like my second mother, and indeed was so, and I felt lost without her. They took up their abode at Brussels. It would be good for Blanche's education, Mrs. Carlen wrote to me. Other people said that the Major had considerably outrun the constable, and went there to economise. Tom Heriot was down at Portsmouth with his regiment.

I think that is all I need say of this part of my life. I liked my profession very much indeed, and got on well in it and with Mr. Brightman and the clerks, and with good old Miss Methold. And so the years passed on.

The first change came when I was close upon twenty years of age: came in the death of Miss Methold. After that, I left Essex Street as a residence, for there was no longer anyone to rule it, and went into Lake's lodgings in Norfolk Street, sharing his sitting-room and securing a bedroom. And still a little more time rolled on.

It was Easter-tide. On Easter Eve, it happened that I had remained in the office after the other clerks had left, to finish some work in hand. In these days Saturday afternoon has become a general holiday; in those days we had to work all the harder. On Saturdays a holiday was unknown.

Writing steadily, I finished my task, and was locking up my desk, which stood near the far window in the front room on the ground floor, when Mr. Brightman, who had also remained late, came downstairs from his private room, and looked in.

"Not gone yet, Charley!"

"I am going now, sir. I have only just finished my work."

"Some of the clerks are coming on Monday, I believe," continued Mr. Brightman. "Are you one of them?"

"Yes, sir. Mr. Lennard told me I might take holiday, but I did not care about it. As I have no friends to spend it with, it would not be much of a holiday to me. Arthur Lake is out of town."

"And Mr. Serjeant Stillingfar on circuit," added Mr. Brightman.

He paused and looked at me, as he stood near the door. I was gathering the pens together.

"Have you no friends to dine with, to-morrow—Easter Day?"

"No, sir. At least, I have not been asked anywhere. I think I shall go for a blow up the river."

"A blow up the river!" he repeated doubtfully. "Don't you go to church?"

"Always. I go to the Temple. I meant in the afternoon, sir."

"Well, if you have no friends to dine with, you may come and dine with me," said Mr. Brightman, after a moment's consideration. "Come down when service is over. You will find an omnibus at Charing Cross."

The invitation pleased me. Some of the clerks would have given their ears for it. Of course I mean the gentlemen clerks; not one of whom had ever been so favoured. I had sometimes wondered that he never asked me, considering his intimacy with my uncle. But, I suppose, to have invited me to his house and left out Miss Methold would have been rather too pointed a slight upon her.

It was a fine day. The Temple service was beautiful, as usual; the anthem, "I know that my Redeemer liveth." Afterwards I went forth to keep my engagement, and in due time reached the entrance-gates of Mr. Brightman's residence.

It was a large, handsome villa, enclosed in fine pleasure-grounds, near Clapham. They lived in a good deal of style, kept seven or eight servants and two carriages: a large barouche, and a brougham in which he sometimes came to town. A well-appointed house, full of comfort and luxury. Mr. Brightman was on the lawn when I reached it.

"Well, Charles! I began to think you were late."

"I walked down, sir. The first two omnibuses were full, and I would not wait for a third."

"Rather a long walk," he remarked with a smile. "But it is what I should have done at your age. Dinner will be ready soon. We dine at three o'clock on Sundays. It allows ourselves and the servants to attend evening as well as morning service."

He had walked towards the house as he spoke, and we went in. The drawing-room and dining-room opened on either side a large hall. In the former room sat Mrs. Brightman. I had seen her occasionally at the office door in her carriage, but had never spoken to her except that first time. She was considerably younger than Mr. Brightman, who must have been then getting towards fifty. A proud woman she looked as she sat there; her hair light and silky, her blue eyes disdainful, her dress a rich purple silk, with fine white lace about it.

"Here is Charles Strange at last," Mr. Brightman said to her, and she replied by a slight bend of the head. She did not offer to shake hands with me.

"I have heard of you as living in Essex Street," she condescended to observe, as I sat down. "Your relatives do not, I presume, live in London?"

"I have not any near relatives," was my answer. "My great-uncle lives in London, but he is away just now."

"You were speaking of that great civil cause, Emma, lately tried in the country; and of the ability of the defendants' counsel, Serjeant Stillingfar," put in Mr. Brightman. "It is Serjeant Stillingfar, if you remember, who is Charles's uncle."

"Oh, indeed," she said; and I thought her manner became rather more gracious. And ah, what a gracious, charming lady she could be when she pleased!—when she was amongst people whom she considered of her own rank and degree.

"Where is Annabel?" asked Mr. Brightman.

"She has gone dancing off somewhere," was Mrs. Brightman's reply. "I never saw such a child. She is never five minutes together in one place."

Presently she danced in. A graceful, pretty child, apparently about twelve, in a light-blue silk frock. She wore her soft brown hair in curls round her head, and they flew about as she flew, and a bright colour rose to her cheeks with every word she spoke, and her eyes were like her father's—dark, tender, expressive. Not any resemblance could I trace to her mother, unless it lay in the same delicately-formed features.

We had a plain dinner; a quarter of lamb, pastry and creams. Mr. Brightman did not exactly apologize for it, but explained that on Sundays they had as little cooking as possible. But it was handsomely served, and there were several sorts of wine. Three servants waited at table, two in livery and the butler in plain clothes.

Some little time after it was over, Mr. Brightman left the room, and Mrs. Brightman, without the least ceremony, leaned back in an easy-chair and closed her eyes. I said something to the child. She did not answer, but came to me on tiptoe.

"If we talk, mamma will be angry," she whispered. "She never lets me make a noise while she goes to sleep. Would you like to come out on the lawn? We may talk there."

I nodded, and Annabel silently opened and passed out at one of the French windows, holding it back for me. I as silently closed it.

"Take care that it is quite shut," she said, "or the draught may get to mamma. Papa has gone to his room to smoke his cigar," she continued; "and we shall have coffee when mamma awakes. We do not take tea until after church. Shall you go to church with us?"

"I dare say I shall. Do you go?"

"Of course I do. My governess tells me never to miss attending church twice on Sundays, unless there is very good cause for doing so, and then things will go well with me in the week. But if I wished to stay at home, papa would not let me. Once, do you know, I made an excuse to stay away from morning service: I said my head ached badly, though it did not. It was to read a book that had been lent me, 'The Old English Baron.' I feared my governess would not let me read it, if she saw it, because it was about ghosts, so that I had only the Sunday to read it in. Well, do you know, that next week nothing went right with me; my lessons were turned back, my drawing was spoilt, and my French mistress tore my translation in two. Oh, dear! it was nothing but scolding and crossness. So at last, on the Saturday, I burst into tears and told Miss Shelley about staying away from church and the false excuse I had made. But she was very kind, and would not punish me, for she said I had already had a whole week of punishment."

Of all the little chatterboxes! "Is Miss Shelley your governess now?" I asked her.

"Yes. But her mother is an invalid, so mamma allows her to go home every Saturday night and come back on Monday morning. Mamma says it is pleasant to have Sunday to ourselves. But I like Miss Shelley very much, and should be dull without her if papa were not at home. I do love Sundays, because papa's here. Did you ever read 'The Old English Baron'?"

"No."

"Shall I lend it you to take home?" continued Annabel, her cheeks glowing, her eyes sparkling with good-nature. "I have it for my own now. It is a very nice book. Have your sisters read it? Perhaps you have no sisters?"

"I have no real sisters, and my father and mother are dead. I have—"

"Oh dear, how sad!" interrupted Annabel, clasping her hands. "Not to have a father and mother! Was it"—after a pause—"you who lived with Miss Methold?"

"Yes. Did you know her?"

"I knew her; and I liked her—oh, very much. Papa used to take me to see her sometimes. With whom do you live now?"

"I live in lodgings."

She stood looking at me with her earnest eyes—thoughtful eyes just then.

"Then who sews the buttons on your shirts?"

I burst into laughter: the reader may have done the same. "My landlady professes to sew them on, Annabel, but the shirts often go without buttons. Sometimes I sew one on myself."

"If you had one off now, and it was not Sunday, I would sew it on for you," said Annabel. "Why do you laugh?"

"At your concern about my domestic affairs, my dear little girl."

"But there's a gentleman who lives in lodgings and comes here sometimes to dine with papa—he is older than you—and he says it is the worst trouble of life to have no one to sew his buttons on. Who takes care of you if you are ill?" she added, after another pause.

"As there is no one to take care of me, I cannot afford to be ill, Annabel. I am generally quite well."

"I am glad of that. Was your father a lawyer, like papa?"

"No. He was a clergyman."

"Oh, don't turn," she cried; "I want to show you my birds. We have an aviary, and they are beautiful. Papa lets me call them mine; and some of them are mine in reality, for they were bought for me. Mamma does not care for birds."

Presently I asked Annabel her age.

"Fourteen."

"Fourteen!" I exclaimed in surprise.

"I was fourteen in January. Mamma says I ought not to tell people my age, for they will only think me more childish; but papa says I may tell everyone."

She was in truth a child for her years; especially as age is now considered. She ran about, showing me everything, her frock, her curls, her eyes dancing: from the aviary to the fowls, from the fowls to the flowers: all innocent objects of her daily pleasures, innocent and guileless as she herself.

A smart-looking maid, with red ringlets flowing about her red cheeks, and wide cap-strings flowing behind them, came up.

"Why, here you are!" she exclaimed. "I've been looking all about for you, Miss Annabel. Your mamma says you are to come in."

"We are coming, Hatch; we were turning at that moment," answered the child. "Is coffee ready?"

"Yes, Miss Annabel, and waiting."

In the evening we went to church, the servants following at some distance. Afterwards we had tea, and then I rose to depart. Mr. Brightman walked with me across the lawn, and we had almost reached the iron gates when there came a sound of swift steps behind us.

"Papa! papa! Is he gone? Is Mr. Strange gone?"

"What is the matter now?" asked Mr. Brightman.

"I promised to lend Mr. Strange this: it is 'The Old English Baron.' He has never read it."

"There, run back," said Mr. Brightman, as I turned and took the book from her. "You will catch cold, Annabel."

"What a charming child she is, sir!" I could not help exclaiming.

"She is that," he replied. "A true child of nature, knowing no harm and thinking none. Mrs. Brightman complains that her ideas and manners are unformed; no style about her, she says, no reserve. In my opinion that ought to constitute a child's chief charm. All Annabel's parts are good. Of sense, intellect, talent, she possesses her full share; and I am thankful that they are not prematurely developed. I am thankful," he repeated with emphasis, "that she is not a forward child. In my young days, girls were girls, but now there is not such a thing to be found. They are all women. I do not admire the forcing system myself; forced vegetables, forced fruit, forced children: they are good for little. A genuine child, such as Annabel, is a treasure rarely met with."

I thought so too.

CHAPTER V

Leaving the omnibus at Charing Cross, I was hastening along the Strand on my way home, when I ran against a gentleman, who was swaggering along in a handsome, capacious cloak as if all the street belonged to him.

"I beg your pardon," I said, in apology. "I—" And there I broke off to stare, for I thought I recognised him in the gaslight.

"Why! It is Major Carlen!"

"Just so. And it is Charles. How are you, Charles?"

"Have you lately come from Brussels?" I asked, as we shook hands. "And how did you leave mamma and Blanche?"

"They are in Gloucester Place," he answered. "We all came over last Wednesday."

"I wonder they did not let me know it."

"Plenty of time, young man. They will not be going away in a hurry. We are settling down here again. You can come up when you like."

"That will be to-morrow then. Good-night, sir."

But it was not until Monday evening that I could get away. Mr. Lennard went out in the afternoon on some private matter of his own, and desired me to remain in to see a client, who had sent us word he should call, although it was Easter Monday. Mr. Brightman did not come to town that day.

Six o'clock was striking when I reached Gloucester Place. Blanche ran to meet me in the passage, and we had a spell of kissing. I think she was then about fourteen; perhaps fifteen. A fair, upright, beautiful girl, with the haughty blue eyes of her childhood, and a shower of golden curls.

"Oh, Charley, I am so glad! I thought you were never, never coming to us."

"I did not know you were here until last night. You should have sent me word."

"I told mamma so; but she was not well. She is not well yet. The journey tired her, you see, and the sea was rough. Come upstairs and see her, Charley. Papa has just gone out."

Mrs. Carlen sat over the fire in the drawing-room in an easy-chair, a shawl upon her shoulders. It was a dull evening, twilight not far off, and she sat with her back to the light. It struck me she looked thin and ill. I had been over once or twice to stay with them in Brussels; the last time, eighteen months ago.

"Are you well, mamma?" I asked as she kissed me—for I had not left off calling her by the fond old childhood's name. "You don't look so."

"The journey tired me, Charley," she answered—just as Blanche had said to me. "I have a little cold, too. Sit down, my boy."

"Have you come back here for good?" I asked.

"Well, yes, I suppose so," she replied with hesitation. "For the present, at all events."

Tea was brought in. Blanche made it; her mother kept to her chair and her shawl. The more I looked at her, the greater grew the conviction that something beyond common ailed her. Major Carlen was dining out, and they had dined in the middle of the day.

Alas! I soon knew what was wrong. After tea, contriving to get rid of Blanche for a few minutes on some plausible excuse, she told me all. An inward complaint was manifesting itself, and it was hard to say how it might terminate. The Belgian doctors had not been very reassuring upon the point. On the morrow she was going to consult James Paget.

"Does Blanche know?" I asked.

"Not yet. I must see Mr. Paget before saying anything to her. If my own fears are confirmed, I shall tell her. In that case I shall lose no time in placing her at school."

"At school!"

"Why, yes, Charley. What else can be done? This will be no home for her when I am out of it. Not at an ordinary school, though. I shall send her to our old home, White Littleham Rectory. Mr. and Mrs. Ravensworth are there still. She takes two or three pupils to bring up with her own daughter, and will be glad of Blanche. There—we will put that subject away for the present, Charley. I want to ask you about something else, and Blanche will soon be back again. Do you see much of Tom Heriot?"

"I see him very rarely indeed. He is not quartered in London, you know."

"Charles, I am afraid—I am very much afraid that Tom is wild," she went on, after a pause. "He came into his money last year: six thousand pounds. We hear that he has been launching out into all sorts of extravagance ever since. That must mean that he is drawing on his capital."

I had heard a little about Tom's doings myself. At least, Lake had done so, which came to the same thing. But I did not say this.

"It distresses me much, Charles. You know how careless and improvident Tom is, and yet how generous-hearted. He will bring himself to ruin if he does not mind, and what would become of him then? Major Carlen says—Hush! here comes Blanche."

I cannot linger over this part of my story. Mrs. Carlen died; and Blanche was sent to White Littleham.

And, indeed, of the next few passing years there is not much to record. I obtained my certificate, as a matter of course. Then I managed, by Mr. Brightman's kindness in sparing me, and by my uncle's liberality, to keep a few terms at Oxford. I was twenty-three when I kept the last term, and then I was sent for some months to Paris, to make myself acquainted with law as administered in the French courts. That over, arrangements were made for my becoming Mr. Brightman's partner. If he had had sons, one of them would probably have filled the position. Having none, he admitted me on easy terms, for I had my brains about me, as the saying runs, and was excessively useful to the firm. A certain sum was paid down by Mr. Serjeant Stillingfar, and the firm became Brightman and Strange. I was to receive at first only a small portion of the profits. And let me say here, that all my expenses of every description, during these past years, had been provided for by that good man, Charles Stillingfar, and provided liberally. So there I was in an excellent position, settled for life when only twenty-four years of age.

After coming home from Paris to enter upon these new arrangements, I found Mr. Brightman had installed a certain James Watts in Essex Street as care-taker and messenger, our former man, Dickory, having become old and feeble. A good change. Dickory, in growing old, had grown fretful and obstinate, and liked his own way and will better than that of his masters. Watts was well-mannered and well-spoken; respectable and trustworthy. His wife's duties were to keep the rooms clean, in which she was at liberty to have in a woman to help once or twice a week if she so minded, and up to the present time to prepare Mr. Brightman's daily luncheon. They lived in the rooms on the bottom floor, one of which was their bedroom.

"I like them both," I said to Mr. Brightman, when I had been back a day or two. "Things will be comfortable now."

"Yes, Charles; I hope you will find them so," he answered.

For it ought to be mentioned that, in becoming Mr. Brightman's partner, it had been settled that I should return as an inmate to the house. He said he should prefer it. And, indeed, I thought I should also. So that I had taken up my abode there at once.

The two rooms on the ground floor were occupied by the clerks. Mr. Lennard had his desk in the back one. Miss Methold's parlour, a few steps lower, was now not much used, except that a client was sometimes taken into it. The large front room on the first floor was Mr. Brightman's private room; the back one was mine; but he had also a desk in it. These two rooms opened to one another. The floor above this was wholly given over to me; sitting-room, bedroom, and dressing-room. The top floor was only used for boxes, and on those rare occasions when someone wanted to sleep at the office. Watts and his wife were to attend to me; she to see to the meals, he to wait upon me.

"I should let her get in everything without troubling, and bring up the bills weekly, were I you, Charles," remarked Mr. Brightman, one evening when he had stayed later than usual, and was in my room, and we fell to talking of the man and his wife. "Much better than for her to be coming to you everlastingly, saying you want this and you want that. She is honest, I feel sure, and I had the best of characters with both of them."

"She has an honest face," I answered. "But it looks sad. And what a silent woman she is. Speaking of her face though, sir, it puts me in mind of someone's, and I cannot think whose."

"You may have seen her somewhere or other," remarked Mr. Brightman.

"Yes, but I can't remember where. I'll ask her."

Mrs. Watts was then coming into the room with some water, which Mr. Brightman had rung for. She looked about forty-five years old; a thin, bony woman of middle height, with a pale, gray, wrinkled face, and gray hairs banded under a huge cap, tied under her chin.

"There's something about your face that seems familiar to me, Mrs. Watts," I said, as she put down the glass and the bottle of water. "Have I ever seen you before?"

She was pouring out the water, and did not look at me. "I can't say, sir," she answered in a low tone.

"Do you remember me? That's the better question."

She shook her head. "Watts and I lived in Ely Place for some years before we came here, sir," she then said. "It's not impossible you may have seen me in the street when I was doing the steps; but I never saw you pass by that I know of."

"And before that, where did you live?"

"Before that, sir? At Dover."

"Ah! well," I said, for this did not help me out with my puzzle; "I suppose it is fancy."

Mr. Brightman caught up the last word as Mrs. Watts withdrew. "Fancy, Charles; that's what it must be. And fancy sometimes plays wonderful tricks with us."

"Yes, sir; I expect it is fancy. For all that, I feel perplexed. The woman's voice and manner seem to strike a chord in my memory as much as her face does."

"Captain Heriot, sir."

Sitting one evening in my room at dusk in the summer weather, the window open to the opposite wall and to the side view of the Thames, waiting for Lake to come in, Watts had thus interrupted me to show in Tom Heriot. I started up and grasped his hands. He was a handsome young fellow, with the open manners that had charmed the world in the days gone by, and charmed it still.

"Charley, boy! It is good to see you."

"Ay, and to see you, Tom. Are you staying in London?"

"Why, we have been here for days! What a fellow you are, not to know that we are now quartered here. Don't you read the newspapers? It used to be said, you remember, that young Charley lived in a wood."

I laughed. "And how are things with you, Tom?"

"Rather down; have been for a long time; getting badder and badder."

My heart gave a thump. In spite of his laughing air and bright smile, I feared it might be too true.

"I am going to the deuce, headlong, Charley."

"Don't, Tom!"

"Don't what? Not go or not talk of it? It is as sure as death, lad."

"Have you made holes in your money?"

"Fairly so. I think I may say so, considering that the whole of it is spent."

"Oh, Tom!"

"Every individual stiver. But upon my honour as a soldier, Charley, other people have had more of it than I. A lot of it went at once, when I came into it, paying off back debts."

"What shall you do? You will never make your pay suffice."

"Sell out, I expect."

"And then?"

Tom shrugged his shoulders in answer. They were very slender shoulders. His frame was slight altogether, suggesting that he might not be strong. He was about as tall as I—rather above middle height.

"Take a clerkship with you, at twenty shillings a week, if you'd give it me. Or go out to the Australian diggings to pick up gold. How grave you look, Charles!"

"It is a grave subject. But I hope you are saying this in joke, Tom."

"Half in joke, half in earnest. I will not sell out if I can help it; be sure of that, old man; but I think it will have to come to it. Can you give me something to drink, Charley? I am thirsty."

"Will you take some tea? I am just going to have mine. Or anything else instead?"

"I was thinking of brandy and soda. But I don't mind if I do try tea, for once. Ay, I will. Have it up, Charley."

I rang the bell, and Mrs. Watts brought it up.

"Anything else, sir?" she stayed to ask.

"Not at present. Watts has gone out with that letter, I suppose?— Why, you have forgotten the milk!"

She gave a sharp word at her own stupidity, and left the room. Tom's eyes had been fixed upon her, following her to the last. He began slowly pushing back his bright brown hair, as he would do in his boyhood when anything puzzled him.

"Oh, I remember," he suddenly exclaimed. "So you have her here, Charley!"

"Who here?"

"Leah."

"Leah! What do you mean?"

"That servant of yours."

"That is our messenger's wife: Mrs. Watts."

"Mrs. Watts she may be now, for aught I know; but she was Leah Williams when we were youngsters, Charley."

"Impossible, Tom. This old woman cannot be Leah."

"I tell you, lad, it is Leah," he persisted. "No mistake about it. At the first moment I did not recollect her. I have a good eye for faces, but she is wonderfully altered. Do you mean to say she has not made herself known to you?"

I shook my head. But even as Tom spoke, little items of remembrance that had worried my brain began to clear themselves bit by bit. Mrs. Watts came in with the milk.

She had put it down on the tray when Tom walked up to her, holding out his hand, his countenance all smiles, his hazel eyes dancing.

"How are you, Leah, after all these years? Shake hands for auld lang syne. Do you sing the song still?"

Leah gave one startled glance and then threw her white apron up to her face with a sob.

"Come, come," said Tom kindly. "I didn't want to startle you, Leah."

"I didn't think you would know me, sir," she said, lifting her woebegone face. "Mr. Charles here did not."

"Not know you! I should know you sooner than my best sweetheart," cried Tom gaily.

"Leah," I interposed, gravely turning to her, "how is it that you did not let me know who you were? Why have you kept it from me?"

She stood with her back against Mr. Brightman's desk, hot tears raining down her worn cheeks.

"I couldn't tell you, Master Charles. I'm sorry you know now. It's like a stab to me."

"But why could you not tell me?"

"Pride, I suppose," she shortly said. "I was upper servant at the Rectory; your mamma's own maid, Master Charles: and I couldn't bear you should know that I had come down to this. A servant of all work—scrubbing floors and washing dishes."

"Oh, that's nothing," struck in Tom cheerfully. "Most of us have our ups and downs, Leah. As far as I can foresee, I may be scouring out pots and pans at the gold-diggings next year. I have just been saying so to Mr. Charley. Your second marriage venture was an unlucky one, I expect?"

Leah was crying silently. "No, it is not that," she answered presently in a low tone. "Watts is a steady and respectable man; very much so; above me, if anything. It—it—I have had cares and crosses of my own, Mr. Tom; I have them always; and they keep me down."

"Well, tell me what they are," said Tom. "I may be able to help you. I will if I can."

Leah sighed and moved to the door. "You are just as kind-hearted as ever, Mr. Tom; I see that; and I thank you. Nobody can help me, sir. And my trouble is secret to myself: one I cannot speak of to anyone in the world."

Just as kind-hearted as ever! Yes, Tom Heriot was that, and always would be. Embarrassed as he no doubt was for money, he slipped a gold piece into Leah's hand as she left the room, whispering that it was for old friendship's sake.

And so that was Leah! Back again waiting upon me, as she had waited when I was a child. It was passing strange.

I spoke to her that night, and asked her to confide her trouble to me. The bare suggestion seemed to terrify her.

"It was a dreadful trouble," she admitted in answer; "a nightly and daily torment; one that at times went well-nigh to frighten her senses away. But she must keep it secret, though she died for it."

And as Leah whispered this to me under her breath, she cast dread glances around the walls on all sides, as if she feared that eaves-droppers might be there.

What on earth could the secret be?

And now, for a time, I retire into the background, and cease personally to tell the story.

CHAPTER VI

BLANCHE HERIOT

On one of those promising days that we now and then see in February, which seem all the more warm and lovely in contrast with the passing winter, the parsonage of White Littleham put on its gayest appearance within—perhaps in response to the fair face of nature without. A group of four girls had collected in the drawing-room. One was taking the brown holland covers from the chairs, sofa, and footstools; another was bringing out certain ornaments, elegant trifles, displayed only on state occasions; the other two were filling glasses with evergreens and hot-house flowers. It was the same room in which you once saw poor Mrs. Strange lying on her road to death. The parsonage received three young ladies to share in the advantages of foreign governesses, provided for the education of its only daughter, Cecilia.

Whilst the girls were thus occupied, a middle-aged lady entered, the mistress of the house, and wife of the Reverend John Ravensworth.

"Oh, Mrs. Ravensworth, why did you come in? We did not want you to see it until it was all finished."

Mrs. Ravensworth smiled. "My dears, it will only look as it has looked many a time before; as it did at Christmas—"

"Mamma, you must excuse my interrupting you," cried the young girl who was arranging the ornaments; "but it will look very different from then. At Christmas we had wretched weather, and see it to-day. And at Christmas we had not the visitors we shall have now."

"We had one of the two visitors, at any rate, Cecilia."

"Oh, yes, we had Arnold. But Arnold is nobody; we are used to him."

"And Major Carlen is somebody," interposed the only beautiful girl present, looking round from the flowers with a laugh. "Thank you, in papa's name, Cecilia."

Very beautiful was she: exceedingly fair, with somewhat haughty blue eyes, delicate features, and fine golden hair. Blanche Heriot (as often as not called Blanche Carlen at the Rectory) stood conspicuous amidst the rest of the girls. They were pleasing-looking and lady-like, but that was all. Rather above middle-height, slender, graceful, she stood as a queen beside her companions. Under different auspices, Blanche Heriot might have become vain and worldly; but, enshrined as she had been for the last few years within the precincts of a humble parsonage, and trained in its doctrines of practical Christianity, Blanche had become thoroughly imbued with the influences around her. Now, in her twentieth year, she was simple and guileless as a child.

It was so long since she had seen her father—as she was pleased to call Major Carlen—that she had partly forgotten what he was like. He was expected now on a two days' visit, and for him the house was being made to look its best. The other visitor, coming by accident at the same time, was Arnold Ravensworth, the Rector's nephew.

Major Carlen's promised visit was an event to the quiet Rector and his wife. All they knew of him was that he was step-father to Blanche, and a man who moved in the gay circles of the world. The interest of Blanche Heriot's money had paid for her education and dress. The Major would have liked the fingering of it amazingly; but to covet is one thing, to obtain is another. Blanche's money was safe in the hands of trustees; but before Mrs. Carlen died she had appointed her husband Blanche's personal guardian, with power to control her residence when she should have attained her eighteenth year. That had been passed some time now, and Major Carlen had just awakened to his responsibilities.

The first to arrive was Arnold Ravensworth, a distinguished-looking man, with a countenance cold, it must be confessed, but full of intellect. And the next to arrive was not the Major. The day passed on to night. The trains came into the neighbouring station, but they did not bring Major Carlen. Blanche cried herself to sleep. She remembered how kind her papa used to be to her—indulging her and taking her about to see sights—and she had cherished a great affection for him. In fact, the Major had always indulged little Blanche.

Neither had he come the next morning. After breakfast, Blanche went to the end of the garden and stood looking out across the field. The shady dingle, where as a little child she had sat to pick violets and primroses, was there; but she was gazing at something else—the path that would bring her father. Arnold Ravensworth came strolling up behind her.

"You know the old saying, Blanche: a watched-for visitor never comes."

"Oh dear, why do you depress me, Arnold? To watch is something. I shall cross the field and look up the road."

They started off in the sunshine. Blanche had a pretty straw hat on. She took the arm Mr. Ravensworth held out to her. Very soon, a stranger turned into the field and came swinging towards them.

"Blanche, is this the Major?"

It was a tall, large-limbed, angular man in an old blue cloak lined with scarlet. He had iron-gray hair and whiskers, gray, hard eyes, a large twisted nose, and very white teeth. Blanche laughed merrily.

"That papa! What an idea you must have of him, Arnold! Papa was a handsome man with black hair, and had lost two of his front teeth. They were knocked out, fighting with the Caffres."

The stranger came on, staring intently at the good-looking young man and the beautiful girl on his arm. Mr. Ravensworth spoke in a low tone.

"Are you quite sure, Blanche? Black hair turns gray, remember; and he has a little travelling portmanteau under that cloak."

Even as he spoke, something in the stranger's face struck upon Blanche Heriot's memory. She disengaged herself and approached him, too agitated to weigh her words.

"Oh—I beg your pardon—are you not papa?"

Major Carlen looked at her closely. "Are you Blanche?"

"Yes, I am Blanche. Oh, papa!"

The Major tucked his step-daughter under his own arm; and Mr. Ravensworth went on to give notice of the arrival.

"Papa, I never saw anyone so much altered!"

"Nor I," interposed the Major. "I was wondering what deuced handsome girl was strolling towards me. You are beautiful, Blanche; more so than your mother was, and she was handsome."

Blanche, confused though she felt at the compliment, could not return it.

"Who is that young fellow?" resumed the Major.

"Arnold Ravensworth; Mr. Ravensworth's nephew. He lives in London, and came down yesterday for a short visit."

"Oh. Does he come often?"

"Pretty often. We wish it was oftener. We like him to be here."

"He seems presuming."

"Dear papa! Presuming! He is not at all so. And he is very talented and clever. He took honours at Oxford, and—"

"I see," interrupted Major Carlen, displaying his large and regular teeth—a habit of his when not pleased. He had rapidly taken up an idea, and it angered him. "Is this the parson, Blanche? He looks very sanctimonious."

"Oh, papa!" she returned, feeling ready to cry at his contemptuous tone. "He is the best man that ever lived. Everyone loves and respects him."

"Hope it's merited, my dear," concluded the Major, as he met the hand of the Reverend John Ravensworth.

Ere middle-day, the Major had scattered a small bombshell through the parsonage by announcing that he had come to take his daughter away. Blanche felt it bitterly. It was her home, and a happy one. To exchange it for the Major's did not look now an inviting prospect. Though she would not acknowledge it to her own heart, she was beginning to regard him with more awe than love. That the resolution must have been suddenly formed she knew, for he had not come down with any intention of removing her.

"Papa, my things can never be ready," was her last forlorn argument, when others had failed.

"Things?" said the Major. "Trunks, and clothes, and rattle-traps? They can be sent after you, Blanche."

"I have a bird," cried Blanche, her eyes filling. "There it is, in the cage."

"Leave it as a souvenir to the Rectory. Blanche, don't be a child. I have pictured you as one hitherto, but now that I see you I find my mistake. You must be thinking of other things, my dear."

And thus Blanche Heriot was hurried away. All the parsonage escorted her to the station, the girls in tears, and she almost heart-broken.

Of late years Major Carlen had been almost always in debt and difficulty. His property was mortgaged. His only certainty was his half-pay; but he was lucky at cards, and often luckier at betting. He retained his club and his visiting connection, and dined out three parts of his time. Just now he was up in the world, having scored a prize on some winter racecourse, and he was back in his house in Gloucester Place. It had been let furnished for three years, portions of which time the Major had spent abroad.

"It will be very dull for me, papa," sighed Blanche, as they were whirling along in an express train. "I dare say you are out all day long, as you used to be."

"Not dull at all," said the Major. "You must make Mrs. Guy take you out and about."

"Mrs. Guy!" exclaimed Blanche, her blue eyes opening widely. "Is she in London?"

"Yes, and a fine old guy she is; more ridiculously nervous than ever," replied the Major. "She arrived unexpectedly from Jersey one evening last week, and quartered herself upon Gloucester Place; for an indefinite period, no doubt. She did this once before, if you remember, in your poor mamma's time."

"She will be something in the way of company for me," said Blanche with another sigh.

"Aye! She is a stupid goose, but you'll be safer under her wing and mine than you would have been ruralising in the fields and the parsonage garden with that Arnold Ravensworth. I have eyes, Miss Blanche."

So had Blanche, especially just then; and they were wide open and fixed upon the Major.

"Doing what, papa?" cried she.

"I saw his drift: 'Blanche' this, and 'Blanche' the other, and his arm put out for you at every turn! No, no; I do not leave you there to be converted into Mrs. Arnold Ravensworth."

Blanche clasped her hands and broke into merry laughter. "Oh, papa, what an idea!—how could you imagine it? Why, he is going to marry Mary Stopford."

Major Carlen looked blank. Had he made all this inconvenient haste for nothing?

"Who the deuce is Mary Stopford?"

"She lives in Devonshire. A pale, gentle girl with nice eyes: I have seen her picture. Arnold wears it attached to a little chain inside his waistcoat. They are to be married in the autumn when the House is up. The very notion of my marrying Arnold Ravensworth!" broke off Blanche with another laugh. A laugh that was quite sufficient to prove the fact that she was heart-whole.

"The House!" repeated the Major. "Who is he, then?"

"He is very well off as to fortune, and is—something. It has to do with the House, not as a Member, though he will be that soon, I believe. I think he is secretary to one of the Ministers. His father was the elder brother, and the Reverend John Ravensworth the younger. There is a very great difference in their positions. Arnold is well-off, and said to be a rising man."

Every word increased Major Carlen's vexation. Even had his fear been correct, it seemed that the young man would not have been an undesirable match for Blanche, and he had saddled himself with her at a most inconvenient moment!

"Well, well," thought he; "she will soon make her mark, unless I am mistaken, and there's as good fish in the sea as ever came out of it."

Mrs. Guy, widow of the late Admiral Guy, vegetating for years past upon her slight income in Jersey, was Major Carlen's younger sister, and a smaller edition of himself. She had the same generally fair-featured face, with the twisted nose and the gray eyes; but while his eyes were hard and fierce, hers were soft and kindly. She was a well-meaning, but indescribably silly woman; and her nervous fears and fancies had so grown upon her that they were becoming a disease. Lying before the fire on a sofa in her bedroom, she received Blanche with a flood of tears, supplemented by several moans. The tears were caused by the pleased surprise; the moans at her having come home on a Friday, for that must surely betoken ill-luck. Blanche was irreverent enough to laugh.

Major Carlen still counted a few acquaintances of consideration in the social world, and Miss Heriot was introduced to them. Mrs. Guy was persuaded to temporarily forget her ailments, and to act as chaperon. The Major gave his sister a new dress and bonnet, and a cap or two; and as she had not yet quite done with vanity (has a woman ever done with it?), she fell before the bribe.

He had been right in his opinion that Blanche's beauty would not fail to make its mark. So charming a girl, so lovely of face and graceful of form, so innocent of guile, had not been seen of late. Before the spring had greatly advanced, a Captain Cross made proposals for her to the Major. He was of excellent family, and offered fair settlements. The Major accepted him, not deeming it at all necessary to consult his daughter.

Blanche rebelled. "I don't care for him, papa," she objected.

The Major gave his nose a twist. He did not intend to have any trouble with Blanche, and would not allow her to begin it.

"Not care!" he exclaimed in surprise. "What does that matter? Captain Cross is a fine man, stands six feet one, and you'll care for him in time."

"But, before I consent to marry him, I ought to know whether I shall like him or not."

"Blanche, you are a dunce! You have been smothered up in that parsonage till you know nothing. Do you suppose that in our class of society it is usual to fall in love, as the ploughboys and milkmaids do? People marry first, and grow accustomed to each other afterwards. Whatever you do, my dear, don't betray gaucherie of that kind."

Blanche Heriot doubted. She never supposed but that he whom she called father had her true interest at heart, and must be so acting. Mrs. Guy, too, unconsciously swayed her. A martyr to poverty herself, she believed that in marrying one so well-off as Captain Cross, a girl must enter upon the seventh heaven of happiness. Altogether, Blanche yielded; yielded against her inclination and her better judgment. She consented to marry Captain Cross, and preparations were begun.

Meanwhile, Arnold Ravensworth had been an occasional visitor at Major Carlen's, the Major making no sort of objection, now that circumstances were explained: indeed, he encouraged him there, and was especially cordial. Major Carlen had invariably one eye on the world and the other on self-interest, and it occurred to him that a rising man, as Arnold Ravensworth beyond doubt was, might prove useful to him in one way or another.

One evening, when it was yet only the beginning of April, Mr. Ravensworth called in Gloucester Place, and found the Major alone.

"Are Mrs. Guy and Blanche out?" he asked.

"They are upstairs with the dressmaker," replied the Major. "We sent to her to-day to spur on with Blanche's things, and she has come to-night for fresh orders."

"Is the marriage being hurried on, Major?"

"Time is creeping on, sir," was the gruff answer.

"Are they getting ahead with the settlements? When I saw you last week, you were in a way at the delay, and said lawyers had only been invented for one's torment."

"They got on, after that, and the deeds were ready and waiting for signature. But I dropped them a note yesterday to say they might burn them, as so much waste paper," returned the Major.

"Burn the settlements!" echoed Mr. Ravensworth.

The Major's eyes, that could look pleasant on occasion, glinted at his astonishment. "Those settlements are being replaced by heavier ones," he said. "Blanche does not marry Captain Cross. It's off. A more eligible offer has been made her, and Cross is dismissed."

Mr. Ravensworth doubted whether he heard aright. Major Carlen resumed. "And she was making herself miserable over it. She cannot endure Cross."

"What a disappointment for Cross! What a mortification! Will he accept his dismissal?"

"He will be obliged to accept it," returned the Major, pulling up his shirt-collar, which was always high enough for two. "He has no other choice left to him. A man does not die of love nowadays; or rush into an action for breach of promise, and become a laughing-stock at his club. Blanche marries Lord Level."

"Lord Level!" Mr. Ravensworth repeated in a curious accent.

"You look as though you doubted the information."

"I do not relish it, for your daughter's sake," replied Mr. Ravensworth. "She never can—can—like Lord Level."

"What's the matter with Lord Level? He may be approaching forty, but—"

Mr. Ravensworth laughed. "Not just yet, Major Carlen."

"Well, say he's thirty-four; thirty-three, if you like. Blanche, at twenty, needs guiding. And if he is not as rich as some peers, he is ten times richer than Cross. He met Blanche out, and came dangling here after her. I did not give a thought to it, for I did not look upon Level as a marrying man: he has been somewhat talked of in another line—"

"Yes," emphatically interrupted Mr. Ravensworth. "Well?"

"Well!" irritably returned the Major: "then there's so much the more credit due to him for settling down. When he found that Cross was really expecting to have Blanche, and that he might lose her altogether, he spoke up, and said he should like her himself."

"Does Blanche approve of the exchange?"

"She was rather inclined to kick at it," returned the Major, in his respectable phraseology, "and we had a few tears.—But if you ask questions in that sarcastic tone, sir, you don't deserve to be answered. Not that Blanche wanted to keep Cross; she acknowledged that she was only too thankful to be rid of him; but, about behaving dishonourably, as she called it. 'My dear,' said I, 'there's your absurd rusticity coming in again. You don't know the world. Such things are done in high life every day.' She believed me, and was reconciled. You look black as a thunder-cloud, Ravensworth. What right have you to do so, pray?"

"None in the world. I beg pardon. I was thinking of Blanche's happiness."

"You had better think of her good," retorted the Major. "She likes Level. I don't say she is yet in love with him: but she did not like Cross. Level is an attractive man, remember."

"Has been rather too much so," cynically retorted Mr. Ravensworth.

"Here she comes. I am going out; so you may offer your congratulations at leisure."

Major Carlen went away, and Blanche entered. She took her seat by the fire, and as Mr. Ravensworth gazed down upon her, a feeling of deep regret and pity came over him. Shame! thought he, to sacrifice her to Level. For in truth that nobleman's name was not in the best odour, and Arnold Ravensworth was a man of strict notions.

It has been asserted that some natures possess an affinity the one for the other; are irresistibly drawn together in the repose of full and perfect confidence. It is a mysterious affinity, not born of love: and it may be experienced by two men or women who have outlived even the remembrance of the passion. Had Blanche Heriot been offered to Arnold Ravensworth, he would have declined her, for he loved another, and she had as much idea of loving the man in the moon as of loving him. Nevertheless, that never-dying, unfathomable part of them, the spirit, was attracted, like finding like. Between such, there can be little reserve.

"What unexpected changes take place, Blanche!"

"Do not blame me," she replied, with a rising colour, her tone sinking to a whisper. "My father says it is right, and I obey him."

"I hope you like Lord Level?"

"Better than I liked someone else," was her answer, as she looked into the fire. "At first the—the change frightened me. It did not seem right, and it was so very sudden. But I am getting over that feeling now. Papa says he is very good."

Papa says he is very good! The old hypocrite of a Major! thought Mr. Ravensworth. But it was not his place to tell her that Lord Level had not been very good.

"Oh, Blanche!" he exclaimed, "I hope you will be happy! Is it to be soon?"

"Yes, they say so. As soon, I think, as the settlements can be ready. Papa sent to-day to hurry on my wedding things. Lord Level is going abroad immediately, and wishes to take me with him."

"They say so!" was his mental repetition. "This poor child, brought up in the innocence of her simple country home, more childish, more tractable and obedient, more inexperienced than are those of less years who have lived in the world, is as a puppet in their hands. But the awakening will come."

"You are going?" said Blanche, as he rose. "Will you not stay and take tea? Mrs. Guy will be down soon."

"Not this evening. Hark! here is the Major back again."

"I do not think it is papa's step," returned Blanche, bending her ear to listen.

It was not. As she spoke, the door was thrown open by the servant. "Lord Level."

Lord Level entered, and took the hand which Mr. Ravensworth released. Mr. Ravensworth looked full at the peer as he passed him: they were not acquainted. A handsome man, with a somewhat free expression—a countenance that Mr. Ravensworth took forthwith a prejudice against, perhaps unjustly. "Who's that, Blanche?" he heard him say as the servant closed the door.

Lord Level was a fine, powerful man, of good height and figure; his dark auburn hair was wavy and worn rather long, in accordance with the fashion of the day. His complexion was fair and fresh, and his features were good. Altogether he was what the Major had called him, an attractive man. Blanche Heriot had danced with him and he had danced with her; the one implies the other, you will say; and a liking for one another had sprung up. It may not have been love on either side as yet—but that is uncertain.

"How lovely!" exclaimed Blanche, as he held out to her a small bouquet of lilies-of-the-valley, and their sweet perfume caught her senses.

"I brought them for you," whispered Lord Level; and he bent his face nearer and took a silent kiss from her lips. It was the first time; and Blanche blushed consciously.

"You did not tell me who that was, Blanche."

"Arnold Ravensworth," she replied. "You have heard me speak of him."

"An ill-tempered looking man!"

"Do you think so? Well, yes, perhaps he did look cross to-night. He had been hearing about—about us—from papa; and I suppose it did not please him."

Archibald Baron Level drew himself up to his full height; his face assumed its haughtiest expression. "What business is it of his?" he asked. "Does he wish to aspire to you himself?"

"Oh, no, no; he is soon to be married. He is a man of strict honour, and I fear he thinks that papa—that I—that we have not behaved well to Captain Cross."

They were standing side by side on the hearth-rug, the fire-light playing on them and on Blanche's shrinking face. How miserably uncomfortable the subject of Captain Cross made her she could never tell.

"See here, Blanche," spoke Lord Level, after a pause. "I was given to understand by Major Carlen that when Captain Cross proposed for you, you refused him; that it was only by dint of pressure and persuasion that you consented to the engagement. Major Carlen told me that as the time went on you became so miserable under it, hating Captain Cross with a greater dislike day by day, that he had resolved before I spoke to save you by breaking it off. Was this the case, or not?"

"Yes, it was. It is true that I felt wretchedly miserable in the prospect of marrying Captain Cross. And oh, how I thank papa for having himself resolved to break it off! He did not tell me that."

"Because I have some honour of my own; and I would not take you sneakingly from Cross, or any other man. You must come to me above-board in all ways, Blanche, or not at all."

Blanche felt her heart beating. She turned to glance at him, fearing what he might mean.

"So that if there is anything behind the scenes which has been kept from me; that is, if it be not of your own good and free will that you marry me; if you gave up Captain Cross liking him, because—because—well, though I feel ashamed to suggest such a thing—because my rank may be somewhat higher than his, or for any other reason: why then matters had better be at an end between us. No harm will have been done, Blanche."

Blanche's face was drawn and white. "Do you mean that you wish to give me up?"

"Wish it! It would be the greatest pain I could ever know in life. My dear, have you failed to understand me? I want you; I want you to be my wife; but not at the sacrifice of my honour. If Captain Cross—"

Blanche broke down. "Oh, don't leave me to him!" she implored. "Of course, I could never, never marry him now; I would rather die. Indeed, I do not quite know what you mean. It was all just as you have been told by papa; there was nothing kept behind."

Lord Level pillowed her head upon his arm. "Blanche, my dear, it was you who invoked this," he whispered, "by talking of Mr. Ravensworth's reflection on you in his 'strict honour.' Be assured I would not leave you to Captain Cross unless compelled to do so, or to any other man."

Her tears were falling. Lord Level kissed them away.

"Shall I buy you, my love?—bind you to me with a golden fetter?" And, taking a small case from his waistcoat-pocket, he slipped upon her marriage finger a hoop of gold, studded with diamonds. His deep-gray eyes were strained upon her through their dark lashes—eyes which had done mischief in their day—and her hand was lingering in his.

"There, Blanche; you see I have bought you; you are my property now—my very own. And, my dear, the ring must be worn always as the keeper of the marriage-ring when you shall be my wife."

It was a most exquisite relief to her. Blanche liked him far better than she had liked Captain Cross. And as Lord Level pressed his last kiss upon her lips—for Mrs. Guy was heard approaching—Blanche could never be sure that she did not return it.

A few more interviews such as these, and the young lady would be in love with him heart and soul.

And it may as well be mentioned, ere the chapter quite closes, that Mr. Charles Strange was out of the way of all this plotting and planning and love-making. The whole of that spring he was over in Paris, watching a case involving English and French interests of importance, that was on before the French courts, and of which Brightman and Strange were the English solicitors.

CHAPTER VII

TRIED AT THE OLD BAILEY

"Oh, Mrs. Guy, he is coming, after all! He is indeed!"

Blanche Heriot's joyful tones, as she read the contents of a short letter brought in by the evening post, aroused old Mrs. Guy, who was dozing over her knitting one Tuesday evening in the May twilight.

"Eh? What, my dear? Who do you say is coming?"

"Tom. He says he must stretch a point for once. He cannot let anyone else give me away."

"The Major is to give you away, Blanche."

"I know he intended to do so if Tom failed me. But Tom is my brother."

"Well, well, child; settle it amongst yourselves. I don't see that it matters one way or the other. There's a knock at the door! Dear me! It must be Lord Level."

"Lord Level cannot be back again before to-morrow. He is at Marshdale, you know," dissented Blanche. "I think it may be Tom. I hope it is Tom. He says here he shall be in town as soon as his letter."

"Mr. Strange," announced a servant, throwing wide the drawing-room door.

Charles Strange had only that morning returned from Paris, having crossed by the night mail. The legal business on which he and Mr. Brightman were just now so much occupied, involving serious matters for a client who lived in Paris, had kept Charles over there nearly all the spring. Blanche ran to his arms. She looked upon him as her brother, quite as much as she looked upon Tom.

"And so, Blanche, we are to lose you," he said, when he had kissed her. "And within a day or two, I hear."

He knew very little of Blanche Heriot's approaching marriage, except that the bridegroom was Archibald, Lord Level. And that little he had heard from Mr. Brightman. Blanche did not write to him about it. She had written to tell him she was going to be married to Captain Cross: but when that marriage was summarily broken off by Major Carlen, Blanche felt a little ashamed, and did not send word to Charles.

"The day after to-morrow, at eleven o'clock in the morning," put in Mrs. Guy, in response to the last remark.

All his attention given to Blanche, Charles Strange really had not observed the old lady. He turned to regard her.

"You cannot have forgotten Mrs. Guy, Charles," said Blanche, noticing his doubtful look.

"I believe I had for the moment," he answered, in those pleasant, cordial tones that won him a way with everyone, as he went up and shook the old lady heartily by both hands. "I heard you were staying here, Mrs. Guy, but I had forgotten it."

They sat down—Blanche and Charles near the open window, Mrs. Guy not moving from her low easy-chair on the hearthrug—and began to talk of the wedding.

"Tom is really coming up to give me away," said Blanche, showing him Captain Heriot's short note. "It is very good of him, for he must be very busy: but Tom was always good. You are aware, Charles, I suppose, that the regiment is embarking for India? Major Carlen saw the announcement this morning in the Times."

At that moment Charles Strange saw, or fancied he saw, a warning look telegraphed to him by Mrs. Guy: and, placing it in conjunction with Blanche's words, he fancied he must know its meaning.

"Yes, I heard the regiment was ordered out," he answered shortly; and turned the subject. "Will Lord Level be here tonight, Blanche? I should like to see him."

"No," she replied. "He went yesterday to Marshdale House, his place in Surrey, and will not return until to-morrow. I think you will like him, Charles."

"I hope you do," replied Charles involuntarily. "That is the chief consideration, Blanche."

He looked at her meaningly as he spoke, and it brought a blush to her face. What a lovely face it was—fair and pure, its blue eyes haughty as of yore, its golden hair brilliant and abundant! She wore a simple evening dress of white muslin, and a blue sash, an inexpensive necklace of twisted blue beads on her neck, no bracelets at all on her arms. She looked what she really was—an inexperienced school-girl. Lord Level's engagement ring on her finger, with its flashing diamonds, was the only ornament of value she had about her.

In the momentary silence that ensued, Blanche left her seat and went to stand at the open window.

"Oh," she exclaimed, an instant later, "I do think this may be Tom! A cab has stopped here."

Charles Strange rose. Mrs. Guy lifted her finger, and he bent down to her. Blanche was still at the window.

"She does not know he has sold out," warningly breathed Mrs. Guy. "She knows nothing of his wild ways, or the fine market he has brought his eggs to, poor fellow. We have kept it from her."

Charles nodded; and the servant opened the door with another announcement.

"Captain Heriot." Blanche flew across the room and was locked in her brother's arms.

Poor Tom Heriot had indeed, as Mrs. Guy expressed it, with more force than elegance, brought his eggs to a fine market. It was some few months now since he sold out of the Army; and what he was doing and how he contrived to exist and flourish without money, his friends did not know. During the spring he had made his appearance in Paris to prefer an appeal for help to Charles, and Charles had answered it to the extent of his power.

Just as gay, just as light-hearted, just as débonnaire as ever was Tom Heriot. To see him and to hear him as he sat this evening with them in Gloucester Place, you might have thought him as free from care as an Eton boy—as flourishing as a duke-royal. Little blame to Blanche that she suspected nothing of the existing state of things.

When Charles rose to say "Good-night," Tom Heriot said it also, and they went away together.

"Charley, lad," said the latter, as the street-door closed behind them, "could you put me up at your place for two nights—until after this wedding is over?"

"To be sure I can. Leah will manage it."

"All right. I have sent a portmanteau there."

"You did not come up from Southampton to-day, Tom? Blanche thought you did."

"And I am much obliged to them for allowing her to think it. I would have staked my last five-pound note, if you'll believe me, Charley, that old Carlen had not as much good feeling in him. I am vegetating in London; have been for some time, Blanche's letter was forwarded to me by a comrade who lets me use his address."

"And what are you doing in London?" asked Charles.

"Hiding my 'diminished head,' old fellow," answered Tom, with a laugh. No matter how serious the subject, he could not be serious over it.

"How much longer do you mean to stand here?" continued Charles—for the Captain (people still gave him his title) had not moved from the door.

"Till an empty cab goes by."

"We don't want a cab this fine night, Tom. Let us walk. Look how bright the moon is up there."

"Ay; my lady's especially bright tonight. Rather too much so for people who prefer the shade. How you stare, Charley! Fact is, I feel safer inside a cab just now than parading the open streets."

"Afraid of being taken for debt?" whispered Charles.

"Worse than that," said Tom laconically.

"Worse than that!" repeated Charles. "Why, what do you mean?"

"Oh, nothing," and Tom Heriot laughed again. "Except that I am in the deuce's own mess, and can't easily get out of it. There's a cab! Here, driver! In with you, Charley."

And on the following Thursday, when his sister's marriage with Lord Level took place, who so gay, who so free from care, who so attractive as Tom Heriot?—when giving her away. Lord Level had never before seen his future brother-in-law (or half brother-in-law, as the more correct term would be), and was agreeably taken with him. A random young fellow, no doubt, given to playing the mischief with his own prospects, but a thorough gentleman, and a very prepossessing one.

"And this is my other brother—I have always called him so," whispered Blanche to her newly-made husband, as she presented Charles Strange to him on their return from church to Gloucester Place. Lord Level shook hands heartily; and Charles, who had been prejudiced against his lordship, of whom tales were told, took rather a liking to the tall, fine man of commanding presence, of handsome face and easy, genial manners.

After the breakfast, to which very few guests were bidden, and at which Mrs. Guy presided, as well as her nerves permitted, at one end of the table and Major Carlen at the other, Lord and Lady Level departed for Dover on their way to the Continent.

And in less than a week after the wedding, poor Thomas Heriot, who could not do an unkind action, who never had been anyone's enemy in the whole world, and never would be anyone's, except his own, was taken into custody on a criminal charge.

The blow came upon Charles Strange as a clap of thunder. That Tom was in a mess of some kind he knew well; nay, in half a dozen messes most likely; but he never glanced at anything so terrible as this.

Tom had fenced with his questions during the day or two he stayed in Essex Street, and laughed them off. What the precise charge was, Charles could not learn at the first moment. Some people said felony, some whispered forgery. By dint of much exertion and inquiry, he at last knew that it was connected with "Bills."

Certain bills had been put into circulation by Thomas Heriot, and there was something wrong about them. At least, about one of them; since it bore the signature of a man who had never seen the bill.

"I am as innocent of it as a child unborn," protested Thomas Heriot to Charles, more solemnly in earnest than he had ever been heard to speak. "True, I got the bills discounted: accommodation bills, you understand, and they were to have been provided for; but that any good name had been forged to one of them, I neither knew nor dreamt of."

"Yet you knew the good name was there?"

"But I thought it had been genuinely obtained."

This was at the first interview Charles held with him in prison. "Whence did you get the bills?" Charles continued.

"They were handed to me by Anstey. He is the true culprit in all this, Charles, and he is slinking out of it, and will get off scot-free. People warned me against the fellow; said he was making a cat's-paw of me; and by Jove it's true! I could not see it then, but my eyes are open now. He only made use of me for his own purposes. He had all, or nearly all, the money."

And this was just the truth of the business. The man Anstey, a gentleman once, but living by his wits for many years past, had got hold of light-headed, careless Tom Heriot, cajoled him of his friendship, and used him. Anstey escaped completely "scot-free," and Tom suffered.

Tom was guilty in the eyes of the law; and the law only takes cognizance of its own hard requirements. After examination, he was committed for trial. Charles Strange was nearly wild with distress; Mr. Brightman was much concerned; Arthur Lake (who was now called to the Bar) would have moved heaven and earth in the cause. Away went Charles to Mr. Serjeant Stillingfar: and that renowned special pleader and good-hearted man threw his best energies into the cause.

All in vain. At the trial, which shortly came on at the Old Bailey, Mr. Serjeant Stillingfar exerted his quiet but most telling eloquence uselessly. He might as well have wasted it on the empty air. Though indeed it did effect something, causing the sentence pronounced upon the unfortunate prisoner to be more lenient than it otherwise would have been. Thomas Heriot was sentenced to be transported for seven years.

Transportation beyond the seas was still in force then. And Thomas Heriot, with a cargo of greater or lesser criminals, was shipped on board the transport Vengeance, to be conveyed to Botany Bay.

It seemed to have taken up such a little space of time! Very little, compared with the greatness of the trouble. June had hardly come in when Tom was first taken; and the Vengeance sailed the beginning of August.

If Mrs. Guy had lamented beforehand the market that poor Tom Heriot had "brought his eggs to," what did she think of it now?

One evening in October a nondescript sort of vehicle, the German makers of which could alone know the name, arrived at a small village not far from the banks of the Rhine, clattering into the yard of the only inn the place contained. A gentleman and lady descended from it, and a parley ensued with the hostess, more protracted than it might have been, in consequence of the travellers' imperfect German, and her own imperfect French. Could madame accommodate them for the night, was the substance of their demand.

"Well—yes," was madame's not very assured answer: "if they could put up with a small bedroom."

"How small?"

She opened the door of—it was certainly not a room, though it might be slightly larger than a boot-closet; madame called it a cabinet-de-toilette. It was on the ground-floor, looking into the yard, and contained a bed, into which one person might have crept, provided he bargained with himself not to turn; but two people, never. Three of her beds were taken up with a milor and miladi Anglais, and their attendants.

Mrs. Ravensworth—a young wife—turned to her husband, and spoke in English. "Arnold, what can we do? We cannot go on in the dark, with such roads as these."

"My love, I see only one thing for it: you must sleep here, and I must sit up."

Madame interrupted; it appeared she added a small stock of English to her other acquirements. "Oh, but dat meeseraable for monsieur: he steef in legs for morning."

"And stiff in arms too," laughed Arnold Ravensworth. "Do try and find us a larger bedroom."

"Perhaps the miladi Anglaise might give up one of her rooms for dis one," debated the hostess, bustling away to ask.

She returned, followed by an unmistakable Englishwoman, fine both in dress and speech. Was she the miladi? She talked enough for one: vowing she would never give up her room to promiscuous travellers, who prowled about with no avant courier, taking their own chance of rooms and beds; and casting, as she spoke, annihilating glances at the benighted wanderers.

"Is anything the matter, Timms?" inquired a gentle voice in the background.

Mr. Ravensworth turned round quickly, for its tones struck upon his remembrance. There stood Blanche, Lady Level; and their hands simultaneously met in surprise and pleasure.

"Oh, this is unexpected!" she exclaimed. "I never should have thought of seeing you in this remote place. Are you alone?"

He drew his wife to his side. "I need not say who she is, Lady Level."

"Are you married, then?"

"Ask Mary."

It was an unnecessary question, seeing her there with him, and Lady Level felt it to be so, and smiled. Timms came forward with an elaborate apology and a string of curtseys, and hoped her room would be found good enough to be honoured by any friends of my lady's.

Lady Level's delight at seeing them seemed as unrestrained as a child's. Exiles from their native land can alone tell that to meet with home faces in a remote spot is grateful as the long-denied water to the traveller in the Eastern desert. And we are writing of days when to travel abroad was the exception, rather than the rule. "There is only one private sitting-room in the whole house, and that is mine, so you must perforce make it yours as well," cried Lady Level, as she laughingly led the way to it. "And oh! what a charming break it will be to my loneliness! Last night I cried till bedtime."

"Is not Lord Level with you?" inquired Mr. Ravensworth.

"Lord Level is in England. While they are getting Timms' room ready, will you come into mine?" she added to Mrs. Ravensworth.

"How long have you been married?" was Lady Level's first question as they entered it.

"Only last Tuesday week."

"Are you happy?"

"Oh yes."

"I knew your husband long before you did," added Lady Level. "Did he ever tell you so? Did he ever tell you what good friends we were? Closer friends, I think, than he and his cousin Cecilia. He used to come to White Littleham Rectory, and we girls there made much of him."

"Yes, he has often told me."

Mrs. Ravensworth was arranging her hair at the glass, and Lady Level held the light for her and looked on. The description given of her by Blanche to her father was a very good one. A pale, gentle girl, with nice eyes, dark, inexpressively soft and attractive. "I shall like you very much," suddenly exclaimed Lady Level. "I think you are very pretty—I mean, you have the sort of face I like to look at." Praise that brought a blush to the cheeks of Mrs. Ravensworth.

The landlady sent them in the best supper she could command at the hour; mutton chops, served German fashion, and soup, which Lady Level's man-servant, Sanders, who waited on them, persisted in calling the potash—and very watery potash it was, flavoured with cabbage. When the meal was over, and the cloth removed, they drew round the fire.

"Do you ever see papa?" Lady Level inquired of Mr. Ravensworth.

"Now and then. Not often. He has let his house again in Gloucester Place, and Mrs. Guy has gone back to the Channel Islands."

"Oh yes, I know all that," replied Blanche.

"The last time I saw Major Carlen he spoke of you—said that you and Lord Level were making a protracted stay abroad."

"Protracted!" Blanche returned bitterly; "yes, it is protracted. I long to be back in England, with a longing that has now grown into a disease. You have heard of the mal du pays that sometimes attacks the Swiss when they are away from their native land; I think that same malady has attacked me."

"But why?" asked Mr. Ravensworth, looking at her.

"I hardly know," she said, with some hesitation. "I had never been out of England before, and everything was strange to me. We went to Switzerland first, then on to Italy, then back again. The longer we stayed away from England, the greater grew my yearning for it. In Savoy I was ill; yes, I was indeed; we were at Chambéry; so ill as to require medical advice. It was on the mind, the doctor said. He was a nice old man, and told Lord Level that I was pining for my native country."

"Then, of course, you left for home at once?"

"We left soon, but we travelled like snails; halting days at one place, and days at another. Oh, I was so sick of it! And the places were all dull and retired, as this is; not those usually frequented by the English. At last we arrived here; to stay also, it appeared. When I asked why we did not go on, he said he was waiting for letters from home."

As Lady Level spoke she appeared to be lost in the past—an expression that you may have observed in old people when they are telling you tales of their youth. Her eyes were fixed on vacancy, and it was evident that she saw nothing of the objects around her, only the time gone by. She appeared to be anything but happy.

"Something up between my lord and my lady," thought Mr. Ravensworth. "Had your husband to wait long for the expected letters?" he asked aloud.

"I do not know: several came for him. One morning he had one that summoned him to England without the loss of a moment, and he said there was not time for me to be ready to accompany him. I prayed to go with him. I said Timms could come on afterwards with the luggage. It was of no use."

"Would he not take you?" exclaimed Mrs. Ravensworth, her eyes full of the astonishment her lips would not express.

Blanche shook her head. "No. He was quite angry with me; said I did not understand my position—that noblemen's wives could not travel in that unceremonious manner. I was on the point of telling him that I wished, to my heart, I had never been a nobleman's wife. Why did he marry me, unless he could look upon me as a companion and friend?" abruptly continued Lady Level, perhaps forgetting that she was not alone. "He treats me as a child."

What answer could be made to this?

"When do you expect him back again?" asked Mr. Ravensworth, after a pause.

"How do I know?" flashed Lady Level, her tone proving how inexpressibly sore was the subject. "He said he should return for me in a few days, but nearly three weeks have gone by, and I am still here. They have seemed to me like three months. I shall be ill if it goes on much longer."

"Of course you hear from him?"

"Oh yes, I hear from him. A few lines at a time, saying he will come for me as soon as he possibly can, and that I must not be impatient. I wanted to go over alone, and he returned me such an answer, asking what I meant by wishing to travel with servants only at my age. I shall do something desperate if I am left here another week."

"As you once did at White Littleham when they forbade your going to a concert, thinking you were too ill!" laughed Mr. Ravensworth.

"Dressed myself up in my best frock, and surprised them in the room. I had ten pages of Italian translation for that escapade."

"Do you like Italy?" he inquired, after a pause.

"No, I hate it!" And the animus in Lady Level's answer was so intense that the husband and wife exchanged stolen glances. Something must be out of gear.

"What parts of Italy did you stay in?"

"Chiefly at Pisa—that is not far from Florence, you know; and a few days at Florence. Lord Level took a villa at Pisa for a month—and why he did so I could not tell, for it was not the season when the English frequent it: no one, so to say, was there. We made the acquaintance of a Mrs. Page Reid, who had the next villa to ours."

"That was pleasant for you—if you liked her."

"But I did not like her," returned Lady Level, her delicate cheeks flushing. "That is, I did and I did not. She was a very pleasant woman, always ready to help us in any way; but she told dreadful tales of people—making one suspect things that otherwise would never have entered the imagination. Lord Level liked her at first, and ended by disliking her."

"Got up a flirtation with her," thought Mr. Ravensworth. But in that he was mistaken. And so they talked on.

It appeared that the mail passed through the village at night time; and the following morning a letter lay on the breakfast-table for Lady Level.

MY DEAR BLANCHE,—I have met with a slight accident, and must again postpone coming to you for a few days. I dare say it will not detain me very long. Rely upon it I shall be with you as soon as I possibly can be.—Ever affectionately yours, LEVEL.

"Short and sweet!" exclaimed Blanche, in her bitter disappointment, as she read the note at the window. "Arnold, when you and your wife leave to-morrow, what will become of me, alone here? If—"

Suddenly, as Lady Level spoke the last word, she started, and began to creep away from the window, as if fearing to be seen.

"Arnold! Arnold! who do you think is out there?" she exclaimed in a timid whisper.

"Why, who?" in astonishment. "Not Lord Level?"

"It is Captain Cross," she said with a shiver. "I would rather meet the whole world than him. My behaviour to him was—was not right; and I have felt ashamed of myself ever since."

Mr. Ravensworth looked out from the window. Captain Cross, seated on the bench in the inn yard, was solacing himself with a cigar.

"I would not meet him for the world! I would not let him see me: he might make a scene. I shall stay in my rooms all day. Why does my husband leave me to such chances as these?"

That Captain Cross had not been well used was certain; but the fault lay with Major Carlen, not with Blanche. Mr. Ravensworth spoke.

"Take my advice, Lady Level. Do not place yourself in Captain Cross's way, but do not run from him. I believe him to be a gentleman; and, if so, he will not say or do anything to annoy you. I will take care he does not, as long as I remain here."

In the course of the morning Captain Cross and Arnold Ravensworth met. "I find Lady Level's here!" the Captain abruptly exclaimed. "Are you staying with her?"

"I and my wife arrived here only last night, and were surprised to meet Lady Level."

"Where's he?" asked Captain Cross.

"In England."

"He in England and she here, and only six months married! Estranged, I suppose. Well, what else could she expect? People mostly reap what they sow."

Arnold Ravensworth laughed good-humouredly. He was not going to give a hint of the state of affairs that he suspected himself.

"You are prejudiced, Cross. Miss Heriot was not to blame for what happened. She was a child: and they did with her as they pleased."

"A child! Old enough to engage herself to one man, and to marry another," retorted Captain Cross, in a burst of angry feeling. "And Level, of all people!"—with sarcastic scorn. "Why does he leave her in Germany whilst he stays gallivanting in England? What do you say? Met with an accident, and can't come for her? That's his tale, I suppose. You may repeat it to the Marines, old boy; it won't do for me. I know Level; knew him of old."

Lady Level was as good as her word: she did not stir out of her rooms all day. On the following morning when Mr. Ravensworth came out of his chamber, he saw, from the corridor window, a travelling-carriage in the yard, packed. By the coat-of-arms he knew it for Lord Level's. Timms moved towards him in a flutter of delight.

"Oh, if you please, sir, breakfast is on the table, and my lady is waiting there, ready dressed. We are going to England, sir."

"Has Lord Level come?"

"No, sir: we are going with you. My lady gave orders, last night, to pack up for home. It is the happiest day I've known, sir, since I set foot in these barbarious countries."

Lady Level met him at the door of the breakfast-room; "ready dressed," as Timms expressed it, for travelling, even to her bonnet.

"Do you really mean to go with us?" he exclaimed.

"Yes," was her decisive reply. "That is, you must go with me. Stay here longer, I will not. I tell you, Arnold, I am sick to death of it. If Lord Level is ill and unable to come for me, I am glad to embrace the opportunity of travelling under your protection: he can't grumble at that. Besides—"

"Besides what?" asked Mr. Ravensworth, for she suddenly stopped.

"I do not choose to remain at an inn in which Captain Cross has taken up his abode: neither would my husband wish me to do so. After you and Mrs. Ravensworth left me last night, I sat over the wood fire, thinking these things over, and made my mind up. If I have not sufficient money for the journey, and I don't think I have, I must apply to you, Arnold."

Whether Mr. Ravensworth approved or disapproved of the decision, he had no power to alter it. Or, rather, whether Lord Level would approve of it. After a hasty breakfast, they went down to the carriage, which had already its array of five horses harnessed to it; Sanders and Timms perched side-by-side in their seat aloft. The two ladies were helped in by Mr. Ravensworth. Captain Cross leaned against the outer wall of the salle-à-manger, watching the departure. He approached Mr. Ravensworth.

"Am I driving her ladyship off?"

"Lady Level is going to England with us, to join her husband. I told you he had met with an accident."

"A merry meeting to them!" was the sarcastic rejoinder. And, as the carriage drove out of the inn-yard, Captain Cross deliberately lifted his hat to Lady Level: but lifted it, she thought, in mockery.

CHAPTER VIII

THE VINE-COVERED COTTAGE AT PISA

That Archibald, Lord Level, had been a gay man, fond of pleasure, fond of talking nonsense to pretty women, the world knew well: and perhaps, world-fashion, admired him none the less for it. But his wife did not know it. When Blanche Heriot became Blanche Level she was little more than an innocent child, entirely unversed in the world's false ways. She esteemed her husband; ay, and loved him, in a measure, and she was happy for a time.

It is true that while they were staying in Switzerland a longing for home came over her. They had halted in Paris for nearly a fortnight on their outward route. Some very nice people whom Lord Level knew were there; they were delighted with the fair young bride, and she was delighted with them. Blanche was taken about everywhere, no one being more anxious for her amusement than Lord Level himself. But one morning, in the very midst of numerous projected expeditions, he suddenly told Blanche that they must continue their journey that day.

"Oh, Archibald!" she had answered in a sort of dismay. "Why, it is this very afternoon that we were going to Fontainebleau!"

"My dear, you shall see Fontainebleau the next time we are in Paris," he said. "I have a reason for wishing to go on at once."

And they went on. Blanche was far too good and dutiful a wife to oppose her own will to her husband's, or to grumble. They went straight on to Switzerland—travelling in their own carriage—but instead of settling himself in one of those pretty dwellings on the banks of Geneva's lake, as he had talked of to Blanche, Lord Level avoided Geneva altogether, and chose a fearfully dull little village as their place of abode. Very lovely as to scenery, it is true; but quite unfrequented by travellers. It was there that Blanche first began to long for home.

Next, they went on to Italy, posting straight to Pisa, and there Lord Level took a pretty villa for a month in the suburbs of the town. Pisa itself was deserted: it was hot weather; and Blanche did not think it had many attractions. Lord Level, however, seemed to find pleasure in it. He knew Pisa well, having stayed at it in days gone by. He made Blanche familiar with the neighbourhood; together they admired and wondered at the Leaning Tower, in its green plain, backed by distant mountains; but he also went out and about a good deal alone.

One English dame of fashion was sojourning in the place—a widow, Mrs. Page Reid. She occupied the next villa to theirs, and called upon them; and she and Lady Level grew tolerably intimate. She was a talkative, gay woman of thirty—and beside her Blanche seemed like a timid schoolgirl.

One evening, when dinner was over, Lord Level strolled out—as he often did—leaving his wife with Mrs. Page Reid, who had dined with them. The two ladies talked together, and sang a song or two; and so whiled away the time.

"Let us go out for a stroll, too!" exclaimed Mrs. Page Reid, speaking on a momentary impulse, when she found the time growing monotonous.

Blanche readily agreed. It was a most lovely night; the moon bright and silvery in the Italian sky. Putting on some fleecy shawls, the ladies went down the solitary road, and turned by-and-by into a narrow lane that looked like a grove of evergreens. Soon they came to a pretty dwelling-place on the left, half villa, half cottage. Vines grew up its trellised walls, flowers and shrubs crowded around it.

"A charming little spot!" cried Mrs. Page Reid, as they halted to peep through the hedge of myrtles that clustered on each side the low entrance-gate. "And two people are sitting there—lovers, I dare say," she added, "telling their vows under the moonbeams."

In front of the vine-wreathed window, on a bench overhung by the branches of the trailing shrubs, the laurels and the myrtles, sat two young people. The girl was tall, slender, graceful; her dark eyes had a flashing fire even in the moonlight; her cheeks wore a rose-red flush.

"How pretty she is!" whispered Blanche. "Look at her long gold earrings! And he— Oh!"

"What's the matter?" cried Mrs. Page Reid, the tone of the last word startling her.

"It is my husband."

"Nonsense!" began Mrs. Page Reid. But after one doubting, disbelieving look, she saw that it was so. Catching Blanche's hand, she drew her forcibly away, and when they had gained the highroad, burst into a long, low laugh.

"Don't think about it, dear," she said to Blanche. "It's nothing. The best of husbands like to amuse themselves behind our backs."

"Perhaps he was—was—inquiring the way—or something," hazarded Blanche, whose breath was coming rather faster than usual.

Mrs. Page Reid nearly choked. "Oh, to be sure!" she cried, when she could speak.

"You don't think so? You think it was—something else?"

"You are only a little goose, my dear, in the ways of the world," rejoined Mrs. Page Reid. "Where's the man that does not like to talk with a pretty woman? Lord Level, of all others, does."

"He does?"

"Well, he used to do so. Of course he has mended his manners. And the women, mind you, liked to talk to him. But don't take up the notion, please, that by saying that I insinuate any unorthodox talking," added Mrs. Page Reid as an after-thought, when she caught a look at Lady Level's tell-tale countenance.

"I shall ask Lord Level—"

"Ask nothing," impressively spoke the elder lady, cutting short the words. "Say nothing to your husband. Take my advice, Lady Level, for it is good. There is no mortal sin a wife can commit so repugnant in her husband's eyes as that of spying upon his actions. It would make him detest her in the end."

"But I was not spying. We saw it by accident."

"All the same. Let it pass from your mind as though it had never been."

Blanche was dubious. If there was no harm, why should she not speak of it?—and she could not think there was harm. And if there was—why, she would not have breathed it to him for the world. Dismissing the subject, she and Mrs. Page Reid sat down to a quiet game at cards. When Lord Level came in, their visitor said good-night.

Blanche sat on in silence and torment. Should she speak, or should she not? Lord Level seemed buried in a reverie.

"Archibald," she presently began.

"Yes," he answered, rousing himself.

"I—we—I and Mrs. Page Reid went out for a little walk in the moonlight. And—"

"Well, my dear?"

"We saw you," Blanche was wishing to say; but somehow her courage failed her. Her breath was short, her throat was beating.

"And it was very pleasant," she went on. "As warm and light as day."

"Just so," said Lord Level. "But the night air is treacherous, apt to bring fever. Do not go out again in it, love."

So her effort to speak had failed. And the silence only caused her to think the more. Blanche Level would have given her best diamond earrings to know who that person was in the gold ones.

An evening or two further on, when she was quite alone, Lord Level having again strolled out, she threw on the same fleecy shawl and betook herself down the road to the cottage in the grove—the cottage that looked like a pretty bower in the evergreens. And—yes—

Well, it was a strange thing—a startling thing; startling, anyway, to poor Blanche Level's heart; but there, on the self-same bench, side by side, sat Lord Level and the Italian girl. Her face looked more beautiful than before to the young wife's jealous eyes; the gold earrings glittered and sparkled in the moonlight. He and she were conversing in a low, earnest voice, and Lord Level was smoking a cigar.

Blanche stood rooted to the spot, shivering a little as she peered through the myrtle hedge, but never moving. Presently the young woman lifted her head, called out "Si," and went indoors, evidently in answer to a summons.

"Nina," sang out Lord Level. "Nina"—raising his voice higher—"I have left my cigar-case on the table; bring it to me when you come out again."

He spoke in English. The next minute the girl returned, cigar-case in hand. She took her place by his side, as before, and they fell to talking again.

Lady Level drew away. She went home with flagging steps and a bitterly rebellious heart.

Not to her husband would she speak; her haughty lips were sealed to him—and should be ever, she resolved in her new pain. But she gave a hint the next day of what she had again seen to Mrs. Page Reid.

That lady only laughed. To her mind it was altogether a rich joke. Not only the affair itself, but Blanche's ideas upon it.

"My dear Lady Level," she rejoined, "as I said before, you are very ignorant of the ways of the world. I assure you our husbands like to chatter to others as well as to us. Nothing wrong, of course, you understand; the mistake is, if we so misconstrue it. Lord Level is a very attractive man, you know, and has had all sorts of escapades."

"I never knew that he had had them."

"Well, it is hardly likely he would tell you of them before you were his wife. He will tell you fast enough some day."

"Won't you tell me some of them now?"

Blanche was speaking very equably, as if worldly wisdom had come to her all at once; and Mrs. Page Reid began to ransack her memory for this, that, or the other that she might have heard of Lord Level. As tales of scandal never lose by carrying, she probably converted mole-hills into mountains; most assuredly so to Blanche's mind. Anyway, she had better have held her tongue.

From that time, what with one doubt and another, Lady Level's regard for her lord was changed. Her feeling towards him became most bitter. Resentment?—indignation?—neither is an adequate word for it.

At the week's end they left Pisa, for the month was up, and travelled back by easy stages to Savoy. Blanche wanted to go direct to England, but Lord Level objected: he said she had not yet seen enough of Switzerland. It was in Savoy that her illness came on—the mal du pays, as they called it. When she grew better, they started towards home; travelling slowly and halting at every available spot. That his wife's manner had changed to him, Lord Level could only perceive, but he had no suspicion of its cause. He put it down to her anger at his keeping her so long away from England.

The morning after they arrived at the inn in Germany (of which mention has been made) Lord Level received a letter, which seemed to disturb him. It was forwarded to him by a banker in Paris, to whom at present all his letters were addressed. Telling Blanche that it contained news of some matter of business upon which he must start for London without delay, he departed; declining to listen to her prayer that she might accompany him, but promising to return for her shortly. It was at that inn that Arnold Ravensworth and his wife found Lady Level: and it was with them she journeyed to England.

And here we must give a few words to Lord Level himself. He crossed the Channel by the night mail to Dover, and reached London soon after daybreak. In the course of the day he called at his bankers', Messrs. Coutts and Co., to inquire for letters: orders having now been given by him to Paris to forward them to London. One only awaited him, which had only just then come in.

As Lord Level read it, he gave utterance to a word of vexation. For it told him that the matter of business upon which he had hurried over was put off for a week: and he found that he might just as well have remained in Germany.

The first thought that crossed his mind was—should he return to his wife? But it was hardly worth while doing so. So he took rooms in Holles Street, at a comfortable house where he had lodged before, and looked up friends and acquaintants at his club. But he did not let that first day pass without calling on Charles Strange.

The afternoon was drawing to an end in Essex Street, and Charles was in his own private room, all his faculties given to a deed, when Lord Level was shown in. It was for Charles he asked, not for Mr. Brightman.

"What an awful business this is!" began his lordship, when greetings had passed.

Charles lifted his hands in dismay. No need to ask to whom the remark applied: or to mention poor Tom Heriot by name.

"Could nothing be done, Mr. Strange?" demanded the peer in his coldest and haughtiest tones. "Were there no means that could have been taken to avert exposure?"

"Yes, I think there might have been, but for Tom's own careless folly: and that's the most galling part of it," returned Charles. "Had he only made a confidant of me beforehand, we should have had a try for it. If I could not have found the money myself, Mr. Brightman would have done so."

"You need only have applied to me," said Lord Level. "I should not have cared how much I paid—to prevent exposure."

"But in his carelessness, you see, he never applied to anyone; he allowed the blow to fall upon him, and then it was too late—"

"Was he a fool?" interjected Lord Level.

"There is this excuse for his not speaking: he did not know that things were so bad, or that the people would proceed to extremities."

The peer drew in his haughty lips. "Did he tell you that pretty fable?"

"Believe this much, Lord Level: what Tom said, he thought. Anyone more reprehensibly light and heedless I do not know, but he is incapable of falsehood. And in saying that he did not expect so grave a charge, or believe there were any grounds on which it could be made, I am sure he spoke only the truth. He was drawn in by one Anstey, and—"

"I read the reports of the trial," interrupted Lord Level. "Do not be at the pain of going over the details again."

"Well, the true culprit was Anstey; there's no doubt of that. But, like most cunning rogues, he was able to escape consequences himself, and throw them upon Tom. I am sure, Lord Level, that Tom Heriot no more knew the bill was forged than I knew it. He knew well enough there was something shady about it; about that and others which had been previously in circulation, and had been met when they came to maturity. This one bill was different. Of course there's all the difference between shady bills of accommodation, and a bill that has a responsible man's name to it, which he never signed himself."

"But what on earth possessed Heriot to allow himself to be drawn into such toils?"

"Ah, there it is. His carelessness. He has been reprehensibly careless all his life. And now he has paid for it. All's over."

"He is already on his passage out in the convict ship Vengeance, is he not?" said Lord Level, with suppressed rage.

"Yes: ever since early in August," shuddered Charles. "How does Blanche bear it?"

"Blanche does not know it."

"Not know it!"

"No. As yet I have managed to keep it from her. I dread its reaching her, and that's the truth. It is a fearful disgrace. She is fond of him, and would feel it keenly."

"But I cannot understand how it can have been kept from her."

"Well, it has been. Why, she does not even know that he sold out! She thinks he embarked with the regiment for India last May! We had been in Paris about ten days—after our marriage, you know—when one morning, happening to take up the Times, I saw in it the account of his apprehension and first examination. They had his name in as large as life—Thomas Heriot. 'Some gross calumny,' I thought; 'Blanche must not hear of this:' and I gave orders for continuing our journey that same day. However, I soon found that it was not a calumny: other examinations took place, and he was committed for trial. I kept my wife away from all places likely to be frequented by the English, lest a word should be dropped to her: and as yet, as I tell you, she knows nothing of it. She is very angry with me in her heart, I can see, for taking her to secluded places, and for keeping her away from England so long, but this has been my sole motive. I want the thought of it to die out of people's minds before I bring her home."

"She is not with you, then?"

"She is in Germany. I had to hasten over here upon a matter of business, and shall return for her when it is finished. I have taken my old rooms in Holles Street for a week. You must look me up there."

"I will," said Charles.

Mr. Brightman came in then, and the trouble was gone over again. Lord Level felt it keenly; there could be no doubt of that. He inquired of the older and more experienced lawyer whether there was any chance of bringing Anstey to a reckoning, so that he might be punished; and as to any expense, great or small, that might be incurred in the process, his lordship added, he would give carte blanche for that with greater delight than he had given money for anything in his whole life.

Charles could not help liking him. With all his pride and his imputed faults, few people could help liking Lord Level.

Meanwhile, as may have been gathered in the last chapter, Lord Level was detained in England longer than he had thought for. Lady Level grew impatient and more impatient at the delay: and then, taking the reins into her own hands, she crossed the Channel with Mr. and Mrs. Arnold Ravensworth.

CHAPTER IX

COMPLICATIONS

Crossing by the night boat from Calais, the travellers reached Dover at a very early hours of the morning. Lady Level, with her servants, proceeded at once to London; but Mrs. Ravensworth, who had been exceedingly ill on the passage, required some repose, and she and her husband waited for a later train.

"Make use of our house, Lady Level," said Mr. Ravensworth—speaking of his new abode in Portland Place. "The servants are expecting me and their mistress, and will have all things in readiness, and make you comfortable."

"Thank you all the same, Arnold," said Lady Level; "but I shall drive straight to my husband's rooms in Holles Street."

"I would not—if I were you," he dissented. "You are not expected, and may not find anything ready in lodgings, so early in the morning. Drive first to my house and have some breakfast. You can go on to Holles Street afterwards."

Sensible advice. And Lady Level took it.

In the evening of that same day, Arnold Ravensworth and his wife reached Portland Place from the London terminus. To Mr. Ravensworth's surprise, who should be swinging from the door as the cab stopped but Major Carlen in his favourite purple and scarlet cloak, his gray hair disordered and his eyes exceeding fierce.

"Here's a pretty kettle-of-fish!" cried he, scarcely giving Arnold time to hand out his wife, and following him into the hall. "You have done a nice thing!"

"What is amiss?" asked Mr. Ravensworth, as he took the Major into a sitting-room.

"Amiss!" returned the excited Major. "I would advise you not to fall into Level's way just now. How the mischief came you to bring Blanche over?"

"We accompanied Lady Level to England at her request: I took no part in influencing her decision. Lady Level is her own mistress."

"Is she, though! She'll find she's not, if she begins to act in opposition to her husband. Before she was married, she had not a wish of her own, let alone a will—and there's where Level was caught, I fancy," added the Major, in a parenthesis, nodding his head knowingly. "He thought he had picked up a docile child, who would never be in his way. What with that and her beauty—anyway, he could not think she would be setting up a will, and an obstinate one, as she's doing now, rely upon that."

Major Carlen was striding from one end of the room to the other, his cloak catching in the furniture as he swayed about. Arnold thought he had been drinking: but he was a man who could take a great deal, and show it very little.

"The case is this," said he, unfastening the troublesome cloak, and flinging it on to a chair. "Level has been in England a week or two; amusing himself, I take it. He didn't want his wife, I suppose; well and good: men like a little society, and as long as they keep their wives in the dark, there's no reason why they shouldn't have it—"

"Major Carlen!" burst forth Mr. Ravensworth. "Lord Level's wife is your daughter. Have you forgotten it?"

"My step-daughter. What if she is? Does that render her different from others? Are you going to climb a pole and cry Morality? You are a young married man, Arnold Ravensworth, and must be on your good behaviour just now; it's etiquette."

Mr. Ravensworth was not easily excited, but the red flush of anger darkened his cheek. He could have thrust the old rascal from the house.

"Level leaves his wife in France, and tells her to remain there. Germany? Well, say Germany, then. My lady chooses to disobey, and comes to England, under your wing: and I wish old Harry had driven you to any place rather than the one she was stopping at. She reaches town to-day, and drives to Lord Level's rooms in Holles Street, whence he had dated his letters to her—and a model of incaution he was for doing it; why couldn't he have dated from his club? My lady finds or hears of something there she does not like. Well, what could she expect? They were his rooms; taken for himself, not for her; and if she had not been a greater simpleton than ever broke loose from keeping, she would have come away, then and there. Not she. She must persist in putting questions as to this and that; so at last she learned the truth, I suppose, or something near it. Then she thought it time to leave the house and come to mine: which is what she ought to have done at first: and there she has been waiting until now to see me, for I have been out all day."

"I thought your house was let?"

"It was let for the season; the people have left it now. I came home only yesterday from Jersey. My sister is lying ill there."

"And may I ask, Major Carlen, how you know that Lord Level has been 'amusing himself' if you have not been here to see?" questioned Mr. Ravensworth sarcastically.

"How do I know it?—why, common sense tells me," stormed the Major. "I have not heard a word about Level, except what Blanche says."

"Is he in Holles Street?"

"Not now. He gave up the rooms a week ago, and went down to Marshdale, his place in Surrey. He is laid up there, having managed to jam his knee against a gatepost; his horse swerved in going through it. A man I met to day, a friend of Level's, told me so. To go back to Blanche. She opened out an indignant tale to me, when I got home just now and found her there, of what she had heard in Holles Street. 'Serve you right, my dear,' I said to her: 'a wife has no business to be looking at her husband through a telescope. If a man chose to fill his rooms with wild tigers, it would not be his wife's province to complain, provided he kept her out of reach of their claws.' 'But what am I to do?' cried Blanche. 'You must return to France, or wherever else you came from,' I answered. 'That I never will: I shall go down to Marshdale, to Lord Level,' asserted Blanche, looking as I had never seen her look before. 'You can't go there,' I said: 'you must not attempt it.' 'I tell you, papa, I will go,' she cried, her eyes flashing. I never knew she had so much passion in her, Ravensworth: Level must have changed her nature. 'I will have an explanation from Lord Level,' she continued. 'Rather than live on as I am living now, I will demand a separation.'—Now, did you put that into her head?" broke off the Major, looking at Mr. Ravensworth.

"I do not think you know what you are saying, Major Carlen. Should I be likely to advise Lady Level to separate from her husband?"

"Someone has; such an idea would never enter Blanche's head unless put there. 'You must lend me the means to go down,' she went on. 'I am quite without money, through paying the bill at the hotel: Mr. Ravensworth had partly to supply my travelling expenses.' 'Then more fool Ravensworth for doing it,' said I; and more fool you were," repeated the Major.

"Anything more, Major?"

"The idea of my lending her money to take her down to Marshdale! And she'd be cunning to get money from me, just now, for I am out at all pockets. The last supplies I had came from Level; I wrote to him when he was abroad. By Jove! I would not cross him now for the universe."

"The selfish old sinner!" thought Mr. Ravensworth—and nearly said so aloud.

"Let me finish; she'll be here in a minute; she said she should come and apply to you. 'Does your husband beat you, or ill-treat you?' I asked her. 'No,' said she, shaking her head in a proud fury; 'even I would not submit to that. Will you lend me some money, papa?' she asked again. 'No, I won't,' I said. 'Then I'll borrow it from Mr. Ravensworth,' she cried, and ran upstairs to put her bonnet on. So then I thought it was time to come too, and explain. Mind you don't supply her with any, Ravensworth."

"What pretext can I have for refusing?"

"Pretext be shot!" irritably returned the Major. "Tell her you won't, as I do. I forbid you to lend her any. There she is! What a passionate knock! Been blundering up wrong turnings, I dare say."

Lady Level came in, looking tired, heated, frightened. Mr. Ravensworth took her hand.

"You have been walking here!" he said. "It is not right that Lady Level should be abroad in London streets at night, and alone."

"What else am I to do without money?" she returned hysterically.

"I sent the servants and the luggage to an hotel this morning, and gave them the few shillings I had left."

"Do sit down and calm yourself. All this is truly distressing."

Calm herself! The emotion, so long pent up, broke forth into sobs. "Yes, it is distressing. I come to England and I find no home; I am driven about from pillar to post, insulted everywhere; I have to walk through the streets, like any poor, helpless girl. Is it right that it should be so?"

"You have brought it all upon yourself, my lady," cried Major Carlen, coming forward from a dark corner.

She turned with a start. "So you are here, papa! Then I hope you have entered into sufficient explanation to spare it to me."

"I have told Ravensworth of your fine exploit, in going to Lord Level's rooms: and he agrees with me that no one except an inexperienced child would have done it."

"The truth, if you please, Major Carlen," struck in Mr. Ravensworth.

"And that what you heard or met with—though as to what it was I'm sure I'm all in a fog about—served you right for going," continued the unabashed Major.

Lady Level threw back her head, the haughty crimson dyeing her cheeks. "I went there expecting to find my husband; was that an inexperienced or a childish action?"

"Yes, it was," roared the Major, completely losing his temper, and showing his fierce teeth. "When men are away from their wives, they fall back into bachelor habits. If they please to turn their sanctums into smoking dens, or boxing dens, or what not, are you to come hunting them up, as I say, with a spyglass that magnifies at both ends?"

"Good men have no need to keep their wives away from them."

The Major gave his nose a twist. "Good men?—bad men?—where's the difference? The good have their wives under their thumb, and the bad haven't, that's all."

"For shame, papa!"

"Tie Lord Level to your apron-string, and keep him there as long as you can," fired the Major; "but don't ferret him up when he is out for a holiday."

"Did I want to ferret up Lord Level?" she retorted. "I went there because I thought it was his temporary home and would be mine. Why did he date his letters thence?"

"There it all lies," cried the Major, changing his tone to one of wrath against the peer. "Better he had dated from the top of the Monument. It is surprising what mistakes men make sometimes. But how was he to think you would come over against his expressed will? You say he had bade you stop there until he could fetch you."

Lady Level would not reply: the respect due to Major Carlen as her step-father was not in the ascendant just then. Turning to Mr. Ravensworth, she requested the loan of sufficient funds to take her down to Marshdale.

"I tell you, Blanche, you must not go there," interrupted the Major. "Better not. Lord Level does not receive strangers at Marshdale."

"Strangers!" emphatically repeated Lady Level.

"Or wives either. They are the same as strangers in a case such as this. I assure you Level told me, long before he married you, that Marshdale was a little secluded place, no establishment kept up in it, except an old servant or two; that he never received company down there, and should never take you to it. Remain at the hotel with your servants, if you will not come to my house, Blanche—there's only a charwoman in it at present, as you know. Then write to Level and let him know that you are there."

"Lady Level had better stay here tonight, at all events," put in Arnold Ravensworth. "My wife is expecting her to do so."

"Ay," acquiesced the old Major: "and write to Marshdale tomorrow, Blanche."

"I go down to Marshdale tomorrow," she replied in tones of determination. "It is too late to go tonight. The old servants that wait upon Lord Level can wait upon me: and if there are none, I will wait upon him myself. Go there I will, and have an understanding. And, unless Lord Level can explain away the aspect that things have taken, I—I—I—"

"Of all the imbeciles that ever gave utterance to folly, you are the worst," was the Major's complimentary retort, when she broke down. "Madam, do you know that you are a peeress of the realm?" he added pompously.

"I do not forget it."

"And you would stand in your own light! You have carriages and finery; you are to be presented next season; you will then have a house in town: what does the earth contain more that you can want?"

"Happiness," said Lady Level.

"Happiness!" repeated the Major, in genuine astonishment. "A pity but you had married a country curate and found it, then. Arnold Ravensworth, you must not lend Lady Level the money she desires; you shall not speed her on this insane journey."

Mr. Ravensworth approached him, and spoke in low tones. "Do you know of any existing reason that may render it inexpedient for her to go there?"

"I know nothing about it," replied the Major, too angry to lower his voice; "absolutely nothing. The Queen and all the princesses might pay it a visit, for aught I know of any reason to the contrary. But it is not Lady Level's place to follow her husband about in this clandestine manner. If he wants her there, he will send for her, once he knows that she is in London. The place is not much more than a farm, I believe, and used to be a hunting-box in the late Lord Level's time."

"Papa, I hope you will forgive me for running counter to your advice—but I shall certainly go down into Surrey tomorrow."

"I wash my hands of it altogether," said the angry Major.

"And you must lend me the money, Arnold."

"I will not refuse you," was his answer: "and I cannot dictate to you; but I think it would be better for you to remain here, and let Lord Level know that you are coming."

Lady Level shook her head. "Good advice, Arnold, no doubt, and I thank you; all the same, I shall go down as I have said."

"You will be very much to blame, sir, if you help on this mad scheme by so much as a sixpence," spoke the Major.

"Papa, listen to a word of common sense," she interposed. "I could go to a dozen places tomorrow, and get any amount of money. I could go to Lord Level's agents, and say I am Lady Level, and they would supply me. I could go to Mr. Brightman, and he would supply me—Charles Strange is in Paris again. I could go to other places. But I prefer to have it from Mr. Ravensworth, and save myself trouble and annoyance. It is not a pleasant thing for a peeress of the realm—as you just now put it—to go about borrowing a five-pound note," she concluded with a faint smile.

"Very well, Blanche. If ill comes of this wild step of yours, remember you were warned against it. I can say no more."

Gathering up his cloak as he spoke, Major Carlen threw it over his shoulders, and went forth, muttering, into the night.

Mr. Ravensworth called his wife, and she took Lady Level upstairs to a hastily-prepared chamber. Sitting down in a low chair, and throwing off her bonnet, Lady Level, worn out with all the excitement she had gone through, burst into a flood of hysterical tears.

"Tell me all about it," said Mary Ravensworth soothingly, drawing the poor wearied head to rest on her shoulder.

"They meant to stop me from going down to my husband, and I will go," sobbed Blanche half defiantly. "If he has met with an accident, and is ill, I ought to be there."

"Of course you ought," said Mary warmly. "But what is all the trouble about?—And what was it that you heard, and did not like, in Holles Street?"

"Oh, never mind that," said Blanche, colouring furiously. "That is what I am going to ask my husband to explain."

Upon Lady Level's arrival in London that morning, she sent her servants and luggage to an hotel, and drove straight to Portland Place herself: where Mr. and Mrs. Ravensworth's servants supplied her with breakfast. Afterwards, she went to Holles Street, arriving there about ten o'clock; walked into the passage, for the house door was open, was met by a young person in green, and inquired for Lord Level.

"Lord Level's not here now, ma'am," was the answer, as she showed Blanche into a parlour. "He has been gone about a week."

"Gone about a week!" repeated Blanche, completely taken back; for she had pictured him as lying at the place disabled.

"About that time, ma'am. He and the lady left together."

Blanche stared, and collected her scattered senses. "What lady?" she asked.

The young person in green considered. "Well, ma'am, I forget the name just now; those foreign names are hard to remember. His lordship called her Nina. A very handsome lady, she was—Italian, I think—with long gold earrings."

Lady Level's heart began to beat loudly. "May I ask if you are Mrs. Pratt?" she inquired, knowing that to be the name of the landlady.

"Dear me, no, ma'am; Mrs. Pratt's my aunt; I'm up here on a visit to her from the country. She is gone out to do her marketings. Lord Level was going down to his seat in Surrey, we understood, when he left here."

"Was the Italian lady going with him?"

The country girl—who was no doubt an inexperienced, simple country maiden, or she might not have talked so freely—shook her head. "We don't know anything about that, ma'am: she might have been. She was related to my lord—his sister-in-law, I think he called her to Mrs. Pratt—or some relation of that sort."

Blanche walked to the window and stood still for a moment, looking into the street, getting up her breath. "Did the lady stay with Lord Level all the time he was here?" she questioned, presently.

"Oh no, ma'am; she came only the day before he went away. Or, stay—the day but one before, I think it was. Yes; for I know they were out together nearly all the intervening day. Mrs. Pratt thought at his lordship's solicitor's. It was about six o'clock in the evening when she first arrived. My lord had spoken to Mrs. Pratt that day in his drawing-room, saying he was expecting a relative from Italy for a day or two, and could we let her have a bedroom, and any other accommodation she might need; and Mrs. Pratt said she would, for we were not full. A very nice lady she seemed to be, ma'am, and spoke English in a very pretty manner."

Lady Level drew in her contemptuous lips. "Did Lord Level meet with any accident while he was here?"

"Accident, ma'am! Not that we heard of. He was quite well when he left."

"Thank you," said Blanche, turning away and drawing her mantle up with a shiver. "As Lord Level is not here, I will not intrude upon you further."

Wishing the young person in green good-morning, she went away to Gloucester Place, feeling that she must scream or cry or fight the air. Blanche knew Major Carlen was about due in London, as his house was vacant again. Yes, the old charwoman said, the Major had got home the previous day, but he had just gone out. Would my lady (for she knew Blanche) like to walk in and wait until he returned?

My lady did so, and had to wait until evening. Then she partly explained to Major Carlen, and partly confused him; causing that gentleman to take up all kinds of free and easy ideas, as to the morals and manners of my Lord Level.

On the following morning Lady Level, pursuing her own sweet will, took train for Marshdale, leaving her servants behind her.

CHAPTER X

THE HOUSE AT MARSHDALE

It was a gloomy day, not far off the gloomy month of November, and it was growing towards mid-day, when a train on a small line, branching from the direct London line, drew up at the somewhat insignificant station of Upper Marshdale. A young and beautiful lady, without attendants, descended from a first-class carriage.

"Any luggage, ma'am?" inquired a porter, stepping up to her.

"A small black bag; nothing else."

The bag was found in the van, and placed on the platform. A family, who also appeared to have arrived at their destination, closed round the van and were tumultuous over a missing trunk, and the lady drew back and accosted a stolid-looking lad, dressed in the railway uniform.

"How far is it to Marshdale?"

"Marshdale! Why, you be at Marshdale," returned the boy, in sulky tones.

"I mean Marshdale House."

"Marshdale House?—That be my Lord Level's place," said the boy, still more sulkily. "It be a matter of two mile."

"Are there any carriages to be hired?"

"There's one—a fly; he waits here when the train comes in."

"Where is it to be found?"

"It stands in the road, yonder. But if ye wants the fly, it's of no use wanting. It have been booked by them folks squabbling over their boxes: they writed here yesterday for it to be ready for 'em."

The more civil porter now came up, and the lady appealed to him. He confirmed the information that there was only this one conveyance to be had, and the family had secured it. Perhaps, he added, the lady might like to wait until they had done with it.

The lady shook her head impatiently, and decided to walk. "Can you come with me to carry my bag and to show me the way?" she asked of the surly boy.

The surly boy, willing or unwilling, had to acquiesce, and they set off to walk. Upon emerging from the station, he came to a standstill.

"Now, which way d'you mean to go?" began he, facing round upon his companion. "There's the road way, and it's plaguy long; two mile, good; and there's the field way, and it's a sight nearer."

"Is it as good as the road?"

"It's gooder—barring the bull. He runs at everybody. And he tosses 'em, if he can catch 'em."

Not caring to encounter so objectionable an animal, the lady chose the road; and the boy strode on before her, bag in hand. It was downhill all the way. In due time they reached Marshdale House, which lay in a hollow. It was a low, straggling, irregular structure, built of dark red brick, with wings and gable ends, and must originally have looked more like a comfortable farm-house than a nobleman's seat. But it had been added to at various periods, without any regard to outward appearance or internal regularity. It was exceedingly retired, and a very large garden surrounded the house, encompassed by high walls and dense trees.

The walls were separated by a pair of handsome iron gates, and a small doorway stood beside them. A short, straight avenue, overhung by trees, led to the front entrance of the house. The surly boy, turning himself and his bag round, pushed backwards against the small door, sent it flying, and branched off into a side-path.

"Is not that the front-door?" said the lady, trying to arrest him.

"'Tain't no manner of use going to it," replied the imperturbable boy, marching on. "The old gentleman and lady gets out o' the way, and the maids in the kitchen be deaf, I think. Last time I came up here with a parcel, I rung at it till I was tired, and nobody heard."

He went up to a side-door, flung it open, and put down the bag. A neat-looking young woman, with her sleeves turned up, came forward, and stared in silence.

"Is Lord Level within?" inquired the lady.

"My lord's ill in bed," replied the servant; "he cannot be seen or spoken to. What do you want with him, please?"

She seemed a good-tempered, ignorant sort of girl, but nothing more. At that moment someone called to her from an inner room, and she turned away.

"Are there not any upper servants in the house, do you know?" inquired the lady of the boy.

"I doesn't think so. There's the missis."

A tinge came over the lady's face. "The mistress! Who is she?"

"She's Mrs. Ed'ards. An old lady, what comes to church with buckles in her shoes. And there's Mr.—"

"What is it that you want here?" interrupted the servant girl, advancing again, and addressing the visitor in a not very conciliatory tone.

"I am Lady Level," was the reply, in a ringing, imperious voice. "Call someone to receive me."

It found its way to the girl's alarm. She looked scared, doubting, and finally turned and flew off down a long, dark passage. The boy heard the announcement without its ruffling his equanimity in the least degree.

"That's all, ain't it?" asked he, giving the bag a condescending touch with his foot.

"How much am I to pay you?" inquired Lady Level.

The boy paused. "You bain't obliged to pay nothing."

"What is the charge?" repeated Lady Level.

"The charge ain't nothing. If folks like to give anything, it's gived as a gift."

She smiled, and, taking out her purse, gave him half-a-crown. He received it with remarkable satisfaction, and then, with an air of great mystery and cunning, slipped it into his boot.

"But, I say, don't you go and tell, over there, as you gived it me," said he, jerking his head in the direction of the railway station. "We are not let take nothing, and there'd be the whole lot of 'em about my ears. You won't tell?"

"No, I will not tell," replied Lady Level, laughing, in spite of her cares and annoyances. And the promising young porter in embryo, giving vent to a shrill whistle, which might have been heard at the two-mile-off station, tore away as fast as his legs would carry him.

The girl came back with a quaint old lady. Her hair was white, her complexion clear and fresh, and her eyes were black and piercing as ever they had been in her youth. She looked in doubt at the visitor, as the servant had done.

"I am told that someone is inquiring for my lord."

"His wife is inquiring for him. I am Lady Level."

Had any doubt been wavering in the old lady's mind, the tones dispelled it. She curtseyed to the ground—the stately, upright, old-fashioned curtsey of the days gone by. A look of distress rose to her face.

"Oh, my lady! That I should live to receive my lord's wife in this unprepared, unceremonious manner! He told me you were in foreign parts, beyond seas."

"I returned to England yesterday, and have left my servants in town. What is the matter with Lord Level?"

"That your ladyship should come to such a house as this, all unfurnished and disordered! and—I beg your pardon, my lady! I cannot take you through these passages," she added, curtseying for Lady Level to go out again. "Deborah, go round and open the front-door."

Lady Level, in the midst of much lamentation, was conducted to the front entrance, and thence ushered into a long, low, uncarpeted room on the left of the dark hall. It was very bare of furniture, chairs and a large table being all that it contained. "It is of no consequence," said Lady Level; "I have come only to see Lord Level, and may not remain above an hour or two. I cannot tell. You are Mrs. Edwards, I think. I have heard Lord Level mention you."

"My name is Edwards, my lady. I was housekeeper in the late lord's time, and, when a young woman, I had the honour of nursing my lord. Since the late lord's death, I and my brother, Jacob Drewitt, have mostly lived here. He used to be house steward at Marshdale."

Lady Level removed her bonnet and cloak, and threw them on the table. She looked impatient and restless, as she listened to the account of her husband's accident. He had received an injury to his knee, when out riding, the day after his arrival at Marshdale; fever had set in, deepening at times to slight delirium.

"I should like to see him," said Lady Level. "Will you take me to his chamber?"

Mrs. Edwards marshalled her upstairs. Curious, in-and-out, wide and shallow stairs they were, with long passages and short turnings branching from them. She gently threw open the door of a large, handsome room. On the bed lay Lord Level, his eyes closed.

"He is dozing again, my lady," she whispered. "He is sure to fall to sleep whenever the fever leaves him."

"There is no fire in the room!" exclaimed Lady Level.

"The doctor says there's not to be any, my lady. In the room opposite to this, across the passage, you will find a good one. It is my lord's sitting-room when he is well. And here," noiselessly opening a door facing the foot of the bed, "is another chamber, that can be prepared for your ladyship, if you remain."

The housekeeper left the room as she spoke, scarcely knowing whether she stood on her head or her heels, so completely was she confounded by this arrival of Lady Level's—and nothing wherewith to receive her! Mrs. Edwards had her head and hands full just then.

As Lady Level moved forward, her dress came into contact with a light chair, and moved it. The invalid started, and raised himself on his elbow.

"Why!—who—is it?"

"It is I, Lord Level," she said, advancing to the bed.

He looked strangely amazed and perplexed. He could not believe his own eyes, and stared at her as though he would discover whether she was really before him, or whether he was in a dream.

"Don't you know me?" she asked gently.

"Is it—Blanche?"

"Yes."

"But where have you come from?—what brings you here?" he slowly ejaculated.

"I came down by train to-day. I have come to speak to you."

"You were in Germany. I left you in Germany!"

"I thought I had been there long enough: too long; and I quitted it. Archibald, I could not stay there. Had I done so, I should have been ill as you are. I think I should have died."

He said nothing for a few moments, and appeared to be lost in thought. Then he drew her face down to his, and kissed it.

"You ought not to have come over without my permission, Blanche."

"I did not travel alone. Mr. and Mrs. Arnold Ravensworth chanced to put up at the inn on their homeward route, and I took the opportunity to come over with them."

The information evidently did not please Lord Level. His brow contracted.

"You wrote me word that you had had an accident," she continued. "How could I be contented to remain away after that? So I came over: and I went to your rooms in Holles Street—"

"Why on earth did you go there?" he sharply interrupted. "When I had left them."

"But I did not know you had left them. How was I to know you had come to Marshdale if you never told me so? When I found you had left Holles Street, I went straight to Gloucester Place. Papa has just come home from Jersey."

"You ought to have remained in Germany until I was able to join you," he reiterated irritably; and Blanche could not avoid seeing that he was growing agitated and feverish. "What's to become of you? Where are you to be?"

"First of all, I want to have an explanation with you," said Blanche. "I came over on purpose to have it; to tell you many things. One is, that I will no longer submit to be treated as a child—"

"Blanche!" he curtly interrupted.

"Well?"

"You are acting as a child now, and as nothing else. This nonsense that you are talking—I am not in a condition to hear it."

"It is not nonsense," said Blanche.

"It is what I will not listen to. It was the height of folly to come here. All you can do now is to go back to London by the next train."

"Go back where?" she passionately asked. "I have no home in London."

"I dare say Major Carlen will receive you for a week. Before that time I hope to be well enough to come up, and prepare a home for you. Where are Sanders and Timms?"

"I did not bring them down with me. They are at an hotel. Why cannot I stay here?"

"Because I won't have it. There is nothing in the place ready for you, or suited to you."

"If it is suited to you, it's suited to me. I say I will not be treated as a child any longer. I could be quite happy here. There is nothing I should like so much as to explore this old house. I never saw such an array of ghostly passages anywhere."

Something in the words seemed dangerously to excite Lord Level. The fever was visibly increasing.

"I forbid you to explore; I forbid you to remain here!" he exclaimed in the deepest agitation. "Do you hear me, Blanche?—you must return by the next train."

"I will not," she replied, quite as obstinate as he. "I will not go hence until I have had an explanation with you. If you are too ill at present, I will wait for it."

He was, indeed, too ill. "Quiet, above all things," the doctor had said when he had paid his early morning visit. But quiet Lord Level had not had; his wife had put an end to that. His talk grew random, his mind wandering; a paroxysm of fever ensued. In terror Lady Level rang the bell.

Mrs. Edwards answered it. Blanche gazed at her with astonishment, scarcely recognising her. She had put on her gala dress of days long gone by: a short, full, red petticoat, a chintz gown looped above it in festoons, high-heeled shoes, buckles, snow-white stockings with worked "clocks," a mob cap of clear lace, large gold earrings, and black mittens. All this she had assumed out of respect to her new lady.

"Is he out of his mind?" gasped Lady Level, terrified at her lord's words and his restless motions.

"It is the fever, my lady," said Mrs. Edwards. "Dear, dear! And we thought him so much better today!"

Close upon that, Dr. Macferraty, the medical man, came in. He was of square-built frame with broad shoulders, very dictatorial and positive considering his years, which did not number more than seven-and-twenty.

"What mischief has been at work here?" he demanded, standing over the bed with Mrs. Edwards. "Who has been with him?"

She explained that Lady Level had arrived and had been talking with his lordship. She—Mrs. Edwards—had begged her ladyship not to talk to him; but—well, the young were heedless and did not think of consequences.

"If she has worried him into brain-fever, she will have herself to thank for it," harshly spoke the doctor. And Lady Level, who was in the adjoining room, overheard the words.

"Something has happened to agitate my patient!" exclaimed Doctor Macferraty, when, in leaving the room, he encountered Lady Level in the passage, and was introduced to her by Mrs. Edwards.

"I am very sorry," she answered. "We were speaking of family affairs, and Lord Level grew excited."

"Then, madam," said the doctor, "do not speak of family affairs again, whilst he is in this weak condition, or of any other affairs likely to excite him. You must, if you please, put off all such topics until he is better."

"How long will that be?" asked Lady Level.

"I cannot say; it may be a week, or it may be a month. When once these intermittent fevers get into the system, it is difficult to shake them off again."

"It will not go on to—to anything worse?" questioned Lady Level timidly, recalling what she had just overheard.

"I hope not; but I cannot answer for it. Your ladyship must be good enough to bear in mind that much depends upon his keeping himself tranquil, and upon those around helping to keep him so."

The doctor withdrew as he spoke, telling Mrs. Edwards that he would look in again at night. Lord Level remained very excited throughout the rest of the day; he had a bad night, the fever continuing, and was no better in the morning. Mrs. Edwards had sat up with him.

Lady Level then made up her mind to remain at Marshdale, consulting neither her lord nor anyone else. As Major Carlen had remarked, Blanche was developing a will of her own. Though, indeed, it might not have been right to leave him in his present condition. She sent for Sanders and Timms, the two servants who had attended her from Germany, and for certain luggage belonging to herself. Mrs. Edwards did the best she could with this influx of visitors to a scantily-furnished house. Lady Level occupied the chamber that opened from her husband's; it also opened on to the corridor.

"Madam," said Dr. Macferraty to her, taking the bull by the horns on one of the earliest days, "you must allow me to give you a word of advice. Do not, just at present, enter Lord Level's chamber; wait until he is a little stronger. He has just asked me whether you had gone back to town, and I did not say no. It is evident that your being here troubles him. The house, as it is at present, is not in a condition to receive you, or he appears to think so. Therefore, so long as he is in this precarious state, do not show yourself to him. Let him think you have returned to London."

"Is his mind quite right again?"

"By no means. But he has lucid intervals. I assure your ladyship it is of the very utmost importance that he should be kept tranquil. Otherwise, I will not answer for the consequences."

Lady Level took the advice in all humility. Bitterly though she was feeling upon some scores towards her husband, she did not want him to die; no, nor to have brain-fever. So she kept the door closed between her room and his, and was as quiet as a mouse at all times. And the days began to pass on.

Blanche found them monotonous. She explored the house, but the number of passages, short and long, their angles and their turnings, confused her. She made the acquaintance of the steward, Mr. Drewitt, an elderly gentleman who went about in a plum-coloured suit and a large cambric frill to his shirt. One autumn morning when Blanche had traversed the long corridor, beyond the rooms which she and Lord Level occupied, she turned into another at right angles with it, and came to a door that was partly open. Passing through it, she found herself in a narrow passage that she had not before seen. Deborah, the good-natured housemaid, suddenly came out of one of the rooms opening from it, carrying a brush and dustpan. Deborah was the only servant kept in the house, so far as Lady Level saw, apart from the cook, who was fat and experienced.

"What a curious old house!" exclaimed Lady Level. "Nothing but dark passages that turn and wind about until you don't know where you are."

"It is that, my lady," answered Deborah. "In the late lord's time the servants took to calling it the maze, it puzzled them so. The name got abroad, and some people call it the maze to this day."

"I don't think I have been in this passage before. Does anyone live or sleep here?" added Lady Level, looking at the household articles Deborah carried.

It was a dark, narrow passage, closed in by a door at each end. The door at the upper end was of oak; heavy, and studded with nails. Four rooms opened from the passage, two on each side.

"All these rooms are occupied by the master and missis," said Deborah, alluding to the steward and his sister. "This is Mrs. Edwards's chamber, my lady," pointing to the one she had just quitted. "That beyond it is Mr. Drewitt's; the opposite room is their sitting-room, and the one beside it is not used."

"Where does that heavy door lead to?" continued Lady Level.

"It leads into the East Wing, my lady," replied Deborah. "I have never entered that wing all the two years I've lived here," continued the gossiping girl. "I am not allowed to do so. The door is kept locked; as well as the door answering to it in the passage below."

"Does no one ever go into it?"

"Why, yes, my lady; Mr. Drewitt does, and spends a good part of his time there. He has a business-room there, in which he keeps his books and papers relating to the estate. Mrs. Edwards is in there, too, with him most days. And my lord goes in when he is down here."

"Then no one really inhabits that wing?"

"Oh yes, my lady, John Snow and his wife live in it; he's the head gardener. A many years he has been in the family; and one of the last things the late lord did before he died was to give him that wing to live in. An easy life Snow has of it now; working or not, just as he pleases. When there's any unusual work to be done, our gardener on this side is had in to help with it."

Lady Level did not feel much interested in the wing, or in Snow the gardener. But it happened that not half an hour after this conversation, she chanced to see Mrs. Snow.

Leaning, in her listlessness, out of an open window that was just above the side entrance, to which she had been conducted by the boy on her way from the station, she was noticing how high the wall was that separated the garden of the house from the garden of the East Wing. Lofty trees, closely planted, also flanked the wall, so that not the slightest glimpse could be had on either side of the other garden. The East Wing, with its grounds, was as completely hidden from view as though it had no existence. While rather wondering at this—for the East Wing was, after all, a part of the house, and not detached from it—Lady Level saw a woman emerge from a little sheltered doorway in the wall, lock it after her, and come up the path, key in hand. This obscure doorway, and another at the foot of the East Wing garden opening to the road, were apparently the only means of entrance to it. To the latter door, always kept locked, was attached a large bell, which awoke the surrounding echoes whenever tradespeople or other applicants rang at it.

"Is that you, Hannah Snow?" cried the cook, stepping forward to meet the other as she came up the path. "And how are you to-day? Do you want anything?"

Catching the name, Lady Level looked out more closely. She saw a tall, strong, respectable woman of middle age, with a smiling, happy face, and laughing hazel eyes. She wore a neat white cap, a clean cotton gown and gray-checked apron.

"Yes, cook," was the answer, given in a merry voice. "I want you to give me a handful of candied peel. I am preparing a batch of cakes for my old man, never supposing I had not all the ingredients at hand, and I find I have no peel. I'm sure I had some; and I tell John he must have stolen it."

"What a shame!" cried the cook, taking the words more literally than they were intended. Mrs. Snow laughed.

"Fact is, I suppose I used the last of it in the bread-and-butter pudding I made last week," said she.

"You are always making cakes for that man o' yours, seems to me, Hannah," grumbled the cook. "We can smell them over here when they're baking, and that's pretty often."

"Seems I am: he's always asking for them," assented Hannah. "He likes to eat one now and then between meals, you see.

"Well, he's a rare one for his inside," retorted the cook, as she went in for the candied peel.

"They seem to do very much as they like here," was the only thought that crossed Lady Level.

On this same day Lord Level, who had grown so much better as to be out of danger, dismissed his doctor. Presenting him with a handsome cheque, he told him that he required no further attendance. Blanche received the news from Mrs. Edwards.

"But is he so well as that?" she asked, in surprise.

"Well, my lady, he is very much better, there's no doubt of that. He will be out of bed to-morrow or the next day, and, if he takes care, will have no relapse," was the housekeeper's answer. "No doubt it might be safer for the doctor to continue to come a little longer, if it were only to enjoin strict quiet; but you see my lord does not like him."

"I fancied he did not."

"He is not our own doctor, as perhaps your ladyship has heard," pursued Mrs. Edwards. "He is a Mr. Hill: a clever, pleasant man, of a certain age, who was very intimate with the late lord. They were close friends, I may say. When his lordship met with this accident, it put him out uncommonly that we had to send for the young man, Dr. Macferraty, Mr. Hill being away."

"If Lord Level is so well as to do without a doctor, I might go into his room. Don't you think so, Mrs. Edwards?"

"Better not for a day or two, my lady; better not, indeed. I'm afraid my lord will be angry at your having stayed here—there being no fitting establishment or accommodation for your ladyship; and—"

"That is such nonsense!" interrupted Lady Level. "With Sanders and Timms here, I am more attended to than is really necessary. And even if I had to put up with discomfort for a short time, I dare say I should survive it."

"And it might cause his lordship excitement, I was about to say," quickly continued Mrs. Edwards. "A very little thing would bring the fever back again."

Blanche sighed rebelliously, but recognised the obligation to condemn herself a little longer to this dreary existence.

CHAPTER XI

THE QUARREL

The following day was charmingly fine: the sun brilliant, the air warm as summer. In the afternoon Lady Level went out to take a walk. Lord Level was not up that day, but would be, all being well, on the morrow. It was the injury to the knee more than his general health that was keeping him in bed now.

Outside the gate Blanche looked about her, and decided to take the way towards the railway station. Upper Marshdale lay close beyond it, and she thought she would see what the little town was like. If she felt tired after exploring it, she could engage the solitary railway fly to bring her home again.

She went along the deserted road, passing a peasant's cottage now and then. Very near to the station she met the surly boy. He was coming along with a leap and a whistle, and stopped dead at sight of Lady Level.

"I say," said he, in a low tone, all his glee and his impudence gone out of him, "be you going there?"

"Yes," answered Lady Level, half smiling, for the boy amused her. He had pointed to indicate the station, but so awkwardly that she thought he pointed to the roofs and chimneys beyond it. "Yes, I am. Why?"

His face fell. "Not to tell of me?" he gasped.

"To tell of you! What should I have to tell of you?"

"About that there half-crown. You give him to me, mind; I never asked. You can't see the station-master if you try: he's a gone to his tea."

"Oh, I won't tell of that," said Lady Level. "I am going to the village, not to the station."

"They'd make such a row," said the boy, somewhat relieved. "The porter'd be mad that it wasn't given to him; he might get me sent away perhaps for't. It's such a lot, you see: a whole half-crown: when anything is given, it's a sixpence. But 'tain't nothing that's given mostly; nothing."

The intense resentment thrown into the last word made Lady Level laugh.

"It's a sight o' time, weeks and weeks, since I've had anything given me afore, barring the three penny pieces from Mr. Snow," went on the grumbling boy. "And what's three penny pieces?"

"Mr. Snow?" repeated Lady Level. "Who is he?"

"He is Lord Level's head gardener, he be. He comes up here to the station one day, not long afore you come down; and he collars the fly for the next down-train. The next down-train comes in and brings my lord and a lady with him. Mr. Snow, he puts the lady inside, and he puts what luggage there were outside. 'Twasn't much, and I helps him, and he dives into his pockets and brings out three penny pieces. And I'll swear that for weeks afore nobody had never given me a single farthing."

Lady Level changed colour. "What's your name?" she suddenly asked the boy, to cover her confusion.

"It be Sam Doughty. That there lady—"

"Oh, I know the lady," she carelessly interrupted, hating herself at the same time for pursuing the subject and the questions. "A lady with black hair and eyes, was it not, and long gold earrings?"

"Well, it were. I noticed the earrings, d'ye see, the sun made 'em sparkle so. Handsome earrings they was; as handsome as she were."

"And Lord Level took her home with him in the fly, did he?"

"That he didn't. She went along of herself, Mr. Snow a-riding on the box. My lord walked across the fields. The station-master told him to mind the bull, but my lord called back that he warn't afraid."

There was nothing more to ask; nothing more that she could ask. But Lady Level had heard enough to disturb her equanimity, and she turned without going on to Upper Marshdale. That the lady with the gold earrings was either in the house, or in its East Wing, and that that was why she was wanted out of it, seemed clearer to her than the sun at noonday.

That same evening, Lady Level's servants were at supper in the large kitchen: where, as no establishment was kept up in the house, they condescended to take their meals. Deborah was partly waiting on them, partly gossiping, and partly dressing veal cutlets and bacon in the Dutch oven for what she called the upstairs supper. The cook had gone to bed early with a violent toothache.

"You have enough there, I hope," cried Timms, as Deborah brought the Dutch oven to the table to turn the cutlets.

"Old Mr. Drewitt has such an appetite; leastways at his supper," answered Deborah.

"I wonder they don't take their meals below; it's a long way to carry them up all them stairs," remarked Mr. Sanders, when Deborah was placing her dish of cutlets on the tray prepared for it.

"Oh, I don't mind it; I'm used to it now," said the good-humoured girl, as she went off with a quick step.

Deborah returned with a quieter step than she had departed. "They are quarrelling like anything!" she exclaimed in a low, frightened voice. "She's gone into my lord's room, and they are having it out over something or other."

Timms, who was then engaged in eating some favourite custard pudding, looked up. "What? Who? Do you mean my lord and my lady? How do you know, Deborah?"

"I heard them wrangling as I went by. I have to pass their rooms, you know, to get to Mr. Drewitt's rooms, and I heard them still louder as I came back. They are quarrelling just like common people. Has she a temper?"

"No," said Timms. "He has, though; that is, he can be frightfully passionate at times."

"He is not thought so in this house," returned Deborah. "To hear my master and mistress talk, my lord is just an angel upon earth."

"Ah!" said Timms, sniffing significantly.

Her supper ended, but not her curiosity, Timms stole a part of the way upstairs, and listened. But she only came in for the end of the dispute, as she related to Mr. Sanders on her return. Lady Level, after some final speech of bitter reproach, passed into her room and shut the door with a force that shook the walls, and probably shook Lord Level, who relieved his wrath by a little delicate language. So much Timms heard; but of what the quarrel had been about, she did not gather the faintest glimmer.

The house went to rest. Silence, probably sleep, had reigned within it for some two hours, and the clock had struck one, when wild calls of alarm, coupled with the ringing of his bell, issued from Lord Level's chamber. The servants rose hastily, in terror. Those cries of fear came not from their lord, but from Lady Level.

Sanders, partly attired, hastened thither; Timms, in a huge shawl, opened her door and stopped him; Deborah came flying down the long corridor. Mrs. Edwards was already in Lord Level's chamber. Lady Level, in a blue silk wrapping-gown, her cries of alarm over, lay panting in a chair, extremely agitated; and Lord Level was in a fainting-fit on his bed, with a stab in his arm, and another in his side, from which blood was flowing.

Some hours later, Mr. and Mrs. Arnold Ravensworth were at breakfast in Portland Place, when Major Carlen entered without ceremony. His purple-and-scarlet cloak, without which he rarely stirred out, had come unfastened and trailed behind him; his face looked scared and crestfallen.

"I must see you, I must see you!" cried the Major, throwing up his hands, as if apologizing for the intrusion. "It's on a matter of life and death."

"We have finished breakfast," said Mrs. Ravensworth; and she rose and left them together.

The Major strode up to Arnold, his teeth actually chattering. "I told you what it would be," he muttered. "I warned you of the consequences, if you helped Blanche to go down there. She has attempted his life."

Mr. Ravensworth gazed at him inquiringly.

"By George she has! They had a blowup last night, it seems, and she has stabbed him. It can be no one else who has done it. When these delicate girls are put up; made jealous, and that sort of thing; they are as bad as their more furious sisters. Witness that character of Scott's—what's her name?—Lucy, in the 'Bride of Lam—'"

"For pity's sake, Major Carlen, what are you saying?" interrupted Mr. Ravensworth, scarcely knowing whether the Major was mad or sane, or had been taking dinner in place of breakfast. "Don't introduce trashy romance into the woes of real life! Has anything happened at Lord Level's, or has it not?"

"He is stabbed, I tell you. One of Lord Level's servants, Sanders, arrived before I was up, with a note from Blanche. Here, read it!" But the Major's hand and the note shook together as he held it out.

Do, dear papa, hasten down! A shocking event has happened to Lord Level. He has been stabbed in bed. I am terrified out of my senses.

BLANCHE LEVEL.

"Now, she has done it," whispered the Major again, his stony eyes turned on Mr. Ravensworth in dread. "As sure as that her name's Blanche Level, it is she who has done it!"

"Nonsense! Impossible. Have you learnt any of the details?"

"A few scraps. As much as the man knew. He says they were awakened by cries in the middle of the night, and found Lord Level had been stabbed; and her ladyship was with him, screaming, and fainting on a chair. 'Who did it, Sanders?' said I. 'It's impossible to make out who did it, sir,' said he; 'there was no one indoors to do it, and all the house was in bed.' 'What do the police say?' I asked. 'The police are not called in, sir,' returned he; 'my lord and my lady won't have it done.' Now, Ravensworth, what can be clearer proof than that? I used to think her mother had a tendency to insanity; I did, by Jove! she went once or twice into such a tantrum with me. Though she had a soft, sweet temper in general, mild as milk."

"Well, you must go down without delay."

The grim old fellow put up his hands, which were trembling visibly. "I wouldn't go down if you gave me a hundred pounds a mile, poor as I am, just now. Look what a state I'm in, as it is: I had to get Sanders to hook my cloak for me, and he didn't half do it. I wouldn't interfere between Blanche and Level for a gold-mine. You must go down for me; I came to ask you to do so."

"It is impossible for me to go down today. I wish I knew more. How did you hear there had been any disagreement between them?"

"Sanders let it out. He said the women-servants heard Level and his wife hotly disputing."

"Where is Sanders?"

"In your hall. I brought him round with me."

The man was called in, and was desired to repeat what he knew of the affair. It was not much, and it has been already stated.

"Someone must have got in, Sanders," observed Mr. Ravensworth, when he had listened.

"Well, sir, I don't know," was the answer. "The curious thing is that there are no signs of it. All the doors and windows had been fastened before we went to bed, and they had not been, so far as we can discover, in the least disturbed."

"Do you suspect anyone in the house?"

"Why—no, sir; there's no one we like to suspect," returned Sanders, coughing dubiously.

"The servants—"

"Oh, none of the servants would do such a thing," interrupted Sanders, very decidedly: and Mr. Ravensworth feared they might be getting upon dangerous ground. He caught Major Carlen's significant glance. It said, as plainly as glance ever yet spoke, "The man suspects his mistress."

"Is Lord Level's bedroom isolated from the rest of the rooms?"

"Pretty well, sir, for that. No one sleeps near him but my lady. Her room opens from his."

"Could he have done it himself, Sanders?" struck in Major Carlen. "He has been light-headed from fever."

"Just at the first moment the same question occurred to me, sir; but we soon saw that it was not at all likely. The fever had abated, my lord was quite collected, and the stab in the arm could not have been done by himself."

"Was any instrument found?"

"Yes, sir: a clasp-knife, with a small, sharp blade. It was found on the floor of my lady's room."

An ominous silence ensued.

"Are the stabs dangerous?" inquired Mr. Ravensworth.

"It is thought they are only slight, sir. The danger will be if they bring back the fever. His lordship will not have a doctor called in—"

"Not have a doctor called in!"

"He forbids it absolutely, sir. When we reached his room, in answer to my lady's cries, he had fainted; but he soon recovered, and hearing Mrs. Edwards speak of the doctor, he refused to have him sent for."

"You ought to have sent, all the same," imperiously spoke Mr. Ravensworth.

Sanders smiled. "Ah, sir, but my lord's will is law."

Mr. Ravensworth turned to a side-table. He wrote a rapid word to Lady Level, promising to be with her that evening, gave it to Sanders, and bade him make the best of his way back to Marshdale. Certain business of importance was detaining him in town for the day.

"When you get down there, Ravensworth, you won't say that I wouldn't go, you know," said the Major. "Say I couldn't."

"What excuse can I make for you?"

"Any excuse that comes uppermost. Say I'm in bed with gout. I have charged Sanders to hold his tongue."

The day had quite passed before Mr. Ravensworth was able to start on his journey. It was dark when he reached Upper Marshdale. There he found Sanders and the solitary fly.

"Is Lord Level better?" was his first question.

"A little better this evening, sir, I believe; but he has again been off his head with fever, and Dr. Macferraty had, after all, to be called in," replied the man. "My lady is pretty nearly beside herself too."

"Have the police been called in yet?"

"No, sir; no chance of it; my lord and my lady won't have it done."

"It appears to be an old-fashioned place, Sanders," remarked Mr. Ravensworth, when they had reached the house.

"It's the most awkward turn-about place inside, sir, you ever saw; nothing but passages. But my lord never lives here; he only pays it promiscuous visits now and then, and brings down no servants with him. He was kept prisoner here, as may be said, through jamming his knee in a gateway; and then my lady came down, and we are putting up with all sorts of inconveniences."

"Who lives here in general?"

"Two old retainers of the Level family, sir: both of 'em sights to look upon; she especially. She dresses up like an old picture."

Waiting within the doorway to receive Mr. Ravensworth was Mrs. Edwards. He could not take his eyes from her. He had never seen one like her in real life, and Sanders's words, "dresses up like an old picture," recurred to him. He had thought this style of dress completely gone out of date, except in pictures; and here it was before him, worn by a living woman! She dropped him a stately curtsey, that would have served for the prelude to a Court minuet in the palmy days of Queen Charlotte.

"Sir, you are the gentleman expected by my lady?"

"Yes—Mr. Ravensworth."

"I'll show you in myself, sir."

Taking up a candle from a marble slab—there was no other light to be seen—she conducted him through the passage, and, turning down another which stood at right angles with it, halted at the door of a room. In answer to a question from Mr. Ravensworth, she said his lordship was much better within the last hour—quite himself again. "What would you be pleased to take, sir?" she added. "I will order it to be brought in to you."

"I require nothing, thank you."

But quite a housekeeper of the old school, and essentially hospitable, she would not take a refusal. "I hope you will, sir: tea—or coffee—or supper—?"

"A little coffee, then."

She dropped another of her ceremonious curtseys, and threw open the door. "The gentleman you expected, my lady."

It was another long, bare room, but not the one already mentioned. Singularly bare and empty it looked to-night. A large fire burned in the grate, halfway down the room, and in an easy-chair before it reclined Lady Level—asleep. Two wax-candles stood on the high carved mantelpiece, and the large oak table behind Lady Level was dark with age. Everything about the room was dreary, excepting the fire, the lights, and the sleeper.

Should he awaken her? He looked at Blanche Level and deliberated. Her feet rested on a footstool, and her head lay on the low back of the chair, a cushion under it. She wore an evening dress of light silk, trimmed with white lace. Her neck and arms, only relieved by the lace, looked cold and bare in the dreary room, for she wore no ornaments; nothing of gold or silver was about her—except her wedding-ring. Was it possible that she had attempted the life of him who had put on that ring? There was a careworn look on her face as she slept, which lessened her beauty, and two indented lines rose in her forehead, not usual to a girl of twenty; her mouth, slightly open, showed her teeth; and very pretty teeth were Lady Level's. No, thought Mr. Ravensworth, guilty of that crime she never had been!

Should he arouse her? A coal fell on to the hearth with a rattle, and settled the question, for Lady Level opened her eyes. A moment's dreamy unconsciousness, and then she started up, her face flushing.

"Oh, Arnold, I beg your pardon! I must have dropped asleep. How good of you to come!"

With a burst of tears she held out her hands; it seemed so glad a relief to have a friend there.

"Arnold, I am so miserable—so frightened! Why did not papa come down this morning?"

"He was—" Mr. Ravensworth searched for an excuse and did not find one easily "Something kept him in town, and he requested me to come down in his stead, and see if I could be of any use to you."

"Have you heard much about it?" she asked, in a whisper.

"Sanders told me and your father what little he knew. But it appeared most extraordinary to both of us. Sit down, Lady Level," he continued, drawing a chair nearer to hers. "You look ill and fatigued."

"I am not ill; unless uncertainty and anxiety can be called illness. Have you dined?"

"Yes; but your housekeeper insists on hospitality, and will send me up some coffee."

"Did you ever see so complete a picture as she is? Just like those engravings we admire in the old frames."

"Will you describe to me this—the details of the business I came down to hear?"

"I am trying to delay it," she said, with a forced laugh—a laugh that caused Mr. Ravensworth involuntarily to knit his brow, for it spoke of insincerity. "I think I will not tell you anything about it until to-morrow morning."

"I must leave again to-night. The last up-train passes—"

"Oh, but you will stay all night," she interrupted nervously. "I cannot be left alone. Mrs. Edwards is preparing a room for you somewhere."

"Well, we will discuss that by-and-by. What is this unpleasant business about Lord Level?"

"I don't know what it is," she replied. "He has been attacked and stabbed. I only know that it nearly frightened me to death."

"By whom was it done?"

"I don't know," she repeated. "They say the doors and windows were all fastened, and that no one could have got in."

Now, strange as it may appear, and firmly impressed as Mr. Ravensworth was with the innocence of Lady Level, there was a tone in her voice, a look in her countenance, as she spoke the last few sentences, that he did not like. Her manner was evasive, and she did not meet his glance openly.

"Were you in his room when it happened?"

"Oh dear no! Since I came down here I have occupied a room next to his; his dressing-room, I believe, when he stays here at ordinary times; and I was in bed and asleep at the time."

"Asleep?"

"Fast asleep. Until something woke me: and when I entered Lord Level's room, I found—I found—what had happened."

"Had it just happened?"

"Just. I was terrified. After I had called the servants, I think I nearly fainted. Lord Level quite fainted."

"But did you not see anyone in the room who could have attacked him?"

She shook her head.

"Nor hear any noise?"

"I—thought I heard a noise; I am positive I thought so. And I heard Lord Level's voice."

"That you naturally would hear. A man whose life is being attempted would not be likely to remain silent. But you must try and give me a better explanation than this. You say something suddenly awoke you. What was it?"

"I cannot tell you," repeated Lady Level.

"Was it a noise?"

"N—o; not exactly. I cannot say precisely what it was."

Mr. Ravensworth deliberated before he spoke again. "My dear Lady Level, this will not do. If these questions are painful to you, if you prefer not to trust me, they shall cease, and I will return to town as wise as I came, without having been able to afford you any assistance or advice. I think you could tell me more, if you would do so."

Lady Level burst into tears and grew agitated. A disagreeable doubt—guilty or not guilty?—stole over Mr. Ravensworth. "Oh, heaven, that it should be so!" he cried to himself, recalling how good and gentle she had been through her innocent girlhood. "I came down, hoping to be to you a true friend," he resumed in a low tone. "If you will allow me to be so, if you will confide in me, Blanche, come what may, I will stand by you."

There was a long silence. Mr. Ravensworth did not choose to break it. He had said his say, and the rest remained with Lady Level.

"Lord Level has made me very angry indeed," she broke out, indignation arresting her tears. "He has made me—almost—hate him."

"But you are not telling me what occurred."

"I have told you," she answered. "I was suddenly aroused from sleep, and then I heard Lord Level's voice, calling 'Blanche! Blanche!' I went into his room, ran up to him, and he put out his arms and caught me to him. Then I saw blood upon his nightshirt, and he told me he had been stabbed. Oh, how I shuddered! I cannot think of it now without feeling sick and ill, without almost fainting," she added, a shiver running through her frame.

Mr. Ravensworth's opinion veered round again. "She do it—nonsense!" Lady Level continued:

"'Don't scream; don't scream, Blanche,' he said. 'I am not much hurt, and I will take care of you,' and he held me to him as though I were in a vice. I thought he did not want me to alarm the house."

"Did he keep you there long?"

"It seemed long to me: I don't suppose it was more than a couple of minutes. His hold gradually relaxed, and then I saw that he had fainted. Oh, the terror of that moment! all the more intense that it had been suppressed. I feared he might bleed to death. I opened the door, and cried and screamed, and called for the servants; I rushed back to the room and rang the bell; and then I fell back in the easy-chair, and could do no more."

"Well, this is a better explanation than you gave me at first," said Mr. Ravensworth encouragingly: and she had spoken more readily, without appearance of disguise. "Then it was Lord Level's calling to you that first aroused you?"

"No; oh no; it was not that. It—" she stopped in confusion. "At least—perhaps it was. It—I can't say."
She had relapsed into evasion again, and once more Mr. Ravensworth was plunged in doubt. He leaned
towards her.

"I am going to ask you a question, Lady Level, and you must of course answer it or not as you please. I
can only repeat that any confidence you repose in me shall never be betrayed. Did Lord Level inflict this
injury on himself?"

"No, that was impossible," she freely answered; "it must have been done to him."

"The weapon, I hear, was found in your room."

"Yes."

"But how could it have come there?"

"As if I knew!"

"Why do you object to the police being called in?"

"It was Lord Level who objected. When he recovered from his faintness, and heard them speaking of the
police, he called Mr. Drewitt to him—who is master of the house under Lord Level—and charged him
that nothing of the kind should be done. I would rather they were here," she added after a pause. "I
should feel safer. This morning I went to my husband and told him if he would not have in the police, the
house searched, and the facts investigated, I should die with terror. He replied, jestingly, then if I chose
to be so foolish, I must die: the hurt was his, not mine, and if he saw no occasion for having in the police,
and did not choose to have them in, surely I need not want them. I was perfectly safe, and so was he, he
continued, and he would see that I was kept so. He would not even have the doctor called in at first; but
towards midday, when the fever returned and he became delirious, Mr. Drewitt sent for him."

"That seems more strange than all—refusing to have a doctor. He—"

The arrival of coffee interrupted them. Sanders brought it in in a silver coffeepot on a silver tray, with
biscuits and other light refreshments; and Mrs. Edwards attended to pour it out. Mr. Ravensworth
repeated to her what he had just said about the doctor.

"The fact is, sir, my lord does not like Dr. Macferraty," she rejoined. "None of us in this house do like
him; we cannot endure him. He has not long been in practice, and we look upon him as an upstart. It is a
great misfortune that Mr. Hill is away just now."

"The usual attendant, I presume, Mrs. Edwards?"

"Yes, sir; and a friend besides. He and the late lord seemed almost like brothers, so intimate were they.
Mr. Hill's mother is going on for ninety; she is beginning to break, and he has gone over to see her. She
lives in the Isle of Man. It is almost a month since he went away."

"The late lord? Let me see. He was the present lord's uncle, was he not?"

"Why, no, sir; he was his father," returned Mrs. Edwards, surprised at the mistake. "The late peer, Archibald Lord Level, had two sons, Mr. Francis the heir, and Mr. Archibald. Mr. Francis died of consumption, and lies buried in the family vault in Marshdale Church; and Mr. Archibald, the only son left, succeeded to his father."

"Yes, yes, I had forgotten," said Mr. Ravensworth. "An idea was floating in my mind that the present peer had not been always the heir-apparent."

CHAPTER XII

MYSTERY

Silence had fallen upon the room. Coffee had been taken, and the tray carried away by Mrs. Edwards. It was yet only eight o'clock. Mr. Ravensworth sat in mental perplexity, believing he had not come to the bottom of this dreadful affair; no, nor half-way to it.

But Lady Level was in still greater perplexity, her mind buried in miserable reverie. A conviction that she was being frightfully wronged in some way, and that she would not bear it, lay uppermost with her. Since meeting with the railway boy, Sam Doughty, the previous afternoon, and hearing the curious information he had disclosed, her temper had been gradually rising. It was temper that had caused her to declare herself to Lord Level while the servants (as related in a former chapter) were at supper in the kitchen, and Mrs. Edwards and the old steward were shut up in their sitting-room, waiting for their own supper to be served. The coast thus clear, in went Blanche to her lord's chamber. Not to open out the budget of her wrongs—he might not be sufficiently well for that—but to announce herself. To let him see that she was still in the house, that she had disregarded his injunction to quit it; and to assure him, in her rebellious spirit, that she meant to remain in it as long as she pleased. Not a word of suspected and unorthodox matters did Lady Level breathe, and the quarrel that arose between them was wholly on the score of her disobedience. Lord Level was passionately angry, thus to have been set at naught. He told her that as his wife she owed him obedience, and must give it to him. She retorted that she would not do so. The dispute went no further than that; but loud and angry words passed on both sides. And the next episode in the drama, some three or four hours later, was the mysterious attack upon Lord Level.

"Arnold," suddenly spoke her ladyship, looking up from her chair, "I mean to take a very decisive step."

"In what way?" he quietly asked, from his seat on the other side of the fireplace. "To send for the police?"

"No, no, no; not that. I shall separate from Lord Level."

"Oh," said Mr. Ravensworth, taken by surprise, and thinking she was jesting.

"As soon as he is well again, and able to discuss matters, I shall demand a separation. I shall insist upon it. If he will not accord it to me privately, I shall apply for it publicly."

"Blanche, you will do no such thing!" he exclaimed, rising in excitement. "You do not know what you are saying."

"And you do not know how much cause I have for saying it," she answered. "Lord Level has—has—insulted me."

"Hush," said Mr. Ravensworth. "I don't quite know what you mean by insult—"

"And I cannot tell you," she interrupted, her pretty black satin slipper beating its indignation on the hearthrug, her cheeks wearing a delicate rose-flush. "It is a thing I can speak of only to himself."

"But—I was going to say—Lord Level does not, I feel sure, intrude personal insult upon you. Anything that may take place outside your knowledge you had better neither notice nor inquire into."

Lady Level shook her head defiantly. "I mean to do it."

"I will not hear another word upon this point," said Mr. Ravensworth sternly. "You are as yet not much more than a child, young lady; when you are a little older and wiser, you will see how foolish such ideas are. For your own sake, Blanche, put them away from you."

"I wish my dear brother Tom were here!" she petulantly returned. "It was a shame his regiment should be sent out to India!"

Mr. Ravensworth drew in his stern lips. He had suspected that of the dreadful fate of Tom Heriot she must still be ignorant. The suspicion was now confirmed.

At that moment the steward, Mr. Drewitt, appeared; and Lady Level introduced him by name. Mr. Ravensworth saw a pale, venerable man of sixty years, still strong and upright, looking like a gentleman of the old, old school, in his plum-coloured suit and white silk stockings, his silver knee-buckles, his low shoes, and his voluminous cambric shirt-frill. He brought a message from his lord, who wished to see Mr. Ravensworth.

"Who told his lordship that Mr. Ravensworth was here?" exclaimed Lady Level quickly.

"Madam, it was I. My lord heard someone being shown in to your ladyship, and inquired who had come. I am sorry he has asked for you, sir," candidly added the steward, as they left the room together. "The fever has abated, but the least excitement will bring it on again."

Lady Level was sorry also. She did not care that Mr. Ravensworth's presence in the house should be known upstairs. The fact was that one day when she and her husband were on their homeward journey from Savoy, and Blanche was indulging in odds and ends of grievances against her lord, as in her ill-feeling towards him she was then taking to do, she had spoken a few words in sheer perverseness of spirit to make him jealous of Arnold Ravensworth. Lord Level said nothing, but he took the words to heart. He had not liked that gentleman before; he hated him now. Blanche blushed for herself as she recalled it.

Of course, it was not the visitor likely to give most pleasure to Lord Level. As the steward introduced Mr. Ravensworth and left them together, Lord Level regarded him with a cold, stern glance.

"So it is you!" he exclaimed. "May I ask what brings you down here? Did my lady send for you?"

"No," answered Mr. Ravensworth, advancing towards the bed. "Major Carlen called at my house this morning and requested me to come down. I could not reach Marshdale before to-night."

"Major Carlen? Oh! very good. Major Carlen dare not interfere between me and my wife; and he knows that."

"So far as I believe, Major Carlen has no intention or wish to interfere. Lady Level sent to him in her alarm, and he requested me to come down in his place."

"If Major Carlen has entered into an arrangement with you to come to my house and pry into matters that concern myself alone—"

"I beg your lordship's pardon," was the curt interruption. "I do not like or respect Major Carlen sufficiently well to enter into any 'arrangement' with him. I came down here, certainly in compliance with his desire, but in a spirit of kindness towards Lady Level, and to be of assistance to yourself if it were possible."

"How came you to bring Lady Level over from Germany?"

"She wished to come over."

"And I wished and desired her to stay there until I could join her. Do you call that interference?"

"It was nothing of the kind. On the morning of our departure from the inn, Lady Level told my wife and myself that she should take the opportunity to travel with us. She and her servants were even then dressed for the journey, and her travelling-carriage stood ready packed in the yard. If she did this against your wish, I am in no way responsible for it. It was not my place to dictate to her; to say she should go, or should remain. Be assured, my lord, I am the last man in the world unduly to interfere with other people; and my coming down now was entirely brought about by Major Carlen."

Lord Level was not insensible to reason. He remained silent for a time, the angry expression gradually leaving his face. Mr. Ravensworth spoke:

"I hope this injury to your lordship will not prove a grave one."

"It is a trifle," was the answer; "nothing but a trifle. It is my knee that keeps me prostrate here more than anything else; and I have intermittent fever with it."

"Can I be of service to you? If so, command me."

"Much obliged. No, I do not want anyone to be of service to me, if you allude to this stabbing business. Some drunken fellow got in, and—"

"The servants say the doors were all left fastened, and were so found."

"The servants say so to conceal their carelessness," cried Lord Level, as a contortion of pain crossed his face. "This knee gives me twinges at times like a red-hot iron."

"If anyone had broken in, especially any—"

"Mr. Ravensworth," imperatively interrupted Lord Level, "it is my pleasure that this affair should not be investigated. I say that some man got in—a poacher, probably, who must have been the worse for drink—and he attacked me, not knowing what he was doing. To have a commotion made over it would only excite me in my present feverish condition. Therefore I shall put up with the injury, and shall be well all the sooner for doing so. You will be so obliging," he added, some sarcasm in his tone, "as to do the same."

But now, Mr. Ravensworth did not show himself wise in that moment. He urged, in all good faith, a different course upon his lordship. The presumption angered and excited Lord Level. In no time, as it seemed, and without sufficient cause, the fever returned and mounted to the brain. His face grew crimson, his eye wild; his voice rose almost to a scream, and he flung his uninjured arm about the bed. Mr. Ravensworth, in self-reproach for what he had done, looked for the bell and rang it.

"Drewitt, are the doors fastened?" raved his lordship in delirium, as the steward hastened in. "Do you hear me, Drewitt? Have you looked to the doors? You must have left one of them open! Where are the keys? The keys, I say, Drewitt!—What brings that man here?"

"You had better go down, sir, out of his sight," whispered the steward, for it was at Mr. Ravensworth the invalid was excitedly pointing. "I knew what it would be if he began talking. And he was so much better!"

"His lordship excites himself for nothing," was the deprecating answer.

"Why, of course," said Mr. Drewitt. "It is the nature of fever-patients to do so."

Mrs. Edwards came in with appliances to cool the heated head, and Mr. Ravensworth returned to the sitting-room below. Blanche was not there. Close upon that, Dr. Macferraty called. After he had been with his patient and dressed the wounds, he came bustling into the sitting-room. This loud young man had a nose that turned straight up, giving an impudent look to the face, and wide-open, round green eyes. But no doubt he had his good points, and was a skilful surgeon.

"You are a friend of the family, I hear, sir," he began. "I hope you intend to order an investigation into this extraordinary affair?"

"I have no authority for doing so. And Lord Level does not wish it done."

"A fig for Lord Level! He does not know what he's saying," cried Dr. Macferraty. "There never was so monstrous a thing heard of as that a nobleman should be stabbed in his own bed and the assassin be let off scot-free! We need not look far for the culprit!"

The last words, significantly spoken, jarred on Mr. Ravensworth's ears. "Have you a suspicion?" he asked.

"I can put two and two together, sir, and find they make four. The windows were fast; the doors were fast; there was no noise, no disturbance, no robbery: well, then, what deduction have we to fall back upon but that the villain, he or she, is an inmate of the house?"

Mr. Ravensworth's pulses beat a shade more quickly. "Do you suspect one of the servants?"

"Yes, I do."

"But the servants are faithful and respectable. They are not suspected indoors, I assure you."

"Perhaps not; they are out-of-doors, though. The whole neighbourhood is in commotion over it; and how Drewitt and the old lady can let these two London servants be at large is the talk of the place."

"Oh, it is the London servants you suspect, then, or one of them?"

"Look here," said Dr. Macferraty, dropping his voice and bending forward in his chair till his face almost touched Mr. Ravensworth's: "that the deed was done by an inmate of the house is certain. No one got in, or could have got in; it is nonsense to suggest it. The inmates consist of Lady Level and the servants only. If you take it from the servants, you must lay it upon her."

No answer.

"Well," went on the doctor, "it is impossible to suspect her. A delicate, refined girl, as she is, could not do so evil a thing. So we must needs look to the servants. Deborah would not do it; the stout old cook could not. She was in bed ill, besides, and slept through all the noise and confusion. The two other servants, Sanders and Timms, are strangers."

"I feel sure they no more did it than I," impulsively spoke Mr. Ravensworth.

"Then you would fall back upon Lady Level?"

"No. No," flashed Mr. Ravensworth. "The bare suggestion of the idea is an insult to her."

Dr. Macferraty drew himself back in his chair. "There's a mystery in the affair, look at it which way you will, sir," he cried raspingly. "My lord says he did not recognise the assassin; but, if he did not, why should he forbid investigation? Put it as you do, that the two servants are innocent—why, then, I fairly own I am puzzled. Another thing puzzles me: the knife was found in Lady Level's chamber, yet she protests that she slept through it all—was only awakened by his lordship calling to her when it was over."

"It may have been flung in."

"No; it was carried in; for blood had dripped from it all along the floor."

"Has the weapon been recognised?"

"Not that I am aware of. No one owns to knowing it. Anyway, it is an affair that ought to be, and that must be, inquired into officially," concluded the doctor from the corridor, as he said good-night and went bustling out.

Mr. Ravensworth, standing at the sitting-room door, saw him meet the steward, who must have overheard the words, and now advanced with cautious steps. Touching Mr. Ravensworth's arm, he drew him within the shadow cast by a remote corner.

"Sir," he whispered, "my lady told Mrs. Edwards that you were a firm friend of hers; a sure friend?"

"I trust I am, Mr. Drewitt."

"Then let it drop, sir; it is no common robber who has done this. Let it drop, for her sake and my lord's."

Mr. Ravensworth felt painfully perplexed. Those few words, spoken by the faithful old steward, were more fraught with suspicion against Lady Level than anything he had yet heard.

Returning to the sitting-room, pacing it to and fro in his perplexity for he knew not how long, he was looking at his watch to ascertain the time, when Lady Level came in. She had been in Lord Level's sitting-room upstairs, she said, the one opposite his bed-chamber. He was somewhat calmer now. Mr. Ravensworth thought that he must now be going.

"I have been of no assistance to you, Lady Level; I do not see that I can be of any," he observed. "But should anything arise in which you think I can help you, send for me."

"What do you expect to arise?" she hastily inquired.

"Nay, I expect nothing."

"Did Lord—" Lady Level suddenly stopped and turned her head. Just within the room stood two policemen. She rose with a startled movement, and shrank close to Mr. Ravensworth, crying out, as for protection. "Arnold! Arnold!"

"Do not agitate yourself," he whispered. "What is it that you want?" he demanded, moving towards the men.

"We have come about this attack on Lord Level, sir," replied one of them.

"Who sent for you?"

"Don't know anything about that, sir. Our superior ordered us here, and is coming on himself. We must examine the fastenings of this window, sir, by the lady's leave."

They passed up the room, and Lady Level left it, followed by Mr. Ravensworth. Outside stood Deborah, aghast.

"They have been in the kitchen this ten minutes, my lady," she whispered, "asking questions of us all—Mr. Sanders and Mrs. Timms and me and cook, all separate. And now they are going round the house to search it, and see to the fastenings."

The men came out again and moved away, Deborah following slowly in their wake: she appeared to regard them with somewhat of the curiosity we give to a wild animal: but Mr. Ravensworth recalled her. Lady Level entered the room again and sat down by the fire. Mr. Ravensworth again observed that he must be going: he had barely time to walk to the station and catch the train.

"Arnold, if you go, and leave me with these men in the house, I will never forgive it!" she passionately uttered.

He looked at her in surprise. "I thought you wished for the presence of the police. You said you should regard them as a protection."

"Did you send for them?" she breathlessly exclaimed.

"Certainly not."

She sank into a reverie—a deep, unpleasant reverie that compressed her lips and contracted her brow. Suddenly she lifted her head.

"He is my husband, after all, Arnold."

"To be sure he is."

"And therefore—and therefore—there had better be no investigation."

"Why?" asked Mr. Ravensworth, scarcely above his breath.

"Because he does not wish it," she answered, bending her face downwards. "He forbade me to call in aid, or to suffer it to be called in; and, as I say, he is my husband. Will you stop those men in their search? will you send them away?"

"I do not think I have power to do so."

"You can forbid them in Lord Level's name. I give you full authority: as he would do, were he capable of acting. Arnold, I will have them out of the house. I will."

"What is it that you fear from them?"

"I fear—I cannot tell you what I fear. They might question me."

"And if they did?—you can only repeat to them what you told me."

"No, it must not be," she shivered. "I—I—dare not let it be."

Mr. Ravensworth paused. "Blanche," he said, in low tones, "have you told me all?"

"Perhaps not," she slowly answered.

"'Perhaps!'"

"There!" she exclaimed, springing up in wild excitement. "I hear those men upstairs, and you stand here idly talking! Order them away in Lord Level's name."

Desperately perplexed, Mr. Ravensworth flew to the stairs. The steward, pale and agitated, met him half-way up. "It must not be looked into by the police," he whispered. "Sir, it must not. Will you speak to them? you may have more weight with them than I. Say you are a friend of my lord's. I strongly suspect this is the work of that meddling Macferraty."

Arnold Ravensworth moved forward as one in a dream, an under-current of thought asking what all this mystery meant. The steward followed. They found the men in one of the first rooms: not engaged in the examination of its fastenings or its closets (and the whole house abounded in closets and cupboards), but with their heads together, talking in whispers.

In answer to Mr. Ravensworth's peremptory demand, made in Lord Level's name, that the search should cease and the house be freed of their presence, they civilly replied that they must not leave, but would willingly retire to the kitchen and there await their superior officer, who was on his road to the house: and they went down accordingly. Mr. Ravensworth returned to the sitting-room to acquaint Lady Level with the fact, but found she had disappeared. In a moment she came in, scared, her hands lifted in dismay, her breath coming in gasps.

"Give me air!" she cried, rushing to the window and motioning to have it opened. "I shall faint; I shall die."

"What ever is the matter?" questioned Mr. Ravensworth, as he succeeded in undoing the bolt of the window, and throwing up its middle compartment. At that moment a loud ring came to the outer gate. It increased her terror, and she broke into a flood of tears.

"My dear young lady, let me be your friend," he said in his grave concern. "Tell me the whole truth. I know you have not done so yet. Let it be what it will, I promise to—if possible—shield you from harm."

"Those men are saying in the kitchen that it was I who attacked Lord Level; I overheard them," she shuddered, the words coming from her brokenly in her agitation.

"Make a friend of me; you shall never have a truer," he continued, for really he knew not what else to urge, and he could not work in the dark. "Tell me all from beginning to end."

But she only shivered in silence.

"Blanche!—did—you—do—it?"

"No," she answered, with a low burst of heartrending sobs. "But I saw it done."

CHAPTER I

SUSPICION

The church-clock of that small country place, Upper Marshdale, was chiming half-past nine on a dark night, as the local inspector turned out of the police-station and made his way with a fleet step across a piece of waste land and some solitary fields beyond it. His name was Poole, and he was hastening to Marshdale House, as Lord Level's place was called. A mysterious occurrence had taken place there the night before: Lord Level, previously an invalid, had been stabbed in his bed.

The officer rang a loud peal at the outer gate, and a policeman, who had been already sent on, came from the house to answer the summons. He waited when they were both within the gate, knowing that he should be questioned. His superior walked half-way up the avenue, and placed his back against a tree.

"What have you learnt, Jekyl? Any clue to the assassin?"

The policeman dropped his voice to a whisper, as though afraid the very trees might hear. "Speak up," sharply interrupted the inspector. "The air carries no tales."

"The case seems as clear, sir, as any we ever came across; a clear case against Lady Level."

It takes a great deal to astonish a police inspector, but this announcement certainly astonished Mr. Inspector Poole. "Against Lady Level?" he repeated.

"She's the guilty one, sir, I fear. But who'd think it, to see her? Only about twenty or so, and with beauty enough to knock you over, and blue eyes that look you down in their pride. She's dressed out like those high-born ladies do dress, in light silk that glistens as she walks, her neck and arms uncovered. There's a gentleman with her now, some friend of the family, and he won't let us go on with our investigation. He came and stopped it, and said we were acting against Lord Level's wishes."

"But why do you suspect Lady Level?" inquired the inspector.

"Listen, sir. It appears certain that no one got in; the doors and windows were left safe, and were found so; hadn't been disturbed at all; there has been no robbery, or anything of that sort, and no suspicion attaches to any of the servants so far as I see. Then there are the facts themselves. The servants were aroused in the middle of the night by Lord Level's bell ringing violently, and my lady screaming. When they got to his room, there he lay, fainted dead off, stabbed in two places, and she pretty near fainting too, and dropped down in a chair in her silk dressing-gown—"

"I am acquainted with the facts so far, Jekyl."

"Well, sir. Not a sign or symptom was there of anybody else being about, or of anybody's having been about. Her ladyship's version is, that she was woke up by Lord Level calling to her, and she found him stabbed and bleeding. That is all she will confess to."

"And he?"

"He says nothing, I hear, except that he will not have the police called in. He did not even want to have a doctor. But his lordship is off his head with fever, and may not know what he is saying."

"How does Lady Level account for the knife being found in her room?"

"There it is," cried the man. "Whenever these people, let them be high or low, do an evil deed, they are certain to commit some act of folly which allows suspicion to creep in. They over-do it, or they under-do it. If anyone else had done it and carried the weapon to her ladyship's room, she must have seen who it was, and would surely have denounced him. And why did she put it there of all places? There's a fatality on them, I say, sir, and they can't escape it."

"But her motive for attacking him?"

"They were on bad terms, it seems. The servants heard them quarrelling violently earlier in the evening."

"Did the servants tell you this, to confirm their suspicions against her?"

"They don't suspect her, sir," replied Jekyl. "I and Cliff have drawn our own deductions by what they have said, and by personal observation."

The inspector mused. He was a kindly-disposed man, possessed his share of common sense, and did not feel so sure about the matter as his subordinate. "It appears scarcely credible that a young woman like Lady Level, hardly six months married, should attempt her husband's life, Jekyl. Where are these servants?"

"In the kitchen, sir. This way. There's no establishment to speak of. When my lord was detained here through damage to his knee, my lady followed him down against his will, it's whispered—and brought only her maid and a man-servant."

"I think you have been listening to a good deal of gossip," remarked Inspector Poole, as he moved on to the house.

Meanwhile Lady Level, in deep agitation, stood at the window which she had had thrown up for air, while she made the confession to Mr. Ravensworth that she had been a witness to the attack on her husband. This she had denied before; and it might never have been wrung from her, but that she overheard the two policemen, already in the house, whispering their suspicions against her.

She was shocked, indignant, terrified. She leaned for support on the window-frame, panting for breath in the cold night air.

"Arnold, am I to bear this?"

He stood with folded arms. He felt for her deeply: were she connected with him by near ties of blood, he could not have been more anxious to protect her; but a strong doubt that she might be guilty was working within him. He supposed she must have received some great provocation from Lord Level.

"How cruel they are to entertain such a suspicion! If they—if they— Oh, Arnold, they never will arrest me!—they never will publicly accuse me!" she uttered, as a new possibility occurred to her.

"Blanche, listen," he rejoined, talking to her as he had talked when she was a child. "All that can be done for you, I will do; but I cannot work in this uncertainty. Tell me the truth; be it good or be it ill, I will stand by you; but, if I am to be of service to you, I must know it. Was it you who struck Lord Level?"

"No. Have I not just told you so?"

"What you told me I do not understand. You say you saw it done—"

"Then I did not see it done," she petulantly interrupted; and no more questions would she answer.

"Let me take you back to the fire," said Mr. Ravensworth, as he shut down the window. "You are trembling with cold."

"Not with cold," was her reply.

Stirring the fire into a blaze, he drew the easy-chair near it for her. He then stood by, saying nothing.

"Suppose they should openly accuse me?" she began, after a silence. "Would they arrest me?"

"Blanche," he retorted, in sharp, ringing, imperative accents, "are you guilty? Tell me, one way or the other, that I may know what to be at."

Lady Level rose and confronted him, her blue eyes wearing their most haughty expression. "You have known me for many years, known me well; how then can you repeat that question? I guilty of attacking Lord Level!"

"I would rather believe myself—I could as soon believe my own wife guilty of such a thing; but why have you equivocated with me? You have not told me the truth, as to what passed that night."

"My husband charged me not to tell anyone."

"Five minutes ago you told me yourself that you saw it done; now you say you did not see it. What am I to think?"

"In saying I saw it done, I spoke hastily; what I ought to have said was, that I saw who did it. And then, to-day, Lord Level insisted that I had been dreaming," she abstractedly continued. "Arnold, do you believe that we can see visions or dream dreams that afterwards wear the semblance of realities?"

"I wish you would not speak in riddles. The time is going on; those men of the law may come in and accuse you, and what defence am I to make for you? You know that you may trust me. What you say shall never pass my lips."

Lady Level deliberated. "I will trust you," she said at length: "there seems to be no help for it. I went to rest last night angry with Lord Level, for we had spoken irritating words to each other. I lay awake, I dare say for an hour, indulging bitter thoughts, and then I dropped asleep. Suddenly something woke me; I cannot tell you what it was: whether it was any noise, or whether it was the opening of the door, which I had closed, between my room and Lord Level's. All I know is, that door was wide open, and someone stood in the doorway with a lighted candle. It was a strange-looking object, and seemed to be dressed in flannel—either a long flannel shirt or a flannel gown. In the confusion of the moment I believed it must be Lord Level, and I was struck with amazement, for Lord Level is not able to get out of bed without assistance, from the injury to his knee, and I thought how long his hair was, and how dark it had grown—that was, you know, when I was between sleeping and waking. Then I saw that it had large, flashing black eyes, so it could not be Lord Level. It crossed the room—"

"Blanche," he interrupted, "you speak just as if you were describing a vision. It—"

"That is what Lord Level now says it was. Let me go on. It crossed the room as far as the dressing-table. I started up in bed then, and the wild eyes turned upon me, and at the same moment Lord Level called out from his own bed, apparently in agitation or pain. The figure dropped something, turned round, and darted back again through the open door to the other chamber. I saw the candle fall from its hand to the floor, and the place was in darkness, except for the little light that came from Lord Level's night-lamp. Terror overwhelmed me, and I cried out, and then my husband called to me by name. I ran to his room, flinging on my warm silk dressing-gown as I went, and there I found him hurt in some way, for he was bleeding from the arm and from the side. Arnold, as I live, as I breathe, that is the whole truth," she concluded with emotion.

"Did you again see the figure? Was it in Lord Level's room?"

"It was not there. I saw no trace of it. I remember I picked up the candlestick, for it was right in my path, and I screamed when I saw the blood upon my husband. He caught me to him by the other arm, as I have told you, telling me not to be frightened, that he would protect me; and I saw how white he looked, and that his brow was damp. Presently I asked him who and what it was; and the question seemed to excite him. 'Say nothing of what you have seen,' he cried; 'I charge you, nothing.' I don't quite know what I replied; it was to the effect that the household must be aroused, and the figure searched for. 'Blanche, you are my wife,' he said solemnly; 'my interests are yours; I charge you, by your duty and obedience to me, that you say nothing. Bury this in silence, as you value your life and mine.' Then he fainted and his hold relaxed, and I screamed out and the servants came. Had my life depended upon it I could not have helped screaming. What the figure had dropped in my room proved to be the knife."

"This is a very strange account!" exclaimed Mr. Ravensworth.

"It is so strange that I lose myself at times, wondering whether I was dreaming or awake. But it was true; it was true; though I could not proclaim it in defiance of my husband."

"Do you think the figure, as you call it, could have been one of the servants in disguise?"

"I am certain it was not. Not one of them has that dark Italian face."

"Italian face!" echoed Mr. Ravensworth. "Why do you call it an Italian face?"

Lady Level bent her head. "The thought somehow struck me," she answered, after a pause. "Not at the time, but since. I fancied it not unlike the Italian faces that one sees in pictures."

"Was it a man or a woman?"

"I do not know. At the time I took it to be a man, quite young. But since, recalling the appearance—well, it seems to me that it is impossible to decide which it was."

"And you saw no signs of this mysterious figure afterwards?"

"None whatever. There were no traces, I tell you, of its having been there, except the injury to Lord Level, the knife, and the fallen candlestick. The candlestick may have been left in Lord Level's room the previous night, for it is precisely like those used in the household, so that the figure may have lighted it from the night-lamp."

Mr. Ravensworth could not make much of all this. It puzzled him. "The curious thing is," he said aloud, "where could the figure have come from?"

"The curious thing is, that Lord Level wants to persuade me now that this was only a dream of the imagination."

"That his wounds are?"

"Not his wounds, of course—or the knife, but a great deal of what I told him. He ridicules the bare idea of its being a 'strange figure,' 'strangely dressed.' He says he caught a full view of the man who attacked him; that he should know him again; that he was dressed in a sort of soft light fustian, and was no more wild-looking than I am, except such wildness as arose from his state of inebriation, and he suspects he was a poacher who must have got in through one of the windows."

Mr. Ravensworth pondered over the tale: and he could not help deeming it a most improbable one. But that traces of some mysterious presence had been left behind, he would have regarded it as her husband appeared partially to regard it—a midnight freak of Lady Level's imagination. "Yet the wounds are realities," said Mr. Ravensworth, speaking aloud, in answer to his own thoughts.

"Arnold, it is all a reality," she said impressively. "There are moments, I say, when I am almost tempted to question it, but in my sober reason I know it to have been true; and while I ask myself, 'Was it a dream?' I hold a perfect, positive conviction that it was only too terrible a reality."

"You have spoken once or twice of its wild appearance. Did it look like a madman?"

"I never saw a madman, that I know of. This creature looked wild enough to be mad. There was one thing I thought curious in connection with finding the knife," proceeded Lady Level. "Timms, who picked it up, while Sanders had gone down for some hot water, brought it into Lord Level's room, calling out that she had found the weapon. 'Why, that's Mr. Drewitt's knife!' exclaimed the housemaid, Deborah, as soon as she saw it; and the steward, who had only just reached the room, asked her how she could make the assertion. 'It is yours, sir,' said Deborah; 'it's your new knife; I have seen it on your table, and should know it anywhere.' 'Deborah, if you repeat that again, I'll have you punished,' sharply called out the housekeeper, without, you understand, turning from Lord Level, to whom she was attending, to ascertain whether it was or was not the knife. Now, Arnold," added Lady Level, "ill and terrified as I felt at the moment, a conviction came across me that it was Mr. Drewitt's knife, but that he and Mrs. Edwards were purposely denying it."

"It is impossible to suspect them of attacking, or conniving at the attack on Lord Level."

"They attack Lord Level! They would rather attack the whole world combined, than that a hair of his head should suffer. They are fondly, devotedly attached to him. And Deborah, it appears, has been convinced out of her assertion. Hark! who is that?"

Mr. Ravensworth opened the door to reconnoitre. The inspector was prowling about the house and passages, exploring the outlets and inlets, followed by his two men, who had done the same before him.

"I thought you had forbidden the men to search," cried Lady Level. "Why are they disobeying you?"

"Their chief is here now, and of course his orders go before mine. Besides, after what you have told me, I consider there ought to be a thorough search," added Mr. Ravensworth.

"In opposition to Lord Level?"

"I think that Lord Level has not taken a sufficiently serious view of the case. The only solution I can come to is, that some escaped madman got into the house before it was closed for the night, and concealed himself in it. If so, he may be in it now."

"Now! In it now!" she exclaimed, turning pale.

"Upon my word, I think it may be so. The doors and windows were all found safely fastened, you see. Therefore he could not escape during the night. And since the doors were opened this morning, the household, I take it, has been so constantly on the alert, that it might be an extremely difficult matter for him to get away unseen. If he, this madman, did enter yesterday evening, he must have found some place of concealment and hidden himself in it for hours, since it was not until one o'clock that he made the attack on Lord Level."

"Oh, Arnold, that is all too improbable," she rejoined doubtingly. "A madman could not plan and do all that."

"Madmen are more cunning than sane ones, sometimes."

"But I—I think it was a woman," said Lady Level, lowering her voice and her eyes.

Mr. Ravensworth looked at her. And for the first time, a feeling flashed into his mind that Lady Level had some suspicion which she would not speak of.

"Blanche," he said sharply, "do you know who it was? Tell me, if you do."

"I do not," she answered emphatically. "I may imagine this and imagine that, but I do not know anything."

"You were speaking, then, from imagination?"

"Y—es. In a case of mystery, such as this, imagination runs riot, and you can't prevent its doing so."

Again there was something about Lady Level that struck Mr. Ravensworth as being not honestly true. Before more could be said, steps were heard approaching the room; and Lady Level, afraid to meet the police, made her escape from it.

Running swiftly upstairs, she was passing Lord Level's door to enter her own, when she heard his voice, speaking collectedly, and peeped in. He saw her, and held out his hand. He appeared now quite rational, though his fine gray eyes were glistening and his fair face was flushed. Mrs. Edwards was standing by the bedside, and it was to her he had been talking.

Blanche advanced timidly. "Are you feeling better?" she softly asked.

"Oh, much better; nearly well: but for my knee I should be up and about," he answered, as he drew her towards him. "Mrs. Edwards, will you close the door? I wish to speak with my wife."

Mrs. Edwards, with a warning glance at her lady, which seemed to say, "He is not fit for it"—at least Blanche so interpreted it—went out and shut the door. Lord Level drew her closer to his side. He was lying propped up by a mound of pillows, almost sitting up in bed, and kept her standing there.

"Blanche," he began in very quiet tones, "I hear the police are in the house."

"Yes," she was obliged to answer, quite taken aback and feeling very much vexed that he had been told, as it was likely to excite him.

"Who sent for them? You?"

"Oh no."

"Then it was your friend; that fellow Ravensworth. I thought as much."

"But indeed it was not," she eagerly answered, shrinking from her husband's scornful tones. "When the two policemen came in—and we do not know who it was sent them—Mr. Ravensworth went to them by my desire to stop the search. I told him that you objected to it."

"Objected to it! I forbade it," haughtily rejoined Lord Level. "And if—if—"

"Oh, pray, Archibald, do not excite yourself; do not, do not!" she interrupted, frightened and anxious. "You know you will become worse again if you do."

"Will you go and end it in my name? End it, and send them away from the house."

"Yes, if you tell me to do so; if you insist upon it," she answered. "But I am afraid."

"Why are you afraid?"

Lady Level bent her head until it was on a level with his. "For this, Archibald," she whispered: "that they might question me—and I should be obliged to answer them."

Lord Level gently drew her cool cheek nearer, that it might rest against his fevered one, and remained silent, apparently pondering the question.

"After I told you all that I saw that night, you bade me be silent," she resumed. "Well, I fear the police might draw it from me if they questioned me."

"But you must not allow them to draw it from you."

"Oh, but perhaps I could not help it," she sighed. "You know what the police are—how they question and cross-question people."

"Blanche, I reminded you last night that you were my wife, and you owed me implicit obedience in all great things."

"Yes, and I am trying to obey you; I am indeed, Archibald," she protested, almost torn by conflicting emotions; for, in spite of her doubts and suspicions, and (as she put it to herself) her "wrongs," she loved her husband yet.

"Well, my dear, you must be brave for my sake; ay, and for your own. Listen, Blanche: you will tell the police nothing; and they must not search the house. I don't care to see them myself to forbid it; I don't want to see them. For one thing, I am hardly strong enough to support the excitement it would cause me. But—"

"Will you tell me something, Archibald?" she whispered. "Is the—the—person—that attacked you in the house now?"

Lord Level looked surprised. "In this house? Why, how could it be? Certainly not."

"Was it—was it a woman?" she breathed, her voice low and tremulous.

He turned angry. "How can you be so silly, Blanche? A woman! Oh yes," changing to sarcasm, "of course it was a woman. It was you, perhaps."

"That is what they are saying, Archibald."

"What are they saying?" he returned, in dangerous excitement—if Blanche had only noticed the signs. For all this was agitating him.

"Why, that," she answered, bursting into tears. "The police are saying so. They are saying that it was I who stabbed you."

Lord Level cried out as a man in agony. And, with that, delirium came on again.

CHAPTER II

NOT LIFTED

My Lady Level sat at the open window of her husband's sitting-room, in the dark, her hot face lifted to the cool night air. Only a moment ago Lord Level had been calling out in his delirium, and Mrs. Edwards was putting cool appliances to his head, and damp, hot bricks to his feet. And Blanche knew that it was she who, by her indiscreet remarks and questioning, had brought on the crisis. She had not meant to harm or excite him; but she had done it; and she was very contrite.

It was now between ten and eleven o'clock. She did not intend to go to bed that night; and she had already slipped off her evening dress, and put on a morning one of soft gray cashmere. With his lordship in a fresh attack of fever, and the police about, the household did not think of going to rest.

Blanche Level sat in a miserable reverie, her lovely face pressed upon her slender hand, the tears standing in her blue eyes. She was suspecting her husband of all kinds of unorthodox things—this has been said before. Not the least disloyal of them being that an individual named Nina, who wore long gold earrings to enhance her charms, was concealed in that east wing, which might almost be called a separate house, and which owned a separate entrance.

And a conviction lay upon Lady Level—caught up since, not at the time—that it was this Nina who had attacked Lord Level. She could not drive away the impression.

Naturally she was bitterly resentful. Not at the attack, but at all the rest of it. She had said nothing yet to her husband, and she did not know whether she ever should say it; for even to speak upon such a topic reflected on herself a shame that stung her. Of course he forbade the search lest this visitor should be discovered, reasoned she; that is, he told her to forbid it: but ought she to obey him? Lady Level, cowering there in the darkness, would have served as a perfect exemplification of a small portion of Collins's "Ode to the Passions."

'Thy numbers, Jealousy, to naught were fixed,
Sad proof of thy distressful state;
Of differing themes the veering song was mixed,
And now it courted love, now raving, called on hate.'

Thus was it here. One moment she felt that she could—and should—put Lord Level away from her for his falsity, his treachery; the next she was conscious that life without him would be one long and bitter penance, for she had learned to love him with her whole heart and soul.

And until that miserable sojourn at Pisa, she had deemed that he returned her love, truly and passionately. Fie on the deceitful wiles of man!

A stir in the passage without. Was there any change in Lord Level, for better or for worse? Despite her resentment, she was anxious, and she opened the door. Mrs. Edwards had come out from the opposite chamber, a basin in hand.

"My lady, he is calmer," whispered the housekeeper, answering the unspoken question which she read in her eyes. "If he could only be kept so, if he had nothing to disturb him, he would soon be well again. It is a most unlucky thing that these police should have come here, where they are not wanted. That of itself must bring excitement to his lordship."

"It is unlucky that these tales should have been carried to him," haughtily reproved the young lady. "I cannot think who does it, or why."

"Nay, my lady, but when his lordship questions of this and that, he must be answered."

Closing the door of the sick-chamber very quietly, Mrs. Edwards passed down the stairs. At the same moment, covert steps were heard ascending them. Lady Level caught a glimpse of Mr. Inspector Poole's head, and stole back out of sight.

Meanwhile Mr. Ravensworth had been trying to gain a little explanation from that official. "Do you know," he said to him, "that you are here against Lord Level's wishes, and in direct opposition to his orders?"

"No, I do not," replied the inspector. "I did not understand it in that light. I certainly was told that his lordship had said he would not have the case officially inquired into, but I understood that he was lightheaded when he spoke, not at all conscious of what he was saying."

"From whom, then, did you receive your instructions, Mr. Poole?"

"From Dr. Macferraty," was the ready answer. "He called in at the station this evening."

"Ah!" cried Arnold Ravensworth.

"It would be a grave mistake, he said, if so monstrous a thing—they were the doctors own words—should be left uninvestigated, because his lordship was off his head," added the inspector. "May I ask, sir, if you entertain any suspicion—in any quarter?"

"Not any," decisively replied Mr. Ravensworth. "The whole thing is to me most mysterious."

The speakers looked at one another. Mr. Poole was deliberating whether he should give a hint of what Jekyl had said about Lady Level. But he was saved the trouble.

"I understand, through overhearing a word or two, that your men have been wondering whether the culprit could have been Lady Level," spoke Mr. Ravensworth in low tones. "The very idea is monstrous: you have but now used the right word. Believe me, she is innocent as a child. But she is most terribly frightened."

"Well, I thought it very unlikely," admitted the inspector.

"But it seems," slowly continued Mr. Ravensworth, weighing well his words, "that she caught sight at the time, or thought she caught sight, of a figure curiously attired in white flannel, who dropped, or flung, the knife down in her chamber. Lord Level says it was not white flannel, but light fustian, such as a countryman might wear. According to that, he must also have seen the individual. The difficulty, however, is, to know whether his lordship is speaking in his senses or out of them."

"Someone must have got in, then, after all; in spite of the doors being found as they were left."

"I think so. I cannot see any other loophole for suspicion to fall back upon. Concealed himself in the house probably beforehand. And, for all we know, may be concealed in it still. I gathered an impression while Lady Level was talking to me that it might really be some escaped madman. All the same, Lord Level persists in forbidding the matter to be investigated."

Keen and practical, the officer revolved what he heard. The story was a curious one altogether, and as yet he did not see his way in it.

"I think, sir," he said with deliberation, "that I shall take the affair into my hands, and act, in the uncertain state of his lordship's mind, upon my own responsibility. First of all, we will just go through the house."

Mr. Ravensworth went with him: they two together. After a thorough search, nothing wrong could they find or discover. The servants and the two policemen remained below; Mrs. Edwards was in close attendance upon his lordship; and the steward, who appeared most exceedingly to resent the presence of these police in the house, had shut himself into his rooms.

In the course of time, the inspector and Mr. Ravensworth approached these rooms. Passing Lord Level's chamber with soft footsteps, they traversed the passages beyond it, until they found themselves stopped by a door, which was fastened.

Mr. Poole shook it. "It must lead to some of the remote rooms," he observed, "and they are uninhabited. Just the spot for an assassin to conceal himself in—or to try to do so."

"I think these may be the steward's apartments," spoke Arnold Ravensworth doubtingly. "I remember Lady Level said they were only divided from his lordship's chamber by a passage or two."

Whose ever rooms they were, no one came to the door in answer to the summons, and the inspector knocked again.

This time it brought forth Mr. Drewitt. They heard him draw a chain, and then he opened the door a few inches, as far as the chain permitted him.

"Will you let us in, Mr. Drewitt? I must search these rooms."

"Search for what?" asked the old man. "It's you, is it, Poole! I cannot have my rooms searched. This morning, after the alarm, I went over them, to be quite sure, and that's sufficient."

"Allow me to search for myself," returned the officer.

"No, sir," answered the steward, with dignity. "No one shall come in to search these rooms in opposition to the wish of my lord. His orders to me were that the affair should be allowed to drop, and I for one will not disobey him, or give help to those who would. His lordship believed that whoever it might be that attacked him came in and went out again. The country might be hunted over, he said, but not his house."

"I must enter here," was all the answer reiterated by the officer.

"It shall be over my body, then," returned the steward, with emotion. "My lord forbade a search, and you have no right whatever to proceed with it."

"My good man, I am a police inspector."

"You may be inspector-general for all I care," retorted the old gentleman, "but you don't come in here. Get my lord's authority first, and then you will be welcome. As to reminding me who you are, Mr. Poole, you must know that to be superfluous. And I beg your pardon, sir," he added, addressing Mr. Ravensworth, "but I would inquire what authority you hold from my lord, that you, a stranger, should set at naught his expressed wishes?"

The door was shut and bolted in their faces, and the inspector leaned against the wall in thought. "Did you notice his agitation?" he whispered to Mr. Ravensworth. "There's more in this than meets the eye."

It certainly wore that appearance. However, for the present they were foiled, and the steward remained master of the position. To attempt to enter those rooms by force would create noise and commotion in the house that might be disastrous to the health of Lord Level.

"There's something in those rooms that has to be concealed," spoke the astute inspector. "If it be the man who attacked Lord Level—"

"But the steward, devoted as he is to his master, would not harbour him," impulsively interrupted Arnold Ravensworth.

"True. Unless—unless, mind you, there exists some cause, which we cannot even guess at, for his lordship's shielding him," said the inspector. "I must say I should like to get into the rooms."

"There is no other way of doing it; no other entrance."

"I don't know that, sir. Unless I am mistaken, these rooms communicate direct with the East Wing. By getting into that, we might find an unsuspected entrance."

He made his way downstairs in silence, musing as he went. At the foot of the staircase he encountered Deborah.

"Which are the passages in this lower part of the house that lead to the East Wing?" he inquired.

"Not any of them, sir," answered Deborah promptly. "At least, not any that are ever opened. At the end of the stone passage there's a heavy door, barred and bolted, that leads to other passages, I believe, and to other heavy bolted doors, and they lead into the East Wing. That's what I have heard say. The only entrance in use is the one through Mr. Drewitt's rooms."

Opposition seemed only to strengthen the will of Mr. Inspector Poole. "Into the rooms I mean to make my way," he said to Mr. Ravensworth, as he retraced his steps up the staircase. "Could you not," he hastily added, "get Lady Level to bring her authority to bear upon old Drewitt?"

It was the appearance of Lady Level that probably induced the thought. She, looking pale, haggard and uneasy, was peeping down at them, and did not escape in time.

Arnold Ravensworth somewhat hesitatingly acceded. They wished to speak to Mr. Drewitt—he put it to her in that way—but he had bolted himself into his rooms; would she use her authority and bid him admit them?

She complied at once, unsuspiciously. Of all parts of the house, that occupied by the steward must be most free from concealment. And she went with them to the barred-up door.

The steward did not presume to dispute Lady Level's mandate, which she gave somewhat imperiously. She entered with them. They found themselves in the old gentleman's sitting-room, and he placed chairs for them. "We have not come to sit down," said Mr. Poole; and he passed into the other rooms in rapid succession: the two bed-chambers and the unoccupied room that had nothing in it but a few trunks. A very cursory inspection convinced him that no person was being harboured there.

"Why could you not have admitted us just now, Mr. Drewitt?" he asked.

"Because you brought not the authority of either my lord or my lady," answered the faithful old retainer.

The inspector strode to the end of the passage and stood before the oaken door already spoken of, examining its heavy fastenings. The others had followed him.

"This must be the door communicating between the house and the East Wing," he remarked. "Will you open it, Mr. Drewitt?"

"No, sir, I will not."

"But we must have it opened," interposed Arnold Ravensworth. "The fact is, we have some reason to fear the midnight assassin may yet be hiding himself on the premises. He does not appear to be in the house, so he may be in the East Wing—and we mean to search it."

"Are you an enemy of my lord's?" returned the old man, greatly agitated.

"Certainly not. I would rather be his friend. I have been the friend, if I may so express it, of Lady Level since she was a child, and I must see that she is protected, her husband being for the time laid aside."

"My lady," called out the old man, visibly trembling, "I appeal to you, as my lord's second self, to forbid these gentlemen from attempting to enter the East Wing."

"Be firm, Blanche," whispered Mr. Ravensworth, as she came forward. "We must search the East Wing, and it is for your sake."

She turned to the steward. "I am sure that they are acting for the best. Open the door."

For one moment the old man hesitated, and then wrung his hands. "That I should be forced to disobey the wife of my lord! My lady, I crave your pardon, but I will not open these rooms unless I have the express authority of his lordship to do so."

"But I wish it done, Mr. Drewitt," she said, blushing hotly.

Police inspectors have generally the means of carrying out their own will. Mr. Poole, after critically regarding the fastenings, produced one or two small instruments from his pockets and a bunch of keys. As he was putting one of the keys into the lock for the purpose of trying whether it would fit it, a curious revulsion came over Lady Level. Possibly the piteous, beseeching countenance of the steward induced it. "He is my husband, after all," she whispered to her own heart.

"Stop!" she said aloud, pushing the key downwards. "I may not have the right to sanction this in opposition to the wish of Lord Level. He has forbidden any search to be made, and I must do the same."

There was a moment's silence. The inspector gazed at her.

"When his lordship shall be sufficiently recovered to see you, sir, you can take instructions from him if he sees well to give them," she added to the officer civilly. "Until then, I must act for him, and I forbid—"

"Highty-tighty, and what's the matter here?" broke in a hearty voice behind them, at which they all turned in surprise. Making his way along the passage was a portly, but rather short man of sixty years, with an intellectual brow and benevolent countenance, a red face and a bald head. The change in Mr. Drewitt's look was remarkable; its piteousness had changed to radiance.

The new-comer shook hands with him. Then he turned and affably shook hands with the inspector, speaking gaily. "You look as if you had the business of all the world on your shoulders, Poole."

"Have you seen my lord, Mr. Hill?" asked the steward.

"I got back home to-night and came on here at once, hearing of the hubbub you are in, and I have seen my lord for a few minutes. And this is my lady—and a very charming lady I am sure she is," he added, bowing to Lady Level with an irresistible smile. "Will she shake hands with the old man who has been doctor-in-ordinary to her lord's family for ages and ages?"

Blanche put her hand into his. She, as she was wont sometimes to tell him in days to come, fell in love with him at once.

"What a blessing that you are back again!" murmured the good old steward.

"Ay," assented Mr. Hill, perhaps purposely misinterpreting the remark: "we will have Lord Level up and about in no time now.—Mr. Poole, I want a private word with you."

The doctor drew him into the steward's sitting-room, and closed the door. The conference did not last more than a minute or two, but it was very effectual. For when Mr. Inspector Poole came forth, he announced his decision of withdrawing all search at present. To be resumed if necessary, he added, when his lordship should have recovered sufficiently to give his own orders.

The only one who did not appear to be altogether satisfied with this summary check was Arnold Ravensworth. He did not understand it. Upon some remark being made as to Lady Level's safety from any attack by the midnight villain, Mr. Hill at once told her he would guarantee that. And though he spoke with a laugh, as if making light of the matter, there was an assurance in his eye and tone that she might implicitly trust to.

"Then—as it seems I cannot be of any further use to you to-night, and as I may just catch the midnight up-train, I will wish you good-bye, Lady Level," said Mr. Ravensworth. "I am easy about you, now Mr. Hill is here. But be sure to write for me if you think I can be of service to you or to Lord Level."

"I will, I will," she answered. "Thank you, Arnold, for coming."

Marshdale House returned to its usual monotony, and a day or two went on. Nothing more was seen or heard of the unknown individual who had so disturbed its peace; the very mention of it was avoided. Nevertheless, Blanche, turning matters over in her mind, could only look at it and at that detestable East Wing with an increased sense of mystery. "But for knowing that someone was there who might not be disclosed to the honest light of day, why should he have forbidden the search?" ran the argument that she was for ever holding with herself; and she steeled her heart yet more against her husband.

On this, the second afternoon after the commotion, she was sitting reading a newspaper in the garden, where the sun was shining hotly, when Mr. Hill, who had been up with Lord Level, appeared.

"Well," said the doctor cheerily, halting before her, "he is a great deal better, and the knee's ever so much stronger. I shall have him up to-morrow. And in a couple of days after that he may venture to travel to town, as he is so anxious to get there."

"Your treatment seems to agree with him better than Dr. Macferraty's did," she answered.

"Ay: I know his constitution, you see. Good-day, Lady Level. I shall be in again to-night."

Soon after the doctor went out, there was heard a shrill whistle at the gate, together with a kicking about of gravel by a pair of rough boots. Lady Level looked up, and saw the boy from the station bringing in a parcel.

"Well, Sam," said she, as the lad approached. "What have you come for?"

"They sent me on with this here parcel—and precious heavy he is for his size," replied Sam Doughty, as without ceremony he tumbled the parcel on to the bench by Lady Level's side. It was addressed to her, and she knew that it contained some books which Mr. Ravensworth had promised to send down. "Come down by the mid-day train," curtly added the boy for her information.

"Do you get paid for delivering parcels, Sam?"

"Me get paid!" returned the youth, with intense aggravation; "no such luck. Unless," added he, a happy thought striking him, "anybody likes to give me something for myself—knowing how weighty they be, and what a lug it is for one's arms."

"This parcel is not at all heavy," said Lady Level.

"I'm sure he is, then, for his size. You should lift, though, what I have to drag along sometimes. Why, yesterday that ever was, I brought a parcel as big as a house to the next door; one that come from Lunnon by the mid-day train just as this'n did; and Mother Snow she never gave me nothing but a jam tart, no bigger nor the round o' your hand. She were taking a tray on 'em out o' the oven."

"Jam tarts for her delectation!" was the thought that flashed through Lady Level's mind. "Who was the parcel for, Sam?" she asked aloud.

"'Twere directed to Mrs. Snow."

"Oh. Not to that lady who is staying there?"

"What lady be that?" questioned Sam.

"The one you told me about. The lady with the long gold earrings."

Sam's stolid countenance assumed a look of doubt, as if he did not altogether understand. His eyes grew wider.

"That un! Her bain't there now, her bain't. Her didn't stop. Her went right away again the next day after she come."

"Did she?" exclaimed Lady Level, taken by surprise. "Are you sure?"

"Be I sure as that's a newspaper in your hand?" retorted Sam. "In course I be sure. The fly were ordered down here for her the next morning, and she come on to the station in it, Mr. Snow a sitting outside."

"She went back to London, then!"

"She went just t'other way," contradicted the boy. "Right on by the down-train. Dover her ticket were took for."

Lady Level fell into a passing reverie. All the conjectures she had been indulging in lately—whither had they flown? At that moment Mrs. Edwards, having seen the boy from the house, came out to ask what he wanted. Sam put on his best behaviour instantly. The respect he failed to show to the young lady was in full force before Mrs. Edwards.

"I come to bring this here parcel, please, ma'am, for Lady Level," said he, touching his old cap.

"Oh, very well," said Mrs. Edwards. "I'll carry it indoors, my lady," she added, taking it up. "You need not wait, Sam."

Lady Level slipped a sixpence into his ready hand, and he went off contented. Mrs. Edwards carried away the parcel.

Presently Lady Level followed, her mind busy as she went upstairs. She was taking some contrition to herself. What if—if it was all, or a great deal of it, only her imagination—that her husband was not the disloyal man she had deemed him?

His chamber door was closed; she passed it and went into her own. Then she opened the door separating the rooms and peeped in. He was lying upon the bed, partly dressed, and wrapped in a warm dressing-gown; his face was turned to the pillow, and he was apparently asleep.

She stole up and stood looking at him. Not a trace of fever lingered in his face now; his fine features looked wan and delicate. Her love for him was making itself heard just then. Cautiously she stooped to imprint a soft, silent kiss upon his cheek; and then another.

She would have lifted her face then, and found she could not do so. His arm was round her in a trice, holding it there; his beautiful gray eyes had opened and were fixed on hers.

"So you care for me a little bit yet, Blanche," he fondly whispered. "Better this than calling me hard names."

She burst into tears. "I should care for you always, Archibald, if—if—I were sure you cared for me."

"You may be very sure of that," he emphatically answered. "Let there be peace between us, at any rate, my dear wife. The clouds will pass away in time."

On the Monday morning following, Lord and Lady Level departed for London. The peace, patched up between them, being honestly genuine and hopeful on his lordship's part, but doubtful on that of my lady.

Still nothing had been said or done to lift the mystery which hung about Marshdale.

CHAPTER III

ONE NIGHT IN ESSEX STREET

We go on now to the following year: and I, Charles Strange, take up the narrative again.

It has been said that the two rooms on the ground-floor of our house in Essex Street were chiefly given over to the clerks. I had a desk in the front office; the same desk that I had occupied as a boy; and I frequently sat at it now. Mr. Lennard's desk stood opposite to mine. On the first floor the large front room was furnished as a sitting-room. It was called Mr. Brightman's room, and there he received his clients. The back room was called my room; but Mr. Brightman had a desk in it, and I had another. His desk stood in the middle of the room before the hearthrug; mine was under the window.

One fine Saturday afternoon in February, when it was getting near five o'clock, I was writing busily at my desk in this latter room, when Mr. Brightman came in.

"Rather dark for you, is it not, Charles?" he remarked, as he stirred the fire and sat down in his arm-chair beside it.

"Yes, sir; but I have almost finished."

"What are you going to do with yourself to-morrow?" he presently asked, when I was putting up my parchments.

"Nothing in particular, sir." I could not help sometimes retaining my old way of addressing him, as from clerk to master. "Last Sunday I was with my uncle Stillingfar."

"Then you may as well come down to Clapham and dine with me. Mrs. Brightman is away for a day or two, and I shall be alone. Come in time for service."

I promised, and drew a chair to the fire, ready to talk with Mr. Brightman. He liked a little chat with me at times when the day's work was over. It turned now on Lord Level, from whom I had heard that morning. We were not his usual solicitors, but were doing a little matter of business for him. He and Blanche had been abroad since the previous November (when they had come up together from Marshdale), and had now been in Paris for about a month.

"Do they still get on pretty well?" asked Mr. Brightman: for he knew that there had been differences between them.

"Pretty well," I answered, rather hesitatingly.

And, in truth, it was only pretty well, so far as I was able to form a judgment. During this sojourn of theirs in Paris I had spent a few days there with a client, and saw Blanche two or three times. That she was living in a state of haughty resentment against her husband was indisputable. Why or wherefore, I knew not. She dropped a mysterious word to me now and then, of which I could make nothing.

While Mr. Brightman was saying this, a clerk came in, handed a letter to him and retired.

"What a nuisance!" cried he, as he read it by fire-light. I looked up at the exclamation.

"Sir Edmund Clavering's coming to town this evening, and wants me to be here to see him!" he explained. "I can't go home to dinner now."

"Which train is he coming by?" I asked.

"One that is due at Euston Square at six o'clock," replied Mr. Brightman, referring to the letter. "I wanted to be home early this evening."

"You are not obliged to wait, sir," I said. I wished to my heart later—oh, how I wished it!—that he had not waited!

"I suppose I must, Charles. He is a good client, and easily takes offence. Recollect that breeze we had with him three or four months ago."

The clocks struck five as he spoke, and we heard the clerks leaving as usual. I have already stated that no difference was made in the working hours on Saturdays in those days. Afterwards, Mr. Lennard came up to ask whether there was anything more to be done.

"Not now," replied Mr. Brightman. "But I tell you what, Lennard," he added, as a thought seemed to occur to him, "you may as well look in again to-night, about half-past seven or eight, if it won't inconvenience you. Sir Edmund Clavering is coming up; I conclude it is for something special; and I may have instructions to give for Monday morning."

"Very well," replied Lennard. "I will come."

He went out as he spoke; a spare, gentlemanly man, with a fair complexion and thin, careworn face. Edgar Lennard was a man of few words, but attentive and always at his post, a most efficient superintendent of the office and of the clerks in general.

He left and Mr. Brightman rose, saying he would go and get some dinner at the Rainbow. I suggested that he should share my modest steak, adding that Leah could as easily send up enough for two as for one: but he preferred to go out. I rang the bell as I heard him close the frontdoor. Watts answered it, and lighted the gas.

"Tell your wife to prepare my dinner at once," I said to him; "or as soon as possible: Mr. Brightman is coming back to-night. You are going out, are you not?"

"Yes, sir, about that business. Mr. Lennard said I had better go as soon as I had had my tea."

"All right. It will take you two or three hours to get there and back again. See to the fire in the next room; it is to be kept up. And, Watts, tell Leah not to trouble about vegetables to-day: I can't wait for them."

In about twenty minutes Leah and the steak appeared. I could not help looking at her as she placed the tray on the table and settled the dishes. Thin, haggard, untidy, Leah presented a strange contrast to the trim, well-dressed upper servant I had known at White Littleham Rectory. It was Watts who generally waited upon me. When Leah knew beforehand that she would have to wait, she put herself straight. Today she had not known. My proper sitting-room upstairs was not much used in winter. This one was warm and comfortable, with the large fire kept in it all day, so I generally remained in it. I was not troubled with clients after office hours.

"I wonder you go such a figure, Leah!" I could not help saying so.

"It is cleaning-day, Mr. Charles. And I did not know I should have to come up here. Watts has just gone out."

"It is a strange thing to me that you cannot get a woman in to help you. I have said so before."

"Ah, sir, nobody knows where the shoe pinches but he who wears it."

With this remark, unintelligible as apropos to the question, and a deep sigh, Leah withdrew. I had finished dinner, and the tray was taken away before Mr. Brightman returned.

"Now I hope Sir Edmund will be punctual," he cried, as we sat together, talking over a glass of sherry. "It is half-past six: time he was here."

"And there he is!" I exclaimed, as a ring and a knock that shook the house resounded in our ears. After five o'clock the front door was always closed.

Watts being out, we heard Leah answer the door in her charming costume. But clients pay little attention to the attire of laundresses in chambers.

"Good heavens! Can Sir Edmund have taken too much!" uttered Mr. Brightman, halting as he was about to enter the other room to receive him. Loud sounds in a man's voice arose from the passage; singing, laughing, joking with Leah. "Open the door, Charles."

I had already opened it, and saw, not Sir Edmund Clavering, but the young country client, George Coney, the son of a substantial and respectable yeoman in Gloucestershire. He appeared to be in exalted spirits, and had a little exceeded, but was very far from being intoxicated.

"What, is Mr. Brightman here? I only expected to see you," cried he, shaking hands with both. "Look here!" holding out a small canvas bag, and rattling it. "What does that sound like?"

"It sounds like gold," said Mr. Brightman.

"Right, Mr. Brightman; thirty golden sovereigns: and I am as delighted with them as if they were thirty hundred," said he, opening the bag and displaying its contents. "Last week I got swindled out of a horse down at home. Thirty pounds I sold him for, and he and the purchaser disappeared and forgot to pay. My father went on at me, like our old mill clacking; not so much for the loss of the thirty pounds, as at my being done: and all the farmers round about clacked at me, like so many more mills. Pleasant, that, for a fellow, was it not?"

"Very," said Mr. Brightman, while I laughed.

"I did not care to stand it," went on George Coney. "I obtained a bit of a clue, and the day before yesterday I came up to London—and I have met with luck. This afternoon I dropped across the very chap, where I had waited for him since the morning. He was going into a public-house, and another with him, and I pinned them in the room, with a policeman outside, and he pretty soon shelled out the thirty pounds, rather than be taken. That's luck, I hope." He opened the bag as he spoke, and displayed the gold.

"Remarkable luck, to get the money," observed Mr. Brightman.

"I expect they had been in luck themselves," continued young Coney, "for they had more gold with them, and several notes. They were for paying me in notes, but 'No, thank ye,' said I, 'I know good gold when I see it, and I'll take it in that.'"

"I am glad you have been so fortunate," said Mr. Brightman. "When do you return home?"

"I did mean to go to-night, and I called to leave with you this small deed that my father said I might as well bring up with me, as I was coming"—producing a thin folded parchment from his capacious pocketbook. "But I began thinking, as I came along, that I might as well have a bit of a spree now I am here, and go down by Monday night's train," added the young man, tying up the bag again, and slipping it into his pocket. "I shall go to a theatre to-night."

"Not with that bag of gold about you?" said Mr. Brightman.

"Why not?"

"Why not? Because you would have no trace of it left to-morrow morning."

George Coney laughed good-humouredly. "I can take care of myself, sir."

"Perhaps so; but you can't take care of the gold. Come, hand it over to me. Your father will thank me for being determined, and you also, Mr. George, when you have cooled down from the seductions of London."

"I may want to spend some of it," returned George Coney. "Let's see how much I have," cried he, turning the loose money out of his pockets. "Four pounds, seven shillings, and a few halfpence," he concluded, counting it up.

"A great deal too much to squander or lose in one night," remarked Mr. Brightman. "Here," added he, unlocking a deep drawer in his desk, "put your bag in here, and come for it on Monday."

George Coney drew the bag from his pocket, but not without a few remonstrative shakes of the head, and put it in the drawer. Mr. Brightman locked it, and restored the bunch of keys to his pocket.

"You are worse than my father is," cried George Coney, half in jest, half vexed at having yielded. "I wouldn't be as close and stingy for anything."

"In telling this story twenty years hence, Mr. George, you will say, What a simpleton I should have made of myself, if that cautious old lawyer Brightman had not been close and stingy!"

George Coney winked at me and laughed. "Perhaps he's right, after all."

"I know I am," said Mr. Brightman. "Will you take a glass of sherry?"

"Well; no, I think I had better not. I have had almost enough already, and I want to carry clear eyes with me to the play. What time does it begin?"

"About seven, I think; but I am not a theatre-goer myself. Strange can tell you."

"Then I shall be off," said he, shaking hands with us, as only a hearty country yeoman knows how to.

He had scarcely gone when Sir Edmund Clavering's knock was heard. Mr. Brightman went with him into the front room, and I sat reading the Times. Leah, by the way, had made herself presentable, and looked tidy enough in a clean white cap and apron.

Sir Edmund did not stay long: he left about seven. I heard Mr. Brightman go back after showing him out, and rake the fire out of the grate—he was always timidly cautious about fire—and then he returned to my room.

"No wonder Sir Edmund wanted to see me," cried he. "There's the deuce of a piece of work down at his place. His cousin wants to dispute the will and to turn him out. They have been serving notices on the tenants not to pay the rent."

"What a curious woman she must be!"

Mr. Brightman smiled slightly, but made no answer.

"He did not stay long, sir."

"No, he is going out to dinner."

As Mr. Brightman spoke, he turned up the gas, drew his chair to the desk and sat down, his back then being towards the fire. "I must look over these letters and copies of notices which Sir Edmund brought with him, and has left with me," he remarked. "I don't care to go home directly."

The next minute he was absorbed in the papers. I put down the Times, and rose. "You do not want me, I suppose, Mr. Brightman," I said. "I promised Arthur Lake to go to his chambers for an hour."

"I don't want you, Charles. Mind you are not late in coming down to me to-morrow morning."

So I wished him good-night and departed. Arthur Lake, a full-fledged barrister now of the Middle Temple, rented a couple of rooms in one of the courts. His papers were in one room, his bed in the other. He was a steady fellow, as he always had been, working hard and likely to get on. We passed many of our evenings together over a quiet chat and a cigar, I going round to him, or he coming in to me. He had grown up a little, dandified sort of man, good-humouredly insolent as ever when the fit took him: but sterling at heart.

Lake was sitting at the fire waiting for me, and began to grumble at my being late. I mentioned what had hindered me.

"And I have forgotten my cigar-case!" I exclaimed as I sat down. "I had filled it, all ready, and left it on the table."

"Never mind," said Lake. "I laid in a parcel to-day."

But I did mind, for Lake's "parcels" were never good. He would buy his cigars so dreadfully strong. Nothing pleased him but those full-flavoured Lopez, whilst I liked mild Cabanas: so, generally speaking, I kept to my own. However, I took one, and we sat, talking and smoking. I smoked it out, abominable though it was, and took another; but I couldn't stand a second.

"Lake, I cannot smoke your cigars," I said, flinging it into the fire. "You know I never can. I must run and fetch my own. There goes eight o'clock."

"What's the matter with them?" asked Lake: his usual question.

"Everything; they are bad all over. I shall be back in a trice."

I went the quickest way, through the passages, which brought me into Essex Street, and had my latch-key ready to open the door with as I approached the house. There were three of these latchkeys. I had one; Lennard another, for it sometimes happened that he had to come in before or after business hours; and Leah had possession of the third. But I had no use for mine now, for the door was open. A policeman, standing by the area railings, recognised me, and wished me good-evening.

'Whose carelessness is this?' thought I, advancing to the top of the kitchen stairs and calling to Leah.

It appeared useless to call: no Leah made her appearance. I shut the front door and went upstairs, wondering whether Mr. Brightman had left.

Left! I started back as I entered; for there lay Mr. Brightman on the floor by his desk, as if he had pushed back his chair and fallen from it.

"What is the matter?" I exclaimed, throwing my hat anywhere, and hastening to raise him. But his head and shoulders were a dead weight in my arms, and there was an awful look upon his face, as the gaslight fell upon it. A look, in short, of death, and not of an easy death.

My pulses beat quicker, man though I was, and my heart beat with them. Was I alone in that large house with the dead? I let him fall again and rang the bell violently. I rushed to the door and shouted over the banisters for Leah; and just as I was leaping down for the policeman I had seen outside, or any other help that might be at hand, I heard a latch-key inserted into the lock, and Lennard came in with Dr. Dickenson. I knew him well, for he had attended Miss Methold in the days gone by.

As he hastened to Mr. Brightman, Lennard turned to me, speaking in a whisper:

"Mr. Strange, how did it happen? Was he ill?"

"I know nothing about it, Lennard. I came in a minute ago, and found him lying here. What do you know? Had you been here before?"

"I came, as Mr. Brightman had directed," he replied. "It was a little before eight; and when I got upstairs he was lying there as you see. I tried to rouse him, but could not, and I went off for the doctor."

"Did you leave the front door open?"

"I believe I did, in my flurry and haste. I thought of it as I ran up the street, but would not lose time in going back to shut it."

"He is gone, Mr. Strange," said Dr. Dickenson, advancing towards me, for I and Lennard had stood near the door. "It is a case of sudden death."

I sat down, bewildered. I could not believe it. How awfully sudden! "Is it apoplexy?" I asked, lifting my head.

"No, I should say not."

"Then what is it?"

"I cannot tell; it may be the heart."

"Are you sure he is dead? Beyond all hope?"

"He is indeed."

A disagreeable doubt rushed over my mind, and I spoke on the impulse of the moment. "Has he come by his death fairly?"

The surgeon paused before he answered. "I see no reason, as yet, to infer otherwise. There are no signs of violence about him."

I cannot describe my feelings as we stood looking down at him. Never had I felt so before. What was I to do next?—how act? A hazy idea was making itself heard that some weighty responsibility lay upon me.

Just then a cab dashed up to the door; we heard it all too plainly in the hushed silence; and someone knocked and rang. Lennard went down to open it, and I told him to send in the policeman and fetch another doctor. Looking over the banisters I saw George Coney come in.

"Such a downfall to my plans, Mr. Strange," he began, seeing me as he ascended the stairs. "I went round to my inn to brush myself up before going to the play, and there I found a letter from my father, which they had forgotten to give me this morning. Our bailiff's been taken ill, cannot leave his bed, and father writes that I had better let the horse and the thirty pounds go for a bad job, and come home, for he can't have me away longer. So my spree's done for, this time, and I am on my way to the station, to catch the nine o'clock train."

"Don't go in until you have heard what is there," I whispered, as he was entering the room. "Mr. Brightman, whom you left well, is lying on the floor, and—"

"And what?" asked young Coney, looking at me.

"I fear he is dead."

After a dismayed pause he went gently into the room, taking off his hat reverently and treading on tiptoe. "Poor fellow! poor gentleman!" he uttered, after looking at him. "What an awful thing! How was he taken?"

"We do not know how. He was alone."

"What, alone when he was taken! no one to help him!" returned the young man. "That was hard! What has he died of?"

"Probably the heart," interposed Dr. Dickenson.

"Last summer a carter of ours fell down as he was standing near us; my father was giving him directions about a load of hay, and when we picked him up he was dead," spoke the young man. "That was the heart, they said. But he looked calm and quiet, not as Mr. Brightman looks. He left seven children, poor chap!"

At that juncture Mr. Lennard returned with the policeman. Another doctor, he said, would be round directly. After some general conversation, George Coney looked at his watch.

"Mr. Strange, my time's up. Would it be convenient to give me that money again? I should like to take it down with me, you see, just to have the laugh against the old folks at home."

"I will give it you," I said.

But for the very life of me, I could not put my hand into the dead man's pocket. I beckoned to Lennard. "Can you take out his keys?"

"Let me do it," said Dr. Dickenson, for Lennard did not seem to relish the task either. "I am more accustomed to death than you are. Which pocket are they in?"

"The right-hand pocket of his trousers; he always kept them there," was my answer.

Dr. Dickenson found the keys and handed them to me. I unlocked the drawer, being obliged to bend over the dead to do so, and young Coney stepped forward to receive the bag.

But the bag was not there.

CHAPTER IV

LEAH'S STORY

Our dismayed faces might have formed a study for a painter, as we stood in my room in Essex Street: the doctor, George Coney, Lennard and myself. On the floor, between the hearthrug and the desk, lay the dead man, the blaze of the fire and the gaslights playing on his features. Mr. Brightman was dead. In my mental pain and emotion I could not realize the fact; would not believe that it was true. He had died thus suddenly, no one near him; no one, so far as was yet known, in the house at the time. And to me, at least, there seemed to be some mystery attaching to it.

But, at this particular moment, we were looking for George Coney's sovereigns, which Mr. Brightman, not much more than an hour before, had locked up in the deep drawer of his desk, returning the keys to his pocket. After Dr. Dickenson had handed me the keys I unlocked and opened the drawer. But the bag was not there.

If the desk itself had disappeared, I could not have been more surprised. Lying in the drawer, close to where the bag had been, was a gold watch belonging to Mrs. Brightman, which had been brought up to town to be cleaned. That was undisturbed. "Coney," I exclaimed, "the money is not here."

"It was put there," replied young Coney. "Next to that watch."

"I know it was," I answered. I opened the drawer on the other side, but that was full of papers. I looked about on the desk; then on my own desk, even unlocking the drawers, though I had had the key in my own pocket; then on the tables and mantelpiece. Not a trace could I see of the canvas bag.

"What bag is it?" inquired Dr. Dickenson, who, of course, had known nothing of this. "What was in it?"

"A small canvas bag containing some gold that Mr. George Coney had wished to leave here until Monday," I answered.

"'Twas one of our sample barley bags; I happened to have it in my pocket when I left home," explained the young man. "My father's initials were on it: S. C."

"How much was in it?" asked Lennard.

"Thirty pounds."

"I fear you will be obliged to go without it, after all," I said, when I had turned everything over, "for it is not to be found. I will remit you thirty pounds on Monday. We send our spare cash to the bank on Saturday afternoons, so that I have not so much in the house: and I really do not know where Mr. Brightman has put the cheque-book. It is strange that he should have taken the bag out of the drawer again."

"Perhaps it may be in one of his pockets," suggested the doctor. "Shall I search them?"

"No, no," interposed George Coney. "I wouldn't have the poor gentleman disturbed just for that. You'll remit it to me, Mr. Strange. Not to my father," he added, with a smile: "to me."

I went down with him, and there sat Leah at the bottom of the stairs, leaning her head against the banisters, almost under the hall lamp. "When did you come in, Leah?" I asked.

She rose hastily, and faced me. "I thought you were out, sir. I have come in only this instant."

"What is the matter?" I continued, struck with the white, strange look upon her face. "Are you ill?"

"No, sir, not ill. Trouble is the lot of us all."

I shook hands with George Coney as he got into his cab and departed, and then returned indoors. Leah was hastening along the passage to the kitchen stairs. I called her back again. "Leah," I said, "do you know what has happened to Mr. Brightman?"

"No, sir," answered she. "What has happened to him?"

"You must prepare for a shock. He is dead."

She had a cloth and a plate in her hand, and laid them down on the slab as she backed against the wall, staring in horror. Then her features relaxed into a wan smile.

"Ah, Master Charles, you are thinking to be a boy again to-night, and are playing a trick upon me, as you used to do in the old days, sir."

"I wish to my heart it was so, Leah. Mr. Brightman is lying upon the floor in my room. I fear there can be no doubt that he is dead."

"My poor master!" she slowly ejaculated. "Heaven have mercy upon him!—and upon us! Why, it's not more than three-quarters of an hour since I took up some water to him."

"Did he ask for it?"

"He rang the bell, sir, and asked for a decanter of water and a tumbler."

"How did he look then, Leah? Where was he sitting?"

"He was sitting at his table, sir, and he looked as usual, for all I saw, but his head was bent over something he was reading. I put some coals on the fire and came away. Mr. Charles, who is up there with him?"

"Dr. Dickenson and—"

A knock at the door interrupted me. It proved to be the other doctor I had sent for.

The medical men proceeded to examine Mr. Brightman more closely. I had sent for the police, and they also were present. I then searched his pockets, a policeman aiding me, and we put their contents carefully away. But there was no bag containing gold amongst them. How had it disappeared?

A most unhappy circumstance was the fact that I could not send for Mrs. Brightman, for I did not know where she was. Mr. Brightman had said she was out of town, but did not say where.

When Watts came home, I despatched him to the house at Clapham, allowing him no time to indulge his grief or his curiosity. Leah had knelt down by Mr. Brightman, tears silently streaming from her eyes.

The fire in the front room was relighted; the fire, the very coals, which he, poor man, had so recently taken off; and I, Lennard and Arthur Lake went in there to talk the matter over quietly.

"Lennard," I said, "I am not satisfied that he has died a natural death. I hope—"

"There are no grounds for any other supposition, Mr. Strange," he interrupted. "None whatever. Are there?" he added, looking at me.

"I trust there are none—but I don't quite like the attendant circumstances of the case. The loss of that bag of money causes all sorts of unpleasant suspicions to arise. When you came to the house, Lennard, did you go straight upstairs?" I added, after a pause.

"No, I went into the front office," replied Lennard. "I thought Sir Edmund Clavering might still be here."

"Was Leah out or in?"

"Leah was standing at the front door, looking—as it seemed to me—down the steps leading to the Thames. While I was lighting my candle by the hall-lamp, she shut the front door and came to me. She was extremely agitated, and—"

"Agitated?" I interrupted.

"Yes," said Lennard; "I could not be mistaken. I stared at her, wondering what could cause it, and why her face was so white—almost as white as Mr. Brightman's is now. She asked—as earnestly as if she were pleading for life—whether I would stop in the house for a few minutes, as Mr. Brightman had not gone, while she ran out upon an errand. I inquired whether Sir Edmund Clavering was upstairs, and she said no; he had left; Mr. Strange was out, and Mr. Brightman was alone."

"Did she go out?"

"Immediately," replied Lennard; "just as she was, without bonnet or shawl. I went up to your room, and tapped at the door. It was not answered, and I went in. At first I thought the room was empty; but in a moment I saw Mr. Brightman lying on the ground. He was dead even then; I am certain of it," added Lennard, pausing from natural emotion. "I raised his head, and put a little water to his temples, but I saw that he was dead."

"It is an awful thing!" exclaimed Lake.

"I can tell you that I thought so," assented Lennard. "I knew that the first thing must be to get in a doctor; but how I found my way up the street to Dickenson's I hardly remember. No wonder I left the front door open behind me."

I turned all this over in my mind. There were two points I did not like—Leah's agitation, and Lennard's carelessness in leaving the door open. I called in one of the policemen from the other room, for they were there still, with the medical men.

"Williams," I began, "you saw me come down the street with my latch-key in my hand?"

"I did, sir, and wished you good-evening," replied Williams. "It wasn't long after the other gentleman," indicating Lennard, "had run out."

"I did not see you," cried Lennard, looking at him. "I wish I had seen you. I wanted help, and there was not a soul in the street."

"I was standing in shadow, at the top of the steps leading to the water," said the man. "You came out, sir, all in a hurry, and went rushing up the street, leaving the door open."

"And it is that door's having been left open that I don't like," I observed. "If this money does not turn up, I can only think some rogue got in and took it."

"Nobody got in, sir," said the policeman. "I had my eye on the door the whole time till you came down. To see two folk running like mad out of a quiet and respectable house roused my suspicions; and I went up to the door and stood near it till you entered."

"How did you see two running out of it?" I inquired. "There was only Mr. Lennard."

"I had seen somebody before that—a woman," replied the officer. "She came out, and went tearing down the steps towards the river, calling to someone out of sight. I think it was your servant, Mrs. Watts, but I was only half-way down the street then, and she was too quick for me."

"Then you are quite sure no one entered?"

"Quite sure, sir. I never moved from the door."

"Setting aside Williams's testimony, there was scarcely time for anyone to get in and do mischief," observed Lake. "And no one could take that gold without first getting the keys out of Mr. Brightman's pocket," he rejoined. "For such a purpose, who would dare rifle the pockets of the dead?"

"And then replace the keys," added Lennard.

"Besides," I said impulsively, "no one knew the money was there. Mr. Brightman, myself, and George Coney were alone cognisant of the fact. The more one thinks of it, the stranger it seems to grow."

The moments passed. The doctors and the police had gone away, and nothing remained but the sad burden in the next room. Lennard also left me to go home, for there was nothing more to be done; and Arthur Lake, who had gone round to his rooms, came in again. His conscience was smiting him, he said, for having deserted me. We sat down in the front room, as before, and began to discuss the mystery. I remarked, to begin with, that there existed not the slightest loophole of suspicion to guide us.

"Except one," said Lake quietly. "And I may pain you, Charley, if I venture to suggest it."

"Nonsense!" I cried. "How could it pain me? Unless you think I took it myself!"

"I fancy it was Leah."

"Leah?"

"Well, I do. She was the only person in the house, except Mr. Brightman. And what did her agitation mean—the agitation Lennard has referred to?"

"No, no, Arthur; it could not have been Leah. Admitting the doubt for a moment, how could she have done it?"

"Only in this way. I have been arguing it out with myself in my rooms: and of course it may be all imagination. Leah took up some water, she says, that Mr. Brightman rang for. Now, it may be that he had the drawer open and she saw the money. Or it may even be that, for some purpose or other, he had the bag upon the table. Was he taken ill whilst she was in the room? and did she, overcome by temptation, steal the money? I confess that this possibility presents itself forcibly to me," concluded Lake. "Naturally she would afterwards be in a state of agitation."

I sat revolving what he said, but could not bring my mind to admit it. Circumstances—especially her agitation—might seem to tell against her, but I believed the woman to be honest as the day.

There is not the slightest doubt that almost every man born into the world is adapted for one especial calling over all others; and it is an unhappy fact that this peculiar tendency is very rarely discovered and followed up. It is the misdirection of talent which causes so many of the failures in life. In my own case this mistake had not occurred. I believe that of all pursuits common to man, I was by nature most fitted for that of a solicitor. At the Bar, as a pleader, I should have failed, and ruined half the clients who entrusted me with briefs. But for penetration, for seizing without effort the different points of a case laid before me, few equalled me. I mention this only because it is a fact: not from motives of self-praise and vanity. Vanity? I am only thankful that my talents were directed into their proper channel. And this judgment, exercised now, told me that Leah was not guilty. I said so to Arthur Lake.

The return of Watts interrupted us. He had brought back with him Mr. Brightman's butler, Perry—a respectable, trustworthy man, who had been long in the family. I shall never forget his emotion as he stood over his dead master, to whom he was much attached. Mrs. and Miss Brightman had gone to Hastings for two or three days, he said, and I determined to go there in the morning and break the sad tidings to them.

Sad tidings, indeed; a grievous calamity for us all. That night I could not sleep, and in the morning I rose unrefreshed. The doubt about Leah and the money also troubled me. Though in one sense convinced that she could not have done it, the possibility that she might be guilty kept presenting itself before me.

She came into the room while I was at breakfast—earlier than I need have been, so far as the train was concerned—and I detained her for a moment.

Very spruce and neat she looked this morning.

"Leah," I began, "there is an unpleasant mystery attending this affair."

"As to what Mr. Brightman has died of, sir?"

"I do not allude to that. But there is some money missing."

"Money!" echoed Leah, in what looked like genuine surprise.

"Last night, after Mr. Brightman came in from dinner, he put a small canvas bag, containing thirty pounds in gold, in the deep drawer of his desk in my room, locked it and put the keys in his pocket. I had occasion to look for that gold immediately after he was found dead, and it was gone."

"Bag and all?" said Leah, after a pause.

"Bag and all."

"Not stolen, surely?"

"I don't see how else it can have disappeared. It could not go without hands; and the question is, did anyone get into the house and take it?"

She looked at me, and I at her: she was apparently thinking. "But how could anyone get in, sir?" she asked in tones of remonstrance.

"I do not see how, unless it was when you went out, Leah. You were out some time, you know. You ran out of the house and down the steps leading to the river, and you were in great agitation. What did it mean?"

Leah threw up her hands in distress. "Oh, Mr. Charles!" she gasped. "Please don't question me, sir. I cannot tell you anything about that."

"I must know it, Leah."

She shook her head. Her tears had begun to fall.

"Indeed you must explain it to me," I continued, speaking gently. "There is no help for it. Don't you see that this will have to be investigated, and—"

"You never suspect me of taking the money, sir?" she exclaimed breathlessly.

"No, I do not," I replied firmly. "It is one thing to be sure of honesty, and quite another thing to wish mysterious circumstances cleared up, where the necessity for doing so exists. What was your mystery last night, Leah?"

"Must I tell you, sir?"

"Indeed you must. I dare say to tell it will not hurt you, or to hear it hurt me."

"I would die rather than Watts should know of it," she exclaimed, in low, impassioned tones, glancing towards the door.

"Watts is in the kitchen, Leah, and cannot hear you. Speak out."

"I never committed but one grave fault in my life," she began, "and that was telling a deliberate lie. The consequences have clung to me ever since, and if things go on as they are going on now, they'll just drive me into the churchyard. When I lived with your people I was a young widow, as you may remember, sir; but perhaps you did not know that I had a little child. Your mamma knew it, but I don't think the servants did, for I was never one to talk of my own affairs. Just your age, Master Charles, was my little Nancy, and when her father died his sister took to her; old Miss Williams—for she was a deal older than him. She had a bit of a farm in Dorsetshire, and I'm afraid Nancy had to work hard at it. But it failed after a time, and Miss Williams died; and Nancy, then about seventeen, had come, I heard, to London. I was at Dover then, not long returned from abroad, and was just married to James Watts; and I found—I found," Leah dropped her voice, "that Nancy had gone wrong. Someone had turned her brain with his vows and his promises, and she had come up to London with him."

"Why don't you sit down whilst you talk, Leah?"

"I had told Watts I had no children," she continued, disregarding my injunction. "And that was the lie, Mr. Charles. More than once he had said in my hearing that he would never marry a ready-made family. For very shame I could not tell him, when I found how things were with Nancy. After we came to London, I searched her out and went to her in secret, begging her to leave the man, but she would not."

A burst of emotion stopped Leah. She soon resumed:

"She would not leave him. In spite of all I could say or do, though I went down on my knees to her, and sobbed and prayed my heart out, she remained with him. And she is with him still."

"All this time?"

"All this time, sir; seven years. He was once superior to her in position, but he has fallen from it now, is unsteady, and drinks half his time away. Sometimes he is in work; oftener without it; and the misery and privation she goes through no tongue can tell. He beats her, abuses her—"

"Why does she not leave him?"

"Ah, sir, why don't we do many things that we ought? Partly because she's afraid he would keep the children. There are three of them. Many a time she would have died of hunger but for me. I help her all I can; she's my own child. Sir, you asked me, only yesterday, why I went shabby; but, instead of buying clothes for myself, I scrape and save to keep her poor body and soul together. I go without food to take it to her; many a day I put my dinner away, telling Watts I don't feel inclined for it then and will eat it by-and-by. He thinks I do so. She does not beg of me; she has never entered this house; she has never told that tyrant of hers that I am her mother. 'Mother,' she has said to me, 'never fear. I would rather die than bring trouble on you.'"

"But about last night?" I interrupted.

"I was at work in the kitchen when a little gravel was thrown against the window. I guessed who it was, and went up to the door. If Watts had been at home, I should have taken no notice, but just have said, 'Drat those street boys again!' or something of that sort. There she was, leaning against the opposite railings, and she crossed over when she saw me. She said she was beside herself with misery and trouble, and I believe she was. He had been beating her, and she had not tasted food since the previous day; not a crumb. She kept looking towards the steps leading to the Thames, and I thought she might have got it in her head, what with her weak condition of body and her misery of mind, to put an end to herself. I tried, sir, to soothe and reason with her; what else could I do? I said I would fetch her some food, and give her sevenpence to buy a loaf to take home to her children."

"Where does she live?" I interposed.

"In this parish, St. Clement Danes; and there are some parts of this parish, you know, sir, as bad as any in London. When I offered to fetch her food, she said, No, she would not take it; her life was too wretched to bear, and she should end it; she had come out to do so. It was just what I feared. I scolded her. I told her to stay there at the door, and I shut it and ran down for the food. But when I got back to the door, I couldn't see her anywhere. Then I heard a voice from the steps call out 'Good-bye!' and I knew she was going to the water. At that moment Mr. Lennard came up, and I asked him to remain in the house whilst I went out for a minute. I was almost frightened out of my senses."

"Did you find her?"

"I found her, sir, looking down at the river. I reasoned her into a little better mood, and she ate a little of the food, and I brought her back up the steps, gave her the sevenpence, and led her up the street and across the Strand, on her way home. And that's the whole truth, Mr. Charles, of what took me out last night; and I declare I know no more of the missing money than a babe unborn. I had just come back with the empty plate and cloth when you saw me sitting on the stairs."

The whole truth I felt sure it was. Every word, every look of Leah's proclaimed it.

"And that's my sad secret," she added; "one I have to bear about with me at all times, in my work and out of my work. Watts is a good husband to me, but he prides himself on his respectability, and I wouldn't have him know that I have deceived him for the universe. I wouldn't have him know that she, being what she is, was my daughter. He said he'd treat me to Ashley's Circus last winter, and gave me two shillings, and I pretended to go. But I gave it to her, poor thing, and walked about in the cold, looking at the late shops, till it was time to come home. Watts asked me what I had seen, and I told him such marvels that he said he'd go the next night himself, for he had never heard the like, and he supposed it must be a benefit night. You will not tell him my secret, sir?"

"No, Leah, I will not tell him. It is safe with me."

With a long drawn sigh she turned to leave the room. But I stopped her.

"A moment yet, Leah. Can you remember at what time you took up the water to Mr. Brightman?"

"It was some time before the stone came to the window. About ten minutes, maybe, sir, after you went out. I heard you come downstairs whistling, and go out."

"No one came to the house during my absence?"

"No one at all, sir."

"Did you notice whether Mr. Brightman had either of the drawers of his desk open when you took up the water?"

Leah shook her head. "I can't say, sir," she answered. "I did not notice one way or the other."

CHAPTER V

The people were coming out of the various churches when I reached Hastings. Going straight to the Queen's Hotel, I asked for Mrs. Brightman. Perry had said she was staying there. It was, I believe, the only good hotel in the place in those days. Hatch, Mrs. Brightman's maid, came to me at once. Her mistress was not yet up, she said, having a bad headache.

Hatch and I had become quite confidential friends during these past years. She was not a whit altered since I first saw her, and to me did not look a day older. The flaming ringlets adorned her face as usual, and sky-blue cap-strings flowed behind them this morning. Hatch was glaringly plain; Hatch had a wonderful tongue, and was ever ready to exercise it, and Hatch's diction and grammar were unique; nevertheless, you could not help liking Hatch.

But to hear that Mrs. Brightman was ill in bed rather checkmated me. I really did not know what to do.

"My business with your mistress is of very great importance, Hatch," I observed. "I ought to see her. I have come down on purpose to see her."

"You might see her this afternoon, Mr. Charles; not before," spoke Hatch decisively. "These headaches is uncommon bad while they last. Perhaps Miss Annabel would do? She is not here, though; but is staying with her aunt Lucy."

"I have brought down bad news, Hatch. I should not like Miss Annabel to be the first to hear it."

"Bad news!" repeated Hatch quickly, as she stared at me with her great green eyes. "Our house ain't burnt down, surely! Is that the news, sir?"

"Worse than that, Hatch. It concerns Mr. Brightman."

Hatch's manner changed in a moment. Her voice became timid. "For goodness' sake, Mr. Charles! he is not ill, is he?"

"Worse, Hatch. He is dead," I whispered.

Hatch backed to a chair and dropped into it: we were in Mrs. Brightman's sitting-room. "The Lord be good to us!" she exclaimed, in all reverence. Her red cheeks turned white, her eloquence for once deserted her.

I sat down and gave her the details in a few brief words: she was a confidential, trusted servant, and had lived with her mistress many years. It affected her even more than I had expected. She wrung her hands, her tears coursed freely.

"My poor master—my poor mistress!" she exclaimed. "What on earth—Mr. Charles, is it sure he is dead? quite dead?" she broke off to ask.

"Nay, Hatch, I have told you."

Presently she got up, and seemed to rally her courage. "Anyway, Mr. Charles, we shall have to meet this, and deal with it as we best may. I mean the family, sir, what's left of 'em. And missis must be told—and, pardon me, sir, but I think I'd best be the one to tell her. She is so used to me, you see," added Hatch, looking at me keenly. "She might take it better from me than from you; that is, it might seem less hard."

"Indeed, I should be only too glad to be spared the task," was my answer.

"But you must tell Miss Brightman, sir, and Miss Annabel. Perhaps if you were to go now, Mr. Charles, while I do the best I can with my missis, we might be ready for the afternoon train. That, you say, will be best to travel by—"

"I said the train would be the best of the trains to-day, Hatch. It is for Mrs. Brightman to consider whether she will go up to-day or to-morrow."

"Well, yes, Mr. Charles, that's what I mean. My head's almost moithered. But I think she is sure to go up to-day."

Miss Brightman, who was Mr. Brightman's only sister, lived in a handsome house facing the sea. Annabel visited her a good deal, staying with her sometimes for weeks together. Mr. Brightman had sanctioned it, Mrs. Brightman did not object to it.

Upon reaching the house, the footman said Miss Brightman was not yet in from church, and ushered me into the drawing-room. Annabel was there. And really, like Hatch, she was not much altered, except in height and years, since the day I first saw her, when she had chattered to me so freely and lent me her favourite book, "The Old English Baron." She was fourteen then: a graceful, pretty child, with charming manners; her dark brown eyes, sweet and tender and bright like her father's, her features delicately carved like her mother's, a rose-blush on her dimpled cheeks. She was twenty now, and a graceful, pretty woman. No, not one whit altered.

She was standing by the fire in her silk attire, just as she had come in from church, only her bonnet-strings untied. Bonnets were really bonnets then, and rendered a lovely face all the more attractive. Annabel's bonnet that day was pink, and its border intermingled, as it seemed, with the waves of her soft brown hair. She quite started with surprise.

"Is it you, Charley!" she exclaimed, coming forward, the sweet rose-blush deepening and the sweet eyes brightening. "Have you come to Hastings? Is papa with you?"

"No, Annabel, he is not with me," I answered gravely, as I clasped her hand. "I wanted to see Miss Brightman."

"She will be here directly. She called in to see old Mrs. Day, who is ill: a great friend of Aunt Lucy's. Did papa—"

But we were interrupted by the return of Miss Brightman, a small, fragile woman, with delicate lungs. Annabel left us together.

How I accomplished my unhappy task I hardly knew. How Miss Brightman subsequently imparted it to Annabel I did not know at all. It must be enough to say that we went to London by an afternoon train, bearing our weight of care. All, except Miss Brightman. Hatch travelled in the carriage with us.

In appearance, at any rate, the news had most affected Mrs. Brightman. Her frame trembled, her pale face and restless hands twitched with nervousness. Of course, her headache went for something.

"I have them so very badly," she moaned to me once during the journey. "They unfit me for everything."

And, indeed, these headaches of Mrs. Brightman's were nothing new to me. She had always suffered from them. But of late, that is to say during the past few months, when by chance I went to Clapham, I more often than not found her ill and invisible from this distressing pain. My intimacy with Mrs. Brightman had not made much progress. The same proud, haughty woman she was when I first saw her, she had remained. Coldly civil to me, as to others; and that was all that could be said.

When about half-way up, whilst waiting for an express to pass, or something of that sort, and we were for some minutes at a standstill, I told Mrs. Brightman about the missing money belonging to George Coney.

"It is of little consequence if it be lost," was her indifferent and no doubt thoughtless comment. "What is thirty pounds?"

Little, I knew, to a firm like ours, but the uncertainty it left us in was a great deal. "Setting aside the mystery attaching to the loss," I remarked, "there remains a suspicion that we may have a thief about us; and that is not a pleasant feeling. Other things may go next."

Upon reaching London we drove to Essex Street. What a painful visit it was! Even now I cannot bear to think of it. Poor Mrs. Brightman grew nervously excited. As she looked down upon him, in his death-stillness, I thought she would have wept her heart away. Annabel strove to be calm for her mother's sake.

After some tea, which Leah and Hatch brought up to us, I saw them safely to Clapham, and then returned home.

Monday morning rose, and its work with it: the immediate work connected with our painful loss, and the future work that was to fall upon me. The chief weight and responsibility of the business had hitherto been his share; now it must be all mine. In the course of the day I sent a cheque to George Coney.

An inquest had to be held, and took place early on Tuesday morning. Mr. Brightman's death was proved, beyond doubt, to have occurred from natural causes, though not from disease of the heart. He had died by the visitation of God. But for the disappearance of the money, my thoughts would never have dwelt on any other issue.

After it was over, Lennard was standing with me in the front-room, from which the jury had just gone out, when we fell to talking about the missing money and its unaccountable loss. It lay heavily upon my mind. Fathom it I could not, turn it about as I would. Edgar Lennard was above suspicion, and he was the only one, so far as he and I knew, who had been in the room after the bag was put there, Leah excepted.

Of her I felt equally certain. Lennard began saying how heartily he wished he had not been told to come back that night; but I requested him to be at ease, for he had quite as much reason to suspect me, as I him.

"Not quite," answered he, smiling; "considering that you had to make it good."

"Well, Lennard, I dare say the mystery will be solved some time or other. Robberies, like murders, generally come out. The worst is, we cannot feel assured that other losses may not follow."

"Not they," returned Lennard, too confidently. "This one has been enough for us."

"Did it ever strike you, Lennard, that Mr. Brightman had been in failing health lately?"

"Often," emphatically spoke Lennard. "I think he had something on his mind."

"On his mind? I should say it was on his health. There were times when he seemed to have neither energy nor spirits for anything. You don't know how much business he has of late left to me that he used to do himself."

"Well," contended Lennard, "it used to strike me he was not at ease; that something or other was troubling him."

"Yes, and now that this fatal termination has ensued, we see that the trouble may have been health," I maintained. "Possibly he knew that something was dangerously wrong with him."

"Possibly so," conceded Lennard.

He was leaving the room for his own, when a clerk met him and said that Sir Edmund Clavering was asking for Mr. Strange. I bade him show up Sir Edmund.

Mr. Brightman had for years been confidential solicitor to Sir Ralph Clavering, a physician, whose baronetcy was a new one. When Sir Ralph gave up practice, and retired to an estate he bought in the country, a Mrs. Clavering, a widow, whose husband had been a distant cousin of Sir Ralph's, entered it with him as his companion and housekeeper. It ended in his marrying her, as these companionships so often end, especially where the man is old, and the woman young, attractive and wily. Mrs. Clavering was poor, and no doubt played for the stake she won. The heir-presumptive to Sir Ralph's title was his nephew, Edmund Clavering, but his fortune he could leave to whom he would.

Sir Ralph Clavering died—only about ten days before Mr. Brightman's own death. The funeral took place on the Tuesday—this very day week of which I am writing. After attending it, Mr. Brightman returned to the office in the evening. The clerks had left, and he came up to my room.

"Take this off my hat, will you, Charles?" he said. "I can't go home in it, of course: and Mrs. Brightman had a superstition against hat-scarves going into the house."

I undid the black silk and laid it on the table. "What am I to do with it, sir?"

"Anything. Give it to Leah for a Sunday apron. My lady treated us to a specimen of her temper when the will was read," he added. "She expected to inherit all, and is not satisfied with the competency left to her."

"Who does inherit?" I asked: for Mr. Brightman had never enlightened me, although I knew that he had made Sir Ralph's will.

"Edmund Clavering. And quite right that he should do so: the estate ought to go with the title. Besides, setting aside that consideration, Sir Edmund is entitled to it quite as much as my lady. More so, I think. There's the will, Charles; you can read it."

I glanced over the will, which Mr. Brightman had brought back with him. Lady Clavering had certainly a competency, but the bulk of the property was left to Sir Edmund, the inheritor of the title. I was very much surprised.

"I thought she would have had it all, Mr. Brightman. Living estranged as Sir Ralph did from his brother, even refusing to be reconciled when the latter was dying, the estrangement extended to the son, Edmund, I certainly thought Lady Clavering would have come in for all. You thought so too, sir."

"I did, until I made the will. And at one time it was Sir Ralph's intention to leave most of it to her. But for certain reasons which arose, he altered his plans. Sufficient reasons," added Mr. Brightman, in a marked, emphatic manner. "He imparted them to me when he gave instructions for his will. I should have left her less."

"May I know them?"

"No, Charles. They were told to me in confidence, and they concern neither you nor me. Is the gas out in the next room?"

"Yes. Shall I light it?"

"It is not worth while. That hand-lamp of yours will do. I only want to put up the will."

I took the lamp, and lighted Mr. Brightman into the front room, his own exclusively. He opened the iron safe, and there deposited Sir Ralph Clavering's will, to be left there until it should be proved.

That is sufficient explanation for the present. Sir Edmund Clavering, shown up by Lennard himself, came into the room. I had never acted for him; Mr. Brightman had invariably done so.

"Can you carry my business through, Mr. Strange?" he asked, after expressing his shock and regret at Mr. Brightman's sudden fate.

"I hope so. Why not, Sir Edmund?"

"You have not Mr. Brightman's legal knowledge and experience."

"Not his experience, certainly; because he was an old man and I am a young one. But, as far as practice goes, I have for some time had chief control of the business. Mr. Brightman almost confined himself to seeing clients. You may trust me, Sir Edmund."

"Oh yes, I dare say it will be all right," he rejoined. "Do you know that Lady Clavering and her cousin John—my cousin also—mean to dispute the will?"

"Upon what grounds?"

"Upon Sir Ralph's incompetency to make one, I suppose—as foul a plea as ever false woman or man invented. Mr. Brightman can prove— Good heavens! every moment I forget that he is dead," broke off Sir Edmund. "How unfortunate that he should have gone just now!"

"But there cannot fail to be ample proof of Sir Ralph's competency. The servants about him must know that he was of sane and healthy mind."

"I don't know what her schemes may be," rejoined Sir Edmund; "but I do know that she will not leave a stone unturned to wrest my rights from me. I am more bitter than gall and wormwood to her."

"Because you have inherited most of the money."

"Ay, for one thing. But there's another reason, more galling to her even than that."

Sir Edmund looked at me with a peculiar expression. He was about my own age, and would have been an exceedingly pleasant man but for his pride. When he could so far forget that as to throw it off, he was warm and cordial.

"Her ladyship is a scheming woman, Mr. Strange. She flung off into a fit of resentment at first, which Mr. Brightman witnessed, but very shortly her tactics changed. Before Sir Ralph had been three days in his grave, she contrived to intimate to me that we had better join interests. Do you understand?"

I did not know whether to understand or not. It was inconceivable.

"And I feel ashamed to enlighten you," said Sir Edmund passionately. "She offered herself to me; my willing wife. 'If you will wed no other woman, I will wed no other man—' How runs the old ballad? Not in so many words, but in terms sufficiently plain to be deciphered. I answered as plainly, and declined. Declined to join interests—declined her—and so made her my mortal enemy for ever. Do you know her?"

"I never saw her."

"Take care of yourself, then, should you be brought into contact with her," laughed Sir Edmund. "She is a Jezebel. All the same, she is one of the most fascinating of women: irresistibly so, no doubt, to many people. Had she been any but my uncle's wife—widow—I don't know how it might have gone with me. By the way, Mr. Strange, did Mr. Brightman impart to you Sir Ralph's reason for devising his property to me? He had always said, you know, that he would not do it. Mr. Brightman would not tell me the reason for the change."

"No, he did not. Sir Ralph intended, I believe, to bequeath most of it to his wife, and altered his mind quite suddenly. So much Mr. Brightman told me."

"Found out Jezebel, perhaps, at some trick or other."

That I thought all too likely; but did not say so. Sir Edmund continued to speak a little longer upon business matters, and then rose.

"The will had better be proved without delay," he paused to say.

"I will see about it the first thing next week, Sir Edmund. It would have been done this week but for Mr. Brightman's unexpected death."

"Why do you sink your voice to a whisper?" asked Sir Edmund, as we were quitting the room. "Do you fear eavesdroppers?"

I was not conscious that I had sunk it, until recalled to the fact. "Every time I approach this door," I said, pointing to the one opening into the other room, "I feel as if I were in the presence of the dead. He is still lying there."

"What—Mr. Brightman?"

"It is where he died. He will be removed to his late residence to-night."

"I think I will see him," cried Sir Edmund, laying his hand on the door.

"As you please. I would not advise you." And he apparently thought better of it, and went down.

I had to attend the Vice-Chancellor's Court; law business goes on without respect to the dead. Upon my return in the afternoon, I was in the front office, speaking to Lennard, when a carriage drove down the street, and stopped at the door. Our blinds were down, but one of the clerks peeped out. "A gentleman's chariot, painted black," he announced: "the servants in deep mourning."

Allen went out and brought back a card. "The lady wishes to see you, sir."

I cast my eyes on it—"Lady Clavering." And an involuntary smile crossed my face, at the remembrance of Sir Edmund's caution, should I ever be brought into contact with her. But what could Lady Clavering want with me?

She was conducted upstairs, and I followed, leaving my business with Lennard until afterwards. She was already seated in the very chair that, not two hours ago, had held her opponent, Sir Edmund: a very handsome woman, dressed as coquettishly as her widow's weeds allowed. Her face was beautiful as to form and colouring, but its free and vain expression spoiled it. Every glance of her coal-black eye, every movement of her head and hands, every word that fell from her lips, was a purposed display of her charms, a demand for admiration. Sir Edmund need not have cautioned me to keep heart-whole. One so vain and foolish would repel rather than attract me, even though gifted with beauty rarely accorded to woman. A Jezebel? Yes, I agreed with him—a very Jezebel.

"I have the honour of speaking to Mr. Strange? Charles Strange, as I have heard Mr. Brightman call you," she said, with a smile of fascination.

"Yes, I am Charles Strange. What can I do for you, madam?"

"Will you promise to do what I have come to ask you?"

The more she spoke, the less I liked her. I am naturally frank in manner, but I grew reserved with her. "I cannot make a promise without knowing its nature, Lady Clavering."

She picked up her long jet chain, and twirled it about in her fingers. "What a frightfully sudden death Mr. Brightman's has been!" she resumed. "Did he lie ill at all?"

"No. He died suddenly, as he was sitting at his desk. And to render it still more painful, no one was with him."

"I read the account in this morning's paper, and came up at once to see you," resumed Lady Clavering. "He was my husband's confidential adviser. Were you in his confidence also?"

I presumed that she meant Mr. Brightman's, and answered accordingly. "Partially so."

"You are aware how very unjustly my poor childish husband strove to will away his property. Of course the will cannot be allowed to stand. At the time of Sir Ralph's funeral, I informed Mr. Brightman that I should take some steps to assert my rights, and I wished him to be my solicitor in the matter. But no; he refused, and went over to the enemy, Edmund Clavering."

"We were solicitors to Mr. Edmund Clavering before he came into the title."

"Mr. Brightman was; you never did anything for him," she hastily interrupted; "therefore no obligation can lie on you to act for him now. I want you to act for me, and I have come all this way to request you to do so."

"I cannot do so, Lady Clavering. I have seen Sir Edmund since Mr. Brightman's death, and have undertaken to carry on his business."

"Seen Sir Edmund since Mr. Brightman's death!"

"I have indeed."

She threw herself back in her chair, and looked at me from under her vain eyelids. "Leave him, Mr. Strange; you can easily make an excuse, if you will. Mr. Brightman held all my husband's papers, knew all about his property, and no one is so fitted to act for me as you, his partner. I will make it worth your while."

"What you suggest is impossible, Lady Clavering. We are enlisted in the interests—I speak professionally—of the other side, and have already advised with Sir Edmund as to the steps to be taken in the suit you purpose to enter against him. To leave him for you, after doing so, would be dishonourable and impossible."

She shot another glance at me from those mischievous eyes. "I will make it well worth your while, I repeat, Mr. Strange."

I could look mischievous too, if I pleased; perhaps did on occasion; but she could read nothing in my gaze then, as it met hers, that was not sober as old Time.

"I can only repeat my answer, Lady Clavering."

Not a word spoke she; only made play with her eyes. Did the woman mean to subdue me? Her gaze dropped.

"I have heard Mr. Brightman speak of Charles Strange not only as a thorough lawyer, but as a gentleman—very fond of the world's vanities."

"Not very fond, Lady Clavering. Joining in them occasionally, in proper time and place."

"I met you once at a large evening party. It was at old Judge Tartar's," she ran on.

"Indeed!" I answered, not remembering it.

"It was before I married Sir Ralph. You came in with your relative, Serjeant Stillingfar. What a charming man he is! I heard you tell someone you had just come down from Oxford. Won't you act for me, Mr. Strange?"

"Indeed, it does not lie in my power."

"Well, I did not think a gentleman"—with another stress upon the word—"would have refused to act on my behalf."

"Lady Clavering must perceive that I have no alternative."

"Who is Edmund Clavering that he should be preferred to me?" she demanded with some vehemence.

"Nay, Lady Clavering, circumstances compel the preference."

A silence ensued, and I glanced at my watch—the lawyer's hint. She did not take it.

"Can you tell me whether, amidst the papers Mr. Brightman held belonging to Sir Ralph, there are any letters of mine?"

"I cannot say."

"Some of my letters, to Sir Ralph and others, are missing, and I think they must have got amongst the papers by mistake. Will you look?"

"I will take an early opportunity of doing so."

"Oh, but I mean now. I want them. Why cannot you search now?"

I did not tell her why. In the first place, most of the Clavering papers were in the room where Mr. Brightman was lying—and there were other reasons also.

"I cannot spare the time, Lady Clavering: I have an appointment out of doors which I must keep. I will search for you in a day or two. But should any letters of yours be here—of which I assure you I am ignorant—you will pardon my intimating that it may not be expedient to give them up."

"What do you mean? Why not?"

"Should they bear at all upon the cause at issue between you and Sir Edmund Clavering—"

"But they don't," she interrupted.

"Then, if they do not, I shall be happy to enclose them to you."

"It is of the utmost consequence to me that I should regain possession of them," she said, with suppressed agitation.

"And, if possible, you shall do so." I rose as I spoke, and waited for her to rise. She did so, but advanced to the window and pulled the blind aside.

"My carriage is not back yet, Mr. Strange. A friend who came up with me has gone to do a commission for herself. It will be here in a few minutes. I suppose I can wait."

I begged her to remain as long as she pleased, but to excuse me, for I was already behind time. She drew up the blind a little and sat down at the window as I left her.

After giving some directions to Lennard, I hastened to keep my appointment, which was at the Temple with a chamber-counsel.

The interview lasted about twenty minutes. As I turned into Essex Street again, Lady Clavering's carriage was bowling up it. I raised my hat, and she bowed to me, leaning before another lady, who sat with her, but she looked white and frightened. What had taken her brilliant colour? At the door, when I reached it, stood the clerks, Lennard amongst them, some with a laugh on their countenances, some looking as white and scared as Lady Clavering.

"Why, what is this?" I exclaimed.

They went back to their desks, and Lennard explained.

"You must have seen Lady Clavering's carriage," he began.

"Yes."

"Just before it came for her, cries and shrieks were heard above; startling shrieks, terrifying us all. We hastened up with one accord, and found that Lady Clavering—"

"Well?" I impatiently cried, looking at Lennard.

"Had gone into the next room, and seen Mr. Brightman," he whispered. "It took three of us to hold her, and it ended with hysterics. Leah came flying from the kitchen, took off her bonnet, and brought some water."

I was sorry to hear it; sorry that any woman should have been exposed to so unpleasant a fright. "But it was her own fault," I said to Lennard. "How could she think of entering a room of which the door was locked?"

"What right had she to attempt to enter it at all, locked or unlocked, I should say, Mr. Strange!" returned Lennard severely. "And the best of it was, she laid the blame upon us, asking what business we had to put dead people into public rooms."

"She is a curious sort of woman, I fancy, Lennard."

And the more I thought of her, the more curious I found her. The door between the two rooms had been locked, and the key was lying in the corner of the mantelpiece. Lady Clavering must have searched for the key before she could open the door and enter the room.

With what motive had she entered it?

CHAPTER VI

THE MISSING WILL

Mr. Brightman was buried on the Thursday, and Mr. Serjeant Stillingfar came up from circuit for the funeral. Three or four other gentlemen attended, and myself. It was all done very quietly. After that the will was read.

He had not left as much money as might have been expected. I suppose the rate at which they lived had absorbed it. Nearly the whole of it was vested in trustees, who would pay the interest to Mrs. Brightman until her death, when it would all descend unconditionally to Annabel. If she married again, one half the yearly income at once went to Annabel. To my surprise, I was left executor. Mr. Brightman had never told me so. Of the two executors originally appointed—for the will had been made many years—one had recently died, and Mr. Brightman had inserted my name in his place. That all the work would fall upon my shoulders I knew, for the other executor had become a confirmed invalid.

With regard to our own articles of partnership, provided for by a recent codicil, they were very favourable to me, though somewhat peculiar. If Mr. Brightman died before I was thirty years of age, two-thirds of the net profits of the business were to be paid to Mrs. Brightman for three years; but if I had passed my thirtieth year when he died, only half the profits would go to her. After the first three years, one-third of the profits would be hers for three years more; and then all would revert to me absolutely.

I wanted some years yet of thirty. But it was an excellent and lucrative practice. Few men fall into so good a thing when they are still young.

"So there you are, Charles, the head of one of the best professional houses in London," remarked my uncle Stillingfar, as he took my arm when we were leaving the house. "Rather different from what your fate might have been, had you carried out your wish of going to the Bar. My boy, you may be thankful that you know nothing of the struggles I had to go through."

"Do you still feel quite well and strong, uncle?" I asked, after a bit.

"Yes, I do, Charles. I suppose you think I am growing old. But I believe I am more capable of work than are many of my juniors who are now on circuit with me. With a sound constitution, never played with, and a temperate way of life, we retain our energies, by God's blessing, to an older age than mine."

That was no doubt true. True also that he must be making heaps of money. I wondered what he meant to do with it. He had been very liberal to me as long as I needed help, but that time was over.

The sad week passed away. On the following Monday I set to professional business in earnest: the previous week had been much given to matters not professional. One of the first things to be attended to was to prove the will of Sir Ralph Clavering, and, in the course of the morning, I unlocked the iron safe in the front room to get it. Nothing was ever placed in that safe but wills and title-deeds, and these were never placed anywhere else. But where this particular will was hiding itself, I could not tell, for I turned over every paper the place contained without coming to it. "More haste less speed," cried I to myself, for I had been doing it in a hurry. "I must have overlooked it."

So I began again and went through the papers carefully, paper by paper. I had not overlooked it, for Sir Ralph's will was certainly not there.

Now, was I awake or dreaming? Was there a fairy in the walls to remove things, or was the house bewitched?—or what was it? I went and examined the Clavering papers, which were in Mr. Brightman's desk in the adjoining room—my room, which had been cleaned and put straight again. But the will was not amongst them. I searched other drawers and desks in vain. Then I called up Lennard.

"Do you know anything of Sir Ralph Clavering's will? I cannot find it."

"It must be in the safe," he replied.

"It is not in the safe. Lennard, this is very strange: first that bag of money, and now the will."

"Oh, but it cannot be," returned Lennard, after a pause. "That the gold went, appears to be too plain, but who would take a will? Money might be a temptation, if any stranger did enter Mr. Brightman's room that night, but—"

"It has been proved almost beyond doubt that no one entered, and yet the money went. Lennard, there's something not canny at work in the house, as the Scotch say."

"Do not think it, Mr. Strange," he replied warmly. "The gold appears to have gone in some mysterious manner, but the will cannot be gone. Depend upon it, it is in the safe."

I had a great respect for Lennard's judgment, but I had as great confidence in my own eyesight. I unlocked the safe again, and, taking out the parchments, one by one, handed them to Lennard that he might read their titles. "There," said I, when we had reached the last; "is the will amongst them?"

Lennard's face had turned grave. "This is very extraordinary!" he exclaimed. "Mr. Brightman would not put it anywhere else."

"He never put a will up in any other place than this since I have been with him, Lennard; and I myself saw him put it in; held the light for him: it was in the evening of last Tuesday week, after he came back from Sir Ralph's funeral. It has gone after the gold."

"No, no," he cried, almost in agitation; "it has not, it has not: I will never believe it."

One very slight hope came to me. Mr. Brightman might have given it into the custody of Sir Edmund Clavering. But then Sir Edmund would surely have said so when he spoke to me about proving the will. The loss of the money was nothing to this, for that had been easily replaced, and there was an end of the matter; but this loss could not be replaced, and there was no knowing what the end would be. It might be little short of ruin to Sir Edmund Clavering, and nothing short of ruin to me: for who would continue to employ a firm liable to lose wills?

I was greatly occupied that day, but the missing will lay upon me as a nightmare, and I forced time for a dash up to Sir Edmund Clavering's hotel in the afternoon, bribing the cabman to double speed. By good luck, I found Sir Edmund in, and inquired if he held possession of the will.

"Mr. Brightman holds the will," he replied. "Held, I should say: I cannot yet speak of him in the past tense, you see. He took it home with him after Sir Ralph's funeral."

"I know he brought it home, Sir Edmund; but I thought it possible he might since then have given it into your possession. I hoped he had, for I cannot find the will. I have searched for it everywhere."

"Not find the will!" he echoed. "Perhaps you have looked in every place but the right one," he added, with a slight laugh. "I can tell you where it is."

"Where?"

"In the iron safe in Mr. Brightman's room."

"It was placed there—we never put wills anywhere else; never—but it is not there now. May I ask how you knew it was there, Sir Edmund?"

"Because on the day but one following the funeral I came to town and had an interview with Mr. Brightman in his room. It was on the Thursday. Perhaps you remember that I was with him that day?"

"Quite well."

"During our consultation we differed in opinion as to a certain clause in the will, and Mr. Brightman took it out of the safe to convince me. He was right, and I was wrong; as, indeed, I might have known, considering that he had made the will. He put it back into the safe at once and locked it up. When are you going to prove the will? It ought to be done now."

"I was going to set about it this very day; but, as I say, I cannot find the will."

"It must be easy enough to find a big parchment like that. If not in the safe, Mr. Brightman must have put it elsewhere. Look in all his pigeon-holes and places."

"I have looked: I have looked everywhere.— Just as I looked some days before for the bag of sovereigns," I mentally added.

But Sir Edmund Clavering was determined to treat the matter lightly: he evidently attached no importance to it whatever, believing that Mr. Brightman had only changed its place.

I went home again, feeling as uncomfortable as I had ever felt in my life. An undefined idea, a doubt, had flashed into my mind whilst I had been talking to Lennard. Imagination is quicker with me, I know, than with many people; and the moment a thing puzzles me, I must dive into its why and wherefore: its various bearings and phases, probable and improbable, natural and unnatural. This doubt—which I had driven away at the time, had been driving away during my gallop to Sir Edmund's, and whilst I was conversing with him—now grew into suspicion.

Let me explain how I arrived at this suspicion. When I found the will had disappeared from the safe— when I searched and searched in vain—I could only come to the conclusion that it had been stolen. But why was it taken? From what motive? Why should that one particular parchment be abstracted, and the others left? Obviously, it could only have been from interested motives. Now, who had an interest in getting possession of the will—so that it might not be proved and acted upon? Only one person in the whole world—Lady Clavering. And Lady Clavering had been alone in the room where the safe was for nearly half an hour.

If she had obtained possession of the will, there was farewell to our ever getting it again. I saw through her character at that first interview: she was a woman absolutely without scruple.

But how could she have got at it? Even supposing she knew the will was in the iron safe, she could not have opened it without the key; and how could she have obtained the key?

Again—if Lady Clavering were the guilty party, what became of my very natural suspicions that the will and the gold were both taken by the same hand? And with the gold Lady Clavering could have had nothing to do. Look at it as I would, perplexities arose; points difficult, if not impossible, to reconcile.

Lennard met me in the passage on my return. "Is it all right? Has Sir Edmund got it, sir?"

"No, no; I told you it was a forlorn hope. Come upstairs, Lennard. Sir Edmund has not the will," I continued, as we entered the front room. "He says that when he was here last Thursday week, Mr. Brightman had occasion to refer to the will, took it from the safe, and put it back again. Therefore it is since that period that the theft has taken place."

"Can you really look upon it as stolen?" Lennard uttered, with emphasis. "Who would steal so valueless a thing as a will?"

"Not valueless to everyone."

"No one in the house would do such a thing. You have a suspicion?" he added.

"Yes, I have, Lennard."

He began to pace the room. Lennard was, in truth, completely upset by this loss. "Of whom?" he presently jerked out. "Surely not of Leah!"

"Of Leah! Oh no!"

"I fancied you suspected her in the matter of the money. I feel sure she was innocent."

"So do I. Leah no more took the money than you or I did, Lennard. And what should she want with the will? If I made her a present of all the wills in the safe, she would only light her fires with them as useless lumber. Try again."

But he only shook his head. "I cannot catch your drift, sir."

"To all persons, two excepted, the will would be as useless as to Leah. One of those two is Sir Edmund; and he has it not: the other is Lady Clavering."

"But surely you cannot suspect her!" exclaimed Lennard. "You cannot suspect Lady Clavering!"

"To say that I suspect her would perhaps be too strong a word, Lennard. If my doubts rest upon her at all, it is because she is the only person who could have an interest in getting possession of the will; and she is the only stranger, as far as I can recollect, who has been alone in this room sufficiently long to take it from the safe."

Lennard was incredulous. "But she had not the key of the safe. She could not have opened it without it."

"I know—I see the improbabilities that encompass my doubts; but I can think of nothing else."

"Where was the key of the safe?" asked Lennard.

"In that back room; and in Mr. Brightman's deep drawer—the drawer from which the gold was taken," was my grave answer. "And she could not have got at it without—without passing him."

Lennard's face grew hot.

"And the key of that drawer was here, in my own pocket, on the bunch." I took out the bunch of keys as I spoke—Mr. Brightman's bunch until within a few days—and shook it before him.

"What mystery has come over the house, about keys, and locks, and things disappearing?" Lennard murmured, as a man bewildered.

"Lennard, it is the question I am asking myself."

"She could never have gone in there and passed him; and stood there while she got the key. A young and beautiful woman like Lady Clavering! Sir, it would be unnatural."

"No more unnatural for beauty than for ugliness, Lennard. Unnatural for most women, though, whether pretty or plain."

"But how could she have divined that the key of the safe was in that drawer, or in that room?" urged Lennard. "For the matter of that, how could she have known that the will was in the safe?"

Truly the affair presented grave perplexities. "One curious part of it is that she should have called you up with her screams, Lennard," I remarked. "If she had only that moment opened the door, and seen—what frightened her, she could not have been already in the room hunting for the key. Were the screams assumed? Was it all a piece of acting?"

"It would take a subtle actress to counterfeit her terror," replied Lennard; "and the best actress breathing could not have assumed her ghastly look. No, Mr. Strange, I believe what she said was the fact: that, weary of waiting for her carriage, she had walked about the room, then opened the door, and passed into the other without any thought except that of distracting her ennui."

"She must have looked about for the key of the door, mind you, Lennard."

A man has rarely been placed in a more disagreeable predicament than I felt to be in then. It was of no use temporising with the matter: I could only meet it boldly, and I sent that evening for Sir Edmund Clavering, and laid it before him. I told him of Lady Clavering's visit, and hinted at the doubt which had forced itself on my mind. Sir Edmund jumped to the conclusion (and into a passion at the same time) that she was the culprit, and declared he would apply for a warrant at Bow Street on the morrow, to take her into custody. With extreme difficulty I got him to hear reason against anything of the sort.

Lennard, who had remained, came round to Sir Edmund's opinion that it must inevitably have been Lady Clavering. Failing her, no shadow of suspicion could attach itself to anyone, sift and search into the matter as we would.

"But neither was there as to the gold," was my rejoinder.

Then after they were gone, and I sat by the fire in the front room, and went over the details dispassionately and carefully, and lay awake the best part of the night, going over them still, my suspicions of Lady Clavering lessened, and I arrived at the conclusion that they were too improbable to be well founded.

Nevertheless, I intended to pursue the course I had decided on: and that was to call upon her. She, like Sir Edmund, was now staying in London, at an hotel. Not to accuse her, but to see if I could not, indirectly, make out something that would confirm or dissipate my suspicion.

I went up in the course of the morning. Lady Clavering was sitting alone, her widow's cap on the sofa beside her. She hurried it on to her head, when the waiter announced me.

"It is so hot and ugly," she exclaimed, in tones of excuse. "I sit without it when I am alone. So you have condescended to return my visit, Mr. Strange. I thought you gentlemen of the law took refuge in your plea of occupation to ignore etiquette."

"Indeed it is not out of deference to etiquette that I have called upon you to-day, Lady Clavering, but—"

"You have thought better of your refusal: you have come to say you will undertake my business!" she interrupted, eyes and looks full of eagerness.

"Nor yet that," I was forced to reply, though, in truth, I should have been glad to conciliate her. "I am sure you will find many an advocate quite as efficient as I should be. The day you were at our house, did you happen to see—"

"Mr. Strange, I must beg you, as a gentleman, not to allude to what I saw," she interposed, in tones of alarm. "I think it was inexcusable on your part not to have informed me what was in the next room."

"Pardon me, Lady Clavering; it would have been an unnecessary and unpleasant piece of information to volunteer: for how could I possibly foresee that you would be likely to enter that room?" I might have added—look for the key, unlock it, and go into it.

"I never saw a dead person in my life," she rejoined; "not even my husband; and I shall not easily recover from the shock. I would give anything rather than have been exposed to it."

"And so would I, and I shall always regret it," was my warm apology.

"Then why do you introduce the subject?"

"I did not intend to allude to that; but to your having sat in the front room I must allude; and I know you will excuse my asking you the question I am about to put to you. Did you happen to see a parchment lying in that front room: on the table, or the side-tables, or—anywhere, in short? We have missed one: and if you chanced to have noticed it, it would be a great assistance to us, as a proof that we need not carry our researches further back than that day."

"I don't remember that I saw any parchment," she carelessly rejoined. "I saw some papers, tied round with pink tape, on the table; I did not notice them particularly. I pray you not to make me think about that afternoon, or you will have me in hysterics again."

"It is not possible—your ladyship will pardon me—that it can have caught your dress in any way, and so have been carried downstairs and out of the house, and—perhaps—lost in the street?" I persisted slowly, looking at her.

Looking at her: but I could detect no emotion on her face; no drooping of the eye; no rise or fall of colour, such as one guilty would have been likely to display. She appeared to take my question literally, and to see nothing beyond it.

"I cannot tell anything about it, Mr. Strange. Had my dress been covered with parchments, I was in too much terror to notice them. Your clerks would be more able to answer you than I, for they had to assist me down to my carriage. But how should a parchment become attached to a lady's dress?" she added, shaking out the folds of her ample skirts. "The crape is quite soft, you perceive. Touch it."

"Quite so," I assented, advancing for a half-moment the extreme tip of my forefinger.

"You will take a glass of wine? Now don't say no. Why can't you be sociable?"

"Not any wine, thank you," I answered with a laugh. "We lawyers have to keep our heads clear, Lady Clavering: we should not do that if we took wine in the daytime."

"Sit still, pray. You have scarcely been here five minutes. I want to speak to you, too, upon a matter of business."

So I resumed my seat, and waited. She was looking at me very earnestly.

"It is about those missing letters of mine. Have you searched for them, Mr. Strange?"

"Partially. I do not think we hold any. There are none amongst the Clavering papers."

"Why do you say 'partially'?" she questioned.

"I have not had time to search amongst the packets of letters in Mr. Brightman's cupboards and places. But I think if there were any of your letters in our possession they would have been with the Clavering papers."

Her gaze again sought mine for a moment, and then faded to vacancy. "I wonder if he burnt them," she dreamily uttered.

"Who? Mr. Brightman?"

"No; my husband. You must look everywhere, Mr. Strange. If those letters are in existence, I must have them. You will look?"

"Certainly I will."

"I shall remain in town until I hear from you. You will go, then!"

"One more question ere I do go, Lady Clavering. Have you positively no recollection of seeing this lost parchment?"

She looked surprised at my pertinacity. "If I had, I should say so. I do not think I saw anything of the sort. But if I had seen it, the subsequent fright would have taken it clean out of my memory."

So I wished her good-morning and departed. "It is not Lady Clavering," I exclaimed to Lennard, when I reached home.

"Are you sure of that, Mr. Strange?"

"I think so. I judge by her manner: it is only consistent with perfect innocence. In truth, Lennard, I begin to see that I was foolish to have doubted her at all, the circumstances surrounding it are so intensely improbable."

And yet, even while I spoke, something of the suspicion crept into my mind again. So prone to inconsistency is the human heart.

CHAPTER VII

ANNABEL

Most men have their romance in life sooner or later. Mine had come in due course, and she who made it for me was Annabel Brightman.

After my first meeting with her, when she was a child of fourteen, and I not much more than a lad of twenty, I had continued to see her from time to time, for Mr. Brightman's first invitation to me was only the prelude to others. I watched her grow up into a good, unaffected woman, lovable and charming as she was when a child. Childhood had passed away now, and thought and gentleness had taken its place; and to my eyes and my heart no other girl in the world could compare with Annabel Brightman.

Her father suspected it. Had he lived only a little longer, he would have learned it beyond doubt, for I should have spoken out more fully upon the matter.

A little less than a year before his death—it was on a Good Friday—I was spending the day at his house, and was in the garden with Annabel. She had taken my arm, and we were pacing the broad walk to the left of the lawn, thinking only of ourselves, when, raising my eyes, I saw Mr. Brightman looking attentively at us from one of the French windows. He beckoned to me, and I went in.

"Charles," said he, when I had stepped inside, "no nonsense. You and Annabel are too young for anything of that sort."

I felt that his eyes were full upon me as I stood before him, and my face flushed to the roots of my hair. But I took courage to ask a question.

"Sir, every year passing over our heads will lessen that objection. Would there be any other?"

"Be quiet, Charles. Time enough to talk of these things when the years shall have passed. You are too young for them, I say."

"I am twenty-five, sir; and Miss Brightman—"

"Twenty-five?" he interrupted. "I was past forty when I thought of marriage. You must not turn Annabel's head with visions of what the years may bring forth, for if you do I will not have you here. Leave that to the future."

But there was sufficient in Mr. Brightman's manner to prove that he had not been blind to the attachment springing up between us, and undoubtedly regarded me as the possible future husband of his daughter. At any rate he continued to invite me to his house. During the past year Annabel had been a great deal at Hastings with Miss Brightman; I wondered that her father and mother would spare her so much.

But Annabel knew nothing of that conversation, and I had never yet spoken of love to her. And now Mr. Brightman, who would, or at least might, have sanctioned it, was gone; and Mrs. Brightman, who would certainly, as I believed, oppose it, remained.

In the days immediately following Mr. Brightman's death, I was literally overwhelmed with business. Apart from the additional work that naturally fell upon me—his share as well as mine—no end of clients came pouring in; and for no earthly purpose, that I could see, excepting curiosity. Besides this, there was the frightful search for Sir Ralph Clavering's will, and the anxiety its loss entailed on me.

On the Wednesday afternoon, just as I had got rid of two clients, Lennard came up with the news that someone else was there. I was then in the front room, seated at Mr. Brightman's desk. Too impatient to hear Lennard out, I told him I could see no one; could not, and would not.

"It is Miss Annabel Brightman," rejoined Lennard quietly.

"Miss Annabel Brightman? Oh, that's very different; I will see her."

Annabel came in, throwing back her crape veil. She had driven up alone in the carriage to bring me a message from her mother. Mrs. Brightman had made an appointment with me for that evening at her house; she had now sent to tell me not to keep it, as she was not well enough to attend to business.

"Mamma wishes you to come to-morrow instead of to-day; early in the afternoon," added Annabel.

That would be impossible, and I said so; my engagements would not at present permit me to give up an afternoon.

"Perhaps to-morrow evening will do," I suggested. "In fact it must do, Annabel. I don't know when I shall have leisure to come down to you in the daytime."

"I dare say it will do," assented Annabel. "At any rate, you can come to us. If mamma is not able to enter into business matters, another time can be appointed."

"Is your mamma so very ill?"

"Sometimes I think so—but she fluctuates," replied Annabel. "She is extremely weak, and her spirits are depressed. She will pass whole hours shut up in her room in solitude. When I ask to go in, Hatch brings out a message that mamma is not able to see even me."

"Her illness must be on the nerves."

"I suppose so. Yesterday she came down and walked with me in the garden in the sunshine. She seemed pretty well then, but not strong. In the evening she shut herself up again."

"I wish you would sit down, Annabel," I said, offering her a chair for the third time.

"I would if I could stay. Mamma charged me to go straight back after leaving the message with you. Are you well?" she continued with hesitation. "You look harassed."

"I am well, Annabel. But you have used the right word—I am harassed; terribly so."

"Poor papa!" she sighed. "It has brought a world of work and care upon you, as well as of grief to us."

"I should not mind work. But—we have had another loss, Annabel. A loss as mysterious as that of the gold; and far more important."

"What is it?" she asked. "More money?"

"No; I wish it were. A will, deposited in the safe there, has disappeared. I cannot even guess at the consequences; ruin probably to me and to one of our best clients. Not only that. If things are to vanish so unaccountably from our strongholds, we must have an enemy at work, and it is impossible to foresee where it may end."

"How very strange! What was the will like? I mean, what did it look like? I have a reason for asking you."

"It was a folded parchment. You saw your father's will, Annabel: it looked very much like that. Why do you ask?"

"Because I remember papa's bringing home a parchment exactly like the one you describe. It was an evening or two before he died: the evening before I and mamma went to Hastings. We left on Saturday, so it must have been Friday. Do you think it could be the missing will?"

"Oh no. I have known Mr. Brightman—though very rarely—take home deeds which required studying; but he was not likely to take home Sir Ralph Clavering's will. He made it himself, and knew every word it contained. Annabel, I did not intend to let out the name, but it will be safe with you."

"Perfectly so; as safe as with yourself. I will not repeat it, even to mamma."

"And what I shall do I cannot tell," I concluded, as I attended her down to the carriage. "I would give every shilling I possess to find it."

More work, and then the afternoon came to an end, my dinner came up, and I was at liberty to enjoy a little rest. I had taken to the front room as my sitting-room, and should speedily remove the desk and iron safe into the other, making that exclusively a business-room, and seeing clients in it. After dinner, the fire clear, my reading-lamp lighted, I took up the newspaper. But for habits of order and self-denying rules, I should never have attained to the position I enjoyed. One of those rules was, never to read the Times or any work of relaxation until my work was over for the day. I could then enjoy my paper and my cigar, and feel that I had earned both.

I took up the Times, and almost the very first paragraph my eye fell upon was the following:

"We hear that the convict ship Vengeance, after encountering stormy weather and contrary winds on her passage out, has been wrecked upon an uninhabited island. It is said that some of the convicts have escaped."

I started up almost as if I had been shot. Tom Heriot had gone out in the Vengeance: was he one of those who had escaped? If so, where was he? and what would be his ultimate fate?

The ship had sailed from our shores in August; this was February: therefore the reader may think that the news had been long enough in reaching England. But it must be remembered that sailing-vessels were at the mercy of the winds and waves, and in those days telegrams and cablegrams had not been invented.

Throwing my cigar into the fire and the newspaper on the table, I fell into an unpleasant reverie. My lucky star did not seem in the ascendant just now. Mr. Brightman's unhappy death; this fresh uncertainty about Tom Heriot; the certain loss of the gold, and the disappearance of the will—

A ring at the visitors' bell aroused me. I listened, as Leah opened the door, curious to know who could be coming after office hours, unless it was Sir Edmund Clavering. Lake was in the country.

"Is Mr. Strange in, Leah?" And the sound of the sweet voice set my heart beating.

"Yes, Miss Brightman. Please go up."

A light foot on the stairs, and Annabel entered, holding up a parchment with its endorsement towards me. "Will of Sir Ralph Clavering."

"Oh, Annabel! you are my guardian angel!"

I seized the deed and her hands together. She smiled, and drew away the latter.

"I still thought the parchment I spoke of might be the missing one," she explained, "and when I got home I looked in papa's secretaire. There it was."

"And you have come back to bring it to me!"

"Of course I have. It would have been cruel to let you pass another night of suspense. I came as soon as I had dined."

"Who is with you?"

"No one; I came in by the omnibus. In two omnibuses really, for the first one only brought me as far as Charing Cross."

"You came in by omnibus! And alone?"

"Why not? Who was to know me, or what could harm me? I kept my veil down. I would not order the carriage out again. It might have disturbed mamma, and she is in bed with one of her worst headaches. And now, Charles, I must hasten back again."

"Wait one moment, Annabel, whilst I lock up this doubly-precious will."

"Why? You are not going to trouble yourself to accompany me, when you are so busy? It is not in the least necessary. I shall return home just as safely as I came here."

"You silly child! That you have come here at night and alone, I cannot help; but what would Mrs. Brightman say to me if I suffered you to go back in the same manner?"

"I suppose it was not quite right," she returned laughingly; "but I only thought of the pleasure of restoring the will."

I locked it up in the safe, and went downstairs with her. Why Mr. Brightman should have taken the will home puzzled me considerably; but the relief to my mind was inexpressible, and I felt quite a gush of remorse towards Lady Clavering for having unjustly suspected her.

The prosy old omnibus, as it sped on its way to Clapham, was to me as an Elysian chariot. And we had it to ourselves the whole way, but never a word passed between us that might not have been spoken before a committee of dowagers. In fact, we talked chiefly of Miss Brightman. I began it by asking how she was.

"Aunt Lucy is very delicate indeed," replied Annabel. "Papa's death has tried her greatly: and anything that tries her at once affects her chest. She says she shall not be able to risk another winter in England, even at Hastings."

"Where would she go?"

"To Madeira. At least, she thinks so now. In a letter mamma received from her yesterday, Aunt Lucy said she should go there in the autumn."

"She will find it very dull and lonely—all by herself."

"Yes," sighed Annabel. "Mamma said she should send me with her. But of course I could not go—and leave mamma. I wish I had a sister! One of us might then accompany Aunt Lucy, and the other remain at home. What do you think that stupid Hatch said?" cried Annabel, running on. "We were talking about it at lunch, and Hatch was in the room. 'It's just the best thing you can do, Miss Annabel, to go with your aunt,' she declared, following up mamma's remark."

"Perhaps Mrs. Brightman may take it into her head to go to Madeira also?"

Annabel made a movement of dissent. "No, I don't think she would do that, Charles. She and Aunt Lucy used to be the very best of friends, but lately there has been some coolness between them. The reason is not known to me, but I fancy Hatch knows it."

"Hatch seems to be quite a confidential attendant on your mamma."

"Oh yes, she is so. She has lived with us so long, you see; and mamma, when she was Miss Chantry, knew Hatch when she was quite a child. They both come from the same place—near Malvern, in

Worcestershire. Aunt Lucy and mamma were intimate in early days, and it was through that intimacy that papa first knew Miss Chantry. Why she and Aunt Lucy should have grown cool to one another now, I cannot tell; but they have done so—and oh, I am sorry for it. I love Aunt Lucy very, very much," added the girl enthusiastically.

"And I'm sure I love the name—Lucy," I said, laughing. "It was my mother's."

The evening was yet early when we reached Mrs. Brightman's, for eight o'clock was striking. Hatch, in her new mourning, came stealing down the stairs with a quiet footfall, her black cap-strings flying as usual.

"Why, Miss Annabel, where have you been?" she cried. "I couldn't imagine what had become of you."

"I had to go out, Hatch—to take a deed to the office that poor papa had brought home and left here. Why? Has mamma wanted me?"

"Not she," returned Hatch. "She has just dropped off into a doze, and I am trying to keep the house free from noise. I thought you had been spirited away, Miss Annabel, and that's the truth."

"Mrs. Brightman has one of her bad headaches?" I remarked.

Hatch looked at me; then quickly at her young mistress: as much as to say: "You've been telling him that, Miss Annabel."

"It is that bad to-night, Mr. Charles, that her temples is fit to split," she answered. "Since master's death she have had 'em a'most constant—and no wonder, with all the worry and the shock it brought her. Are you going already, sir?"

"Will you not stay for tea?" asked Annabel.

"Not to-night, thank you," I replied.

"I'll let you out quietly," said Hatch, advancing towards the hall-door. "And mind, Miss Annabel, you are not to go anigh your mamma's room to waken her," she added, looking back dictatorially. "When one is racked with pain, body and mind, sleep is more precious than gold."

Hatch had lived there during the whole of Annabel's life, and could not always lay aside the authoritative manner she had exercised towards the child; possibly did not try to do so.

Great sway was held by Hatch in the household, and Mrs. Brightman appeared to sanction it. Certainly she never in any way interfered with it. But Hatch, always kindly, was a favourite with the servants.

With her shrewdness, capability and strong sense, it seemed a marvel that she should not have improved in manners and in her way of speaking. But she remained very much the same rough diamond that she had always been. Strangers were wont to feel surprise that Mrs. Brightman, herself so refined a woman, should put up with Hatch as her personal attendant; and in her attacks of illness Hatch would be in her mistress's room for hours together. At this time I knew nothing of Hatch's antecedents, very little of Mrs. Brightman's; or of matters relating to the past; and when circumstances brought me into

Hatch's confidence, she enlightened me upon some points of the family history. A few of her communications I cannot do better than insert here, improving somewhat upon her parts of speech.

I recall the scene now. It was a lovely moonlit evening, not long after the time of which I am writing. I had gone to Clapham to inquire after Mrs. Brightman, who was then seriously ill, and kept her chamber. Strolling about the garden in the soft twilight, wishing Annabel was at home instead of at Hastings, Hatch came out and joined me, and at once fell to chatting without ceremony. I made a remark, quite by chance, that touched upon the subject of Mrs. Brightman's early life; it was immediately taken up by Hatch and enlarged upon. I heard much to which I had hitherto been a stranger.

"Colonel Chantry and his wife, who was the daughter of Lord Onyx, lived at their seat, Chantry Hall, a beautiful place not far from Malvern in Worcestershire. They had three children—George, Frederic and Emma, who were reared in all the pride and pomp of the Chantry family. The property was strictly entailed. It would descend to George Chantry at his father's death; and as Colonel Chantry had no other property whatever, and as he lived not only up to his income but beyond it, the future look-out for the younger son and the daughter was not a very great one.

"Such a dash they kept up," said Hatch, warming with her subject. "The Colonel liked show and parade, and Madam, as we always called her, had been born to it. She was the Honourable Mrs. Chantry, you see, sir, and chose to live according. They visited all the noble families round about, and were visited back again. The Somers' at Eastnor Castle, the Lyons' at Maddresfield, the Foleys at Whitley, the other Foleys at Stoke Edith, the Coventrys over at Croome, the Lechmeres at the Rhydd, the Hornyholds at Blacknore Park, and the Parkingtons at Ombersley—but there'd be no end if I stopped to tell you the half of 'em. Besides that, Mrs. Chantry counted a near relative in one of the cathedral prebendaries at Worcester—and for pride and exclusiveness some of those old prebendaries capped the world. So that—"

"But, Hatch, why are you telling me this?" I interrupted.

"To give you a notion of what my mistress was accustomed to when she was Miss Emma Chantry," promptly replied Hatch. "Well, Mr. Charles, they grew up, those three children, and I watched 'em grow; not that I was as old as they were; and I looked upon 'em as the finest and grandest young people in the world. The two sons spent a good deal more than they ought. Mr. Frederic especially, and the Colonel had to find a lot o' money, for 'twas wanted on all sides, and folks wondered how he did it. The end to it came all on a sudden—death."

"Whose death?"

"The Colonel's, sir. Mr. George, who was then Captain Chantry, and about twenty-seven years old, took the estate. But it was frightfully encumbered, and he complained bitterly to his mother that he should be a poor man for years and years to come. Madam resented what he said, and a quarrel ensued. She would not remain at the Hall, as he had expected her to do, but took a cottage at Malvern, and went into it with her daughter, with a parade of humility. She did not live very long after that, and Miss Emma was thrown on the world. Captain Chantry was married, then, to an earl's daughter; but his wife and Miss Emma did not get on together. Miss Emma refused to make her home at the Hall with Lady Grace, and she came to London on a visit to Miss Lucy Brightman, whose mother was living there. She and Miss Lucy had been at a finishing school together years before, and they had kept up their friendship. It was there she first saw Mr. Brightman, who was a great many years older than his sister; and it ended in their being married."

"And you came into their service, I suppose, Hatch?"

"I did, sir. They had been married near upon twelve months when young Mrs. Brightman found occasion to discharge two or three of her servants: and she wrote to the late housekeeper at Chantry Hall, asking her to find her some from our neighbourhood. London servants were frightful, she said: fine, lazy, extravagant and insolent. Mother heard about it, and spoke for me to go as under-housemaid. Well, I was engaged, Mr. Charles, and I came up here to Clapham: and I was called 'Hatch' from the beginning, because my Christian name, Emma, was the same as my lady's. Soon after this, Miss Annabel was born. It was my duty to wait upon the nurse and the sick-room; and my lady—who was ill and weakly for a long while—grew to like to have me there. She would talk about the old place to me, for you see I knew all the people in it as well as she did. Next, she made me upper-housemaid; and in a very few years, for she had found out how clever I was at dressmaking and with the needle generally, I became her maid."

"And you are in her confidence, Hatch?" I rejoined. "Deservedly so, I am sure."

"In a measure I am, Mr. Charles. A lady like my Missis, who never loses her pride day nor night, cannot descend to be over-confidential with an inferior. But I know she values me—and so did my poor master. I mayn't be polished, Mr. Charles, but I'd go through fire and water for them any day."

And I am sure she would have done so.

Well, this was a portion of what Hatch told me. But I must now go back to the night whose events were interrupted for the purpose of recording these details. Not that there is anything more to relate of the night in question. Leaving a message that I would call on Mrs. Brightman in good time the following evening, wishing Annabel good-night, and Hatch also, I returned home.

CHAPTER VIII

PERRY'S REVELATION

DEAR STRANGE,—Have you seen the news in to-day's paper? I have just caught sight of it. If the Vengeance has foundered, or whatever the mishap may be, and Tom Heriot should be one of the escaped prisoners, he will be sure to make his way home. Rely upon it he has not grown less reckless than he was, but probably has become more so. What trouble may not come of it? Do try and get at the particulars officially, as to whether there's truth in the report, or not; and let me know without delay.

Very truly yours,

LEVEL.

Letters from Paris and the Continent generally were then usually delivered about mid-day. I was talking with Lennard in the front office when this one arrived. The clerks had gone to dinner.

"Have you heard the rumour about the ship Vengeance, Lennard?" I asked, laying down Lord Level's letter.

"I read it yesterday," he answered.

"I wonder how I could learn whether there's any foundation for it?"

Before he could answer me, we were interrupted by Major Carlen. He was in his usual state of excitement; his face lengthened, his arms thrown about, and his everlasting blue cloak trailing about him. I slipped the letter into my desk.

"Here's a pretty go, Charles!" he exclaimed. "Have you heard of it yet? That convict ship's gone to the bottom, and Tom Heriot has escaped."

"You should not assert that so positively, Major Carlen," I remonstrated. "It is not certain that any of the men have escaped, I suppose. If they have, Tom Heriot may not be one of them."

"But they have escaped," stuttered the gray old man, plumping himself down on a stool, around which his cloak fell like so much drapery. "Five have got off, and Tom is one of them."

"How do you know that?"

"How do I know it? How could I tell you if I didn't know it? Half an hour ago I met Percival in Downing Street, and he told me."

What little hope had been left within me took wings and flew away. Percival was First Lord of the Admiralty. He would certainly know the truth.

"Government has had official news of it," went on the Major gloomily; "and with it a list of the fugitives."

"And Tom's name is amongst them?"

"Tom's name is amongst them."

There was a pause. Lennard had gone into the other room. Major Carlen rose, saying something about lunch waiting for him at his club.

"Mark you, Charles: if Tom takes it into that rattle-pate of his to worm his way back to these shores, there may be the devil to pay. I hope with all my heart Level won't hear of this. The disgrace has been a precious thorn to him from the first."

"Blanche knows nothing at all of the matter as yet. She thinks Tom is with his regiment in India. The last time I saw her in Paris, not long before Mr. Brightman's death, she asked me what could be the reason Tom did not write to her."

"Much better tell her, and get it over," spoke the Major. "I should, if I were Level. He is more careful of her than she deserves—silly chit!"

Major Carlen and his cloak swung out again, the clerks came back, and the day and its duties went on. I wrote to Lord Level; giving him the substance of what the Major had heard, and telling him that I thought there could be little fear of Tom Heriot's venturing back to England. He could never be so reckless as to risk the danger.

Dinner over, I started for Mrs. Brightman's, and was admitted by the butler, who told me, in answer to my inquiry, that his mistress had been ill all day and had not come down. Tea waited on the drawing-room table, but no one was in the room. Presently Annabel entered.

"I am sorry you should have had the trouble to come, when perhaps you could not spare the time," she said. "Mamma is not well enough to see you."

"I was not busy to-night, Annabel. Perry has just told me your mamma has not been down to-day. Is her illness anything more than would be caused by these bad headaches? Do you fear anything serious?"

"Yes—no. I—I hope not."

Her voice and manner were excessively subdued, as if she could scarcely speak from fear of breaking down. She turned to the table, evidently to avoid my notice, and busied herself with the teacups.

"What is the matter, Annabel?"

"Nothing," she faintly answered, though her tears were even then falling. But I knew that some great trouble must be upon her.

"Is Mrs. Brightman vexed with you for having come up last night with that deed?"

"No; oh no! I told mamma about it this morning, and she said I had done quite right to take it up, but that I ought to have gone in the carriage."

"What, then, is causing you this grief?"

"You cannot expect me to be in very good spirits as yet," she replied: which was a decided evasion. "There are times—when I feel—the loss—"

She fairly broke down, and, sinking into a chair, cried bitterly and without concealment. I waited until she had become calmer.

"Annabel, my dear, sorrow for your loss is not all that disturbs your peace to-night. What else is there?"

"It is true that I have had something to vex me," she admitted after a pause. "But I cannot tell you about it."

"It is a momentary trouble, I hope; one that will pass away—"

"It will never pass away," she interrupted, with another burst of emotion. "It will be a weight and a grief upon me as long as life shall last. I almost wish I had died with my father, rather than have to live and bear it."

I took her hands in mine, and spoke deliberately. "If it be so serious a trouble as that, I must know it, Annabel."

"And if it were of a nature to be spoken of, you should know it. But it is not, and I can tell you nothing."

"Could you speak of it to your father, were he still living?"

"We should be compelled to speak of it, I fear. But—"

"Then, my dear, you can speak of it to me. From henceforth you must look upon me as in his place; your protector; your best friend: one who will share your cares, perhaps more closely than he could have done; who will strive to soothe them with a love that could not have been his. In a short time, Annabel, I shall ask you to give me the legal right to be and do this."

"It can never be," she replied, lifting her tearful eyes to mine.

I looked at her with an amused smile. I knew she loved me—and what other obstacle could exist? Mrs. Brightman might oppose it at first, but I did not despair of winning her over in the end.

"Not quite yet, I know," I answered her. "In a few months' time."

"Charles, you misunderstand me. I said it could never be. Never."

"I certainly do not understand that. Had your father lived, it would have been; and I do not say this without reason for the assertion. I believe that he would have given you to me, Annabel, heartily, with all his good will."

"Yes, that may be true; I think you are right; but—"

"But what, then? One word, Annabel: the objection would not surely come from your heart?"

"No, it would not," she softly answered, blushing deeply. "Please do not speak of these things."

"I did not intend to speak of them so soon. But I wish to remind you that I do possess a right to share your troubles, of whatever nature those troubles may be. Come, my darling, tell me your grief."

"Indeed I cannot," she answered, "and you know I am not one to refuse anything from caprice. Let me go, Charles; I must make the tea."

I did let her go; but I bent over her first, without warning, and kissed her fervently.

"Oh, Charles!"

"As an earnest of a brother's love and care for you, Annabel, if you object for the present to the other," I whispered.

"Yes, yes; be a brother to me," she returned, with strange yearning. "No other tie can now be ours."

"My love, it shall be."

She rang for the urn, which Perry brought in, and then sat down to the table. I placed myself opposite to her and drew the dry toast towards me. "Mrs. Brightman prefers this, I believe; shall I prepare some for her?"

Annabel did not answer, and I looked up. She was struggling with her tears again. "I fear mamma is not well enough to eat," she said, in a stifled voice.

"Annabel!" I suddenly exclaimed, a light flashing upon me: "your mother is worse than you have confessed: it is her illness which is causing you this pain."

Far greater than any that had gone before was the storm of emotion that shook her now. I rose in consternation and approached her, and she buried her face in her hands. It was very singular. Annabel Brightman was calm, sensible, open as the day. She seemed to-night to have borrowed another character. Suddenly she rose, and nervously putting my hand aside, walked once or twice up and down the room, evidently to obtain calmness. Then she dried her eyes, and sat down again to the tea-tray. I confess that I looked on in amazement.

"Will you be kind enough to ring, Charles? Twice, please. It is for Hatch."

I did so, and returned to my seat. Hatch appeared in answer to her signal. Annabel held the cup of tea she had poured out.

"Mamma's tea, Hatch."

"She won't take none, miss."

It is impossible to resist the temptation of now and then giving the grammar and idioms Hatch had brought from her country home, and had never since attempted to alter or improve. But what Hatch lacked in accuracy she made up in fluency, for a greater talker never flourished under the sun.

"If you could get her to drink a cup, it might do her good," pursued Hatch's young mistress. "Take it up, and try."

Hatch flirted round, giving me full view of her black streamers, and brought forward a small silver waiter. "But 'twon't be of no manner of use, Miss Annabel."

"And here's some toast, Hatch," cried I.

"Toast, sir! Missis wouldn't look at it. I might as well offer her a piece of Ingy-rubbins to eat. Miss Annabel knows—"

"The tea will be cold, Hatch; take it at once," interposed Miss Annabel.

"Annabel, who is attending your mamma? Mr. Close, I suppose."

"Mr. Close. She never will have anyone else. I fear mamma must have been ill for some time; but I have been so much away with Aunt Lucy that I never noticed it before."

"Ay; Hastings and your aunt will miss you. I suppose Mrs. Brightman will not spare you now as she has hitherto done."

Annabel bent her head over the tea-tray, and a burning colour dyed her face. What had my words contained to call up the emotion? Presently she suddenly rose and left the room, saying she must see whether the tea had been taken. She returned with the empty cup, looking somewhat more cheerful.

"See, Charles, mamma has taken it: I do believe she would take more nourishment, if Hatch would only press it upon her. She is so very weak and depressed."

Annabel filled the cup again, and Hatch came in for it. "Suppose you were to take up a little toast as well; mamma might eat it," suggested Annabel, placing the cup on the waiter.

"Oh, well, not to contrairy you, Miss Annabel," returned Hatch. "I know what use it will be, though."

She held out the waiter, and I was putting the small plate of toast upon it, when screams arose from the floor above. Loud, piercing screams; screams of fear or terror; and I felt sure that they came from Mrs. Brightman. Hatch dropped the waiter on to the table, upsetting the tea, and dashed out of the room.

I thought nothing less than that Mrs. Brightman was on fire, and should have been upstairs as speedily as Hatch; but Annabel darted before me, closed the drawing-room door, and stood against it to prevent my exit, her arms clasping mine in the extremity of agitation, the shrieks above still sounding in our ears.

"Charles, you must not go! Charles, stay here! I ask it of you in my father's name."

"Annabel, are you in your senses? Your mother may be on fire! She must be on fire: do you not hear her screams?"

"No; it is nothing of that sort. I know what it is. You could do no good; only harm. I am in my own house—its mistress just now—and I tell you that you must not go up."

I looked down at Annabel. Her face was the hue of death, and though she shook from head to foot, her voice was painfully imperative. The screams died away.

A sound of servants was heard in the hall, and Annabel turned to open the door. "You will not take advantage of my being obliged to do so, Charles?" she hurriedly whispered. "You will not attempt to go up?"

She glided out and stood before the servants, arresting their progress as she had arrested mine. "It is only a similar attack to the one mamma had last night," she said, addressing them. "You know that it arises from nervousness, and your going up would only increase it. She prefers that Hatch alone should be with her; and if Hatch requires help, she will ring."

They moved away again slowly; and Annabel came back to the drawing-room.

"Charles," she said, "I am going upstairs. Pray continue your tea without waiting for me; I will return as soon as possible."

And all this time she was looking like a ghost and shaking like an aspen leaf.

I crossed to the fire almost in a dream and stood with my back to it. My eyes were on the tea-table, but they were eyes that saw not. All this seemed very strange. Something attracted my attention. It was the tea that Hatch had spilt, slowly filtering down to the carpet. I rang the bell to have it attended to.

Perry answered the ring. Seeing what was wrong, he brought a cloth and knelt down upon the carpet. I stood where I was, and looked on, my mind far away.

"Curious thing, sir, this illness of mistress's," he remarked.

"Is it?" I dreamily replied.

"The worst is, sir, I don't know how we shall pacify the maids," he continued. "I and Hatch both told them last night what stupids they were to take it up so, and that what missis saw could not affect them. But now that she has seen it a second time—and of course there was no mistaking the screams just now—they are turning rebellious over it. The cook's the most senseless old thing in the world! She vows she won't sleep in the house to-night; and if she carries out her threat, sir, and goes away, she'll spread it all over the neighbourhood."

Was Perry talking Sanscrit? It was about as intelligible to me as though he had been. He was still over the carpet, and in matter-of-fact tones which shook with his exertion, for he was a fat man, and was rubbing vehemently, he continued:

"I'm sure I couldn't have believed it. I wouldn't have believed it, sir, but that I have been in the house and a witness to it, as one may say; at any rate, heard the screams. For a more quieter, amiabler, and peaceabler man never lived than my master, kind to all about him, and doing no harm to anybody; and why he should 'Walk' is beyond our comprehension."

"Why he should—what?" I exclaimed.

"Walk, sir," repeated Perry. "Hatch says it's no doubt on account of his dying a sudden death; that he must have left something untold, and won't be laid till he has told it. It's apparent, I take it, that it concerns Mrs. Brightman, by his appearing to her."

"What is it that has appeared to Mrs. Brightman?" I asked, doubting my ears.

Perry arrested his occupation, and raised himself to look at me. "My dead master, sir," he whispered mysteriously. "Master's ghost."

"Your master's—ghost!" I echoed.

"Yes, sir. But I thought my young lady had told you."

I felt an irreverent inclination to laugh, in spite of the serious surroundings of the topic. Ghosts and I had never had any affinity with each other. I had refused to believe in them as a child, and most unhesitatingly did so as a man. When I returned "The Old English Baron" to Annabel, some years before, she wished she had never lent it to me, because I declined to accept the ghost.

"I am sure, sir, I never supposed but what Miss Annabel must have imparted it to you," repeated Perry, as if doubting his own discretion in having done so. "But somebody ought to know it, if it's only to advise; and who so fit as you, sir, master's friend and partner? I should send for a clergyman, and let him try to lay it; that's what I should do."

"Perry, my good man," and I looked at his bald head and rotund form, "you are too old, and I should have thought too sensible, to believe in ghosts. How can you possibly listen for a moment to stories so absurd as these?"

"Well, sir," argued Perry, "my mistress did see it or she didn't; and if she didn't, why should she scream and say she did? You heard her screams just now; and they were worse yesterday."

"Did you see the ghost?"

"No, sir; I was not up there. Hatch thought she saw it as she went into the room. It was in a corner, and wore its shroud: but when we got up there it was gone."

"When was all this?"

"Last night, sir. When you left, Miss Annabel took off her bonnet in the drawing-room and rang for tea, which I carried in. Presently Hatch ran in at the front door, and Miss Annabel told me to call her in. 'Has mamma had her tea, Hatch?' said my young lady. 'Yes, she has,' returned Hatch; which was a downright falsehood, for she had not had any. But Hatch is master and missis too, as far as we servants go, and nobody dares contradict her. Perhaps she only said it to keep Mrs. Brightman undisturbed, for she knows her ailments and her wants and ways better than Miss Annabel. So, sir, I went down, and Hatch went up, but not, it seems, into Mrs. Brightman's room, for she thought she was asleep. In two or three minutes, sir, the most frightful shrieks echoed through the house; those to-night were nothing half as bad. Hatch was first in the chamber, Miss Annabel next, and we servants last. My mistress stood at the foot of the bed, which she must have left—"

"Was she dressed?" I interrupted.

"No, sir; she was in her night-gown, or a dressing-gown it might have been. She looked like—like—I don't hardly know what to say she looked like, Mr. Strange, but as one might suppose anybody would look who had seen a ghost. She was not a bit like herself. Her eyes were starting and her face was red with terror; almost all alight, as one may say; indeed, she looked mad. As to her precise words, sir, I can't tell you what they were, for when we gathered that it was master's ghost which she had seen, appearing in its shroud in the corner by the wardrobe, the women servants set up a cry and ran away. That stupid cook went into hysterics, and declared she wouldn't stop another night in the house."

"What was done with Mrs. Brightman?"

"Miss Annabel—she seemed terrified out of her senses, too, poor young lady—bade me hasten for Mr. Close; but Hatch put in her word and stopped me, and said the first thing to be done was to get those shrieking maids downstairs. Before I and John had well done it—and you'd never have forgot it, sir, had you seen 'em hanging on to our coat tails—Hatch followed us down, bringing her mistress's orders that Mr. Close was not to be fetched; and indeed, as Hatch remarked, of what use could a doctor be in a ghost affair? But this morning Miss Annabel sent for him."

"Mrs. Brightman must have had a dream, Perry."

"Well, sir, I don't know; it might have been; but she is not one given to dreams and fancies. And she must have had the same dream again now."

"Not unlikely. But there's no ghost, Perry; take my word for it."

"I hope it will be found so, sir," returned Perry, shaking his head as he retired; for he had done his work and had no further pretext for lingering.

CHAPTER IX

SOMEONE ELSE SEEN

Standing with my back to the fire in the drawing-room, waiting for Annabel's return, the tea growing cold on the table, I puzzled over what I had just heard, and could make nothing of it. That Mr. Brightman's spirit should appear to his wife seemed to be utterly incomprehensible; was, of course, incredible. That many people believed in the reappearance of the dead, I well knew; but I had not yet made up my mind to become one of them.

It was inexplicable that a woman in this enlightened age, moving in Mrs. Brightman's station, could yield to so strange a delusion. But, allowing that she had done so, did this sufficiently explain Annabel's deep-seated grief? or the remark that her grief would end only with her life? or the hint that she could never be my wife? And why should she refuse to confide these facts to me? why, indeed, have prevented my going upstairs? I might have reassured Mrs. Brightman far more effectually than Hatch; who, by Perry's account, was one of the believers in the ghost theory. It was altogether past comprehension, and I was trying hard to arrive at a solution when Hatch came in, her idioms in full play.

"My young lady's complemens, sir, and will you excuse her coming down again to-night? she is not equal to seeing nobody. And she says truth, poor child," added Hatch, "for she's quite done over."

"How is your mistress now, Hatch?"

"Oh, she's better, she is. Her nerves have been shook, sir, of late, you know, through the shock of master's unexpected death, and in course she starts at shadders. I won't leave the room again, without the gas a-burning full on."

"What is this tale about Mr. Brightman?"

Hatch and her streamers swung round, and she closed the door before answering. "Miss Annabel never told you that; did she, sir?"

"No; but I have heard a word or two elsewhere. You fancy you saw a ghost?"

"Missis do."

"Oh, I thought you did also."

"I just believe it's a delusion of hers, Mr. Charles, and nothing more," returned Hatch confidently. "If master had been a bad sort of character, or had taken his own life, or anything of that, why, the likelihood is that he might have walked, dying sudden. But being what he was, a Christian gentleman that never missed church, and said his own prayers at home on his knees regular—which I see him a doing of once, when I went bolt into his dressing-room, not beknowing he was in it—why, it is not likely, sir, that he comes again. I don't say as much to them downstairs; better let them be frightened at his ghost than at—at—anybody else's. I wish it was master's ghost, and nothing worse," abruptly concluded Hatch.

"Nothing worse! Some of you would think that bad enough, were it possible for it to appear."

"Yes, sir, ghosts is bad enough, no doubt. But realities is worse."

So it was of no use waiting. I finished my cup of cold tea, and turned to go, telling Hatch that I would come again the following evening to see how things were progressing.

"Yes, do, Mr. Charles; you had better," assented Hatch, who had a habit, not arising from want of respect, but from her long and confidential services, and the plenitude of her attachment, of identifying herself with the family in the most unceremonious manner. "Miss Annabel's life hasn't been a bed of roses since this ghost appeared, and I fear it is not likely to be, and if there's anybody that can say a word to comfort her, it must be you, sir; for in course I've not had my eyes quite blinded. Eyes is eyes, sir, and has their sight in 'em, and we can't always shut 'em, if we would."

Hatch was crossing the hall to open the door for me, and I had taken my great-coat from the stand, when Annabel flew down the stairs, her face white, her voice sharp with terror.

"Hatch! Hatch! mamma is frightened again!"

Hatch ran up, two stairs at a time, and I went after her. Mrs. Brightman had followed Annabel, and now stood outside her chamber-door in her white dressing-gown, trembling violently. "He is watching me again," she panted: "he stands there in his grave-clothes!"

"Don't you come," cried Hatch, putting Annabel back unceremoniously. "I shall get my missis round best alone; I'm not afraid of no ghostesses, not I. Give a look to her, sir," she added, pointing to Annabel, as she drew Mrs. Brightman into her chamber, and fastened the door.

Annabel, her hands clasped on her chest, shook as she stood. I put my arm round her waist and took her down to the drawing-room. I closed the door, and Annabel sat down on the sofa near the fire.

"My darling, how can I comfort you?"

A burst of grief prevented her from replying—grief that I had rarely witnessed. I let it spend itself; you can do nothing else with emotion so violent: and when it was over I sat down beside her.

"Annabel, you might have confided this to me at first. It can be nothing but a temporary delusion of Mrs. Brightman's, arising from a relaxed state of the nervous system. Imaginary spectral appearances—"

"Who told you about that?" she interrupted, in agitation. "How came you to hear it?"

"My dear, I heard it from Perry. But he did not break faith in speaking of it, for he thought you had already told me. There can be no reason why I should not know it; but I am sorry that it has penetrated to the servants."

Poor Annabel laid her head on the arm of the sofa, and moaned.

"I do not like to leave you or Mrs. Brightman either, in this distress. Shall I remain in the house to-night? I can send a message to Leah—"

"Oh no, no," she hastily interrupted, as if the proposal had startled her. And then she continued slowly, hesitatingly, pausing between her words: "You do not—of course—believe that—that papa—"

"Of course I do not," was my hearty reply, relieving her from her embarrassing question. "Nor you either, Annabel: although, as a child, you devoured every ghost-story you came near."

She made no confirmatory reply, only looked down, and kept silence. I gazed at her wonderingly.

"It terrified me so much last night," she whispered.

"What terrified you, Annabel?"

"I was terrified altogether; at mamma's screams, at her words, at the nervous state she was in. Mr. Close has helped to frighten me, too, for I heard him say this morning to Hatch that such cases have been known to end in madness."

"Mr. Close is not worth a rush," cried I, suppressing what I had been about to utter impulsively. "So he knows of this fancy?"

"Yes, Hatch told him. Indeed, Charles, I do not see that there was any help for it."

"He will observe discretion, I suppose. Still, I almost wish you had called in someone who is a stranger to the neighbourhood."

"Mamma will not have a stranger, and you know we must not act in opposition to her will. She seemed so much better this morning; quite herself again."

"Of course. With the return of daylight these fancies subside. But as it seems there is nothing I can do for you, Annabel, I must be going, and will come again to-morrow evening."

The conclusion seemed to startle her. "Had—you—better come?" she cried, with much hesitation.

"Yes, Annabel, I had better come," I firmly replied. "And I cannot understand why you should wish me not to do so, as I can see you do."

"Only—if mamma should be ill again—it is all so uncomfortable. I dare say you never even finished your tea," glancing at the table. All trivial excuses, to conceal her real and inexplicable motive, I felt certain. "Good-night, Charles."

She held out her hand to me. I did not take it: I took her instead, and held her to my heart. "You are not yourself to-night, Annabel, for there is some further mystery in all this, and you will not tell it me. But the time will soon come, my dearest, when our mysteries and our sorrows must be shared in common." And all the answer I received was a look of despair.

In passing through the iron gates, I met Mr. Close. The moon to-night was obscured by clouds, but the gas-lamps revealed us plainly to each other. "How is Mrs. Brightman?" he asked.

"Very ill and very strange," I answered. "Do you apprehend any serious result?"

"Well—no," said he; "not immediately. Of course, it will tell upon her in the long-run."

"She has had another attack of nervous terror to-night; in fact, two attacks."

"Ay; seen the ghost again, I suppose. I suspected she would, so thought I would just call in."

"Would it not be as well—excuse me, Mr. Close, but you are aware how intimately connected I was with Mr. Brightman—to call in a consultation? Not that there is the slightest doubt of your skill and competency, but it appears to be so singular a malady; and in the multitude of counsellors there is safety, you know."

"It is the commonest malady we have to deal with," returned he; and the answer was so unexpected that I could only stare in silence.

"Have a consultation if you think it more satisfactory, Mr. Strange. But it will not produce the slightest benefit; and the less this matter is allowed to transpire the better. I assure you that all the faculty combined could not do more for Mrs. Brightman than I am doing. It is a lamentable disease, but it is one that must run its course."

He went on to the house, and I got outside an omnibus that was passing the end of the road, and lighted my cigar, more at sea than ever. If seeing ghosts was the commonest malady doctors had to deal with, where had I lived all my life not to have learned it?

The next afternoon I was surprised by a visit from Perry. He brought word from his mistress that she was very much better, though not yet able to see me on business matters; when she felt equal to it, she would let me know. Miss Annabel, concluded the butler, was gone to Hastings.

"To Hastings!" I exclaimed.

"Well, yes, sir. My mistress decided upon it this morning, and I have just seen her off by train, with Sarah in attendance on her. Fact is, sir," added Perry, dropping his voice to a confidential key: "Hatch whispered to me that it was thought best the poor young lady should be out of the house while it is so troubled."

"Troubled!" I repeated, half in scorn.

"Why, yes, sir, you know what it is that's in it," rejoined Perry simply. "Mr. Close, too, he said Miss Annabel ought to be away from it just now."

When every hour of the day is occupied, time glides on insensibly. A week passed. I heard no news of or from Mrs. Brightman, and did not altogether care to intrude upon her, unbidden. But when the second week was also quickly passing, I determined to take an evening to go to Clapham. Dinner over, I was going downstairs, and met Leah coming up.

"If anyone calls, I am out for the evening, Leah," I said to her. "And tell Watts when he comes in that I have left the Law Times on the table for Mr. Lake. He must take it round to him."

"Very well, sir."

I was nearing the top of Essex Street when I met the postman.

"Anything for me?" I inquired, for I had expected an important letter all day.

"I think there is, sir," he replied, looking over his letters under the gas-lamp. "'Messrs. Brightman and Strange;' there it is, sir."

I opened it by the same light. It was the expected letter, and required an immediate answer. So I returned, and letting myself in with my latch-key, went into the front office to write it.

Leah had not heard me come in. She was upstairs, deep in one of the two favourite ballads which now appeared to comprise all her collection. During office hours Leah was quiet as a mute; but in the evening she would generally croon over one of these old songs in an undertone, if she thought that I was out and she had the house to herself. As she was thinking now, for she sang out in full key, but in a doleful, monotonous sort of chant. Her voice was still very sweet, but had lost much of the power of its earlier days. One of these two songs was a Scotch fragment, beginning "Woe's me, for my heart is breaking;" the other was "Barbara Allen." Fragmentary also, apparently; for as Leah sang it there appeared to be neither beginning nor ending to it.

"And as she wandered up and down,
She heard the bells a-ringing,
And as they rang they seemed to say,

'Hard-hearted Barbara Allen.'

"She turned her body round and round,
She saw his corpse a-coming;
'Oh, put him down by this blade's side,
That I may gaze upon him!'

"The more she looked, the more she laughed,
The further she went from him;
Her friends they all cried out, 'For shame,
Hard-hearted Barbara Allen!'"

Whether this is the correct version of the ballad or not, I do not know; it was Leah's version. Many and many a time had I heard it; and I was hearing it again this evening, when there came a quiet ring at the door bell. My door was pushed to but not closed, and Leah came bustling down. Barbara Allen was going on still, but in a more subdued voice.

"Do Mr. Strange live here?" was asked, when the door was opened.

"Yes, he does," responded Leah. "He is out."

"Oh, I don't want him, ma'am. I only wanted to know if he lived here. What sort of a man is he?"

"What sort of a man?" repeated Leah. "A very nice man."

"Yes; but in looks, I mean."

"Well, he is very good-looking. Blue eyes, and dark hair, and straight features. Why do you want to know?"

"Ay, that's him. But I don't know about the colour of his eyes; I thought they was dark. Blue in one light and brown in another, maybe. A tallish, thinnish man."

"He's pretty tall; not what can be called a maypole. A little taller than Mr. Brightman was."

"Brightman and Strange, that's it? T'other's an old gent, I suppose?" was the next remark; while I sat, amused at the colloquy.

"He was not old. He is just dead. Have you any message?"

"No, I don't want to leave a message; that's not my business. He told me he lived here, and I came to make sure of it. A pleasant, sociable man, ain't he; no pride about him, though he is well off and goes cruising about in his own yacht."

"No pride at all with those he knows, whether it's friends or servants," returned Leah, forgetting her own pride, or at any rate her discretion, in singing my praises. "Never was anybody pleasanter than he. But as to a yacht—"

"Needn't say any more, ma'am; it's the same man. Takes a short pipe and a social dram occasionally, and makes no bones over it."

"What?" retorted Leah indignantly. "Mr. Strange doesn't take drams or smoke short pipes. If he just lights a cigar at night, when business is over, it's as much as he does. He's a gentleman."

"Ah," returned the visitor, his tones expressing a patronizing sort of contempt for Leah's belief in Mr. Strange: "gents that is gents indoors be not always gents out. Though I don't see why a man need be reproached with not being a gent because he smokes a honest clay pipe, and takes a drop short; and Mr. Strange does both, I can tell ye."

"Then I know he does not," repeated Leah. "And if you knew Mr. Strange, you wouldn't say it."

"If I knew Mr. Strange! Perhaps I know him as well as you do, ma'am. He don't come courting our Betsy without my knowing of him."

"What do you say he does?" demanded Leah, suppressing her wrath.

"Why, I say he comes after our Betsy; leastways, I'm a'most sure of it. And that's why I wanted to know whether this was his house or not, for I'm not a-going to have her trifled with. She's my only daughter, and as good as he is. And now that I've got my information I'll say good-night, ma'am."

Leah shut the door, and I opened mine. "Who was that, Leah?"

"My patience, Mr. Charles!" she exclaimed in astonishment. "I thought you were out, sir."

"I came in again. Who was that man at the door?"

"Who's to know, sir—and what does it matter?" cried Leah. "Some half-tipsy fellow who must have mistaken the house."

"He did not speak as though he were tipsy at all."

"You must have heard what he said, sir."

"I heard."

Leah turned away, but came back hesitatingly, a wistful expression in her eyes. I believe she looked upon me as a boy still, and cared for me as she did when I had been one. "It is not true, Mr. Charles?"

"Of course it is not true, Leah. I neither take drams short, nor go courting Miss Betsys."

"Why, no, sir, of course not. I believe I must be getting old and foolish, Mr. Charles. I should just like to wring that man's neck for his impudence!" she concluded, as she went upstairs again.

But what struck me was this: either that one of my clerks was playing pranks in my name—passing himself off as Mr. Strange, to appear great and consequential; and if so, I should uncommonly like to know which of them it was—or else that something was being enacted by those people who made the sorrow of Leah's life; that daughter of hers and the husband—as we will call him. For the voice at the door had sounded honest and the application genuine.

Posting my letter, I made the best of my way to Clapham. But I had my journey for nothing, and saw only Perry. His mistress had been getting much better, he said, but a day or two ago she had a relapse and was again confined to her room, unable to see anyone. Mr. Close had ordered her to be kept perfectly quiet. Annabel remained at Hastings.

"And what about that fright, Perry, that you were all so scared with a fortnight ago?" I asked, as he strolled by my side back to the iron gates: for it was useless for me to go in if I could not see Mrs. Brightman. "Has the house got over it yet?"

"Sir, it is in the house still," he gravely answered.

"Do you mean the scare?"

"I mean the ghost, sir. Poor master's spirit."

I turned to look at his face, plainly enough to be discerned in the dimness of the foggy night. It was no less grave than his words had been.

"The figure does not appear every night, sir; only occasionally," he resumed; "and always in the same place—in the corner by the wardrobe in Mrs. Brightman's bedroom. It stands there in its grave-clothes."

What with the dark trees about us, the weird evening, and Perry's shrinking tones, I slightly shivered, for all my unbelief.

"But, Perry, it is impossible, you know. There must be delusion somewhere. Mrs. Brightman's nerves have been unstrung by her husband's death."

"Hatch has seen it twice, Mr. Strange," he rejoined. "Nobody can suspect Hatch of having nerves. The last time was on Sunday night. It stood in its shroud, gazing at them—her and the mistress—with a mournful face. Master's very own face, sir, Hatch says, just as it used to be in life; only white and ghastly."

It was a ghastly subject, and the words haunted me all the way back to town. Once or twice I could have declared that I saw Mr. Brightman's face, pale and wan, gazing at me through the fog. Certainly Hatch had neither nerves nor fancies; no living woman within my circle of acquaintance possessed less. What did it all mean? Where could the mystery lie?

Stirring the fire into a blaze when I got into my room, I sat before it, and tried to think out the problem. But the more I tried, the more effectually it seemed to elude me.

With the whir-r-r that it always made, the clock on the mantelpiece began to strike ten. I started. At the same moment, the door opened slowly and noiselessly, and Leah glided in. Mysteriously, if I may so express it: my chamber candlestick carried in one hand, her shoes in the other. She was barefooted; and, unless I strangely mistook, her face was as ghastly as the one Perry had been speaking of that night.

Putting the candlestick on a side-table, slipping her feet into her shoes, and softly closing the door, she turned to me. Her lips trembled, her hands worked nervously; she seemed unable to speak.

"Why, Leah!" I exclaimed, "what is the matter?"

"Sir," she then said, in the deepest agitation; "I have seen to-night that which has almost frightened me to death. I don't know how to tell you about it. Watts has dropped asleep in his chair in the kitchen, and I took the opportunity to steal up here. I wouldn't let him hear it for the world. He is growing suspicious, fancying I'm a bit odd at times. He'd be true in this, I know, but it may be as well to keep it from him."

"But what is it, Leah?"

"When I saw him, I thought I should have dropped down dead," she went on, paying no attention to the question. "He stood there with just the same smile on his face that it used to wear. It was himself, sir; it was, indeed."

May I be forgiven for the folly that flashed over me. Occupied as my mind was with the apparition haunting the house at Clapham, what could I think but that Leah must have seen the same?

"You mean Mr. Brightman," I whispered.

"Good heavens!" she exclaimed, approaching nearer to me, whilst glancing over her shoulder as if in dread that the ghost were following her: "does he come again, Mr. Charles? Have you seen him? Is he in the house?"

"No, no; but I thought you meant that, Leah. Who is it that you have seen?"

"Mr. Tom, sir. Captain Heriot."

CHAPTER X

PROWLING ABOUT

So the blow had fallen. What we were dreading had come to pass. Tom Heriot was back again.

I sat half-paralyzed with terror. Leah stood before me on the hearthrug, pouring out her unwelcome disclosure with eager words now that her first emotion had subsided. She went on with her tale more coherently, but in undertones.

"After you had gone out this evening, Mr. Charles, I was in the kitchen, when one of those small handfuls of gravel I dread to hear rattled against the window. 'Nancy,' I groaned, my heart failing me. I could not go to the door, lest Watts should come up and see me, for I expected him back every minute; and, sure enough, just then I heard his ring. I gave him the Law Times, as you bade me, sir, telling him he was to take it round to Mr. Lake at once. When he was gone I ran up to the door and looked about, and saw Nancy in the shadow of the opposite house, where she mostly stands when waiting for me. I could not speak to her then, but told her I would try and come out presently. Her eldest boy, strolling away with others at play, had been run over by a cab somewhere in Lambeth; he was thought to be dying; and Nancy had come begging and praying me with tears to go with her to see him."

"And you went, I suppose, Leah. Go on."

"You know her dreadful life, Mr. Charles, its sorrows and its misery; how could I find it in my heart to deny her? When Watts came back from Mr. Lake's, I had my bonnet and shawl on. 'What, going out?' said he, in surprise, and rather crossly—for I had promised him a game at cribbage. 'Well,' I answered, 'I've just remembered that I have to fetch those curtains home to-night that went to be dyed; and I must hasten or the shop may be shut up. I've put your supper ready in case they keep me waiting, but I dare say I shall not be long.'"

To attempt to hurry Leah through her stories when once she had entered upon them, was simply waste of words; so I listened with all the patience I had at command.

"The boy had been carried into a house down Lambeth way, and the doctor said he must not be moved; but the damage was not as bad, sir, as was at first thought, and I cheered Nancy up a bit by saying he would get all right and well. I think he will. Leaving her with the lad, I was coming back alone, when I missed my way. The streets are puzzling just there, and I am not familiar with them. I thought I'd ask at a book-stall, and went towards it. A sailor was standing outside, fingering the books and talking to somebody inside that I couldn't see. Mr. Charles, I had got within a yard of him, when I saw who it was— and the fright turned me sick and faint."

"You mean the sailor?"

"Yes, sir, the sailor. It was Captain Heriot, disguised. Oh, sir, what is to be done? The boy that I have often nursed upon my knee—what will become of him if he should be recognised?"

The very thought almost turned me sick and faint also, as Leah expressed it. How could Tom be so foolhardy? An escaped convict, openly walking about the streets of London!

"Did he see you, Leah?"

"No, sir; I stole away quickly; and the next turning brought me into the right road again."

"How did he look?"

"I saw no change in him, sir. He wore a round glazed hat, and rough blue clothes, with a large sailor collar, open at the throat. His face was not hidden at all. It used to be clean-shaved, you know, except the whiskers; but now the whiskers are gone, and he wears a beard. That's all the difference I could see in him."

Could this possibly be Tom? I scarcely thought so; scarcely thought that even he would be as reckless of consequences.

"Ah, Mr. Charles, do you suppose I could be mistaken in him?" cried Leah, in answer to my doubt. "Indeed, sir, it was Captain Heriot. He and the man inside—the master of the shop, I suppose—seemed talking as if they knew one another, so Mr. Tom may have been there before. Perhaps he is hiding in the neighbourhood."

"Hiding!" I repeated, in pain.

"Well, sir—"

"Leah! have you gone up to bed?"

The words came floating up the staircase in Watts's deep voice. Leah hurried to the door.

"I came up to bring the master's candle," she called out, as she went down. "If you hadn't gone to sleep, you might have heard him ring for it."

All night I lay awake, tormented on the score of Tom Heriot. Now looking at the worst side of things, now trying to see them at their best, the hours dragged along, one after the other, until daybreak. In spite of Leah's statement and her own certainty in the matter, my mind refused to believe that the sailor she had seen could be Tom. Tom was inconceivably daring; but not daring enough for this. He would have put on a more complete disguise. At least, I thought so.

But if indeed it was Tom—why, then there was no hope. He would inevitably be recaptured. And this meant I knew not what of heavier punishment for himself; and for the rest of us further exposure, reflected disgrace, and mental pain.

Resolving to go myself at night and reconnoitre, I turned to my day's work. In the course of the morning a somewhat curious thing happened. The old saying says that "In looking for one thing you find another," and it was exemplified in the present instance. I was searching Mr. Brightman's small desk for a paper that I thought might be there, and, as I suppose, accidentally touched a spring, for the lower part of the desk suddenly loosened, and I found it had a false bottom to it. Lifting the upper portion, I found several small deeds of importance, letters and other papers; and lying on the top of all was a small packet, inscribed "Lady Clavering," in Mr. Brightman's writing.

No doubt the letters she was uneasy about, and which I had hitherto failed to find. But now, what was I to do? Give them back to her? Well, no, I thought not. At any rate, not until I had glanced over them. Their being in this secret division proved the importance attaching to them.

Untying the narrow pink ribbon that held them together, there fell out a note of Sir Ralph Clavering's, addressed to Mr. Brightman. It was dated just before his death, and ran as follows:

I send you the letters I told you I had discovered. Read them, and keep them safely. Should trouble arise with her after my death, confront her with them. Use your own discretion about showing them or not to my nephew Edmund. But should she acquiesce in the just will I have made, and when all things are settled on a sure foundation, then destroy the letters, unseen by any eye save your own; I do not wish to expose her needlessly.—R. C.

Lady Clavering had not acquiesced in the will, and she was still going on with her threatened and most foolish action. I examined the letters. Some were written to her; not by her husband, though; some were written by her: and, take them for all in all, they were about as damaging a series as any it was ever my fate to see.

"The senseless things these women are!" thought I. "How on earth came she to preserve such letters as these?"

I sent a messenger for Sir Edmund Clavering. Mr. Brightman was to use his own discretion: I hardly thought any was left to me. It was more Sir Edmund's place to see them than mine. He came at once.

"By George!" he exclaimed, when he had read two or three of them, his handsome face flushing, his brow knit in condemnation. "What a despicable woman! We have the cause in our own hands now."

"Yes; she cannot attempt to carry it further."

We consulted a little as to the best means of making the truth known to Lady Clavering—an unthankful office that would fall to me—and Sir Edmund rose to leave.

"Keep the letters safely," he said; almost in the very words Sir Ralph had written. "Do not bring them within a mile of her hands: copies, if she pleases, as many as she likes. And when things are upon a safe footing, as my uncle says, and there's no longer anything to fear from her, then they can be destroyed."

"Yes. Of course, Sir Edmund," I continued, in some hesitation, "she must be spared to the world. This discovery must be held sacred between us—"

"Do you mean that as a caution?" he interrupted in surprise. "Why, Strange, what do you take me for?"

He clasped my hand with a half-laugh, and went out. Yes, Lady Clavering had contrived to damage herself, but it would never transpire to her friends or her enemies.

Leah had noticed the name of the street containing the book-stall, and when night came I put on a discarded old great-coat and slouching hat, and set out for it. It was soon found: a narrow, well-frequented street, leading out of the main thoroughfare, full of poor shops, patronized by still poorer customers.

The book-stall was on the right, about half-way down the street. Numbers of old books lay upon a board outside, lighted by a flaring, smoking tin lamp. Inside the shop they seemed chiefly to deal in tobacco and snuff. Every now and then the master of the shop—whose name, according to the announcement above the shop, must be Caleb Lee—came to the door to look about him, or to answer the questions of some outside customer touching the books. But as yet I saw no sign of Tom Heriot.

Opposite the shop, on the other side the way, was a dark entry; into that entry I ensconced myself to watch.

Tired of this at last, I marched to the end of the street, crossed over, strolled back on the other side the way, and halted at the book-stall. There I began to turn the books about: anything to while away the time.

"Looking for any book in particular, sir?"

I turned sharply at the question, which came from the man Lee. The voice sounded familiar to my ear. Where had I heard it?

"You have not an old copy of the 'Vicar of Wakefield,' I suppose?"—the work flashing into my mind by chance.

"No, sir. I had one, but it was bought last week. There's 'Fatherless Fanny,' sir; that's a very nice book; it was thought a deal of some years ago. And there's the 'Water Witch,' by Cooper. That's good, too."

I remembered the voice now. It was that of Leah's mysterious visitor of the night before, who had been curiously inquisitive about me. Recognition came upon me with a shock, and opened up a new fear.

Taking the "Water Witch"—for which I paid fourpence—I walked on again. Could it be possible that Tom Heriot was passing himself off for me? Why, this would be the veriest folly of all. But no; that was altogether impossible.

Anxious and uneasy, I turned about again and again. The matter ought to be set at rest, yet I knew not how to do it.

I entered the shop, which contained two small counters: the one covered with papers, the other with smoking gear. Lee stood behind the former, serving a customer, who was inquiring for last week's number of the Fireside Friend. Behind the other counter sat a young girl, pretty and modest. I turned to her.

"Will you give me a packet of bird's-eye?"

"Yes, sir," she answered in pleasant tones; and, opening a drawer, handed me the tobacco, ready wrapped up. It would do for Watts. Bird's-eye, I knew, was his favourite mixture.

"Thank you, sir," she said, returning me the change out of a florin. "Anything else, sir?"

"Yes; a box of wax matches."

But the matches were not to be found, and the girl appealed to her father.

"Wax matches," returned the man from across the shop. "Why, they are on the shelf behind you, Betsy."

The matches were found, the girl took the money for them, and thanked me again. All very properly and modestly. The girl was evidently as modest and well-behaved as a girl could be.

So that was Betsy! But who was it that was courting her in my name? One of my office clerks—or Captain Thomas Heriot?

Captain Thomas Heriot did not make his appearance, and I began to hope that Leah had been mistaken. It grew late. I was heartily tired, and turned to make my way home.

Why I should have looked round I cannot tell, but I did look round just as I reached the end of the street. Looming slowly up in the distance was a sailor, with a sailor's swaying walk, and he turned into the shop.

I turned back also, all my pulses quickened. I did not follow him in, for we might have betrayed ourselves. I stood outside, occupied with the old books again, and pulled the collar of my coat well up, and my hat well down. Not here must there be any mutual recognition.

How long did he mean to stay there? For ever? He and Lee seemed to be at the back of the shop, talking together. I could not hear the voices sufficiently to judge whether one of them was that of Tom Heriot.

He was coming now! Out he came, puffing at a fresh-lighted pipe, his glazed hat at the back of his head, his face lifted to the world.

"Tell you we shall, master. Fine to-morrow? not a bit of it. Rain as sure as a gun. This dampness in the air is a safe sign on't. Let a sailor alone for knowing the weather."

"At sea, maybe," retorted Caleb Lee. "But I never yet knew a sailor who wasn't wrong about the weather on shore. Good-night, sir."

"Good-night to you, master," responded the sailor.

He lounged slowly away. It was not Tom Heriot. About his build and his fair complexion, but shorter than Tom. A real, genuine Jack-tar, this, unmistakably. Was he the man Leah had seen? This one wore no beard, but bushy, drooping whiskers.

"Looking for another book, sir?"

In momentary confusion, I caught up the book nearest to hand. It proved to be "Fatherless Fanny," and I said I'd take it. While searching for the money, I remarked that the sailor, just gone away, had said we should have rain to-morrow.

"I don't see that he is obliged to be right, though he was so positive over it," returned the man. "I hate a rainy day: spoils our custom. Thankye, sir. Sixpence this time. That's right."

"Do many sailors frequent this neighbourhood?"

"Not many; we've a sprinkling of 'em sometimes. They come over here from the Kent Road way."

Well, and what else could I ask? Nothing. And just then a voice came from the shop.

"Father," called out Miss Betsy, "is it not time to shut up?"

"What do you ask? Getting a little deaf, sir, in my old age. Coming, Betsy."

He turned into the shop, and I walked away for the night: hoping, ah! how earnestly, that Leah had been mistaken.

"Mr. Strange, my lord."

It was the following evening. Restlessly anxious about Tom Heriot, I betook myself to Gloucester Place as soon as dinner was over, to ask Major Carlen whether he had learnt anything further. The disreputable old man was in some way intimate with one or two members of the Government. To my surprise, Sanders, Lord Level's servant, opened the door to me, and showed me to the dining-room. Lord Level sat there alone over his after-dinner claret.

"You look as if you hardly believed your eyes, Charles," he laughed as he shook hands. "Sit down. Glasses, Sanders."

"And surprised I may well look to see you here, when I thought you were in Paris," was my answer.

"We came over to-day; got here an hour ago. Blanche was very ill in crossing and has gone to bed."

"Where is Major Carlen?"

"Oh, he is off to Jersey to see his sister, Mrs. Guy. At least, that is what he said; but he is not famous for veracity, you know, and it is just as likely that he may be catching the mail train at London Bridge en route for Homburg, as the Southampton train from Waterloo. Had you been half an hour earlier, you might have had the pleasure of assisting at his departure. I have taken this house for a month, and paid him in advance," added Lord Level, as much as to say that the Major was not altogether out of funds.

A short silence ensued. The thoughts of both of us were no doubt busy. Level, his head bent, was slowly turning his wine-glass round by its stem.

"Charles," he suddenly said, in a half-whisper, "what of Tom Heriot?"

I hardly knew how to take the question.

"I know nothing more of him," was my answer.

"Is he in London, think you? Have you heard news of him, in any way?"

Now I could not say that I had heard news: for Leah's information was not news, if (as I hoped) she was mistaken. And I judged it better not to speak of it to Lord Level until the question was set at rest. Why torment him needlessly?

"I wrote you word what Major Carlen said: that Tom was one of those who escaped. The ship was wrecked upon an uninhabited island, believed to be that of Tristan d'Acunha. After a few days some of the convicts contrived to steal a boat and make good their escape. Of course they were in hope of being picked up by some homeward-bound ship, and may already have reached England."

"Look here," said Lord Level, after a pause: "that island lies, no doubt, in the track of ships bound to the colonies, but not in the track of those homeward-bound. So the probability is, that if the convicts were sighted and picked up, they would be carried further from England, not brought back to it."

I confess that this view had not occurred to me; in fact, I knew very little about navigation, or the courses taken by ships. It served to strengthen my impression that Leah had been in error.

"Are you sure of that?" I asked him.

"Sure of what?" returned Lord Level.

"That the island would be out of the track of homeward-bound vessels."

"Quite sure. Homeward-bound vessels come round Cape Horn. Those bound for the colonies go by way of the Cape of Good Hope."

"My visit here to-night was to ask Major Carlen whether he had heard any further particulars."

"I think he heard a few more to-day," said Lord Level. "The Vengeance was wrecked, it seems, on this island. It is often sighted by ships going to the colonies, and the captain was in hope that his signals from the island would be seen, and some ship would bear down to them. In vain. After the convicts—five of them, I believe—had made their escape, he determined to send off the long-boat, in charge of the chief officer, to the nearest Australian coast, for assistance. On the 10th of December the boat set sail, and on Christmas Day was picked up by the Vernon, which reached Melbourne the last day of the year."

"But how do you know all these details?" I interrupted in surprise.

"They have been furnished to the Government, and Carlen was informed of them this morning," replied Lord Level. "On the following day, the 1st of January, the ship Lightning sailed from Melbourne for England; she was furnished with a full account of the wreck of the Vengeance and what succeeded to it. The Lightning made a good passage home, and on her arrival laid her reports before the Government. That's how it is."

"And what of the escaped convicts?"

"Nothing is known of them. The probability is that they were picked up by an outward-bound ship and landed in one of the colonies. If not, they must have perished at sea."

"And if they were so picked up and landed, I suppose they would have reached England by this time?"

"Certainly—seeing that the Lightning has arrived. And the convicts had some days' start of the long-boat. I hope Tom Heriot will not make his way here!" fervently spoke Lord Level. "The consequences would three-parts kill my wife. No chance of keeping it from her in such a hullabaloo as would attend his recapture."

"I cannot think how you have managed to keep it from her as it is."

"Well, I have been watchful and cautious—and we have not mixed much with the gossiping English. What! are you going, Charles?"

"Yes, I have an engagement," I answered, as we both rose. "Good-night. Give my love to Blanche. Tell her that Charley will see her to-morrow if he can squeeze out a minute's leisure for it."

Taking up the old coat I had left in the passage, I went out with it on my arm, hailed a cab that was crossing Portman Square and was driven to Lambeth. There I recommenced my watch upon the book-stall and the street containing it, not, however, disclosing myself to Lee that night. But nothing was to be seen of Tom Heriot.

CHAPTER XI

MRS BRIGHTMAN

"Sur this coms hoppin youle excuse blundurs bein no skollerd sur missis is worse and if youle com ive got som things to tell you I darnt keep um any longer your unbil servint emma hatch but doant say to peri as i sent."

This remarkable missive was delivered to me by the late afternoon post. The schoolmaster must have been abroad when Hatch received her education.

I had intended to spend the evening with Blanche. It was the day subsequent to her arrival from France with Lord Level, and I had not yet seen her. But this appeared to be something like an imperative summons, and I resolved to attend to it.

"The more haste, the less speed." The proverb exemplifies itself very frequently in real life. Ordering my dinner to be served half an hour earlier than usual, I had no sooner eaten it than a gentleman called and detained me. It was close upon eight o'clock when I reached Clapham.

Perry, the butler, received me as usual. "Oh, sir, such a house of sickness as it is!" he exclaimed, leading the way to the drawing-room. "My mistress is in bed with brain-fever. They were afraid of it yesterday, but it has quite shown itself to-day. And Miss Annabel is still at Hastings. I say she ought to be sent for; Hatch says not, and tells me to mind my own business: but—"

Hatch herself interrupted the sentence. She came into the room and ordered Perry out of it. The servants, even Perry, had grown into the habit of obeying her. Closing the door, she advanced to me as I stood warming my hands at the fire, for it was a sharp night.

"Mr. Strange, sir," she began in a low tone, "did you get that epistle from me?"

I nodded.

"You've not been down here much lately, sir. Last night I thought you might come, the night afore I thought it. The last time you did come you never stepped inside the door."

"Where is the use of coming, Hatch, when I am always told that Mrs. Brightman cannot see me—and that Miss Annabel remains at Hastings?"

"And a good thing that she do remain there," returned Hatch. "Perry, the gaby, says, 'Send for Miss Annabel: why don't you write for Miss Annabel?' But that his brains is no bigger than one o' them she-gooses' on Newland Common, he'd have found out why afore now. Sir," continued Hatch, changing her tone, "I want to know what I be to do. I'm not a person of edication or book-learning, but my wits is alive, and they serves me instead. For this two or three days past, sir, I've been thinking that I ought to tell out to somebody responsible what it is that's the matter with my missis, and I know of nobody nearer the family than you, sir. There's her brother, in course, at the Hall, Captain Chantrey, but my missis has held herself aloof from him and Lady Grace, and I know she'd be in a fine way if I spoke to him. Three or four days ago I said to myself, 'The first time I see Mr. Strange, I'll tell him the truth.' Last night she was worse than she has been at all, quite raving. I got frightened, which is a complaint I'm not given to, and resolved not to let another day pass, and then, whether she lived or died, the responsibility would not lie upon my back."

Straightening myself, I stood gazing at Hatch. She had spoken rapidly. If I had caught all the words, I did not catch their meaning.

"Yes?" I said mechanically.

"And so, with morning light, sir, I wrote you that epistle."

"Yes, yes; never mind all that. What about Mrs. Brightman?"

Hatch dropped her voice to a lower and more mysterious whisper. "Sir, my missis gives way, she do."

"Gives way," I repeated, gazing at Hatch, and still unable to see any meaning in the words. "What do you say she does?"

Hatch took a step forward, which brought her on the hearthrug, close to me. "Yes, sir; missis gives way."

"Gives way to what?" I reiterated. "To her superstitious fancies?"

"No, sir, to stimilinks."

"To—" The meaning, in spite of Hatch's obscure English, dawned upon me now. A cold shiver ran through me. Annabel's mother! and honoured Henry Brightman's wife!

"She takes stimulants!" I gasped.

"Yes, sir; stimilinks," proceeded Hatch. "A'most any sort that comes anigh her. She likes wine and brandy best; but failing them, she'll drink others."

Question upon question rose to my mind. Had it been known to Mr. Brightman? Had it been a prolonged habit? Was it deeply indulged in? But Annabel was her child, and my lips refused to utter them.

"It has been the very plague of my life and my master's to keep it private these many months past," continued Hatch. "'Hatch does this in the house, and Hatch does the other,' the servants cry. Yes; but my master knew why I set up my authority; and missis knew it too. It was to screen her."

"How could she have fallen into the habit?"

"It has grown upon her by degrees, sir. A little at first, and a little, and then a little more. As long as master was here, she was kept tolerably in check, but since his death there has been nobody to restrain her, except me. Whole days she has been in her room, shutting out Miss Annabel, under the excuse of headaches or lowness, drinking all the time; and me there to keep the door. I'm sure the black stories I have gone and invented, to pacify Miss Annabel and put her off the right scent, would drive a parson to his prayers."

"Then Miss Annabel does not know it?"

"She do now," returned Hatch. "The first night there was that disturbance in the house about missis seeing the ghost, her room was thrown open in the fright, and all the house got in. I turned the servants out: I dared not turn out Miss Annabel, and she couldn't fail to see that her mother was the worse for drink. So then I told her some, and Mr. Close told her more next morning."

Annabel's strange grief, so mysterious to me, was accounted for now. Hatch continued:

"You see now, sir, why Miss Annabel has been kept so much at Hastings. Master would never have her at home for long together, afeared her mother might betray herself. He wanted to keep the child in ignorance of it, as long as it was possible. Miss Brightman knew it. She found it out the last time she was visiting here; and she begged my missis on her bended knees to be true to herself and leave it off. Missis promised—and such a bout of crying they two had together afore Miss Lucy went away! For a time she did get better; but it all came back again. And then came master's death—and the shock and grief of that has made her give way more than she ever did. And there it is, sir. The secret's got too weighty for me; I couldn't keep it to myself any longer."

"Perry says Mrs. Brightman is now lying ill with brain-fever."

"We call it brain-fever to the servants, me and Mr. Close; it's near enough for them," was Hatch's cool reply. "The curious thing is that Perry don't seem to suspect; he sees more of his missis than the rest do, and many a time must have noticed her shaking. Last night her fit of shaking was dreadful—and her fever too, for the matter of that. She is as close as she well can be upon that disorder that comes of drink. If it goes on to a climax, nothing can save the disgrace from coming out downstairs."

Nothing could or would save it, in my opinion, downstairs or up, indoors or out. What a calamity!

"But she is a trifle better to-night," continued Hatch. "The medicines have taken effect at last, and put her into a deep sleep, or else I couldn't be talking here."

"Did you invent the episode of Mr. Brightman's ghost, Hatch, by way of accounting for Mrs. Brightman's state to the servants?" I inquired.

"I invent it!" returned Hatch. "I didn't invent it. My missis did see it. Not, I take it, that there was any ghost to see, in one sense; but when these poor creatures is in the shakes, they fancy they see all kinds of things—monkeys and demons, and such-like. I can't believe it was master. I don't see why he should come back, being a good man; and good men that die in peace be pretty sure to rest in their graves. Still, I'd not be too sure. It may be that he comes back, as my missis fancies, to silently reproach her. It's odd that she always sees him in the same place, and in his shroud. Several times she has seen him now, and her description of how he looks never varies. Nothing will ever persuade her, sick or well, that it is fancy."

"You have seen him also, I hear?"

"Not I," said Hatch. "I have upheld what my missis says. For which was best, Mr. Strange, sir—to let the servants think she is shaking and raving from fear of a ghost, or to let 'em get to suspect her the worse for drink?"

Hatch's policy had no doubt been wise in this. I told her so.

"I have seen the shakes before to-day; was used to 'em when a child, as may be said," resumed Hatch. "I had a step-uncle, sir, mother's half-brother, who lived next door to us; he was give to drink, and he had 'em now and then. Beer were his chief weakness; wine is missis's. If that step-uncle of mine had been put to stand head downwards in a beer barrel, Mr. Charles, he'd not have thought he had enough. He'd be always seeing things, he would; blue and red and green imps that crawled up his bed-posts, and horrid little black devils. He used to start out of doors and run away for fear of 'em. Once he ran out stark naked, all but his shoes; he tore past the cottages all down the village, and flung himself into the pond opposite the stocks. All the women watching him from their doors and windows followed after him. The men thought it were at least a mad dog broke loose, seeing the women in pursuit like that; whereas it were nothing but my step-uncle in one of his bouts—stripped. Mrs. Brightman would never do such a thing as that, being a lady; but they be all pretty much alike for sense when the fit is on 'em."

"And Mr. Brightman knew of this, you say? Knew that she was given to—to like stimulants?"

"He couldn't be off knowing of it, sir, habiting, as he did, the same rooms: and it has just bittered his life out. She has never had a downright bad attack, like this one, therefore we could hide it from the servants and from Miss Annabel, but it couldn't be hided from him. He first spoke to me about it six or seven months ago, when he was having an iron bedstead put up in the little room close to hers; until then he had made believe to me not to see it. Sometimes I know he talked to her, all lovingly and persuasively, and I would see her with red eyes afterwards. I once heard her say, 'I will try, Henry; indeed I will;' and I do believe she did. But she got worse, and then master spoke to Mr. Close."

"Has it been long growing upon her?" I asked, in a low voice.

"Sir," returned Hatch, looking at me with her powerful eyes, "it has been growing for years and years. I think it came on, first, from idleness—"

"From idleness!"

"I mean what I say, sir. She married master for a home, as it were, and she didn't care for him. She cared for somebody else—but things wouldn't work convenient, and they had to part. Miss Emma Chantrey was high-born and beautiful, but she had no money, and the gentleman had no money either, so it would not do. It was all over and done with long before she knew Mr. Brightman. Well, sir, she married and come home here. But she never liked the place; commercial, she said, these neighbourhoods was, round London, and the people were beneath her. So she wouldn't visit, and she wouldn't sew nor read; she'd just sit all day long with her hands afore her, a-doing of nothing. I saw that as soon as I took service here. 'Wait,' said I to myself, 'till the baby comes.' Well, it came, sweet little Miss Annabel, but it didn't make a pin's difference: missis got a maid for it, and then a governess, and turned her over to them. No more babies followed; pity but what a score of 'em had; they might have roused her from her apathy."

"But surely she did not give way, as you call it, then?"

"No, not then. She was just ate up with weariness; she found no pleasure in life, and she did no work in it; when morning broke she'd wish the day was over; and when night came she'd wish it was morning; and so the years went by. Then she got to say—it come on quite imperceptible—'Hatch, get me a glass of wine; I'm so low and exhausted.' And I used to get her one, thinking nothing. She took it then, just because she wanted something to rouse her, and didn't know what. That was the beginning of it, Mr. Charles."

"A very unfortunate beginning."

"But," continued Hatch, "after a while, she got to like the wine, and in course o' time she couldn't do without it; a glass now and a glass then between her meals, besides what she took with them, and it was a great deal; pretty nigh a bottle a-day I fancy, altogether. Master couldn't make out how it was his wine went, and he spoke sharp to Perry; and when missis found that, she took to have some in on her own account, unbeknowing to him. Then it grew to brandy. Upon the slightest excuse, just a stitch in her side, or her finger aching, she would say, 'Hatch, I must have half a glass of hot brandy-and-water.' Folks don't stop at the first liquor, sir, when it gets to that pitch; my step-uncle would have swallowed vitriol sooner than have kept to beer."

"Hatch, this is a painful tale."

"And I've not finished of it," was Hatch's response. "Missis had an illness a year or eighteen months back; I dare say you remember it, sir. Weak enough she was when she began to get about; some people thought she wouldn't live. 'She must take stimilinks to strengthen her,' says Close. 'She don't want stimilinks,' says I; 'she'll get better without 'em;' for she was a taking of 'em then in secret, though he didn't know it. 'Mrs. Brightman must take stimilinks,' says he to master. 'Whatever you thinks necessary,' returns master—though if he hadn't begun to suspect then, it's odd to me. And my missis was not backward to take Close's stimilinks, and she took her own as well; and that I look upon as the true foundation of it all; it might never have grown into a habit but for that; and since then matters have been going from bad to worse. It's a dangerous plan for doctors to order stimilinks to weak people," added Hatch reflectively; "evil comes of it sometimes."

I had heard that opinion before; more than once. I had heard Mr. Brightman express it to a client, who was recovering from an illness. Was he thinking of his wife?

"And for the last six months or so my missis has been getting almost beyond control," resumed Hatch; "one could hardly keep her within bounds. Me and master tried everything. We got Miss Annabel out of the way, not letting her come home but for two or three days at a time, and them days—my patience! if I hadn't to watch missis like a cat! She didn't wish to exceed in the daytime when Miss Annabel was here, though she would at night; but you know, sir, these poor creatures can't keep their resolves; and if she once got a glass early, then all her prudence went to the winds. I did my best; master did his best; and she'd listen, and be reasonable, and say she'd touch nothing. But upon the least temptation she'd give way. My belief is, she couldn't help it; when it comes to this stage it's just a disease. A disease, Mr. Charles, like the measles or the yellow jaundice, and they can't put it from 'em if they would."

True.

"On the Thursday night, it was the Thursday before the master died, there was a quarrel," Hatch went on. "Mrs. Brightman was not fit to appear at the dinner-table, and her dinner was sent up to her room, and master came upstairs afterwards, and they had words. Master said he should send Miss Annabel to Hastings in the morning and keep her there, for it would be impossible to hide matters from her longer if she stayed at home. Mrs. Brightman, who was not very bad, resented that, and called him harsh names: generally speaking, she was as humble as could be, knowing herself in the wrong and feeling ashamed of it. They parted in anger. Master was as good as his word; he sent Miss Annabel with Sarah down to Hastings on the Friday morning to Miss Brightman. In the evening, when he came home to dinner, missis was again the worse for drink. But on the Saturday morning she was up betimes, afore the household even, and had ordered the carriage, and went whirling off with me to the station to take the first train for Hastings. 'I shall return on Monday and bring back Annabel,' she said to master, when she was stepping into the carriage at the door, and he ran out to ask where she was going, for he had not seen nor heard nothing about it. 'Very well,' said he in a whisper; 'only come back as you ought to come.' Mr. Charles, I think those were the only words that passed between them after the quarrel."

"You mean the quarrel on the Thursday night?"

"Yes, sir; there was no other quarrel. We went to the Queen's Hotel. And on the Sunday, if you remember, you came down to tell us of the master's sudden death. Mrs. Brightman was ill that morning, really ill, I mean, with one of her dreadful headaches—which she did have at times, and when she didn't they was uncommon convenient things for me to fall back upon if I needed an excuse for her. She had meant to go to church, but was not able. She had had too much on the Saturday night, though she was always more prudent out than at home, and was worried in mind besides. But, to be sure, how she did take on about master's death when alone with me. They had parted bad friends: leastways had not made it up after the quarrel; she knew how aggravating she had been to him in it, and a notion got hold of her that he might have poisoned himself. When she learnt the rights of it, that he had died peaceful and natural, she didn't get much happier. She was perpetually saying to me, as the days went on, that her conduct had made him miserable. She drank then to drown care; she fancied she saw all sorts of things, and when it came to master's ghost—"

"She could not have been sober when she fancied that."

"Nor was she," returned Hatch. "Half-and-half like; had enough to betray herself to Miss Annabel. 'Now don't you go and contradict about the ghost,' I says to her, poor child; 'better let the kitchen think it's a ghost than brandy-and-water.' Frightful vexed and ashamed missis was, when she grew sober, to find that Miss Annabel knew the truth. She told her she must go to her aunt at Hastings for a time: Mr. Close, he said the same. Miss Annabel would not go; she said it was not right that she should leave her mother, and there was a scene; miss sobbing and crying, mistress angry and commanding; but it ended in her going. 'I don't want no spies upon me,' says missis to me, 'and she shall stop at Hastings for good.' Since then she has been giving way unbearable, and the end of it is, she has got the shakes."

What a life! What a life it had been for Mr. Brightman! Lennard had thought of late that he appeared as a man who bore about him some hidden grief! Once, when he had seemed low-spirited, I asked whether anything was amiss. "We all have our trials, Charles; some more, some less," was the answer, in tones that rather shut me up.

Hatch would fain have talked until now: if wine was her mistress's weakness, talking was hers; but she was interrupted by the arrival of Mr. Close, and had to attend him upstairs. On his return he came into the drawing-room.

"This is a disagreeable business, Mr. Strange. Hatch tells me she has informed you of the true nature of the case."

A disagreeable business! The light words, the matter-of-fact tone seemed as a mockery. The business nearly overwhelmed me.

"When you met me the other night, at the gate, and spoke of Mrs. Brightman's illness, I was uncertain how to answer you," continued Mr. Close. "I thought it probable you might be behind the curtain, connected as you are with the family, but I was not sure."

"I never had the faintest suspicion of such a thing, until Hatch's communication to me to-night. She says her young mistress, even, did not know of it."

"No; they have contrived to keep it from Annabel."

"Will Mrs. Brightman recover?"

"From this illness? oh dear yes! She is already in a fair way for it, having dropped into the needed sleep; which is all we want. If you mean will she recover from the habit—why, I cannot answer you. It has obtained a safe hold upon her."

"What is to be done?"

"What can be done?" returned the surgeon. "Mrs. Brightman is her own mistress, subject to no control, and has a good income at command. She may go on drinking to the end."

Go on drinking to the end! What a fearful thought! what a fearful life! Could nothing be done to prevent it; to recall her to herself; to her responsibility for this world and the next?

"I have seen much of these cases," continued Mr. Close; "few medical men more. Before I came into this practice I was assistant-surgeon to one of the debtors' prisons up in town: no school equal to that in all Europe for initiating a man into the mysteries of the disorder."

"Ay, so I believe. But can Mrs. Brightman's case be like those cases?"

"Why should it differ from them? The same habits have induced it. Of course, she is not yet as bad as some of them are, but unless she pulls up she will become so. Her great chance, her one chance, I may say, would be to place herself under some proper control. But this would require firm resolution and self-denial. To begin with, she would have to leave her home."

"This cannot be a desirable home for Annabel."

"No. Were she my child, she should not return to it."

"What is to be done when she recovers from this attack?"

"In what way?"

In what way, truly! My brain was at work over the difficulties of the future. Was Mrs. Brightman to live on in this, her home, amidst her household of curious servants, amidst the prying neighbours, all of whom would revel in a tale of scandal?

"When she is sufficiently well she should have change of air," proceeded the doctor, "and get her nerves braced up. Otherwise she may be seeing that ghost for six months to come. A strange fancy that, for her to take up—and yet, perhaps, not so very strange, taking all things into consideration. She is full of remorse, thinking she might have done her duty better by her husband, made him less unhappy, and all that. Mrs. Brightman is a gentlewoman of proud, elevated instincts: she would be only too thankful to leave off this demoralizing habit; in a way, I believe she strives to do it, but it is stronger than she is."

"It has become worse, Hatch says, since Mr. Brightman died."

"Undoubtedly," concluded Mr. Close. "She had taken it to drown care."

CHAPTER XII

MY LORD AND MY LADY

The breakfast-table was laid in Gloucester Place, waiting for Lord and Lady Level. It was the day following the one recorded in the last chapter. A clear, bright morning, the sun shining hotly.

Blanche came in, wearing a dainty white dress. Her face, though thin, was fair and lovely as ever; her eyes were as blue and brilliant. Ringing for the coffee to be brought in, she began turning over the letters on the table: one for herself, which she saw was from Mrs. Guy; three for her husband. Of these, one bore the Paris postmark.

"Here is a letter from Paris, Archibald," she said to him as he entered. "I think from Madame Sauvage; it is like her writing. I hope it is to say that she has sent off the box."

"That you may regain possession of your finery," rejoined Lord Level, with a light, pleasant laugh. "Eh, Blanche?"

"Well, my new lace mantle is in it. So stupid of Timms to have made the mistake!"

"So it was. I dare say the box is on its road by this time."

Blanche began to pour out the coffee. Lord Level had gone to the window, and was looking up and down the street. As he took his seat to begin breakfast, he pushed the letters away idly without opening them, and remarked upon the fineness of the morning.

They were fairly good friends, these two; always courteous, save when Blanche was seized with a fit of jealousy, persuading herself, rightly or wrongly, that she had cause for it. Then she would be cross, bitter, snappish. Once in a way Lord Level retorted in kind; though on the whole he was patient and gentle with her. In the midst of it all she loved him passionately at heart, and sometimes let him know it.

"As it is so fine a day, Archibald, you might take me to Kensington, to call on Mrs. Page Reid, this afternoon. She sent us her address, you know."

"I would rather not, Blanche, unless you particularly wish it. I don't care to keep up Mrs. Page Reid's acquaintance. She's good for nothing but to talk scandal."

"I do not much care for her either," acknowledged Blanche. "We are not in the least obliged to renew her acquaintance."

"I will take you somewhere else instead," said he, pleased at her acquiescence. "We will go out after luncheon and make an afternoon of it—like Darby and Joan."

Presently, when breakfast was nearly over, Blanche opened her letter from Mrs. Guy; reading out scraps of it to her husband. It told of Major Carlen's arrival—so that he had really gone to Jersey. Then she took up the Times. An unusual thing for her to do. She did not care for newspapers, and Lord Level did not have them sent to him when in Paris: he saw the English journals at the club. No doubt he had his reasons for so doing.

Meanwhile he was opening his own letters. The one from Paris came last. Had his wife been looking at him, she might have seen a sudden change pass over his face as he read it, as though startled by some doubt or perplexity.

"Archibald, what can this mean?" exclaimed Blanche in breathless tones. "Listen: 'The names of the five convicts said to have escaped from the ship Vengeance after her wreck on the island, supposed to be that of Tristan d'Acunha, are the following: George Ford, Walter Green, John Andison, Nathaniel Markham, and Thomas Heriot.' That is Tom's name."

Cramming all his letters into his breastpocket with a hurried movement, Lord Level quietly took the paper from his wife's hands. This was the very contretemps he had so long striven to guard against.

"My dear Blanche, do you suppose there is only one Thomas Heriot in the world?" cried he carelessly. "'Ship Vengeance?' 'Escape of convicts?' Oh, it is something that has happened over at Botany Bay."

"Well, the name startled me, at the moment. I'm sure Tom might as well be a convict as anything else for all the news he sends us of himself."

"He was always careless, you know, and detested letter-writing."

Carrying away the paper, Lord Level left the room and went to the one behind it, of which he made a sort of study. There he sat down, spread the letter from Paris before him on the table, and reperused it.

"Confound the woman!" remarked his lordship. "I shall have to go down there now!"

Breakfast removed, Blanche began at once to write to Mrs. Guy, whose letter required an answer. That over, she put on her bonnet to call on Mrs. Arnold Ravensworth in Langham Place. She had called on the previous day, but found Mr. and Mrs. Ravensworth out of town: they were expected home that evening. So now Blanche went again.

Yes, they had arrived; and had brought with them Blanche's old friend, Cecilia Ravensworth, from White Littleham Rectory.

How happy they were together, these two! It seemed an age since they had parted, and yet it was not in reality so very long ago. Lady Level remained the best part of the morning, talking of the old days of her happy, yet uneventful, girlhood.

Strolling leisurely through Cavendish Square on her way home, Blanche fell to thinking of the afternoon: speculating where it might be that her husband meant to take her. Perhaps to Hampton Court: she had never seen it, and would like to do so: she would ask him to take her there. Quickening her pace, she soon reached her own door, and saw an empty cab drawn up before it.

"Is any visitor here?" she asked of Sanders, when admitted.

"No, my lady. I have just called the cab for his lordship."

Lord Level came out of the study at the sound of her voice, and turned with her into the front room. She thought he looked vexed—hurried.

"Blanche," he began, "I find I have to run down to Marshdale. But I shall not be away more than a night if I can help it. I shall be back to-morrow if possible; if not, you may expect me the next day for certain."

"To Marshdale!" she repeated, in surprise and vexation. "Then you will not be able to take me out this afternoon! I was hoping it might be to Hampton Court."

"You shall go to Hampton Court when I return."

"Take me with you to Marshdale."

"I cannot," he replied decisively. "I am going down on business."

"Why did you not tell me of it this morning? Why have proposed to—"

"I did not know of it then," he interrupted. "How dismayed you look, Blanche!" he added, half laughing.

"I shall be very lonely, Archibald—all by myself here!"

He said no more, but stooped to kiss her, and left the room, looking at his watch.

"I did not think it was quite so late!" he exclaimed. Turning sharply, for he had been about to enter the study, he approached the front door, hesitated, then turned again, and went into the study.

"No, I can't stop," he said, coming to a final decision, as he once more came forth, shut the study door after him, and locked it, but did not take out the key. "Blanche, don't let anyone come in here; I have left all my papers at sixes and sevens. If I wait to put them up I shall not catch Jenning."

"Are you going to the train now, Archibald?"

"No, no; I want to see Jenning. I shall come back before going to the train."

Getting into the cab, Lord Level was whirled away. Sanders closed the house-door. And Blanche, ascending the stairs to her chamber, in the slow manner we are apt to assume after experiencing some unexpected check, and untying her bonnet as she went up, came upon her maid, Timms. Timms appeared to be in trouble: her face was gloomy and wet with tears.

"What is the matter?" exclaimed her mistress.

"My lady, I can't understand it. My belief is she has stole it, and nothing less. But for that dreadful sea-passage, there and back, I'd go over myself to-day, if your ladyship would spare me."

"Now, Timms, what are you talking about?"

"Why, of the box, my lady. I was that vexed at its being left behind that I scribbled a few lines to Victorine from Dover, telling her to get Sauvage not to delay in sending it on. And I've got her answer this morning, denying that any box has been left. Leastways, saying that she can't see it."

While Timms was speaking, she had pulled a note out of her pocket, and offered it to her mistress. It was from their late chambermaid, and written in curious English for Timms' benefit, who was no French scholar, and it certainly denied that the box inquired for, or any other box, had been left behind, so far as she, Victorine, could ascertain.

When departing from Paris three days before, Timms, counting over the luggage with Sanders, discovered at the station that one of the boxes was missing, left behind in their apartments by her own carelessness. The train was on the point of starting, and there was no time to return; but Lord Level despatched a message by a commissionaire to the concierge, Sauvage, to send it on to London by grande vitesse. The box contained wearing apparel belonging to Lady Level, and amidst it a certain dark silk dress which Timms had long coveted. Altogether she was in a state of melancholy self-reproach and had written to Victorine from Dover, urging speed. Victorine's answer, delivered this morning, had completely upset Timms.

Lady Level laughed gaily. "Cheer up, Timms," she said; "the box is on its road. His lordship has had a letter from Madame Sauvage this morning." The concierge himself was no scribe, and his wife always did the writing for him.

Timms dashed her tears away. "Oh, my lady, how thankful I am! What could Victorine mean, I wonder? When was the box sent off? Does your ladyship know?"

"No—o. I—don't know what the letter does say," added Lady Level, calling to mind that she was as yet ignorant of its contents. "I forgot all about it after Lord Level opened it."

Timms did not quite comprehend. "But—I beg your pardon, my lady—I suppose Madame Sauvage does say they have sent it off?"

"I dare say she does. What else should she write for?"

The maid's countenance fell considerably.

"But, my lady," she remonstrated, wise in her superior age and experience, "if—if your ladyship has not read the letter, it may be just the opposite. To pretend, like Victorine, that they have not found the box. Victorine may have spirited it away without their knowledge. She would uncommonly like to get some of those dresses for herself."

This view scarcely appeared feasible to Lady Level. "How silly you are, Timms!" she cried. "You can only look at the dark side of the case. As if Lord Level would not have told me had it been that news! I wonder where he put the letter? I will look for it."

"If you would be so kind, my lady! so as to set the doubt at rest."

That she should find the letter on her husband's table, Blanche no more doubted than that it was written by Madame Sauvage to announce the despatch of the box. She ran down to the study, unlocked the door, and entered.

The table was covered with quite a confused mass of papers, heaped one upon another. It seemed as though Lord Level must have been looking for some deed or other. A despatch-box, usually crammed full of papers, stood on the table, open and empty. At the opposite corner was his desk; but that was locked.

For a moment Blanche thought she would abandon her search. The confusion looked too formidable to be meddled with. Well for her own peace of mind that she had not done so!

Bending forward, for papers lay on the carpet as well as the table, she let her eyes range over the litter, slightly lifting with her thumb and forefinger a paper here and there, hoping to discern the required letter. Quite by a stroke of good fortune she came upon it. Good fortune or ill—which?

It lay, together with the two letters which had come with it, under an open parchment, close before Lord Level's chair. One of these letters was from Mr. Jenning, his confidential solicitor, requesting his lordship to be with him at twelve o'clock that morning on a special matter; but that had nothing to do with Blanche, or with us either. She opened the envelope of the one she wished to see, and took out its letter.

But it was not a letter; not, at least, as letters run in general. It was only a piece of thin paper folded once, which bore a few lines in a fine, pointed Italian hand, and in faint-coloured ink, somewhat difficult to decipher.

Now it must be premised that Lady Level had no more thought of prying into what concerned her husband, and did not concern herself, than a child could have had. She would not have been guilty of such a thing for the world. Any one of those parchments or papers, lying open before her eyes, she would have deemed it the height of dishonour to read a word of. This letter from the wife of their late concierge, containing news of her own lost box, was a different matter.

But though the address to Lord Level was undoubtedly in the handwriting of Madame Sauvage, the inside was not. Blanche strained her eyes over it.

"I arrive to-day at Paris, and find you departed for England with your wife and servants. I come straight on from Pisa, without halting, to inform you of a discovery we have made; there was no time to write. As I am so near, it is well to use the opportunity to pay a short visit to Marshdale to see the child, and I start this evening for it; you can join me there. Pardon the trouble I give you.—NINA."

With her face flaming, with trembling hands, and shortened breath, Lady Level gathered in the words and their meaning. Nina! It was the Italian girl, the base woman who had troubled before her peace of mind, and who must have got Madame Sauvage to address the letter. Evidently she did not mean, the shameless siren, to let Lord Level be at rest. And—and—and what was the meaning of that allusion about "the child"?

Leaving the letter precisely as she had found it, under the sheet of parchment, Lady Level quitted the room and turned the key in the door again. Not for very shame, now that this shameful secret had been revealed to her, would she let her husband know that she had entered. Had she found only what she sought, she would have said openly to him on his return: "Archibald, I went in for Madame Sauvage's note, and I found it. I hope you don't mind—we were anxious about the box." But somehow her eyes were now opened to the fact that she had been guilty of a dishonourable action, one that could not be excused or justified. Had he not locked his door against intruders—herself as well as others?

Passing into the front room, where the table was now being laid for luncheon, which they took at one o'clock, she drew a chair near the fire, mechanically watching Sanders as he placed the dishes on the table, in reality seeing nothing; her mind was in a tumult, very painful and rebellious.

Timms came stealing in. How any lady could be so indifferent as her lady when a box of beautiful clothes was at stake, Timms could not understand: sitting quietly there over the fire, and never coming back to set a body's mind at rest with yes or no.

"I beg pardon for intruding," began Timms, with deprecation, "but did your ladyship find Madame Sauvage's letter?"

"No," curtly replied Lady Level. "I dare say the box is lost. Not much matter if it is."

Timms withdrew, lifting her hands in condemning displeasure when she got outside. "Not much matter! if ever I heard the like of that! A whole trunk full! and some of 'em lovely!"

"Will you sit down, now, my lady, or wait for his lordship?" inquired Sanders.

Lady Level answered the question by taking her place at table. She felt as though she should never care to wait for his lordship again, for luncheon or anything else. In a few minutes a cab dashed up to the door, bringing him.

"That's right, Blanche; I am glad you did not wait for me," he began. "Sanders, is my hand-bag ready?"

"Quite, my lord."

"Put it into the cab, then."

He hastened into the study as he spoke, and began putting things straight there with a deft and rapid hand. In an incredibly short time, the papers were all in order, locked up in their various receptacles, and the table was cleared.

"Good-bye, my love," said he, returning to the front room.

"Do you not take anything to eat?" asked Blanche, in short and sullen tones, which he was in too great a hurry to notice.

"No: or I should lose the train."

He caught her to him. Blanche turned her face away.

"You silly child! you are cross with me for leaving you. My dear, believe me, I could not help it. Charley is coming up to dine with you this evening."

Leaving his kisses on her lips, but getting none in return, Lord Level went out to the cab. As it drove away, there came up to the door a railway luggage van. The lost box had arrived from Paris. Timms knelt down with extra fervour that night to offer up her thanksgivings.

Lord Level had snatched a moment to look in upon me, and ask me to dine with Blanche that evening.

"She is not pleased at being left alone," he said; "but I am obliged to run down to Marshdale. And, Charley, she saw something about Tom in the paper this morning: I had to turn it off in the best way I could: so be cautious if she mentions it to you."

I had meant to look again after Tom Heriot that evening, but could not refuse this. Blanche was unusually silent throughout dinner.

"Is anything the matter, Blanche?" I asked her, when we were in the drawing-room.

"A great deal is the matter," she replied resentfully. "I am not going to put up with it."

"Put up with what?"

"Oh—with Lord Level. With his—his deceit. But I can't tell you now, Charles: I shall speak to himself first."

I laughed. "More jealousy cropping up! What has he done now, Blanche?"

"What has he gone to Marshdale for?" retorted Blanche, her cheeks flaming. "And what did he go to Pisa for when we were last in Paris?" continued she, without any pause. "He did go. It was in December; and he was away ten days."

"Well,' I suppose some matter or other called him there," I said. "As to Marshdale—it is his place; his home. Why should this annoy you, Blanche? A man cannot carry his wife with him everywhere."

"I know," she said, catching up her fan, and beginning to use it sharply. "I know more than you do, Charles. More than he thinks for—a great deal more."

"It strikes me, my dear, that you are doing your best to estrange your husband from you—if you speak to him as you are speaking now. That will not enhance your own happiness, Blanche."

"The fault is his," she cried, turning her hot face defiantly upon me.

"It may be. I don't think so."

"He does not care for me at all. He cares for—for—somebody else."

"You may be mistaken. I should be sorry to believe it. But, even should it be so—listen, Blanche—even should it be so, you will do well to change your tactics. Try and win him back to you. I tell it you for the sake of your own happiness."

Blanche tossed back her golden curls, and rose. "How old-fashioned you are, Charles! it is of no use talking to you. Will you sing our old duet with me—'I've wandered in dreams'?"

"Ay. But I am out of practice."

She had taken her place on the music-stool, and was playing the first bars of the song, when a thought struck her, and she turned round.

"Charley, such a curious thing happened this morning. I saw in the Times a list of some escaped convicts, who had been on their way to Van Diemen's Land, and amongst them was the name of Thomas Heriot. For a moment it startled and frightened me."

Her eyes were upon my face, so was the light. Having a piece of music in my hand, I let it fall, and stooped to pick it up.

"Was it not strange, Charles?"

"Not particularly so. There may be a hundred Tom Heriots in the world."

"That's what Archibald said—or something to the same effect. But, do you know, I cannot get it out of my head. And Tom's not writing to us from India has seemed to me all day more strangely odd than it did before."

"India is a regular lazy place. The heat makes people indolent and indifferent."

"Yes, I know. Besides, as papa said to me in the few minutes we were talking together before he went away, Tom may have written, and the letters not have reached us. The mail from India is by no means a safe one, he says; letters often get lost by it."

"By no means safe: no end of letters are lost continually," I murmured, seconding old Carlen's invention, knowing not what else to say. "Let us go on, Blanche. It is I who begin, I think—'I've wandered in dreams.'"

Wandered in dreams! If this misery connected with Tom Heriot were only a dream, and not a reality!

VOLUME III

CHAPTER I

ON THE WATCH

Mr. Serjeant Stillingfar sat at dinner in his house in Russell Square one Sunday afternoon. A great cause, in which he was to lead, had brought him up from circuit, to which he would return when the Nisi Prius trial was over. The cloth was being removed when I entered. He received me with his usual kindly welcome.

"Why not have come to dinner, Charles? Just had it, you say? All the more reason why we might have had it together. Sit down, and help yourself to wine."

Declining the wine, I drew my chair near to his, and told him what I had come about.

A few days had gone on since the last chapter. With the trouble connected with Mrs. Brightman, and the trouble connected with Tom Heriot, I had enough on my mind at that time, if not upon my shoulders. As regarded Mrs. Brightman, no one could help me; but regarding the other—

Was Tom in London, or was he not? How was I to find out? I had again gone prowling about the book-stall and its environs, and had seen no trace of him. Had Leah really seen him, or only some other man who resembled him?

Again I questioned Leah. Her opinion was not to be shaken. She held emphatically to her assertion. It was Tom that she had seen, and none other.

"You may have seen some other sailor, sir; I don't say to the contrary; but the sailor I saw was Captain Heriot," she reiterated. "Suppose I go again to-night, sir? I may, perhaps, have the good luck to see him."

"Should you call it good luck, Leah?"

"Ah well, sir, you know what I mean," she answered. "Shall I go to-night?"

"No, Leah; I am going myself. I cannot rest in this uncertainty."

Rest! I felt more like a troubled spirit or a wandering ghost. Arthur Lake asked what had gone wrong with me, and where I disappeared to of an evening.

Once more I turned out in discarded clothes to saunter about Lambeth. It was Saturday night and the thoroughfares were crowded; but amidst all who came and went I saw no trace of Tom.

Worried, disheartened, I determined to carry the perplexity to my Uncle Stillingfar. That he was true as steel, full of loving-kindness to all the world, no matter what their errors, and that he would aid me with his counsel—if any counsel could avail—I well knew. And thus I found myself at his house on that Sunday afternoon. Of course he had heard about the escape of the convicts; had seen Tom's name in the list; but he did not know that he was suspected of having reached London. I told him of what Leah had seen, and added the little episode about "Miss Betsy."

"And now, what can be done, Uncle Stillingfar? I have come to ask you."

His kindly blue eyes became thoughtful whilst he pondered the question. "Indeed, Charles, I know not," he answered. "Either you must wait in patience until he turns up some fine day—as he is sure to do if he is in London—or you must quietly pursue your search for him, and smuggle him away when you have found him."

"But if I don't find him? Do you think it could be Tom that Leah saw? Is it possible that he can be in London?"

"Quite possible. If a homeward vessel, bound, it may be, for the port of London, picked them up, what more likely than that he is here? Again, who else would call himself Charles Strange, and pass himself off for you? Though I cannot see his motive for doing it."

"Did you ever know any man so recklessly imprudent, uncle?"

"I have never known any man so reckless as Tom Heriot. You must do your best to find him, Charles."

"I don't know how. I thought you might possibly have suggested some plan. Every day increases his danger."

"It does: and the chances of his being recognised."

"It seems useless to search further in Lambeth: he must have changed his quarters. And to look about London for him will be like looking for a needle in a bottle of hay. I suppose," I slowly added, "it would not do to employ a detective?"

"Not unless you wish to put him into the lion's mouth," said the Serjeant. "Why, Charles, it would be his business to retake him. Rely upon it, the police are now looking for him if they have the slightest suspicion that he is here."

At that time one or two private detectives had started in business on their own account, having nothing to do with the police: now they have sprung up in numbers. It was to these I alluded.

Serjeant Stillingfar shook his head. "I would not trust one of them, Charles: it would be too dangerous an experiment. No; what you do, you must do yourself. Once let Government get scent that he is here, and we shall probably find the walls placarded with a reward for his apprehension."

"One thing I am surprised at," I said as I rose to leave: "that if he is here, he should not have let me know it. What can he be doing for money? An escaped convict is not likely to have much of that about him."

Serjeant Stillingfar shook his head. "There are points about the affair that I cannot fathom, Charles. Talking of money—you are well-off now, but if more than you can spare should be needed to get Tom Heriot away, apply to me."

"Thank you, uncle; but I don't think it will be needed. Where would you recommend him to escape to?"

"Find him first," was the Serjeant's answer.

He accompanied me himself to the front door. As we stood, speaking a last word, a middle-aged man, with keen eyes and spare frame, dressed as a workman, came up with a brisk step. Mr. Serjeant Stillingfar met the smile on the man's face as he glanced up in passing.

"Arkwright!" he exclaimed. "I hardly knew you. Some sharp case in hand, I conclude?"

"Just so, Serjeant; but I hope to bring it to earth before the day's over. You know—"

Then the man glanced at me and came to a pause.

"However, I mustn't talk about it now, so good-afternoon, Serjeant." And thus speaking, he walked briskly onwards.

"I wonder what he has in hand? I think he would have told me, Charles, but for your being present," cried my uncle, looking after him. "A keen man is Arkwright."

"Arkwright!" I echoed, the name now impressing itself upon me. "Surely not Arkwright the famous detective!"

"Yes, it is. And he has evidently got himself up as a workman to further some case that he has in hand. He knew you, Charles; depend upon that; though you did not know him."

A fear, perhaps a foolish one, fell upon me. "Uncle Stillingfar," I breathed, "can his case be Tom's? Think you it is he who is being run to earth?"

"No, no. That is not likely," he answered, after a moment's consideration. "Anyway, you must use every exertion to find him, for his stay in London is full of danger."

It will readily be believed that this incident had not added to my peace of mind. One more visit I decided to pay to the old ground in Lambeth, and after that—why, in truth, whether to turn east, west, north or south, I knew no more than the dead.

Monday was bright and frosty; Monday evening clear, cold and starlight. The gaslights flared away in the streets and shops; the roads were lined with wayfarers.

Sauntering down the narrow pavement on the opposite side of the way, in the purposeless manner that a hopeless man favours, I approached the book-stall. A sailor was standing before it, his head bent over the volumes. Every pulse within me went up to fever heat: for there was that in him that reminded me of Tom Heriot.

I crossed quietly to the stall, stood side by side with him, and took up a handful of penny dreadfuls. Yes, it was he—Tom Heriot.

"Tom," I cried softly. "Tom!"

I felt the start he gave. But he did not move hand or foot; only his eyes turned to scan me.

"Tom," I whispered again, apparently intent upon a grand picture of a castle in flames, and a gentleman miraculously escaping with a lady from an attic window. "Tom, don't you know me?"

"For goodness' sake don't speak to me, Charley!" he breathed in answer, the words barely audible. "Go away, for the love of heaven! I've been a prisoner here for the last three minutes. That policeman yonder would know me, and I dare not turn. His name's Wren."

Three doors off, a policeman was standing at the edge of the pavement, facing the shops, as if waiting to pounce upon someone he was expecting to pass. Even as Tom spoke, he wheeled round to the right, and marched up the street. Tom as quickly disappeared to the left, leaving a few words in my ear.

"I'll wait for you at the other end, Charley; it is darker there than here. Don't follow me immediately."

So I remained where I was, still bending an enraptured gaze upon the burning castle and the gallant knight and damsel escaping from it at their peril.

"Betsy says the account comes to seven shillings, Mr. Strange."

The address gave me almost as great a thrill as the sight of Tom had done. It came from the man Lee, now emerging from his shop. Involuntarily I pulled my hat lower upon my brow. He looked up and down the street.

"Oh, I beg pardon—thought Mr. Strange was standing here," he said. And then I saw my error. He had not spoken to me, but to Tom Heriot. My gaze was still fascinated by the flaming picture.

"Anything you'd like this evening, sir?"

"I'll take this sheet—half a dozen of them," I said, putting down sixpence.

"Thank you, sir. A fine night."

"Yes, very. Were you speaking to the sailor who stood here?" I added carelessly "He went off in that direction, I think," pointing to the one opposite to that Tom had taken.

"Yes," answered the man; "'twas Mr. Strange. He had asked me to look how much his score was for tobacco. I dare say he'll be back presently. Captain Strange, by rights," added Lee chattily.

"Oh! Captain of a vessel?"

"Of his own vessel—a yacht. Not but what he has been about the world in vessels of all sorts, he tells us; one voyage before the mast, the next right up next to the skipper. But for them ups and downs where, as he says, would sailors find their experience?"

"Very true. Well, this is all I want just now. Good-evening."

"Good-evening, sir," replied Caleb Lee.

The end of the street to which Tom had pointed was destitute of shops; the houses were small and poor; consequently, it was tolerably dark. Tom was sauntering along, smoking a short pipe.

"Is there any place at hand where we can have a few words together in tolerable security?" I asked.

"Come along," briefly responded Tom. "You walk on the other side of the street, old fellow; keep me in view."

It was good advice, and I took it. He increased his pace to a brisk walk, and presently turned down a narrow passage, which brought him to a sort of small, triangular green, planted with shrubs and trees. I followed, and we sat down on one of the benches.

"Are you quite mad, Tom?"

"Not mad a bit," laughed Tom. "I say, Charley, did you come to that book-stall to look after me?"

"Ay. And it's about the tenth time I have been there."

"How the dickens did you find me out?"

"Chance one evening took Leah into the neighbourhood, and she happened to see you. I had feared you might be in England."

"You had heard of the wreck of the Vengeance, I suppose; and that a few of us had escaped. Good old Leah! Did I give her a fright?"

We were sitting side by side. Tom had put his pipe out, lest the light should catch the sight of any passing stragglers. We spoke in whispers. It was, perhaps, as safe a place as could be found; nevertheless, I sat upon thorns.

Not so Tom. By the few signs that might be gathered—his light voice, his gay laugh, his careless manner—Tom felt as happy and secure as if he had been attending one of her Majesty's levées, in the full glory of scarlet coat and flashing sword-blade.

"Do you know, Tom, you have half killed me with terror and apprehension? How could you be so reckless as to come back to London?"

"Because the old ship brought me," lightly returned Tom.

"I suppose a vessel picked you up—and the comrades who escaped with you?"

"It picked two of us up. The other three died."

"What, in the boat?"

He nodded. "In the open boat at sea."

"How did you manage to escape? I thought convicts were too well looked after."

"So they are, under ordinary circumstances. Shipwrecks form the exception. I'll give you the history, Charley."

"Make it brief, then. I am upon thorns."

Tom laughed, and began:

"We were started on that blessed voyage, a cargo of men in irons, and for some time made a fair passage, and thought we must be nearing the other side. Such a crew, that cargo, Charles! Such an awful lot! Villainous wretches, who wore their guilt on their faces, and suffered their deserts; half demons, most of them. A few amongst them were no doubt like me, innocent enough; wrongfully accused and condemned—"

"But go on with the narrative, Tom."

"I swear I was innocent," he cried, with emotion, heedless of my interruption. "I was wickedly careless, I admit that, but the guilt was another's, not mine. When I put those bills into circulation, Charles, I knew no more they were forged than you did. Don't you believe me?"

"I do believe you. I have believed you throughout."

"And if the trial had not been hurried on I think it could have been proved. It was hurried on, Charles, and when it was on it was hurried over. I am suffering unjustly."

"Yes, Tom. But won't you go on with your story?"

"Where was I? Oh, about the voyage and the shipwreck. After getting out of the south-east trades, we had a fortnight's light winds and calms, and then got into a steady westerly wind, before which we ran quietly for some days. One dark night, it was the fifteenth of November, and thick, drizzling weather, the wind about north-west, we had turned in and were in our first sleep, when a tremendous uproar arose on deck; the watch shouting and tramping, the officers' orders and the boatswain's mate's shrill piping rising above the din. One might have thought Old Nick had leaped on board and was giving chase. Next came distinctly that fearful cry, 'All hands save ship!' Sails were being clewed up, yards were being swung round. Before we could realize what it all meant, the ship had run ashore; and there she stuck, bumping as if she would knock her bottom out."

"Get on, Tom," I whispered, for he had paused, and seemed to be spinning a long yarn instead of a short one.

"Fortunately, the ship soon made a sort of cradle for herself in the sand, and lay on her starboard bilge. To attempt to get her off was hopeless. So they got us all out of the ship and on shore, and put us under tents made of the sails. The skipper made out, or thought he made out, the island to be that of Tristan d'Acunha: whether it was or not I can't say positively. At first we thought it was uninhabited, but it turned out to have a few natives on it, sixty or eighty in all. In the course of a few days every movable thing had been landed. All the boats were intact, and were moored in a sort of creek, or small natural harbour, their gear, sails and oars in them."

"Hush!" I breathed, "or you are lost!"

A policeman's bull's-eye was suddenly turned upon the grass. By the man's size, I knew him for Tom's friend, Wren. We sat motionless. The light just escaped us, and the man passed on. But we had been in danger.

"If you would only be quicker, Tom. I don't want to know about boats and their gear."

He laughed. "How impatient you are, Charles! Well, to get on ahead. A cargo of convicts cannot be kept as securely under such circumstances as had befallen us as they could be in a ship's hold, and the surveillance exercised was surprisingly lax. Two or three of the prisoners were meditating an escape, and thought they saw their way to effecting it by means of one of the boats. I found this out, and joined the party. But there were almost insurmountable difficulties in the way. It was absolutely necessary that we should put on ordinary clothes—for what vessel, picking us up, but would have delivered us up at the first port it touched at, had we been in convict dress? We marked the purser's slop-chest, which was under a tent, and well filled, and—"

"Do get on, Tom!"

"Here goes, then! One calm, but dark night, when other people were sleeping, we stole down to the creek, five of us, rigged ourselves out in the purser's toggery, leaving the Government uniforms in exchange, unmoored one of the cutters, and got quietly away. We had secreted some bread and salt meat; water there had been already on board. The wind was off the land, and we let the boat drift before it a bit before attempting to make sail. By daylight we were far enough from the island; no chance of their seeing us—a speck on the waters. The wind, hitherto south, had backed to the westward. We shaped a course by the sun to the eastward, and sailed along at the rate of five or six knots. My comrades were not as rough as they might have been; rather decent fellows for convicts. Two of them were from Essex; had been sentenced for poaching only. Now began our lookout: constantly straining our eyes along the horizon for a sail, but especially astern for an outward-bounder, but only saw one or two in the distance that did not see us. What I underwent in that boat as day after day passed, and no sail appeared, I won't enter upon now, old fellow. The provisions were exhausted, and so was the water. One by one three of my companions went crazy and died. The survivor and I had consigned the last of them to the deep on the twelfth day, and then I thought my turn had come; but Markham was worse than I was. How many hours went on, I knew not. I lay at the bottom of the boat, exhausted and half unconscious, when suddenly I heard voices. I imagined it to be a dream. But in a few minutes a boat was alongside the cutter, and two of its crew had stepped over and were raising me up. They spoke to me, but I was too weak to understand or answer; in fact, I was delirious. I and Markham were taken on board and put to bed. After some days, passed in a sort of dreamy, happy delirium, well cared for and attended to, I woke up to the realities of life. Markham was dead: he had never revived, and died of exposure and weakness some hours after the rescue."

"What vessel had picked you up?"

"It was the Discovery, a whaler belonging to Whitby, and homeward bound. The captain, Van Hoppe, was Dutch by birth, but had been reared in England and had always sailed in English ships. A good and kind fellow, if ever there was one. Of course, I had to make my tale good and suppress the truth. The passenger-ship in which I was sailing to Australia to seek my fortune had foundered in mid-ocean, and those who escaped with me had died of their sufferings. That was true so far. Captain Van Hoppe took up my misfortunes warmly. Had he been my own brother—had he been you, Charley—he could not have treated me better or cared for me more. The vessel had a prosperous run home. She was bound for the port of London; and when I put my hand into Van Hoppe's at parting, and tried to thank him for his goodness, he left a twenty-pound note in it. 'You'll need it, Mr. Strange,' he said; 'you can repay me when your fortune's made and you are rich.'"

"Strange!" I cried.

Tom laughed.

"I called myself 'Strange' on the whaler. Don't know that it was wise of me. One day when I was getting better and lay deep in thought—which just then chanced to be of you, Charley—the mate suddenly asked me what my name was. 'Strange,' I answered, on the spur of the moment. That's how it was. And that's the brief history of my escape."

"You have had money, then, for your wants since you landed," I remarked.

"I have had the twenty pounds. It's coming to an end now."

"You ought not to have come to London. You should have got the captain to put you ashore somewhere, and then made your escape from England."

"All very fine to talk, Charley! I had not a sixpence in my pocket, or any idea that he was going to help me. I could only come on as far as the vessel would bring me."

"And suppose he had not given you money—what then?"

"Then I must have contrived to let you know that I was home again, and borrowed from you," he lightly replied.

"Well, your being here is frightfully dangerous."

"Not a bit of it. As long as the police don't suspect I am in England, they won't look after me. It's true that a few of them might know me, but I do not think they would in this guise and with my altered face."

"You were afraid of one to-night."

"Well, he is especially one who might know me; and he stood there so long that I began to think he might be watching me. Anyway, I've been on shore these three weeks, and nothing has come of it yet."

"What about that young lady named Betsy? Miss Betsy Lee."

Tom threw himself back in a fit of laughter.

"I hear the old fellow went down to Essex Street one night to ascertain whether I lived there! The girl asked me one day where I lived, and I rapped out Essex Street."

"But, Tom, what have you to do with the girl?"

"Nothing; nothing. On my honour. I have often been in the shop, sometimes of an evening. The father has invited me to some grog in the parlour behind it, and I have sat there for an hour chatting with him and the girl. That's all. She is a well-behaved, modest little girl; none better."

"Well, Tom, with one imprudence and another, you stand a fair chance—"

"There, there! Don't preach, Charley. What you call imprudence, I call fun."

"What do you think of doing? To remain on here for ever in this disguise?"

"Couldn't, I expect, if I wanted to. I must soon see about getting away."

"You must get away at once."

"I am not going yet, Charley; take my word for that; and I am as safe in London, I reckon, as I should be elsewhere. Don't say but I may have to clear out of this particular locality. If that burly policeman is going to make a permanent beat of it about here, he might drop upon me some fine evening."

"And you must exchange your sailor's disguise, as you call it, for a better one."

"Perhaps so. That rough old coat you have on, Charley, might not come amiss to me."

"You can have it. Why do you fear that policeman should know you, more than any other?"

"He was present at the trial last August. Was staring me in the face most of the day. His name's Wren."

I sighed.

"Well, Tom, it is getting late; we have sat here as long as is consistent with safety," I said, rising.

He made me sit down again.

"The later the safer, perhaps, Charley. When shall we meet again?"

"Ay; when, and where?"

"Come to-morrow evening, to this same spot. It is as good a one as any I know of. I shall remain indoors all day tomorrow. Of course one does not care to run needlessly into danger. Shall you find your way to it?"

"Yes, and will be here; but I shall go now. Do be cautious, Tom. Do you want any money? I have brought some with me."

"Many thanks, old fellow; I've enough to go on with for a day or two. How is Blanche? Did she nearly die of the disgrace?"

"She did not know of it. Does not know it yet."

"No!" he exclaimed in astonishment. "Why, how can it have been kept from her? She does not live in a wood."

"Level has managed it, somehow. She was abroad during the trial, you know. They have chiefly lived there since, Blanche seeing no English newspapers; and, of course, her acquaintances do not gratuitously speak to her about it. But I don't think it can be kept from her much longer."

"But where does she think I am—all this time?"

"She thinks you are in India with the regiment."

"I suppose he was in a fine way about it!"

"Level? Yes—naturally; and is still. He would have saved you, Tom, at any cost."

"As you would, and one or two more good friends; but, you see, I did not know what was coming upon me in time to ask them. It fell upon my head like a thunderbolt. Level is not a bad fellow at bottom."

"He is a downright good one—at least, that's my opinion of him."

We stood hand locked in hand at parting. "Where are you staying?" I whispered.

"Not far off. I've a lodging in the neighbourhood—one room."

"Fare you well, then, until to-morrow evening."

"Au revoir, Charley."

CHAPTER II

TOM HERIOT

I found my way straight enough the next night to the little green with its trees and shrubs. Tom was there, and was humming one of our boyhood's songs taught us by Leah:

"Young Henry was as brave a youth
As ever graced a martial story;
And Jane was fair as lovely truth:
She sighed for love, and he for glory.

"To her his faith he meant to plight,
And told her many a gallant story:
But war, their honest joys to blight,
Called him away from love to glory.

"Young Henry met the foe with pride;
Jane followed—fought—ah! hapless story!
In man's attire, by Henry's side,
She died for love, and he for glory."

He was still dressed as a sailor, but the pilot-coat was buttoned up high and tight about his throat, and the round glazed hat was worn upon the front of his head instead of the back of it.

"I thought you meant to change these things, Tom," I said as we sat down.

"All in good time," he answered; "don't quite know yet what costume to adopt. Could one become a negro-melody man, think you, Charley—or a Red Indian juggler with balls and sword-swallowing?"

How light he seemed! how supremely indifferent! Was it real or only assumed? Then he turned suddenly upon me:

"I say, what are you in black for, Charley? For my sins?"

"For Mr. Brightman."

"Mr. Brightman!" he repeated, his tone changing to one of concern. "Is he dead?"

"He died the last week in February. Some weeks ago now. Died quite suddenly."

"Well, well, well!" softly breathed Tom Heriot. "I am very sorry. I did not know it. But how am I likely to know anything of what the past months have brought forth?"

It would serve no purpose to relate the interview of that night in detail. We spent it partly in quarrelling. That is, in differences of opinion. It was impossible to convince Tom of his danger. I told him about the Sunday incident, when Detective Arkwright passed the door of Serjeant Stillingfar, and my momentary fear that he might be looking after Tom. He only laughed. "Good old Uncle Stillingfar!" cried he; "give my love to him." And all his conversation was carried on in the same light strain.

"But you must leave Lambeth," I urged. "You said you would do so."

"I said I might. I will, if I see just cause for doing so. Plenty of time yet. I am not sure, you know, Charles, that Wren would know me."

"The very fact of your having called yourself 'Strange' ought to take you away from here."

"Well, I suppose that was a bit of a mistake," he acknowledged. "But look here, brother mine, your own fears mislead you. Until it is known that I have made my way home no one will be likely to look after me. Believing me to be at the antipodes, they won't search London for me."

"They may suspect that you are in London, if they don't actually know it."

"Not they. To begin with, it must be a matter of absolute uncertainty whether we got picked up at all, after escaping from the island; but the natural conclusion will be that, if we were, it was by a vessel bound for the colonies: homeward-bound ships do not take that course. Everyone at all acquainted with navigation knows that. I assure you, our being found by the whaler was the merest chance in the world. Be at ease, Charley. I can take care of myself, and I will leave Lambeth if necessary. One of these fine mornings you may get a note from me, telling you I have emigrated to the Isle of Dogs, or some such enticing quarter, and have become 'Mr. Smith.' Meanwhile, we can meet here occasionally."

"I don't like this place, Tom. It must inevitably be attended with more or less danger. Had I not better come to your lodgings?"

"No," he replied, after a moment's consideration. "I am quite sure that we are safe here, and there it's hot and stifling—a dozen families living in the same house. And I shall not tell you where the lodgings are, Charles: you might be swooping down upon me to carry me away as Mephistopheles carried away Dr. Faustus."

After supplying him with money, with a last handshake, whispering a last injunction to be cautious, I left the triangle, and left him within it. The next moment found me face to face with the burly frame and wary glance of Mr. Policemen Wren. He was standing still in the starlight. I walked past him with as much unconcern as I could muster. He turned to look after me for a time, and then continued his beat.

It gave me a scare. What would be the result if Tom met him unexpectedly as I had done? I would have given half I was worth to hover about and ascertain. But I had to go on my way.

"Can you see Lord Level, sir?"

It was the following Saturday afternoon, and I was just starting for Hastings. The week had passed in anxious labour. Business cares for me, more work than I knew how to get through, for Lennard was away ill, and constant mental torment about Tom. I took out my watch before answering Watts.

"Yes, I have five minutes to spare. If that will be enough for his lordship," I added, laughing, as we shook hands: for he had followed Watts into the room.

"You are off somewhere, Charles?"

"Yes, to Hastings. I shall be back again to-morrow night. Can I do anything for you?"

"Nothing," replied Lord Level. "I came up from Marshdale this morning, and thought I would come round this afternoon to ask whether you have any news."

When Lord Level went to Marshdale on the visit that bore so suspicious an aspect to his wife, he had remained there only one night, returning to London the following day. This week he had been down again, and stayed rather longer—two days, in fact. Blanche, as I chanced to know, was rebelling over it. Secretly rebelling, for she had not brought herself to accuse him openly.

"News?" I repeated.

"Of Tom Heriot."

Should I tell Lord Level? Perhaps there was no help for it. When he had asked me before I had known nothing positively; now I knew only too much.

"Why I should have it, I know not; but a conviction lies upon me that he has found his way back to London," he continued. "Charles, you look conscious. Do you know anything?"

"You are right. He is here, and I have seen him."

"Good heavens!" exclaimed Lord Level, throwing himself back in his chair. "Has he really been mad enough to come back to London?"

Drawing my own chair nearer to him, I bent forward, and in low tones gave him briefly the history. I had seen Tom on the Monday and Tuesday nights, as already related to the reader. On the Thursday night I was again at the trysting-place, but Tom did not meet me. The previous night, Friday, I had gone again, and again Tom did not appear.

"Is he taken, think you?" cried Lord Level.

"I don't know: and you see I dare not make any inquiries. But I think not. Had he been captured, it would be in the papers."

"I am not so sure of that. What an awful thing! What suspense for us all! Can nothing be done?"

"Nothing," I answered, rising, for my time was up. "We can only wait, and watch, and be silent."

"If it were not for the disgrace reflected upon us, and raking it up again to people's minds, I would say let him be re-taken! It would serve him right for his foolhardiness."

"How is Blanche?"

"Cross and snappish; unaccountably so: and showing her temper to me rather unbearably."

I laughed—willing to treat the matter lightly. "She does not care that you should go travelling without her, I take it."

Lord Level, who was passing out before me, turned and gazed into my face.

"Yes," said he emphatically. "But a man may have matters to take up his attention, and his movements also, that he may deem it inexpedient to talk of to his wife."

He spoke with a touch of haughtiness. "Very true," I murmured, as we shook hands and went out together, he walking away towards Gloucester Place, I jumping into the cab waiting to take me to the station.

Mrs. Brightman was better; I knew that; and showing herself more self-controlled. But there was no certainty that the improvement would be lasting. In truth, the certainty lay rather the other way. Her mother's home was no home for Annabel; and I had formed the resolution to ask her to come to mine.

The sun had set when I reached Hastings, and Miss Brightman's house. Miss Brightman, who seemed to grow less strong day by day, which I was grieved to hear, was in her room lying down. Annabel sat at the front drawing-room window in the twilight. She started up at my entrance, full of surprise and apprehension.

"Oh, Charles! Has anything happened? Is mamma worse?"

"No, indeed; your mamma is very much better," said I cheerfully. "I have taken a run down for the pleasure of seeing you, Annabel."

She still looked uneasy. I remembered the dreadful tidings I had brought the last time I came to Hastings. No doubt she was thinking of it, too, poor girl.

"Take a seat, Charles," she said. "Aunt Lucy will soon be down."

I drew a chair opposite to her, and talked for a little time on indifferent topics. The twilight shades grew deeper, passers-by more indistinct, the sea less bright and shimmering. Silence stole over us—a sweet silence all too conscious, all too fleeting. Annabel suddenly rose, stood at the window, and made some slight remark about a little boat that was nearing the pier.

"Annabel," I whispered, as I rose and stood by her, "you do not know what I have really come down for."

"No," she answered, with hesitation.

"When I last saw you at your own home, you may remember that you were in very great trouble. I asked you to share it with me, but you would not do so."

She began to tremble, and became agitated, and I passed my arm round her waist.

"My darling, I now know all."

Her heart beat violently as I held her. Her hand shook nervously in mine.

"You cannot know all!" she cried piteously.

"I know all; more than you do. Mrs. Brightman was worse after you left, and Hatch sent for me. She and Mr. Close have told me the whole truth."

Annabel would have shrunk away, in the full tide of shame that swept over her, and a low moan broke from her lips.

"Nay, my dear, instead of shrinking from me, you must come nearer to me—for ever. My home must be yours now."

She did not break away from me, and stood pale and trembling, her hands clasped, her emotion strong.

"It cannot, must not be, Charles."

"Hush, my love. It can be—and shall be."

"Charles," she said, her very lips trembling, "weigh well what you are saying. Do not suffer the— affection—I must speak fully—the implied engagement that was between us, ere this unhappiness came to my knowledge and yours—do not suffer it to bind you now. It is a fearful disgrace to attach to my poor mother, and it is reflected upon me."

"Were your father living, Annabel, should you say the disgrace was also reflected upon him?"

"Oh no, no. I could not do so. My good father! honourable and honoured. Never upon him."

I laughed a little at her want of logic.

"Annabel, my dear, you have yourself answered the question. As I hold you to my heart now, so will I, in as short a time as may be, hold you in my home and at my hearth. Let what will betide, you shall have one true friend to shelter and protect you with his care and love for ever and for ever."

Her tears were falling.

"Oh please, please, Charles! I am sure it ought not to be. Aunt Lucy would tell you so."

Aunt Lucy came in at that moment, and proved to be on my side. She would be going to Madeira at the close of the summer, and the difficulty as to what was to be done then with Annabel had begun to trouble her greatly.

"I cannot take her with me, you see, Charles," she said. "In her mother's precarious state, the child must not absent herself from England. Still less can I leave her to her mother's care. Therefore I think your proposal exactly meets the dilemma. I suppose matters have been virtually settled between you for some little time now."

"Oh, Aunt Lucy!" remonstrated Annabel, blushing furiously.

"Well, my dear, and I say it is all for the best. If you can suggest a better plan I am willing to hear it."

Annabel sat silent, her head drooping.

"I may tell you this much, child: your father looked forward to it and approved it. Not that he would have allowed the marriage to take place just yet had he lived; I am sure of that; but he is not living, and circumstances alter cases."

"I am sure he liked me, Miss Brightman," I ventured to put in, as modestly as I could; "and I believe he would have consented to our marriage."

"Yes, he liked you very much; and so do I," she added, laughing. "I wish I could say as much for Mrs. Brightman. The opposition, I fancy, will come from her."

"You think she will oppose it?" I said—and, indeed, the doubt had lain in my own mind.

"I am afraid so. Of course there will be nothing for it but patience. Annabel cannot marry without her consent."

How a word will turn the scales of our hopes and fears! That Mrs. Brightman would oppose and wither our bright prospects came to me in that moment with the certainty of conviction.

"Come what come may, we will be true to each other," I whispered to Annabel the next afternoon. We were standing at the end of the pier, looking out upon the calm sea, flashing in the sunshine, and I imprisoned her hand momentarily in mine. "If we have to exercise all the patience your Aunt Lucy spoke of, we will still hope on, and put our trust in Heaven."

"Even so, Charles." The evening was yet early when I reached London, and I walked home from the station. St. Mary's was striking half-past seven as I passed it. At the self-same moment, an arm was inserted into mine. I turned quickly, wondering if anyone had designs upon my small hand-bag.

"All right, Charley! I'm not a burglar."

It was only Lake. "Why, Arthur! I thought you had gone to Oxford until Monday!"

"Got news last night that the fellow could not have me: had to go down somewhere or other," he answered, as we walked along arm-in-arm. "I say, I had a bit of a scare just now."

"In what way?"

"I thought I saw Tom pass. Tom Heriot," he added in a whisper.

"Oh, but that's impossible, you know, Lake," I said, though I felt my pulses quicken. "All your fancy."

"It was just under that gas-lamp at the corner of Wellington Street," Lake went on. "He was sauntering along as if he had nothing to do, muffled in a coat that looked a mile too big for him, and a red comforter. He lifted his face in passing, and stopped suddenly, as if he had recognised me, and were going to speak; then seemed to think better of it, turned on his heel and walked back the way he had been coming. Charley, if it was not Tom Heriot, I never saw such a likeness as that man bore to him."

My lips felt glued. "It could not have been Tom Heriot, Lake. You know Tom is at the antipodes. We will not talk of him, please. Are you coming home with me?"

"Yes. I was going on to Barlow's Chambers, but I'll come with you instead."

CHAPTER III

AN EVENING VISITOR

The spring flowers were showing themselves, and the may was budding in the hedges. I thought how charming it all looked, as I turned, this Monday afternoon, into Mrs. Brightman's grounds, where laburnums drooped their graceful blossoms, and lilacs filled the air with their perfume; how significantly it all spoke to the heart of renewed life after the gloom of winter, the death and decay of nature.

Mrs. Brightman was herself, enjoying the spring-tide. She sat, robed in crape, on a bench amidst the trees, on which the sun was shining. What a refined, proud, handsome face was hers! but pale and somewhat haggard now. No other trace of her recent illness was apparent, except a nervous trembling of the hands.

"This is a surprise," she said, holding out one of those hands to me quite cordially. "I thought you had been too busy of late to visit me in the day-time."

"Generally I am very busy, but I made time to come to-day. I have something of importance to say to you, Mrs. Brightman. Will you hear me?"

She paused to look at me—a searching, doubtful look. Did she fear that I was about to speak to her of her failing? The idea occurred to me.

"Certainly," she coldly replied. "Business must, of course, be attended to. Would you prefer to go indoors or to sit out here?"

"I would rather remain here. I am not often favoured with such a combination of velvet lawn and sunshine and sweet scents."

She made room for me beside her. And, with as little circumlocution as possible, I brought out what I wanted—Annabel. When the heart is truly engaged, a man at these moments can only be bashful, especially when he sees it will be an uphill fight; but if the heart has nothing to do with the matter, he can be as cool and suave as though he were merely telling an everyday story.

Mrs. Brightman, hearing me to the end, rose haughtily.

"Surely you do not know what you are saying!" she exclaimed. "Or is it that I fail to understand you? You cannot be asking for the hand of my daughter?"

"Indeed—pardon me—I am. Mrs. Brightman, we—"

"Pardon me," she interrupted, "but I must tell you that it is utterly preposterous. Say no more, Mr. Strange; not another word. My daughter cannot marry a professional man. I did so, you may reply: yes, and have forfeited my proper place in the world ever since."

"Mr. Brightman would have given Annabel to me."

"Possibly so, though I think not. As Mr. Brightman is no longer here, we may let that supposition alone. And you must allow me to say this much, sir—that it is scarcely seemly to come to me on any such subject so soon after his death."

"But—" I stopped in embarrassment, unable to give my reason for speaking so soon. How could I tell Mrs. Brightman that it was to afford Annabel a home and a protector: that this, her mother's home, was not fitting for a refined and sensitive girl?

But I pressed the suit. I told her I had Annabel's consent, and that I had recently been with her at Hastings. I should like to have added that I had Miss Brightman's, only that it might have done more harm than good. I spoke very slightly of Miss Brightman's projected departure from England, when her house would be shut up and Annabel must leave Hastings. And I added that I wanted to make a home for her by that time.

I am sure she caught my implied meaning, for she grew agitated and her hands shook as they lay on her crape dress. Her diamond rings, which she had not discarded, flashed in the sunlight. But she rallied her strength. All her pride rose up in rebellion.

"My daughter has her own home, sir; her home with me—what do you mean? During my illness, I have allowed her to remain with her aunt, but she will shortly return to me."

And when I would have urged further, and pleaded as for something dearer than life, she peremptorily stopped me.

"I will hear no more, Mr. Strange. My daughter is descended on my side from the nobles of the land— you must forgive me for thus alluding to it—and it is impossible that I can forget that, or allow her to do so. Never, with my consent, will she marry out of that grade: a professional man is, in rank, beneath her. This is my decision, and it is unalterable. The subject is at an end, and I beg of you never again to enter upon it."

There was no chance of my pursuing it then, at any rate. Hatch came from the house, a folded cloak on her arm, and approached her mistress.

"The carriage is at the gate, ma'am."

Mrs. Brightman rose at once: she was going for a drive. After what had just passed, I held out my arm to her with some hesitation. She put the tips of her fingers within it, with a stiff "Thank you," and we walked to the gate in silence. I handed her into the open carriage; Hatch disposed the cloak upon her knees, assisted by the footman. With a cold bow, Mrs. Brightman, who had already as coldly shaken hands with me, drove away.

Hatch, always ready for a gossip, stood within the little iron gate while she spoke to me.

"We be going away for a bit, sir," she began. "Did you know it?"

"No. Mrs. Brightman has not mentioned the matter to me."

"Well, we be, then," continued Hatch; "missis and me and Perry. Mr. Close have got her to consent at last. I don't say that she was well enough to go before; Close thought so, but I didn't. He wants her gone, you see, Mr. Charles, to get that fancy out of her head about master."

"But does she still think she sees him?"

"Not for the past few days," replied Hatch. "She has changed her bedroom, and taken to the best spare one; and she has been better in herself. Oh, she'll be all right now for a bit, if only—"

"If only what?" I asked, for Hatch had paused.

"Well, you know, sir. If only she can control herself. I'm certain she is trying to," added Hatch. "There ain't one of us would be so glad to find it got rid of for good and all as she'd be. She's put about frightfully yet at Miss Annabel's knowing of it."

"And where is it that you are going to?"

"Missis talked of Cheltenham; it was early, she thought, for the seaside; but this morning she got a Cheltenham newspaper up, and saw that amid the company staying there were Captain and Lady Grace Chantrey. 'I'm not going where my brother and that wife of his are,' she says to me in a temper—for, as I dare say you've heard, Mr. Charles, they don't agree. And now she talks of Brighton. Whatever place she fixes on, Perry is to be sent on first to take lodgings."

"Well, Hatch," I said, "the change from home will do your mistress good. She is much better. I trust the improvement will be permanent."

"Ah, if she would but take care! It all lies in that, sir," concluded Hatch, as I turned away from the gate, and she went up the garden.

We must go back for a moment to the previous evening. Leaving behind us the church of St. Clement Danes and its lighted windows, Lake and I turned into Essex Street, arm-in-arm, went down it and reached my door. I opened it with my latch-key. The hall-lamp was not lighted, and I wondered at Watts's neglect.

"Go on up to my room," I said to Lake. "I'll follow you in a moment."

He bounded up the stairs, and the next moment Leah came up from the kitchen with a lighted candle, her face white and terrified.

"It is only myself, Leah. Why is the lamp not alight?"

"Heaven be good to us, sir!" she cried. "I thought I heard somebody go upstairs."

"Mr. Lake has gone up."

She dropped her candlestick upon the slab, and backed against the wall, looking more white and terrified than ever. I thought she was about to faint.

"Mr. Charles! I feel as if I could die! I ought to have bolted the front door."

"But what for?" I cried, intensely surprised. "What on earth is the matter, Leah?"

"He is up there, sir! Up in your front sitting-room. I put out the hall-lamp, thinking the house would be best in darkness."

"Who is up there?" For in the moment's bewilderment I did not glance at the truth.

"Mr. Tom, sir. Captain Heriot."

"Mr. Tom! Up there?"

"Not many minutes ago, soon after Watts had gone out to church—for he was late to-night—there came a ring at the doorbell," said Leah. "I came up to answer it, thinking nothing. A rough-looking man stood, in a wide-awake hat, close against the door there. 'Is Mr. Strange at home?' said he, and walked right in. I knew his voice, and I knew him, and I cried out. 'Don't be stupid, Leah; it's only me,' says he. 'Is Mr. Charles upstairs? Nobody with him, I hope.' 'There's nobody to come and put his head in the lion's mouth, as may be said, there at all, sir,' said I; and up he went, like a lamplighter. I put the hall-lamp out. I was terrified out of my senses, and told him you were at Hastings, but I expected you in soon. And Mr. Charles," wound up Leah, "I think he must have gone clean daft."

"Light the lamp again," I replied. "It always is alight, you know. If the house is in darkness, you might have a policeman calling to know what was the matter."

Tom was in a fit of laughter when I got upstairs. He had taken off his rough overcoat and broad-brimmed hat, and stood in a worn—very much worn—suit of brown velveteen breeches and gaiters. Lake stared at him over the table, a comical expression on his face.

"Suppose we shake hands, to begin with," said Lake. And they clasped hands heartily across the table.

"Did you know me just now, in the Strand, Lake?" asked Tom Heriot.

"I did," replied Lake, and his tone proved that he meant it. "I said to Charley, here, that I had just seen a fellow very like Tom Heriot; but I knew who it was, fast enough."

"You wouldn't have known me, though, if I hadn't lifted my face to the lamp-light. I forget myself at moments, you see," added Tom, after a pause. "Meeting you unexpectedly, I was about to speak as in the old days, and recollected myself only just in time. I say"—turning himself about in his velveteens—"should you take me for a gamekeeper?"

"No, I should not: you don't look the thing at all," I put in testily, for I was frightfully vexed with him altogether. "I thought you must have been taken up by your especial friend, Wren. Twice have I been to the trysting-place as agreed, but you did not appear."

"No; but I think he nearly had me," replied Tom.

"How was that?"

"I'll tell you," he answered, as we all three took chairs round the fire, and I stirred it into a blaze. "On the Wednesday I did not go out at all; I told you I should not. On the Thursday, after dusk, I went out to meet you, Charley. It was early, and I strolled in for a smoke with Lee and a chat with Miss Betsy. The old man began at once: 'Captain Strange, Policeman Wren has been here, asking questions about you.' It seems old Wren is well known in the neighbourhood—"

"Captain Strange?" cried Lake. "Who is Captain Strange?"

"I am—down there," laughed Tom. "Don't interrupt, please. 'What questions?' I said to Lee. 'Oh, what your name was, and where you came from, and if I had known you long, and what your ship was called,' answered Lee. 'And you told him?' I asked. 'Well, I should have told him, but for Betsy,' he said. 'Betsy spoke up, saying you were a sailor-gentleman that came in to buy tobacco and newspapers; and that was all he got out of us, not your name, captain, or anything. As Betsy said to me afterwards, it was not our place to answer questions about Captain Strange: if the policeman wanted to know anything, let him apply to the captain himself. Which I thought good sense,' concluded Lee. As it was."

"Well, Tom?"

"Well, I thought it about time to go straight home again," said Tom; "and that's why I did not meet you, Charley. And the next day, Friday, I cleared out of my diggings in that quarter of the globe, rigged myself out afresh, and found other lodgings. I am nearer to you now, Charley: vegetating in the wilds over Blackfriars Bridge."

"How could you be so imprudent as to come here to-night? or to be seen in so conspicuous a spot as the Strand?"

"The fit took me to pay you a visit, old fellow. As to the Strand—it is a fine thoroughfare, you know, and I had not set eyes on it since last summer. I walked up and down a bit, listening to the church bells, and looking about me."

"You turn everything into ridicule, Tom."

"Better that, Charley, than into sighing and groaning."

"How did you know that Leah would open the door to you? Watts might have done so."

"I had it all cut-and-dried. 'Is Mrs. Brown at home?' I should have said, in a voice Watts would never have known. 'Mrs. Brown don't live here,' old Watts would have answered; upon which I should have politely begged his pardon and walked off."

"All very fine, Tom, and you may think yourself amazingly clever; but as sure as you are living, you will run these risks once too often."

"Not I. Didn't I give old Leah a scare! You should have heard her shriek."

"Suppose it had been some enemy—some stickler for law and justice—that I had brought home with me to-night, instead of Lake?"

"But it wasn't," laughed Tom. "It was Lake himself. And I guess he is as safe as you are."

"Be sure of that," added Lake. "But what do you think of doing, Heriot? You cannot hide away for ever in the wilds of Blackfriars. I would not answer for your safety there for a day."

"Goodness knows!" said Tom. "Perhaps Charley could put me up here—in one of his top bedrooms?"

Whether he spoke in jest or earnest, I knew not. He might remember that I was running a risk in concealing him even for an hour or two. Were it discovered, the law might make me answer for it.

"I should like something to eat, Charley."

Leaving him with Lake, I summoned Leah, and bade her bring up quickly what she had. She speedily appeared with the tray.

"Good old Leah!" said Tom to her. "That ham looks tempting."

"Mr. Tom, if you go on like this, loitering in the open streets and calling at houses, trouble will overtake you," returned Leah, in much the same tone she had used to reprimand him when a child. "I wonder what your dear, good mother would say to it if she saw you throwing yourself into peril. Do you remember, sir, how often she would beg of you to be good?"

"My mother!" repeated Tom, who was in one of his lightest moods. "Why, you never saw her. She was dead and buried and gone to heaven before you knew anything of us."

"Ah well, Master Tom, you know I mean Mrs. Heriot—afterwards Mrs. Strange. It wouldn't be you, sir, if you didn't turn everything into a jest. She was a good mother to you all."

"That she was, Leah. Excused our lessons for the asking, and fed us on jam."

He was taking his supper rapidly the while; for, of course, he had to be away before church was over and Watts was home again. The man might have been true and faithful; little doubt of it; but it would have added one more item to the danger.

Lake went out and brought a cab; and Tom, his wide-awake low on his brow, his rough coat on, and his red comforter round about his throat, vaulted into it, to be conveyed over Blackfriars Bridge to any point that he might choose to indicate.

"It is an amazing hazard his going about like this," cried Lake, as we sat down together in front of the fire. "He must be got out of England as quickly as possible."

"But he won't go."

"Then, mark my words, Charles, bad will come of it."

CHAPTER IV

RESTITUTION

Time had gone on—weeks and weeks—though there is little to tell of passing events. Things generally remained pretty much as they had been. The Levels were abroad again. Mrs. Brightman on the whole was better, but had occasional relapses; Annabel spent most of her time at Hastings; and Tom Heriot had not yet been taken.

Tom was now at an obscure fishing village on the coast of Scotland, passing himself off as a fisherman, owning a small boat and pretending to fish. This did not allay our anxiety, which was almost as great as ever. Still, it was something to have him away from London. Out of Great Britain he refused to move.

Does the reader remember George Coney's money, that so strangely disappeared the night of Mr. Brightman's death? From that hour to this nothing has been seen or heard of it: but the time for it was now at hand. And what I am about to relate may appear a very common-place ending to a mystery— though, indeed, it was not yet quite the ending. In my capacity of story-teller I could have invented a hundred romantic incidents, and worked them and the reader up to a high point of interest; but I can only record the incident as it happened, and its termination was a very matter-of-fact one.

I was sitting one evening in the front room: a sitting-room now—I think this has been said before— smoking my after-dinner cigar. The window was open to the summer air, which all day long had been intensely hot. A letter received in the morning from Gloucestershire from Mr. Coney, to which his son had scrawled a postscript: "Has that bag turned up yet?" had set me thinking of the loss, and from that I fell to thinking of the loss of the Clavering will, which had followed close upon it. Edmund Clavering, by the way, had been with me that day to impart some news. He was going to be married—to a charming girl, too—and we were discussing settlements. My Lady Clavering, he said, was figuring at Baden-Baden, and report ran that she was about to espouse a French count with a fierce moustache.

Presently I took up the Times, not opened before that day, and was deep in a police case, which had convulsed the court in Marlborough Street with laughter, and was convulsing me, when a vehicle dashed down Essex Street. It was the van of the Parcels Delivery Company.

"Mr. Strange live here?" was the question I heard from the man who had descended from the seat beside the driver, when Watts went out.

"All right," said Watts.

"Here's a parcel for him. Nothing to pay."

The driver whipped up his horse, then turned sharply round, and—overturned the van. It was not the first accident of a similar nature, or the last by many, that I have seen in that particular spot. How it is I don't know, but drivers, especially cabmen, have an unconquerable propensity for pulling their horses round in a perilously short fashion at the bottom of Essex Street, and sometimes the result is that they come to grief. I threw down my newspaper and leaned out at the window watching the fun. The street was covered with parcels, and the driver and his friend were throwing off their consternation in choice language. One hamper could not be picked up: it had contained wine loosely packed, and the broken bottles were lying in a red pool. Where the mob collected from, that speedily arrived to assist, was a marvel. The van at length took its departure up the street, considerably shorn of the triumph with which it had dashed down.

This had taken up a considerable space of time, and it was growing too dark to resume my newspaper. Turning from the window, I proceeded to examine the parcel which Watts had brought up on its arrival and placed on the table. It was about a foot square, wrapped in brown paper, sealed and tied with string; and, in what Tony Lumpkin would have called a confounded cramped, up-and-down hand, where you could not tell an izzard from an R, was directed "C. Strange, Esquire."

I took out my penknife, cut the string, and removed the paper; and there was disclosed a pasteboard-box with green edges, also sealed. I opened it, and from a mass of soft paper took out a small canvas bag, tied round with tape, and containing thirty golden sovereigns!

From the very depth of my conviction I believed it to be the bag we had lost. It was the bag; for, on turning it round, there were Mr. Coney's initials, S. C., neatly marked with blue cotton, as they had been on the one left by George. It was one of their sample barley bags. I wondered if they were the same sovereigns. Where had it been? Who had taken it? And who had returned it?

I rang the bell, and then called to Watts, who was coming up to answer it, to bring Leah also. It was my duty to tell them, especially Leah, of the money's restitution, as they had been inmates of the house when it was lost.

Watts only stared and ejaculated; but Leah, with some colour, for once, in her pale cheeks, clasped her hands. "Oh, sir, I'm thankful you have found it again!" she exclaimed. "I'm heartily thankful!"

"So am I, Leah, though the mystery attending the transaction is as great as ever; indeed, more so."

It certainly was. They went down again, and I sat musing over the problem. But nothing could I make out of it. One moment I argued that the individual taking it (whomsoever it might be) must have had temporary need of funds, and, the difficulty over, had now restored the money. The next, I wondered whether anyone could have taken the bag inadvertently, and had now discovered it. I locked the bag safely up, wrote a letter to George Coney, and then went out to confide the news to Arthur Lake.

Taking the short cuts and passages that lead from Essex Street to the Temple, as I generally did when bound for Lake's chambers, I was passing onwards, when I found myself called to—or I thought so. Standing still in the shade, leaning against the railings of the Temple Gardens, was a slight man of middle height: and he seemed to say "Charley."

Glancing in doubt, half stopping as I did so, yet thinking I must have been mistaken, I was passing on, when the voice came again.

"Charley!"

I stopped then. And I declare that in the revulsion it brought me you might have knocked me down with a feather; for it was Tom Heriot.

"I was almost sure it was you, Charles," he said in a low voice; "but not quite sure."

I had not often had such a scare as this. My heart, with pain and dismay, beat as if it meant to burst its bonds.

"Can it possibly be you?" I cried. "What brings you here? Why have you come again?"

"Reached London this morning. Came here when dusk set in, thinking I might have the luck to see you or Lake, Charley."

"But why have you left Scotland? You were safer there."

"Don't know that I was. And I had grown tired to death of it."

"It will end in death, or something like it, if you persist in staying here."

Tom laughed his gay, ringing laugh. I looked round to see that no one was about, or within hearing.

"What a croaker you are, old Charley! I'm sure you ought to kill the fatted calf, to celebrate my return from banishment."

"But, Tom, you know how dangerous it is, and must be, for you to be here in London."

"And it was becoming dangerous up there," he quickly rejoined. "Since the summer season set in, those blessed tourists are abroad again, with their staves and knapsacks. No place is safe from them, and the smaller and more obscure it is, the more they are sure to find it. The other day I was in my boat in my fishing toggery, as usual, when a fellow comes up, addresses me as 'My good man,' and plunges into queries touching the sea and the fishing-trade. Now who do you think that was, Charles?"

"I can't say."

"It was James Lawless, Q.C.—the leader who prosecuted at my trial."

"Good heavens!"

"I unfastened the boat, keeping my back to him and my face down, and shot off like a whirlwind, calling out that I was behind time, and must put out. I took good care, Charles, not to get back before the stars were bright in the night sky."

"Did he recognise you?"

"No—no. For certain, no. But he would have done so had I stayed to talk. And it is not always that I could escape as I did then. You must see that."

I saw it all too plainly.

"So I thought it best to make myself scarce, Charles, and leave the tourists' haunts. I sold my boat; no difficulty in that; though, of course, the two men who bought it shaved me; and came over to London as fast as a third-class train would bring me. Dare not put my nose into a first-class carriage, lest I should drop upon some one of my old chums."

"Of all places, Tom, you should not have chosen London."

"Will you tell me, old fellow, what other place I could have pitched upon?"

And I could not tell.

"Go where I will," he continued, "it seems that the Philistines are likely to find me out."

We were pacing about now, side by side, keeping in the shade as much as possible, and speaking under our breath.

"You will have to leave the country, Tom; you must do it. And go somewhere over the seas."

"To Van Diemen's Land, perhaps," suggested Tom.

"Now, be quiet. The subject is too serious for jesting. I should think—perhaps—America. But I must have time to consider. Where do you mean to stay at present? Where are you going to-night?"

"I've been dodging about all day, not showing up much; but I'm going now to where I lodged last, down Blackfriars way. You remember?"

"Yes, I remember: it is not so long ago."

"It is as safe as any other quarter, for aught I can tell. Any way, I don't know of another."

"Are you well, Tom?" I asked. He was looking thin, and seemed to have a nasty cough upon him.

"I caught cold some time ago, and it hangs about me," he replied. "Oh, I shall be all right now I'm here," he added carelessly.

"You ought to take a good jorum of something hot when you get to bed to-night—"

Tom laughed. "I am likely to get anything of that sort in any lodging I stand a chance of to-night. Well done, Charley! I haven't old Leah to coddle me."

And somehow the mocking words made me realize the discomforts and deprivations of Tom Heriot's present life. How would it all end?

We parted with a hand-shake: he stealing off on his way to his lodging, I going thoughtfully on mine. It was a calm summer evening, clear and lovely, the stars twinkling in the sky, but all its peace had gone out for me.

It was impossible to foresee what the ending would or could be. At any moment Tom might be recognised and captured, so long as he inhabited London; and it might be difficult to induce him to leave it. Still more difficult to cause him to depart altogether for other lands and climes.

Not long before, I had consulted with Mr. Serjeant Stillingfar as to the possibility of obtaining a pardon for Tom. That he had not been guilty was indisputable, though the law had deemed him so. But the Serjeant had given me no encouragement that any such movement would be successful. The very fact, as he pointed out, of Tom Heriot's having escaped clandestinely, would tell against him. What, I said then, if Tom gave himself up? He smiled, and told me I had better not ask his opinion upon the practical points of the case.

So the old trouble was back again in full force, and I knew not how to cope with it.

The summer sun, glowing with light and heat, lay full upon Hastings and St. Leonard's. The broad expanse of sea sparkled beneath it; the houses that looked on the water were burning and blistering under the fierce rays. Miss Brightman, seated at her drawing-room window, knitting in hand, observed that it was one of the most dazzling days she remembered.

The remark was made to me and to Annabel. We sat at the table together, looking over a book of costly engravings that Miss Brightman had recently bought. "I shall leave it with you, Charles," she said, "when I go away; you will take care of it. And if it were not that you are tied to London, and it would be too far for you to go up and down daily, I would leave you my house also—that you might live in it, and take care of that during my absence."

Mrs. Brightman had come to her senses. Very much, I confess, to my astonishment, much also I think to Annabel's, she had put aside her prejudices and consented to our marriage. The difficulty of where her daughter was to be during Miss Brightman's sojourn in Madeira had in a degree paved the way for it. Annabel would, of course, have returned to her mother; she begged hard to be allowed to do so: she believed it her duty to be with her. But Miss Brightman would not hear of it, and, had she yielded, I should have interposed my veto in Mr. Brightman's name. In Hatch's words, strong in sense but weak in grammar, "their home wasn't no home for Miss Annabel."

Mrs. Brightman could only be conscious of this. During her sojourn at Brighton, and for some little time after her return home, she had been very much better; had fought resolutely with the insidious foe, and conquered. But alas! she fell away again. Now she was almost as bad as ever; tolerably sober by day, very much the opposite by night.

Miss Brightman, dating forward, seeing, as she feared, only shoals and pitfalls, and most anxious for Annabel, had journeyed up to Clapham to her sister-in-law, and stayed there with her a couple of days. What passed between them even Hatch never knew; but she did know that her mistress was brought to a penitent and subdued frame of mind, and that she promised Lucy Brightman, with many tears, to strive to overcome her fatal habit for the good God's sake. And it was during this visit that she withdrew her opposition to the marriage; when Miss Brightman returned home she carried the consent with her.

And my present visit to Hastings was to discuss time and place and other matters; more particularly the question of where our home was to be. A large London house we were not yet rich enough to set up, and I would not take Annabel to an inferior one; but I had seen a charming little cottage at Richmond that might suit us—if she liked the locality.

Closing the book of engravings, I turned to Miss Brightman, and entered upon the subject. Suddenly her attention wavered. It seemed to be attracted by something in the road.

"Why, bless my heart, it is!" she cried in astonishment. "If ever I saw Hatch in my life, that is Hatch—coming up the street! Annabel, child, give me the glasses."

The glasses were on the table, and I handed them to her. Annabel flew to the window and grew white. She was never free from fears of what might happen in her mother's house. Hatch it was, and apparently in haste.

"What can be the matter?" she gasped. "Oh, Aunt Lucy!"

"Hatch is nodding heartily, as if not much were wrong," remarked Miss Brightman, who was watching her through the glasses. "Hatch is peculiar in manner, as you are aware, Mr. Charles, but she means no disrespect by it."

I smiled. I knew Hatch quite as well as Miss Brightman knew her.

"Now what brings you to Hastings?" she exclaimed, rising from her chair, when Hatch was shown in.

"My missis brought me, ma'am," returned Hatch, with composure. "Miss Annabel, you be looking frighted, but there's nothing wrong. Yesterday morning, all in a flurry like, your mamma took it into her head to come down here, and we drove down with—"

"Drove down?"

"Yes, ma'am, with four posters to the carriage. My missis can't abear the rail; she says folks stare at her: and here we be at the Queen's Hotel, she, and me, and Perry."

"Would you like to take a chair, Hatch?" said Miss Brightman.

"My legs is used to standing, ma'am," replied Hatch, with a nod of thanks, "and I've not much time to linger. It was late last night when we got here. This morning, up gets my missis, and downstairs she comes to her breakfast in her sitting-room, and me with her to wait upon her, for sometimes her hands is shaky, and she prefers me to Perry or anybody else—"

"How has your mistress been lately?" interposed Miss Brightman.

"Better, ma'am. Not always quite the thing, though a deal better on the whole. But I must get on about this morning," added Hatch impressively. "'Waiter,' says my missis when the man brings up the coffee. 'Mum?' says he. 'I am subject to spadical attacks in the chest,' says she, 'and should like to have some brandy in my room: they take me sometimes in the middle of the night. Put a bottle into it, the very best French, and a corkscrew. Or you may as well put two bottles,' she goes on; 'I may be here some time.' 'It shall be done, mum,' says he. I was as vexed as I could be to hear it," broke off Hatch, "but what could I do? I couldn't contradict my missis and tell the man that no brandy must be put in her room, or else she'd drink it. Well, ma'am, I goes down presently to my own breakfast with Perry, and while we sat at it a chambermaid comes through the room: 'I've put two bottles of brandy in the lady's bedroom, as was ordered,' says she. With that Perry looks at me all in a fluster—he have no more wits to turn things off than a born idiot. 'Very well,' says I to her, eating at my egg as if I thought nothing; 'I hopes my missis won't have no call to use 'em, but she's took awful bad in the chest sometimes, and it's as well for us to be ready.' 'I'm sure I pities her,' says the girl, 'for there ain't nothing worse than spasms. I has 'em myself occasional—'"

When once Hatch was in the full flow of a narrative, there was no getting in a word edgeways, and Miss Brightman had to repeat her question twice: "Does Perry know the nature of the illness that affects Mrs. Brightman?"

"Why, in course he does, ma'am," was Hatch's rejoinder. "He couldn't be off guessing it for himself, and the rest I told him. Why, ma'am, without his helping, we could never keep it dark from the servants at home. It was better to make a confidant of Perry, that I might have his aid in screening the trouble, than to let it get round to everybody. He's as safe and sure as I be, and when it all first came out to him, he cried over it, to think of what his poor master must have suffered in mind before death took him. Well, ma'am, I made haste over my breakfast, and I went upstairs, and there was the bottles and the corkscrew, so I whips 'em off the table and puts them out of sight. Mrs. Brightman comes up presently, and looks about and goes down again. Three separate times she comes up, and the third time she gives the bell a whirl, and in runs the chambermaid, who was only outside. 'I gave orders this morning,' says my lady, 'to have some brandy placed in the room.' 'Oh, I have got the brandy,' says I, before the girl could speak; 'I put it in the little cupboard here, ma'am.' So away goes the girl, looking from the corners of her eyes at me, as if suspicious I meant to crib it for my own use: and my mistress began: 'Draw one of them corks, Hatch.' 'No, ma'am,' says I, 'not yet; please don't.' 'Draw 'em both,' says missis—for there are times," added Hatch, "when a trifle puts her out so much that it's hazardous to cross her. I drew the cork of one, and missis just pointed with her finger to the tumbler on the wash-handstand, and I brought it forward and the decanter of water. 'Now you may go,' says she; so I took up the corkscrew. 'I told you to leave that,' says she, in her temper, and I had to come away without it, and the minute I was gone she turned the key upon me. Miss Annabel, I see the words are grieving of you, but they are the truth, and I can but tell them."

"Is she there now—locked in?" asked Miss Brightman.

"She's there now," returned Hatch, with solemn enunciation, to make up for her failings in grammar, which was never anywhere in times of excitement; "she is locked in with them two bottles and the corkscrew, and she'll just drink herself mad—and what's to be done? I goes at once to Perry and tells him. 'Let's get in through the winder,' says Perry—which his brains is only fit for a gander, as I've said many a time. 'You stop outside her door to listen again downright harm,' says I, 'that's what you'll do; and I'll go for Miss Brightman.' And here I'm come, ma'am, running all the way."

"What can I do?" wailed Miss Brightman.

"Ma'am," answered Hatch, "I think that if you'll go back with me, and knock at her room door, and call out that you be come to pay her a visit, she'd undo it. She's more afeared of you than of anybody living. She can't have done herself much harm yet, and you might coax her out for a walk or a drive, and then bring her in to dinner here—anything to get her away from them two dangerous bottles. If I be making too free, ma'am, you'll be good enough to excuse me—it is for the family's sake. At home I can manage her pretty well, but to have a scene at the hotel would make it public."

"What is to be the ending?" I exclaimed involuntarily as Miss Brightman went in haste for her bonnet.

"Why, the ending must be—just what it will be," observed Hatch philosophically. "But, Mr. Charles, I don't despair of her yet. Begging your pardon, Miss Annabel, you'd better not come. Your mamma won't undo her door if she thinks there's many round it."

Annabel stood at the window as they departed, her face turned from me, her eyes blinded with tears. I drew her away, though I hardly knew how to soothe her. It was a heavy grief to bear.

"My days are passed in dread of what tidings may be on the way to me," she began, after a little time given to gathering composure. "I ought to be nearer my mother, Charles; I tell Aunt Lucy so almost every day. She might be ill and dead before I could get to her, up in London."

"And you will be nearer to her shortly, Annabel. My dear, where shall our home be? I was thinking of Richmond—"

"No, no," she interrupted in sufficient haste to show me she had thoughts of her own.

"Annabel! It shall not be there: at your mother's. Anywhere else."

"It is somewhere else that I want to be."

"Then you shall be. Where is it?"

She lifted her face like a pleading child's, and spoke in a whisper. "Charles, let me come to you in Essex Street."

"Essex Street!" I echoed in surprise. "My dear Annabel, I will certainly not bring you to Essex Street and its inconveniences. I cannot do great things for you yet, but I can do better than that."

"They would not be inconveniences to me. I would turn them into pleasures. We would take another servant to help Watts and Leah; or two if necessary. You would not find me the least encumbrance; I would never be in the way of your professional rooms. And in the evening, when you had finished for the day, we would dine, and go down to mamma's for an hour, and then back again. Charles, it would be a happy home: let me come to it."

But I shook my head. I did not see how it could be arranged; and said so.

"No, because at present the idea is new to you," returned Annabel. "Think it over, Charles. Promise me that you will do so."

"Yes, my dear; I can at least promise you that."

There was less trouble with Mrs. Brightman that day than had been anticipated. She opened her door at once to her sister-in-law, who brought her back to the Terrace. Hatch had been wise. In the afternoon we all went for a drive in a fly, and returned to dinner. And the following day Mrs. Brightman, with her servants, departed for London in her travelling-carriage, no scandal whatever having been caused at the Queen's Hotel. I went up by train early in the morning.

It is surprising how much thinking upon a problem simplifies it. I began to see by degrees that Annabel's coming to Essex Street could be easily managed; nay, that it would be for the best. Miss Brightman strongly advocated it. At present a large portion of my income had to be paid over to Mrs. Brightman in accordance with her husband's will, so that I could not do as I would, and must study economy. Annabel would be rich in time; for Mrs. Brightman's large income, vested at present in trustees, must eventually descend to Annabel; but that time was not yet. And who knew what expenses Tom Heriot might bring upon me?

Changes had to be made in the house. I determined to confine the business rooms to the ground floor; making Miss Methold's parlour, which had not been much used since her death, my own private consulting-room. The front room on the first floor would be our drawing-room, the one behind it the dining-room.

Leah was in an ecstasy when she heard the news. The workmen were coming in to paint and paper, and then I told her.

"Of course, Mr. Charles, it—is—"

"Is what, Leah?"

"Miss Annabel."

"It should be no one else, Leah. We shall want another servant or two, but you can still be major-domo."

"If my poor master had only lived to see it!" she uttered, with enthusiasm. "How happy he would have been; how proud to have her here! Well, well, what turns things take!"

CHAPTER V

CONFESSION

October came in; and we were married early in the month, the wedding taking place from Mrs. Brightman's residence, as was of course only right and proper. It was so very quiet a wedding that there is not the least necessity for describing it—and how can a young man be expected to give the particulars of his own? Mr. Serjeant Stillingfar was present; Lord and Lady Level, now staying in London, drove down for it; and Captain Chantrey gave his niece away. For Mrs. Brightman had chosen to request him to accept her invitation to do so, and to be accompanied by his wife, Lady Grace. Miss Brightman was also present, having travelled up from Hastings the day before. Three or four days later on, she would sail for Madeira.

I could not spare more than a fortnight from work, leaving Lennard as my locum tenens. Annabel would have been glad to spare less, for she was haunted by visions of what might happen to her mother. Though there was no especial cause for anxiety in that quarter just now, she could never feel at ease. And on my part I was more anxious than ever about Tom Heriot, for more reasons than one.

The fortnight came to an end, all too soon: and late on the Saturday evening we reached home. Watts threw open the door, and there stood Leah in a silk gown. The drawing-room, gayer than it used to be, was bright with a fire and preparations for tea.

"How homelike it looks!" exclaimed Annabel. "Charles," she whispered, turning to me with her earnest eyes, as she had been wont to do when a child: "I will not make the least noise when you have clients with you. You shall not know I am in the house: I will take care not to drop even a reel of cotton on the carpet. I do thank you for letting me come to Essex Street: I should not have seemed so completely your wife had you taken me to any but your old home."

The floors above were also in order, their chambers refurnished. Leah went up to them with her new mistress, and I went down to the clerks' office, telling Annabel I should not be there five minutes. One of the clerks, Allen, had waited; but I had expected Lennard.

"Is Mr. Lennard not here?" I asked. "Did he not wait? I wrote to him to do so."

"Mr. Lennard has not been here all day, sir," was Allen's reply. "A messenger came from him this morning, to say he was ill."

We were deep in letters and other matters, I and Allen, when the front door opened next the office door, and there stood Arthur Lake, laughing, a light coat on his arm.

"Fancy! I've been down the river for a blow," cried he. "Just landed at the pier here. Seeing lights in your windows, I thought you must have got back, Charley."

We shook hands, and he stayed a minute, talking. Then, wishing good-night to Allen, he backed out of the room, making an almost imperceptible movement to me with his head. I followed him out, shutting the office door behind me. Lake touched my arm and drew me outside.

"I suppose you've not heard from Tom Heriot since you were away," breathed Lake, in cautious tones, as we stood together on the outer step.

"No; I did not expect to hear. Why?"

"I saw him three days ago," whispered Lake. "I had a queer-looking letter on Wednesday morning from one Mr. Dominic Turk, asking me to call at a certain place in Southwark. Of course, I guessed it was Tom, and that he had moved his lodgings again; and I found I was right."

"Dominic Turk!" I repeated. "Does he call himself that?"

Lake laughed. "He is passing now for a retired schoolmaster. Says he's sure nobody can doubt he is one as long as he sticks to that name."

"How is he? Has any fresh trouble turned up? I'm sure you've something bad to tell me."

"Well, Charley, honestly speaking, it is a bad look-out, in more ways than one," he answered. "He is very ill, to begin with; also has an idea that a certain policeman named Wren has picked up an inkling of his return, and is trying to unearth him. But," added Lake, "we can't very well talk in this place. I've more to say—"

"Come upstairs, and take tea with me and Annabel," I interrupted.

"Can't," said he; "my dinner's waiting. I'm back two hours later than I expected to be; it has been frizzling, I expect, all the time. Besides, old fellow, I'd rather you and I were alone. There's fearful peril looming ahead, unless I'm mistaken. Can you come round to my chambers to-morrow afternoon?"

"No: we are going to Mrs. Brightman's after morning service."

"It must be left until Monday, then; but I don't think there's much time to be lost. Good-night."

Lake hastened up the street, and I returned to Allen and the letters.

With this interruption, and with all I found to do, the five minutes' absence I had promised my wife lengthened into twenty. At last the office was closed for the night, Allen left, and I ran upstairs, expecting to have kept Annabel waiting tea. She was not in the drawing-room, the tea was not made, and I went up higher and found her sobbing in the bedroom. It sent me into a cold chill.

"My love, what is this? Are you disappointed? Are you not happy?"

"Oh, Charles," she sobbed, clinging to me, "you know I am happy. It is not that. But I could not help thinking of my father. Leah got talking about him; and I remembered once his sitting in that very chair, holding me on his knee. I must have been about seven years old. Miss Methold was ill—"

At that moment there came a knock and a ring at the front door. Not a common knock and ring, but sharp, loud and prolonged, resounding through the house as from some impatient messenger of evil. It startled us both. Annabel's fears flew to her mother; mine to a different quarter, for Lake's communication was troubling and tormenting me.

"Charles! if—"

"Hush, dear. Listen."

As we stood outside on the landing, her heart beating against my encircling hand, and our senses strained to listen, we heard Watts open the front door.

"Has Mr. Strange come home?" cried a voice hurriedly—that of a woman.

"Yes," said Watts.

"Can I speak to him? It is on a matter of life and death."

"Where do you come from?" asked Watts, with habitual caution.

"I come from Mr. Lennard. Oh, pray do not waste time!"

"All right, my darling; it is not from your mother," I whispered to Annabel, as I ran down.

A young woman stood at the foot of the stairs; I was at a loss to guess her condition in life. She had the face and manner of a lady, but her dress was poor and shabby.

"I have come from my father, sir—Mr. Lennard," she said in a low tone, blushing very much. "He is dangerously ill: we fear he is dying, and so does he. He bade me say that he must see you, or he cannot die in peace. Will you please be at the trouble of coming?"

One hasty word despatched to my wife, and I went out with Miss Lennard, hailing a cab, which had just set down its freight some doors higher up. "What is the matter with your father?" I questioned, as we whirled along towards Blackfriars Bridge, in accordance with her directions.

"It is an attack of inward inflammation," she replied. "He was taken ill suddenly last night after he got home from the office, and he has been in great agony all day. This evening he grew better; the pain almost subsided; but the doctor said that might not prove a favourable symptom. My father asked for the truth—whether he was dying, and the answer was that he might be. Then my father grew terribly uneasy in mind, and said he must see you if possible before he died—and sent me to ascertain, sir, whether you had returned home."

The cab drew up at a house in a side street, a little beyond Blackfriars Bridge. We entered, and Miss Lennard left me in the front sitting-room. The remnants of faded gentility were strangely mixed with bareness and poverty. Poor Lennard was a gentleman born and bred, but had been reduced by untoward misfortune. Trifling ornaments stood about; "antimacassars" were thrown over the shabby chairs. Miss Lennard had gone upstairs, but came down quickly.

"It is the door on the left, sir, on the second landing," said she, putting a candle in my hand. "My father is anxiously expecting you, but says I am not to go up."

It was a small landing, nothing in front of me but a bare white-washed wall, and two doors to the left. I blundered into the wrong one. A night-cap border turned on the bed, and a girlish face looked up from under it.

"What do you want?" she said.

"Pardon me. I am in search of Mr. Lennard."

"Oh, it is the next room. But—sir! wait a moment. Oh, wait, wait!"

I turned to her in surprise, and she put up two thin white hands in an imploring attitude. "Is it anything bad? Have you come to take him?"

"To take him! What do you mean?"

"You are not a sheriff's officer?"

I smiled at her troubled countenance. "I am Mr. Strange—come to see how he is."

Down fell her hands peacefully. "Sir, I beg your pardon: thank you for telling me. I know papa has sometimes been in apprehension, and I lie here and fear things till I am stupid. A strange step on the stairs, or a strange knock at the door, sets me shaking."

The next room was the right one, and Lennard was lying in it on a low bed; his face looked ghastly, his eyes wildly anxious.

"Lennard," I said, "I am sorry to hear of your illness. What's the matter?"

"Sit down, Mr. Strange; sit down," he added, pointing to a chair, which I drew near. "It is an attack of inflammation: the pain has ceased now, but the doctor says it is an uncertain symptom: it may be for better, or it may be for worse. If the latter, I have not many hours to live."

"What brought it on?"

"I don't know: unless it was that I drank a draught of cold water when I was hot. I have not been very strong for some time, and a little thing sends me into a violent heat. I had a long walk, four miles, and I made nearly a run of it half the way, being pressed for time. When I got in, I asked Leah for some water, and drank two glasses of it, one after the other. It seemed to strike a chill to me at the time."

"It was at the office, then. Four miles! Why did you not ride?"

"It was not your business I was out on, sir; it was my own. But whether that was the cause or not, the illness came on, and it cannot be remedied now. If I am to die, I must die; God is over all: but I cannot go without making a confession to you. How the fear of death's approach alters a man's views and feelings!" he went on, in a different tone. "Yesterday, had I been told I must make this confession to you, I should have said, Let me die, rather; but it appears to me now to be an imperative duty, and one I must nerve myself to perform."

Lennard lay on his pillow, and looked fixedly at me, and I not less fixedly at him. What, in the shape of a "confession," could he have to make to me? He had been managing clerk in Mr. Brightman's office long before I was in it, a man of severe integrity, and respected by all.

"The night Mr. Brightman died," he began under his panting breath, "the bag of gold was missing—George Coney's. You remember it."

"Well?"

"I took it."

Was Lennard's mind wandering? He was no more likely to take gold than I was. I sat still, gazing at him.

"Yes, it was I who took it, sir. Will you hear the tale?"

A deep breath, and the drawing of my chair closer to his bedside, was my only answer.

"You are a young man, Mr. Strange. I have taken an interest in you since you first came, a lad, into the office, and were under my authority—Charles, do this; Charles, do the other. Not that I have shown any especial interest, for outwardly I am cold and undemonstrative; but I saw what you were, and liked you in my heart. You are a young man yet, I say; but, liking you, hoping for your welfare, I pray Heaven that it may never be your fate, in after-life, to be trammelled with misfortunes as I have been. For me they seem to have had no end, and the worst of them in later years has been that brought upon me by an undutiful and spendthrift son."

In a moment there flashed into my mind my later trouble in Tom Heriot: I seemed to be comparing the one with the other. "Have you been trammelled with an undutiful son?" I said aloud.

"I have been, and am," replied Lennard. "It has been my later cross. The first was that of losing my property and position in life, for, as you know, Mr. Strange, I was born and reared a gentleman. The last cross has been Leonard—that is his name, Leonard Lennard—and it has been worse than the first, for it has kept us down, and in a perpetual ferment for years. It has kept us poor amongst the poor: my salary, as you know, is a handsome one, but it has chiefly to be wasted upon him."

"What age is he?"

"Six-and-twenty yesterday."

"Then you are not forced to supply his extravagance, to find money for his faults and follies. You are not obliged to let him keep you down."

"By law, no," sighed poor Lennard. "But these ill-doing sons sometimes entwine themselves around your very heartstrings; far rather would you suffer and suffer than not ward off the ill from them. He has tried his hand at many occupations, but remains at none; the result is always trouble: and yet his education and intellect, his good looks and perfect, pleasant manners, would fit him for almost any responsible position in life. But he is reckless. Get into what scrape he would, whether of debt, or worse, here he was sure of a refuge and a welcome; I received him, his mother and sisters loved him. One of them is bedridden," he added, in an altered tone.

"I went first by mistake into the next room. I probably saw her."

"Yes, that's Maria. It is a weakness that has settled in her legs; some chronic affection, I suppose; and there she has lain for ten months. With medical attendance and sea air she might be restored, they tell me, but I can provide neither. Leonard's claims have been too heavy."

"But should you waste means on him that ought to be applied to her necessities?" I involuntarily interrupted.

He half raised himself on his elbow, and the effort proved how weak he was, and his eyes and his voice betrayed a strange earnestness. "When a son, whom you love better than life itself, has to be saved from the consequences of his follies, from prison, from worse disgrace even than that, other interests are forgotten, let them be what they may. Silent, patient needs give way to obtrusive wants that stare you in the face, and that may bear fear and danger in their train. Mr. Strange, you can imagine this."

"I do. It must ever be so."

"The pecuniary wants of a young man, such as my son is, are as the cry of the horse-leech. Give! give! Leonard mixes sometimes with distant relatives, young fellows of fashion, who are moving in a sphere far above our present position, although I constantly warn him not to do it. One of these wants, imperative and to be provided for in some way or other, occurred the beginning of February in this year. How I managed to pay it I can hardly tell, but it stripped me of all the money I could raise, and left me with some urgent debts upon me. The rent was owing, twelve months the previous December, and some of the tradespeople were becoming clamorous. The landlord, discerning the state of affairs, put in a distress, terrifying poor Maria, whose illness had then not very long set in, almost to death. That I had the means to pay the man out you may judge, when I tell you that we had not the money to buy a joint of meat or a loaf of bread."

Lennard paused to wipe the dew from his brow.

"Maria was in bed, wanting comforts; Charlotte was worn out with apprehension; Leonard was away again, and we had nothing. Of my wife I will not speak: of delicate frame and delicately reared, the long-continued troubles have reduced her to a sort of dumb apathy. No credit anywhere, and a distress in for rent! In sheer despair, I resolved to disclose part of my difficulty to Mr. Brightman, and ask him to advance me a portion of my next quarter's salary. I hated to do it. A reduced gentleman is, perhaps, over-fastidious. I know I have been so, and my pride rose against it. In health, I could not have spoken to you, Mr. Charles, as I am now doing. I went on, shilly-shallying for a few days. On the Saturday morning Charlotte came to me with a whisper: 'That man in the house says if the rent is not paid to-night, the things will be taken out and sold on Monday: it is the very last day they'll give.' I went to the office, my mind made up at length, and thinking what I should say to Mr. Brightman. Should I tell him part of the truth, or should I urge some plea, foreign to it? It was an unusually busy day: I dare say you remember it, Mr. Charles, for it was that of Mr. Brightman's sudden death. Client after client called, and no opportunity offered for my speaking to him in private. I waited for him to come down, on his way out in the evening, thinking I would speak to him then. He did not come, and when the clients left, and I went upstairs, I found he was stopping in town to see Sir Edmund Clavering. I should have spoken to him then, but you were present. He told me to look in again in the course of the evening, and I hoped I might find him alone then. You recollect the subsequent events of the night, sir?"

"I shall never forget them."

"When I came in, as he directed me, between seven and eight o'clock, there occurred that flurry with Leah—the cause of which I never knew. She said Mr. Brightman was alone, and I went up. He was lying in your room, Mr. Charles; had fallen close to his own desk, the deep drawer of which stood open. I tried to raise him; I sprinkled water on his face, but I saw that he was dead. On the desk lay a small canvas bag. I took it up and shook it. Why, I do not know, for I declare that no wrong thought had then come into my mind. He appeared to have momentarily put it out of the drawer, probably in search of something, for his private cheque-book and the key of the iron safe, that I knew were always kept in the drawer, lay near it. I shook the bag, and its contents sounded like gold. I opened it, and counted thirty sovereigns. Mr. Brightman was dead. I could not apply to him; and yet money I must have. The temptation upon me was strong, and I took it. Don't turn away from me, sir. There are some temptations too strong to be resisted by a man in his necessities."

"Indeed, I am not turning from you. The temptation was overwhelmingly great."

"Indeed," continued the sick man, "the devil was near me then. I put the key and the cheque-book inside, and I locked the drawer, and placed the keys in Mr. Brightman's pocket, where he kept them, and I leaped down the stairs with the bag in my hand. It was all done in a minute or two of time, though it seems long in relating it. Where should I put the bag, now I had it? Upon my person? No: it might be missed directly, and inquired for. I was in a tumult—scarcely sane, I believe—and I dashed into the clerks' office, and, taking off the lid of the coal-box, put it there. Then I tore off for a surgeon. You know the rest. When I returned with him you were there; and the next visitor, while we were standing round Mr. Brightman, was George Coney, after his bag of money. I never shall forget the feeling when you motioned me to take Mr. Brightman's keys from his pocket to get the bag out of the drawer. Or when— after it was missed—you took me with you to search for it, in the very office where it was, and I moved the coal-box under the desk. Had you only happened to lift the lid, sir!"

"Ah!"

"When the search was over, and I went home, I had put the bag in my breastpocket. The gold saved me from immediate trouble, but—"

"You have sent it back to me, you know—the bag and the thirty pounds."

"Yes, I sent it back—tardily. I could not do it earlier, though the crime coloured my days with remorse, and I never knew a happy moment until it was restored. But Leonard had been back again, and restoration was not easy."

Miss Lennard opened the door at this juncture. "Papa, the doctor is here. Can he come up? He says he ought to see you."

"Oh, certainly, he must come up," I interposed.

"Yes, yes, Charlotte," said Lennard.

The doctor came in, and stood looking at his patient, after putting a few questions. "Well," said he, "you are better; you will get over it."

"Do you really think so?" I asked joyfully.

"Decidedly I do, now. It has been a sharp twinge, but the danger's over. You see, when pain suddenly ceases, mortification sometimes sets in, and I could not be sure. But you will do this time, Mr. Lennard."

Lennard had little more to say; and, soon after the doctor left, I prepared to follow him.

"There's a trifle of salary due to me, Mr. Strange," he whispered; "that which has been going on since Quarter Day. I suppose you will not keep it from me?"

"Keep it from you! No. Why should I? Do you want it at once? You can have it if you do."

Leonard looked up wistfully. "You do not think of taking me back again? You will not do that?"

"Yes, I will. You and I shall understand each other better than ever now."

The tears welled up to his eyes. He laid his other hand—I had taken one—across his face. I bent over him with a whisper.

"What has passed to-night need never be recurred to between us; and I shall never speak of it to another. We all have our trials and troubles, Lennard. A very weighty one is lying now upon me, though it is not absolutely my own—brought upon me, you see, as yours was. And it is worse than yours."

"Worse!" he exclaimed, looking at me.

"More dangerous in its possible consequences. Now mind," I broke off, shaking him by the hand, "you are not to attempt to come to Essex Street until you are quite strong enough for it. But I shall see you here again on Monday, for I have two or three questions to ask you as to some of the matters that have transpired during my absence. Good-night, Lennard; keep up a good heart; you will outlive your trials yet."

And when I left him he was fairly sobbing.

CHAPTER VI

DANGER

Mrs. Brightman was certainly improving. When I reached her house with Annabel on the following day, Sunday, between one and two o'clock, she was bright and cheerful, and came towards the entrance-gates to meet us. She, moreover, displayed interest in all we told her of our honeymoon in the Isle of Wight, and of the places we had visited. Besides that, I noticed that she took water with her dinner.

"If she'll only keep to it," said Hatch, joining me in her unceremonious fashion as I strolled in the garden later, smoking a cigar. "Yes, Mr. Charles, she's trying hard to put bad habits away from her, and I hope she'll be able to do it."

"I hope and trust she will!"

"Miss Brightman went back to Hastings the day after the wedding-day," continued Hatch; "but before she started she had a long interview with my mistress, they two shut up in missis's bedroom alone. For pretty nigh all the rest of the day, my missis was in tears, and she has not touched nothing strong since."

"Nothing at all!" I cried in surprise, for it seemed too good to be true. "Why, that's a fortnight ago! More than a fortnight."

"Well, it is so, Mr. Charles. Not but that missis has tried as long and as hard before now—and failed again."

It was Monday evening before I could find time to go round to Lake's—and he did not come to me. He was at home, poring over some difficult law case by lamp-light.

"Been in court all day, Charley," he cried. "Have not had a minute to spare for you."

"About Tom?" I said, as I sat down. "You seemed to say that you had more unpleasantness to tell me."

"Aye, about Tom," he replied, turning his chair to face me, and propping his right elbow upon his table. "Well, I fear Tom is in a bad way."

"In health, you mean?"

"I do. His cough is frightful, and he is more like a skeleton than a living being. I should say the illness has laid hold of his lungs."

"Has he had a doctor?"

"No. Asks how he is to have one. Says a doctor might (they were his own words) smell a rat. Doctors are not called in to the class of people lodging in that house unless they are dying: and it would soon be seen by any educated man that Tom is not of their kind. My opinion is, that a doctor could not do him much good now," added Lake.

He looked at me as he spoke; to see, I suppose, whether I took in his full meaning. I did—unhappily.

"And what do you think he is talking of now, Charles?" returned Lake. "Of giving himself up."

"Giving himself up! What, to justice?"

Lake nodded. "You know what Tom Heriot is—not much like other people."

"But why should he think of that? It would end everything."

"I was on the point of asking him why," said Lake. "Whether I should have had a satisfactory answer, I cannot say; I should think he could not give one; but we were interrupted. Miss Betsy Lee came in."

"Who? What?" I cried, starting from my chair.

"The young lady you told me of who lives in Lambeth—Miss Betsy Lee. Sit down, Charley. She came over to bring him a pot of jelly."

"Then he has let those people know where he is, Lake! Is he mad?"

"Mad as to carelessness," assented Lake. "I tell you Tom Heriot's not like other people."

"He will leave himself no chance."

"She seems to be a nice, modest little woman," said Lake; "and I'll go bail her visit was quite honest and proper. She had made this jelly, she told Tom, and she and her father hoped it would serve to strengthen him, and her father sent his respects, and hopes to hear that Captain Strange was feeling better."

"Well, Lake, the matter will get beyond me," I said in despair. "Only a word dropped, innocently, by these people in some dangerous quarter, and where will Tom be?"

"That's just it," said Lake. "Policeman Wren is acquainted with them."

"Did you leave the girl there?"

"No. Some rough man came into the room smoking, and sat down, evidently with the intention of making an evening of it; he lives in the same house and has made acquaintance with Tom, or Tom with him. So I said good-night, and the girl did the same, and we went down together. 'Don't you think Captain Strange looks very ill, sir?' said she as we got into the street. 'I'm afraid he does,' I answered. 'I'm sure he does, sir,' she said. 'It's a woeful pity that somebody should be coming upon him for a big back debt just now, obliging him to keep quiet in a low quarter!' So that is what Tom has told his Lambeth friends," concluded Lake.

Lake gave me the address in Southwark, and I determined to see Tom the next evening. In that, however, I was disappointed. One of our oldest clients, passing through London from the country on his way to Pau, summoned me to him on the Tuesday evening.

But I went on Wednesday. The stars were shining overhead as I traversed the silent street, making out Tom's lodgings. He had only an attic bedroom, I found, and I went up to it. He was partly lying across the bed when I entered.

I almost thought even then that I saw death written in his face. White, wan, shadowy it looked; much changed, much worn from what it was three weeks before. But it lighted up with a smile, as he got up to greet me.

"Halloa, Charley!" cried he. "Best congratulations! Made yourself into a respectable man. All good luck to yourself and madam. I'm thinking of coming to Essex Street to pay the wedding visit."

"Thank you," said I, "but do be serious. My coming here is a hazard, as you know, Tom; don't let us waste in nonsense the few minutes I may stay."

"Nonsense!" cried Tom. "Why, do you think I should be afraid to venture to Essex Street?—what nonsense is there in that? Look here, Charley!"

From some box in a dark corner of the room, he got out an old big blue cloak lined with red, and swung it on. The collar, made of some black curly wool, stood up above his ears. He walked about the small room, exhibiting himself.

"Would the sharpest officer in Scotland Yard take me for anyone but old Major Carlen?" laughed he. "I'm sure I look like his double in this elegant cloak. It was his, once."

"His! What, Major Carlen's?"

"Just so. He made me a present of it."

"You have seen him, then!"

"I sent for him," answered Tom, putting off the old cloak and coughing painfully after his recent exertion. "I thought I should like to see the old fellow; I was not afraid he'd betray me; Carlen would not do that; and I dropped a quiet note to his club, taking the chance of his being in town."

"Taking the chance! Suppose he had not been in town, Tom, and the note had fallen into wrong hands—some inquisitive waiter, let us say, who chose to open it?"

"Well—what then? A waiter would only turn up his nose at Mr. Dominic Turk, the retired schoolmaster, and close up the note again for the Major."

"And what would Major Carlen make of Mr. Dominic Turk?"

"Major Carlen would know my handwriting, Charley."

"And he came in answer to it?"

"He came: and blew me up in a loud and awful fashion; seemed to be trying to blow the ceiling off. First, he threatened to go out and bring in the police; next, he vowed he would go straight to Blanche and tell her all. Finally, he calmed down and promised to send me one of his cast-off cloaks to disguise me, in case I had to go into the streets. Isn't it a beauty?"

"Well, now, Tom, if you can be serious for once, what is going to become of you, and what is to be done? I've come to know."

"Wish I could tell you; don't know myself," said he lightly.

"What was it you said to Lake about giving yourself up?"

"Upon my word of honour, Charley, I sometimes feel inclined to do it. I couldn't be much worse off in prison than I am here. Sick and sad, lad, needing comforts that can't be had in such a place as this; no one to see after me, no one to attend to me. Anyway, it would end the suspense."

I sat turning things about in my mind. It all seemed so full of hazard. That he must be got away from his present quarters was certain. I told him so.

"But you are so recklessly imprudent, you see, Tom," I observed, "and it increases the risk. You have had Miss Betsy Lee here."

Tom flung himself back with a laugh. "She has been here twice, the good little soul. The old man came once."

"Don't you think you might as well take up your standing to-morrow on the top of the Monument, and proclaim yourself to the public at large? You try me greatly, Tom!"

"Try you because I see the Lees! Come, Charley, that's good. They are as safe as you are."

"In intention perhaps. How came you to let them know you were to be found here?"

"How came I?" he carelessly rejoined. "Let's see? Oh, I remember. One evening when I was hipped, fit to die of it all and of the confinement to this wretched room, I strolled out. My feet took me to the old ground—Lambeth—and to Lee's. He chanced to see me, and invited me in. Over some whisky and water, I opened out my woes to them; not of course the truth, but as near as might be. Told them of a curmudgeon creditor of past days that I feared was coming down upon me, so that I had to be in close hiding for a bit."

"But you need not have told them where."

"Oh, they'll be cautious. Miss Betsy was so much struck with my cough and my looks that she said she should make some jelly for me, of the kind she used to make for her mother before she died; and the good little girl has brought me some over here twice in a jar. They are all right, Charley."

It was of no use contending with him. After sitting a little time longer, I promised that he should shortly see me again or hear from me, and took my departure. Full of doubt and trouble, I wanted to be alone, to decide, if possible, what was to be done.

What to do about Tom I knew not. That he required nursing and nourishment, and that he ought to be moved where he could have it, was indisputable. But—the risk!

Three-parts of the night I lay awake, thinking of different plans. None seemed feasible. In the morning I was hardly fit for my day's work, and set to it with unsteady nerves and a worried brain. If I had only someone to consult with, some capable man who would help me! I did think of Mr. Serjeant Stillingfar; but I knew he would not like it, would probably refuse advice. One who now and again sat in the position of judge, sentencing men himself, would scarcely choose to aid in concealing an escaped convict.

I was upstairs in the dining-room at one o'clock, taking luncheon with Annabel, when the door was thrown back by Watts and there loomed into the room the old blue cloak with the red lining. For a moment I thought it was the one I had seen the past night in Southwark, and my heart leaped into my mouth. Watts's quiet announcement dispelled the alarm.

"Major Carlen, sir."

The Major unclasped his cloak after shaking hands with us, and flung it across the sofa, just as Tom had flung his on the bed. I pointed to the cold beef, and asked if he would take some.

"Don't mind if I do, Charles," said he, drawing a chair to the table: "I'm too much bothered just now to eat as I ought. A pretty kettle of fish this is, lad, that you and I have had brought upon us!"

I gave him a warning look, glancing at Annabel. The old fellow understood me—she had not been trusted with the present trouble. That Tom Heriot had effected his escape, Annabel knew; that it was expected he would make his way home, she knew; but that he had long been here, and was now close at hand, I had never told her. Why inflict upon her the suspense I had to endure?

"Rather a chilly day for the time of year," observed the Major, as he coughed down his previous words. "Just a little, Mrs. Strange; underdone, please."

Annabel, who carved at luncheon-time, helped him carefully. "And what kettle of fish is it that you and Charles are troubled with, Major?" she inquired, smiling.

"Ah—aw—don't care to say much about it," answered the Major, more ready at an excuse than I should have deemed him. "Blanche is up to her ears in anger against Level; says she'll get a separation from him, and all that kind of nonsense. But you and I may as well not make it our business, Charles, I expect: better let married folk fight out their own battles. And have you heard from your Aunt Lucy yet, Mrs. Strange?"

So the subject was turned off for the time; but down below, in my office, the Major went at it tooth and nail, talking himself into a fever. All the hard names in the Major's vocabulary were hurled at Tom. His original sin was disgraceful enough, never to be condoned, said the Major; but his present imprudent procedure was worse, and desperately wicked.

"Are Blanche and her husband still at variance?" I asked, when he had somewhat cooled down on the other subject.

"They just are, and are likely to remain so," growled the Major. "It's Blanche's fault. Men have ways of their own, and she's a little fool for wishing to interfere with his. Don't let your wife begin that, Charles; it's my best advice to you. You are laughing, young fellow! Well, perhaps you and Level don't row in quite the same boat; but you can't foresee the shoals you may pitch into. No one can."

We were interrupted by Lennard, who had come back on the previous day, pale and pulled down by his sharp attack of illness, but the same efficient man of business as ever. A telegram had been delivered, which he could not deal with without me.

"I'll be off, then," said the Major; "I suppose I'm only hindering work. And I wish you well through your difficulties, Charles," he added significantly. "I wish all of us well through them. Good-day, Mr. Lennard."

The Major was ready enough to wish that, but he could not suggest any means by which it might be accomplished. I had asked him; and he confessed himself incompetent to advise. "I should send him off to sea in a whaling-boat and keep him there," was all the help he gave.

Lennard stayed beyond time that evening, and was ready in my private room to go over certain business with me that had transpired during my own absence. I could not give the necessary attention to it, try as earnestly as I would: Tom and his business kept dancing in my brain to the exclusion of other things. Lennard asked me whether I was ill.

"No," I answered; "at least, not in body." And as I spoke, the thought crossed me to confide the trouble to Lennard. He had seen too much trouble himself not to be safe and cautious, and perhaps he might suggest something.

"Let Captain Heriot come to me," he immediately said. "He could not be safer anywhere. Sometimes we let our drawing-room floor; it is vacant now, and he can have it. My wife and my daughter Charlotte will attend to his comforts and nurse him, if that may be, into health. It is the best thing that can be done with him, Mr. Charles."

I saw that it was, seeming to discern all the advantages of the proposal at a grasp, and accepted it. We consulted as to how best to effect Tom's removal, which Lennard himself undertook. I dropped a hasty note to "Mr. Turk" to prepare him to be in readiness the following evening, and Lennard posted it when he went out. He had no sooner gone, than the door of my private room slowly opened, and, rather to my surprise, Leah appeared.

"I beg your pardon, sir, for presuming to disturb you here," she said; "but I can't rest. There's some great trouble afloat; I've seen it in your looks and ways, sir, ever since Sunday. Your face couldn't deceive me when you were my little nursling, Master Charles, and it can't deceive me now. Is it about Mr. Tom?"

"Well, yes, it is, Leah."

Her face turned white. "He has not got himself taken, surely!"

"No; it's not so bad as that—yet."

"Thank Heaven for it!" she returned. "I knew it was him, and I'm all in a twitter about him from morning till night. I can't sleep or eat for dreading the news that any moment may bring of him. It seems to me, Mr. Charles, that one must needs be for ever in a twitter in this world; before one trouble is mended, another turns up. No sooner am I a bit relieved about poor Nancy, that unfortunate daughter of mine, than there comes Mr. Tom."

The relief that Leah spoke of was this: some relatives of Leah's former husband, Nancy's father, had somehow got to hear of Nancy's misfortunes. Instead of turning from her, they had taken her and her cause in hand, and had settled her and her three children in a general shop in Hampshire near to themselves, where she was already beginning to earn enough for a good living. The man who was the cause of all the mischief had emigrated, and meant never to return to Europe.

And Leah had taken my advice in the matter, and disclosed all to Watts. He was not in the least put out by it, as she had feared he would be; only told her she was a simpleton for not having told him before.

My Dear Charles,—I particularly wish you to come to me. I want some legal advice, and I would rather you acted for me than anyone else. Come up this morning, please. Your affectionate sister, BLANCHE.

The above note, brought from Gloucester Place on Monday morning by one of Lady Level's servants, reached me before ten o'clock. By the dashing character of the handwriting, I judged that Blanche had not been in the calmest temper when she penned it.

"Is Lord Level at home?" I inquired of the man Sanders.

"No, sir. His lordship went down to Marshdale yesterday evening. A telegram came for him, and I think it was in consequence of that he went."

I wrote a few words to Blanche, telling her I would be with her as soon as I could, and sent it by Sanders.

But a lawyer's time is not always his own. One client after another kept coming in that morning, as if on purpose; and it was half-past twelve in the day when I reached Gloucester Place.

The house in Gloucester Place was, and had been for some little time now, entirely rented by Lord Level of Major Carlen. The Major, when in London, had rooms in Seymour Street, but lived chiefly at his club.

"Her ladyship has gone out, sir," was Sanders's greeting to me, when he answered my ring at the door-bell.

"Gone out?"

"Just gone," confirmed Major Carlen, who was there, it seemed, and came forward in the wake of Sanders. "Come in, Charles."

He turned into the dining-room, and I after him. "Blanche ought to have waited in," I remarked. "I have come up at the greatest inconvenience."

"She has gone off in a tantrum," cried the Major, lowering his voice as he carefully closed the door and pushed a chair towards me, just as if the house were still in his occupancy.

"But where has she gone?" I asked, not taking the chair, but standing with my elbow on the mantelpiece.

"Who's to know? To you, in Essex Street, I shouldn't wonder. She was on the heights of impatience at your not coming."

"Not to Essex Street, I think, Major. I should have seen her."

"Nonsense! There's fifty turnings and windings between this and Essex Street, where you might miss one another; your cab taking the straight way and she the crooked," retorted the Major. "When Blanche gets her back up, you can't easily put it down."

"Something has gone contrary, I expect."

"Nothing has gone contrary but herself," replied the Major, who seemed in a cross and contrary mood on his own part. "Women are the very deuce for folly."

"Well, what is it all about, sir? I suppose you can tell me?"

The Major sat down in Lord Level's easy-chair, pushed back his cloak, and prepared to explain.

"What it's all about is just nothing, Charles; but so far as Madam Blanche's version goes, it is this," said he. "They were about to sit down, yesterday evening, to dinner—which they take on Sundays at five o'clock (good, pious souls!), and limit their fare to roast beef and a tart—when a telegram arrived from Marshdale. My lord seemed put out about it; my lady was no doubt the same. 'I must go down at once, Blanche,' said he, speaking on the spur of the moment. 'But why? Where's the need of it?' returned she. 'Surely there can be nothing at Marshdale to call you away on Sunday and in this haste?' 'Yes,' said he, 'there is; there's illness.' And then, Blanche says, he tried to cough down the words, as if he had made a slip of the tongue. 'Who is ill?' said Blanche. 'Let me see the telegram.' Level slid the telegram into his pocket, and told her it was Mr. Edwards, the old steward. Down he sat again at the table, swallowed a mouthful of beef, sent Sanders to put up a few things in his small portmanteau, and was off in a cab like the wind. Fact is," added the Major, "had he failed to catch that particular train, he would not have got down at all, being Sunday; and Sanders says that catching it must have been a near shave for his lordship."

"Is that all?"

"No. This morning there was delivered here a letter for his lordship; post-mark Marshdale, handwriting a certain Italian one that Blanche has seen before. She has seen the writer, too, it seems—a fair lady called Nina. Blanche argues that as the letter came from Marshdale, the lady must be at Marshdale, and she means to know without delay, she says, who and what this damsel is, and what the tie may be that binds her to Lord Level and gives her the right to pursue him, as she does, and the power to influence his movements, and to be at her beck and call. The probability is," added the shrewd Major, "that this person wrote to him on the Saturday, but, being a foreigner, was not aware that he would not receive her letter on Sunday morning. Finding that he did not arrive at Marshdale on the Sunday, and the day getting on, she despatched the telegram. That's how I make it out, Charles; I don't know if I am right."

"You think, then, that some Italian lady is at Marshdale?"

"Sure of it," returned the Major. "I've heard of it before to-day. Expect she lives there, making journeys to her own land between whiles, no doubt. The best and the worst of us get homesick."

"You mean that she lives there in—in—well, in a manner not quite orthodox, and that Lord Level connives at it?"

"Connives at it!" echoed the old reprobate. "Why, he is at the top and bottom of it. Level's a man of the world, always was, and does as the world does. And that little ignorant fool, Blanche, ferrets out some inkling of this, and goes and sets up a fuss! Level's as good a husband to her as can be, and yet she's not content! Commend me to foolish women! They are all alike!"

In his indignation against women in general, Major Carlen rose from his chair and began striding up and down the room. I was pondering on what he had said to me.

"What right have wives to rake up particulars of their husbands' private affairs?" he demanded fiercely. "If Level does go off to Marshdale for a few days' sojourn now and again, is it any business of Blanche's what he goes for, or what he does there, or whom he sees? Suppose he chose to maintain a whole menagerie of—of—Italian monkeys there, ought Blanche to interfere and make bones over it?"

"But—"

"He does not offend her; he does not allow her to see that anything exists to offend her: why, then, should she suspect this and suspect that, and peep and peer after Level as if she were a detective told off expressly to watch his movements?" continued the angry man. "Only an ignorant girl would dream of doing it. I am sick of her folly."

"Well now, Major Carlen, will you listen to me for a moment?" I said, speaking quietly and calmly as an antidote to his heat. "I don't believe this. I think you and Blanche are both mistaken."

He brought himself to an anchor on the hearthrug, and stared at me under his thick, grizzled eyebrows. "What is it that you don't believe, Charles?"

"This that you insinuate about Marshdale. I have faith in Lord Level; I like Lord Level; and I think you are misjudging him."

"Oh, indeed!" responded the Major. "I suppose you know what a wild blade Level always was?"

"In his early days he may have been. But you may depend upon it that when he married he left his wild ways behind him."

"All right, young Charles. And, upon my word, you are pretty near as young in the world's depths as Blanche herself is," was the Major's sarcastic remark. "Do you wish to tell me there's nothing up at Marshdale, with all these mysterious telegrams to Level, and his scampers back in answer? Come!"

"I admit that there seems to be some mystery at Marshdale. Something that we do not understand, and that Lord Level does not intend us to understand; but I must have further proof before I can believe it is of any such nature as you hint it, Major. For a long time past, Lord Level has appeared to me like a man in trouble; as if he had some anxiety on his mind."

"Well," acquiesced the Major equably, "and what can trouble a man's mind more than the exactions of these foreign syrens? Let them be Italian, or Spanish, or French—what you will—they'll worry your life out of you in the long-run. What does that Italian girl do at Marshdale?"

"I cannot say. For my own part I do not know that one is there. But if she be, if there be a whole menagerie of Italian ladies there, as you have just expressed it, Major—"

"I said a menagerie of monkeys," he growled.

"Monkeys, then. But whether they be monkeys or whether they be ladies, I feel convinced that Lord Level is acting no unworthy part—that he is loyal to his wife."

"You had better tell her so," nodded the Major; "perhaps she'll believe you. I told her the opposite. I told her that when women marry gay and attractive men, they must look out for squalls, and learn to shut their eyes a bit in going through life. I bade her bottle up her fancies, and let Marshdale and her husband alone, and not show herself a simpleton before the public."

"What did she say to that?"

"Say? It was that piece of advice which raised the storm. She burst out of the room like a maniac, declaring she wouldn't remain in it to listen to me. The next thing was, I heard the street-door bang, and saw my lady go out, putting on her gloves as she went. You came up two minutes afterwards."

I was buried in thought again. He stood staring at me, as if I had no business to have any thought.

"Look here, Major: one thing strikes me forcibly: the very fact of Lord Level allowing these telegrams to come to him openly is enough to prove that matters are not as you and Blanche suspect. If—"

"How can a telegram come secretly?" interrupted the Major.

"He would take care that they did not come at all—to his house."

"Oh, would he?" cried the old reprobate. "I should like to know how he could hinder it if any she-fiend chooses to send them."

"Rely upon it he would hinder it. Level is not one to be coerced against his will by either man or woman. Have you any idea how long Blanche will remain out?"

"Just as much as you have, Charley. She may remain away till night, for all I know."

It was of no use, then, my staying longer; and time, that day, was almost as precious to me as gold. Major Carlen threw on his cloak, and we went out together.

"I should not wonder if my young lady has gone to Seymour Street," remarked the Major. "The thought has just occurred to me."

"To your lodgings, you mean?" I asked, thinking it very unlikely.

"Yes; Mrs. Guy is there. The poor old thing arrived from Jersey on Saturday. She has come over on her usual errand—to consult the doctors; grows more ridiculously fanciful as she grows older. You might just look in upon her now, Charles; it's close by: and then you'll see whether Blanche is there or not."

I spared a few minutes for it. Poor Mrs. Guy looked very poorly indeed; but she was meek and mild as ever, and burst into tears as I greeted her. Her ailments I promised to go and hear all about another time. Yes, Blanche was there. When we went in, she was laughing at something Mrs. Guy had said, and her indignation seemed to have subsided.

I could not stay long. Blanche came out with me, thinking I should go back with her to Gloucester Place. But that was impossible; I had already wasted more time than I could well spare. Blanche was vexed.

"My dear, you should not have gone out when you were expecting me. You know how very much I am occupied."

"Papa vexed me, and drove me to it," she answered. "He said—oh, such wicked things, that I could not and would not stay to listen. And all the while I knew it was not that he believed them, but that he wanted to make excuses for Lord Level."

I did not contradict her. Let her retain, and she could, some little veneration for her step-father.

"Charles, I want to have a long conversation with you, so you must come to me as soon as you can," she said. "I mean to have a separation from my husband; perhaps a divorce, and I want you to tell me how I must proceed in it. I did think of applying to Jennings and Ward, Lord Level's solicitors, but, perhaps, you will be best."

I laughed. "You don't suppose, do you, Blanche, that Lord Level's solicitors would act for you against him."

"Now, Charles, you are speaking lightly; you are making game of me. Why do you laugh? I can tell you it is more serious than you may think for! and I am serious. I have talked of this for a long time, and now I will act. How shall I begin?"

"Do not begin at all, Blanche," I said, with earnestness. "Do nothing. Were your father living—were your mother living, they would both give you this advice—and this is not the first time I have enjoined it on you. Ah, my dear, you do not know—you little guess what misery to the wife such a climax as this which you propose would involve."

Blanche had turned to the railings round the interior of Portman Square, and halted there, apparently looking at the shrubs. Her eyes were full of tears.

"On the other hand, Charles, you do not know, you cannot guess, what I have to bear—what a misery it makes of my life."

"Are you sure of the facts that make the misery?"

"Why, of course I am."

"I think not, Blanche. I think you are mistaken."

She turned to me in surprise. "But I can't be mistaken," she said. "How can I be? If Lord Level does not go to Marshdale to—to—to see people, what does he go for?"

"He may go for something quite different. My dear, I have more confidence in your husband than you have, and I think you are wrong. I must be off; I've not another moment; but these are my last words to you, Blanche.—Take no action. Be still. Do nothing."

By half-past four o'clock, the most pressing of my work was over for the day, and then I took a cab to Lincoln's Inn to see Mr. Serjeant Stillingfar. He had often said to me, good old uncle that he was: "Come to me always, Charles, when you are in any legal doubt or difficulty, or deem that my opinion may be of use to you." I was in one of those difficulties now. Some remarkably troublesome business had been laid before me by a client; I could not see my way in it at all, and was taking it to Serjeant Stillingfar.

The old chambers were just as they used to be; as they were on the day which the reader has heard of, when I saw them for the first time. Running up the stairs, there sat a clerk at the desk in the narrow room, where young Lake, full of impudence, had sat that day, Mr. Jones's empty place beside it now, as it was then.

"Is the Serjeant in?" I asked the clerk.

"No, sir; he's not out of Court yet. Mr. Jones is in."

I went on to the inner room. Old Jones, the Serjeant's own especial clerk, was writing at his little desk in the corner. Nothing was changed; not even old Jones himself. He was not, to appearance, a day older, and not an ounce bigger. Lake used to tell him he would make his fortune if he went about the country in a caravan and called himself a consumptive lamp-post.

"My uncle is not back from Court, Graham says," I observed to the clerk, after shaking hands.

"Not yet," he answered. "I don't think he'll be long. Sit down, Mr. Strange."

I took the chair I had taken that first day years ago, and waited. Mr. Jones finished the writing he was about, arranged his papers, and then came and stood with his back to the fire, having kept his quill in his hand. It must be a very hot day indeed which did not see a fire in that grate.

"If the Serjeant is not back speedily, I think I must open my business to you, and get your opinion, Mr. Jones," I said. "I dare say you could give me one as well as he."

"Some complicated case that you can't quite manage?" he rejoined.

"It's the most complicated, exasperating case I nearly ever had brought to me," I answered. "I think it is a matter more for a detective officer to deal with than a solicitor. If Serjeant Stillingfar says the same, I shall throw it up."

"Curious things, some of those detective cases," remarked Mr. Jones, gently waving his pen.

"They are. I wouldn't have to deal with them, as a detective, for the world. Shall I relate this case to you?"

He took out his watch and looked at it. "Better wait a bit longer, Mr. Charles. I expect the Serjeant every minute now."

"Don't you wonder that my uncle continues to work?" I cried presently. "He is old now. I should retire."

"He is sixty-five. If you were not young yourself, you would not call that old."

"Old enough, I should say, for work to be a labour to him."

"A labour that he loves, and that he is as capable of performing as he was twenty years ago," returned old Jones. "No, Mr. Charles, I do not wonder that he should continue to work."

"Did you know that he had been offered a judgeship?"

Old Jones laughed a little. I thought it was as much as to say there was little which concerned the Serjeant that he did not know.

"He has been offered a judgeship more than once—had it pressed upon him, Mr. Charles. The last time was when Mr. Baron Charlton died."

"Why! that is only a month or two ago!"

"Just about nine weeks, I fancy."

"And he declined it?"

"He declines them all."

"But what can be his motive? It would give him more rest than he enjoys now—"

"I don't altogether know that," interrupted the clerk. "The judges are very much over-worked now. It would increase his responsibility; and he is one to feel that, perhaps painfully."

"You mean when he had to pass the dread sentence of death. A new judge must always feel that at the beginning."

"I heard one of our present judges say—it was in this room, too, Mr. Charles—that the first time he put on the black cap he never closed his eyes the whole night after it. All the Bench are not so sensitive as that, you know."

A thought suddenly struck me. "Surely," I cried, "you do not mean that that is the reason for my uncle's refusing a seat on the Bench!"

"Not at all. He'd get over that in time, as others do. Oh no! that has nothing to do with it."

"Then I really cannot see what can have to do with it. It would give him a degree of rest; yes, it would; and it would give him rank and position."

"But it would take from him half his income. Yes, just about half, I reckon," repeated Mr. Jones, attentively regarding the feather of the pen.

"What of that? He must be putting by heaps and heaps of money—and he has neither wife nor child to put by for."

"Ah!" said the clerk, "that is just how we all are apt to judge of a neighbour's business. Would it surprise you very much, sir, if I told you that the Serjeant is not putting by?"

"But he must be putting by. Or what becomes of his money?"

"He spends it, Mr. Charles."

"Spends it! Upon what?"

"Upon other people."

Mr. Jones looked at me from across the hearthrug, and I looked at him. The assertion puzzled me.

"It's true," he said with a nod. "You have not forgotten that great calamity which happened some ten or twelve years ago, Mr. Charles? That bank which went to pieces, and broke up homes and hearts? Your money went in it."

As if I could forget that!

"The Serjeant's money, all he had then saved, went in it," continued the clerk. "Mortifying enough, of course, but he was in the full swing of his prosperity, and could soon have replaced it. What he could not so easily replace, Mr. Charles, was the money he had been the means of placing in the bank belonging to other people, and which was lost. He had done it for the best. He held the bank to be thoroughly sound and prosperous; he could not have had more confidence in his own integrity than he had in that bank; and he had counselled friends and others whom he knew, who were not as well off as he was, to invest all they could spare in it, believing he was doing them a kindness. Instead of that, it ruined them."

I thought I saw what the clerk was coming to. After a pause, he went on:

"It is these people that he has been working for, Mr. Charles. Some of them he has entirely repaid—the money, you know, which he caused them to lose. He considered it his duty to recompense them, so far as he could; and to keep them, where they needed to be kept, until he had effected that. For those who were better off and did not need present help, he put money by as he could spare it, investing it in the funds in their name: I dare say your name is amongst them. That's what Mr. Serjeant Stillingfar does with his income, and that's why he keeps on working."

I had never suspected this.

"I believe it is almost accomplished now," said the clerk. "So nearly that I thought he might, perhaps, have taken the judgeship on this last occasion. But he did not. 'Just a few months longer in harness, Jones,' he said to me, 'and then—?' So I reckon that we shall yet see him on the Bench, Mr. Charles."

"He must be very good."

"Good!" echoed old Jones, with emotion; "he is made of goodness. There are few people like him. He would help the whole world if he could. I don't believe there's any man who has ever done a single service for him of the most trifling nature but he would wish to place beyond the reach of poverty. 'I've put a trifle by for you, Jones,' he said to me the other day, 'in case you might be at a loss for another such place as this when my time's over.' And when I tried to thank him—"

Mr. Jones broke down. Bringing the quill pen under his eyes, as if he suddenly caught sight of a flaw thereon, I saw a drop of water fall on to it.

"Yes, Mr. Charles, he said that to me. It has taken a load from my mind. When a man is on the downhill of life and is not sure of his future, he can't help being anxious. The Serjeant has paid me a liberal salary, as you may well guess, but he knows that it has not been in my power to put by a fraction of it. 'You are too generous with your money, Serjeant,' I said to him one day, a good while ago. 'Ah no, Jones, not at all,' he answered. 'God has prospered me so marvellously in these later years, what can I do but strive to prosper others?' Those were his very words."

And with these last words of Jones's our conference came to an end. The door was abruptly thrown open by Graham to admit the Serjeant. Mr. Jones helped him off with his wig and gown, and handed him the little flaxen top that he wore when not on duty. Then Jones, leaving the room for a few moments, came back with a glass of milk, which he handed to his master.

"Would not a glass of wine do you more good, uncle?" I asked.

"No, lad; not so much. A glass of milk after a hard day's work in Court refreshes me. I never touch wine except at a dinner. I take a little then; not much."

Sitting down together when Mr. Jones had again left us, I opened my business to the Serjeant as concisely as possible. He listened attentively, but made no remark until the end.

"Now go over it all again, Charles." I did so: and this second time I was repeatedly interrupted by remarks or questions. After that we discussed the case.

"I cannot see any reason why you should not take up the matter," he said, when he had given it a little silent consideration. "I do not look upon it quite as you do; I think you have formed a wrong judgment. It is intricate at present; I grant you that; but if you proceed in the manner I have suggested, you will unravel it."

"Thank you, Uncle Stillingfar. I can never thank you enough for all your kindness to me."

"Were you so full of anxiety over this case?" he asked, as we were shaking hands, and I was about to leave. "You look as though you had a weight of it on your brow."

"And so I have, uncle; but not about this case. Something nearer home."

"What is it?" he returned, looking at me.

"It is— Perhaps I had better not tell it you."

"I understand," he slowly said. "Tom Heriot, I suppose. Why does he not get away?"

"He is too ill for that at present: confined to his room and his bed. Of course, he does not run quite so great a risk as he did when he persisted in parading the streets, but danger is always imminent."

"He ought to end the danger by getting away. Very ill, is he?"

"So ill that I think danger will soon be all at an end in another way; it certainly will be unless he rallies."

"What is the matter with him?"

"I cannot help fearing that consumption has set in."

"Poor fellow! Oh, Charles, how that fine young man has spoilt his life! Consumption?—Wait a bit—let me think," broke off the Serjeant. "Why, yes, I remember now; it was consumption that Colonel Heriot's first wife died of—Tom's mother."

"Tom said so the last time I saw him."

"Ah. He knows it, then. Better not see him too often, Charles. You are running a risk yourself, as you must be aware."

"Yes; I know I am. It is altogether a trial. Good-day, uncle."

I shook hands with Jones as I passed through his room, and ran down the stairs, feeling all the better for my interview with him and with his patron, Mr. Serjeant Stillingfar.

CHAPTER VIII

AN ACCIDENT

The drawing-room floor at Lennard's made very comfortable quarters for Tom Heriot, and his removal from the room in Southwark had been accomplished without difficulty. Mrs. Lennard, a patient, mild, weak woman, who could never have been strong-minded, made him an excellent nurse, her more practical and very capable daughter, Charlotte, aiding her when necessary.

A safer refuge could not have been found in London. The Lennards were so often under a cloud themselves as regarded pecuniary matters, so beset at times by their unwelcome creditors—the butcher, baker and grocer—that the chain of their front door was kept habitually fastened, and no one was admitted within its portals without being first of all subjected to a comprehensive survey. Had some kind friend made a rush to the perambulating policeman of the district, to inform him that the domicile of those Lennards was again in a state of siege, he would simply have speculated upon whether the enemy was this time the landlord or the Queen's taxes. It chanced to be neither; but it was well for the besieged to favour the impression that it was one or the other, or both. Policemen do not wage war with unfortunate debtors, and Mr. Lennard's house was as safe as a remote castle.

"Mr. Brown" Tom was called there; none of the household, with the exception of its master, having any idea that it was not his true name. "One of the gentlemen clerks in Essex Street, who has no home in London; I have undertaken to receive him while he is ill," Mr. Lennard had carelessly remarked to his wife and daughters before introducing Tom. They had unsuspecting minds, except as regarded their own creditors, those ladies—ladies always, though fallen from their former state—and never thought to question the statement, or to be at all surprised that Mr. Strange himself took an interest in his clerk's illness, and paid an evening visit to him now and then. The doctor who was called in, a hard-worked practitioner named Purfleet, did his best for "Mr. Brown," but had no time to spare for curiosity about him in any other way, or to give so much as a thought to his antecedents.

And just at first, after being settled at Lennard's, Tom Heriot seemed to be taking a turn for the better. The warmth of the comfortable rooms, the care given to him, the strengthening diet, and perhaps a feeling that he was in a safer asylum than he had yet found, all had their effect upon him for good.

"Hatch!" called out Mrs. Brightman.

Hatch ran in from the next room. "Yes, ma'am."

"Let Perry go and tell the gardener to cut some of his best grapes, white and purple, and do you arrange them in a basket. I shall go up to Essex Street and see my daughter this afternoon, and will take them to her. Order the carriage for half-past two o'clock."

"Miss Annabel will be finely pleased to see you, ma'am!" remarked Hatch.

"Possibly so. But she is no longer Miss Annabel. Go and see about the grapes."

When Mrs. Brightman's tones were cold and haughty, and they sounded especially so just now, she brooked no dilatoriness in those who had to obey her behests. Hatch turned away immediately, and went along talking to herself.

"She's getting cross and restless again. I'm certain of it. In a week's time from this we shall have her as bad as before. And for ever so many weeks now she has been as cautious and sober as a judge! Hang the drink, then! Doctors may well call it a disease when it comes to this stage with people. Here—I say, Perry!"

The butler, passing along the hall, heard Hatch's call, and stopped. She gave her cap-strings a fling backwards as she advanced to him.

"You are to go and tell Church to cut a basket of grapes, and to mix 'em, white and black. The very best and ripest that is in the greenhouse; they be for Miss Annabel."

"All right, I'll go at once," answered Perry. "But you need not snap a man's nose off, Hatch, or look as if you were going to eat him. What has put you out?"

"Enough has put me out; and you might know that, old Perry, if you had any sense," retorted Hatch. "When do I snap people's noses off—which it's my tone, I take it, that you mean—except I'm that bothered and worried I can't speak sweet?"

"Well, what's amiss?" asked Perry.

They were standing close together, and Hatch lowered her voice to a whisper. "The missis is going off again; I be certain sure on't."

"No!" cried Perry, full of dismay. "But, look here, Hatch"—suddenly diving into one of his jackets—"she can't have done it; here's the cellar-key. I can be upon my word that there's not a drain of anything out."

"You always did have the brains of a turkey, you know, Perry," was Hatch's gracious rejoinder; "and I'm tired of reminding you of it. Who said missis had took anything? Not me. She haven't—yet. As you observe, there's nothing up for her to take. But she'll be ordering you to bring something up before to-morrow's over; perhaps before to-day is."

"Dear, dear!" lamented the faithful servant. "Don't you think you may be mistaken, Hatch? What do you judge by?"

"I judge by herself. I've not lived with my missis all these years without learning to notice signs and tokens. Her manner to-day and her restlessness is just as plain as the sun in the sky. I know what it means, and you'll know it too, as soon as she gives you her orders to unlock the cellar."

"Can nothing be done?" cried the unhappy Perry. "Could I lose the key of the cellar, do you think, Hatch? Would that be of any good?"

"It would hold good just as long as you'd be in getting a hammer and poker to break it open with; you've not got to deal with a pack of schoolboys that's under control," was Hatch's sarcastic reproof. "But I think there's one thing we might try, Perry, and that is, run round to Mr. Close and tell him about it. Perhaps he could give her something to stop the craving."

"I'll go," said Perry. "I'll slip round when I've told Church about the grapes."

"And the carriage is ordered early—half-past two; so mind you are in readiness," concluded Hatch.

Perry went to the surgeon's, after delivering his orders to the gardener. But Mr. Close was not at home, and the man came away again without leaving any message; he did not choose to enter upon the subject with Mr. Dunn, the assistant. The latter inquired who was ill, and Perry replied that nobody was; he had only come to speak a private word to Mr. Close, which could wait. In point of fact, he meant to call later.

But the curiosity of Mr. Dunn, who was a very inquisitive young man, fonder of attending to other people's business than of doing his own, had been aroused by this. He considered Perry's manner rather mysterious, as well as the suppression of the message, and he enlarged upon the account to Mr. Close when he came in. Mr. Close made no particular rejoinder; but in his own mind he felt little doubt that Mrs. Brightman was breaking out again, and determined to go and see her when he had had his dinner.

Perry returned home, and waited on his mistress at luncheon, quaking inwardly all the time, as he subsequently confessed to Hatch, lest she should ask him for something that was not upon the table. However, she did not do so; but she was very restless, as Perry observed; ate little, drank no water, and told Perry to bring her a cup of coffee.

At half-past two the carriage stood at the gate, the silver on the horses' harness glittering in the sun. Quickly enough appeared the procession from the house. Mrs. Brightman, upright and impassive, walking with stately step; Hatch, a shawl or two upon her arm, holding an umbrella over her mistress to shade her from the sun; Perry in the background, carrying the basket of grapes. Perry would attend his mistress in her drive, as usual, but not Hatch.

The servants were placing the shawls and the grapes in the carriage, and Mrs. Brightman, who hated anything to be done after she had taken her seat, was waiting to enter it, when Mr. Close, the surgeon, came bustling up.

"Going for a drive this fine day!" he exclaimed, as he shook hands with Mrs. Brightman. "I'm glad of that. I had been thinking that perhaps you were not well."

"Why should you think so?" asked she.

"Well, Perry was round at my place this morning, and left a message that he wanted to see me. I—"

Mr. Close suppressed the remainder of his speech as his gaze suddenly fell on Perry's startled face. The man had turned from the carriage, and was looking at him in helpless, beseeching terror. A faithful retainer was Perry, an honest butler; but at a pinch his brains were no better than what Hatch had compared them with—those of a turkey.

Mrs. Brightman, her countenance taking its very haughtiest expression, gazed first at the doctor, then at Perry, as if demanding what this might mean; possibly, poor lady, she had a suspicion of it. But Hatch, ready Hatch, was equal to the occasion: she never lost her presence of mind.

"I told Perry he might just as well have asked young Mr. Dunn for 'em, when he came back without the drops," said she, facing the surgeon and speaking carelessly. "Your not being in didn't matter. It was some cough-drops I sent him for; the same as those you've let us have before, Mr. Close. Our cook's cough is that bad, she can't sleep at night, nor let anybody else sleep that's within earshot of her room."

"Well, I came round in a hurry, thinking some of you might be suffering from this complaint that's going about," said Mr. Close, taking up the clue in an easy manner.

"That there spasadic cholera," assented Hatch.

"Cholera! It's not cholera. There's nothing of that sort about," said the surgeon. "But there's a good bit of influenza; I have half a dozen patients suffering from it. A spell of bright weather such as this, though, will soon drive it away. And I'll send you some of the drops when I get back, Hatch."

Mrs. Brightman advanced to the carriage; the surgeon was at hand to assist her in. Perry stood on the other side his mistress. Hatch had retreated to the gate and was looking on.

Suddenly a yell, as of something unearthly, startled their ears. A fierce-looking bull, frightened probably by the passers-by on the road, and the prods given to it by the formidable stick of its driver, had dashed behind the carriage on to the foot-path, and set up that terrible roar. Mr. Close looked round, Perry did the same; whilst Mrs. Brightman, who was in the very act of getting into her carriage, and whose nerves were more sensitive than theirs, turned sharply round also and screamed.

Again Hatch came to the rescue. She had closed the umbrella and lodged it against the pillar of the gate, for here they were under the shade of trees. Seizing the umbrella now, she opened it with a great dash and noise, and rushed towards the bull, pointing it menacingly. The animal, no doubt more startled than they were, tore away and gained the highroad again. Then everyone had leisure to see that Mrs. Brightman was lying on the ground partly under the carriage.

She must have fallen in turning round, partly from fright, partly from the moving of the carriage. The horses had also been somewhat startled by the bull's noise, and one of them began to prance. The coachman had his horses well in hand, and soon quieted them; but he had not been able to prevent the movement, which had no doubt chiefly caused his mistress to fall.

They quickly drew her from under the carriage and attempted to raise her; but she cried out with such tones of agony that the surgeon feared she was seriously injured. As soon as possible she was conveyed indoors on a mattress. Another surgeon joined Mr. Close, and it was found that her leg was broken near the ankle.

When it had been set and the commotion was subsiding, Perry was despatched to Essex Street with the carriage and the bad news—the carriage to bring back Annabel.

"What was it you really came to my surgery for, Perry?" Mr. Close took an opportunity of asking him before he started.

"It was about my mistress, sir," answered the man. "Hatch felt quite sure, by signs and tokens, that Mrs. Brightman was going to—to—be ill again. She sent me to tell you, sir, and to ask if you couldn't give her something to stop it."

"Ah, I thought as much. But when I saw you all out there, your mistress looking well and about to take a drive, I concluded I had been mistaken," said the surgeon.

I had run upstairs during the afternoon to ask a question of Annabel, and was standing beside her at the drawing-room window, where she sat at work, when a carriage came swiftly down the street, and stopped at the door.

"Why, it is mamma's!" exclaimed Annabel, looking out.

"But I don't see her in it," I rejoined.

"Oh, she must be in it, Charles. Perry is on the box."

Perry was getting down, but was not quite so quick in his movements as a slim young footman would be. He rang the door-bell, and I was fetched down to him. In two minutes afterwards I had disclosed the news to my wife, and brought Perry upstairs that she might herself question him. The tears were coursing down her cheeks.

"Don't take on, Miss Annabel," said the man, feeling quite too much lost in the bad tidings to remember Annabel's new title. "There's not the least bit of danger, ma'am; Mr. Close bade me say it; all is sure to go on well."

"Did you bring the carriage for me, Perry?"

"Yes, ma'am, I did. And it was my mistress herself thought of it. When Mr. Close, or Hatch—one of 'em it was, I don't know which—told her they were going to send me for you, she said, 'Let Perry take the carriage.' Oh, ma'am, indeed she is fully as well as she could be: it was only at first that she seemed faintish like."

Annabel went back in the carriage at once. I promised to follow her as early in the evening as I could get away. Relying upon the butler's assurance that Mrs. Brightman was not in the slightest danger; that, on the contrary, it would be an illness of weeks, if not of months, there was no necessity for accompanying Annabel at an inconvenient moment.

"It is, in one sense, the luckiest thing that could have happened to her," Mr. Close remarked to me that evening when we were conversing together.

"Lucky! How do you mean?"

"Well, she must be under our control now," he answered in significant tones, "and we were fearing, only to-day, that she was on the point of breaking out again. A long spell of enforced abstinence, such as this, may effect wonders."

Of course, looking at it in that light, the accident might be called fortunate. "There's a silver lining to every cloud."

Annabel took up her abode temporarily at her mother's: Mrs. Brightman requested it. I went down there of an evening—though not every evening—returning to Essex Street in the morning. Tom's increasing illness kept me in town occasionally, for I could not help going to see him, and he was growing weaker day by day. The closing features of consumption were gaining upon him rapidly. To add to our difficulties, Mr. Policeman Wren, who seemed to follow Tom's changes of domicile in a very ominous and remarkable manner, had now transferred his beat from Southwark, and might be seen pacing before Lennard's door ten times a day.

One morning when I had come up from Clapham and was seated in my own room opening letters, Lennard entered. He closed the door with a quiet, cautious movement, and waited, without speaking.

"Anything particular, Lennard?"

"Yes, sir; I've brought rather bad news," he said. "Captain Heriot is worse."

"Worse? In what way? But he is not Captain Heriot, Lennard; he is Mr. Brown. Be careful."

"We cannot be overheard," he answered, glancing at the closed door. "He appeared so exceedingly weak last night that I thought I would sit up with him for an hour or two, and then lie down on his sofa for the rest of the night. About five o'clock this morning he had a violent fit of coughing and broke a blood-vessel."

"What did you do?"

"I know a little of the treatment necessary in such cases, and we got the doctor to him as soon as possible. Mr. Purfleet does not give the slightest hope now. In fact, he thinks that a very few days more will bring the ending."

I sat back in my chair. Poor Tom! Poor Tom!

"It is the best for him, Mr. Charles," spoke Lennard, with some emotion. "Better, infinitely, than that of which he has been running the risk. When a man's life is marred as he has marred his, heaven must seem like a haven of refuge to him."

"Has he any idea of his critical state?"

"Yes; and, I feel sure, is quite reconciled to it. He remarked this morning how much he should like to see Blanche: meaning, I presume, Lady Level."

"Ah, but there are difficulties in the way, Lennard. I will come to him myself, but not until evening. There's no immediate danger, you tell me, and I do not care to be seen entering your house during the day while he is in it. The big policeman might be on the watch, and ask me what I wanted there."

Lennard left the room and I returned to my letters. The next I took up was a note from Blanche. Lord Level was not yet back from Marshdale, she told me in it; he kept writing miserable scraps of notes in which he put her off with excuses from day to day, always assuring her he hoped to be up on the morrow. But she could see she was being played with; and the patience which, in obedience to me and Major Carlen, she had been exercising, was very nearly exhausted. She wrote this, she concluded by saying, to warn me that it was so.

Truth to say, I did wonder what was keeping Level at Marshdale. He had been there more than a week now.

CHAPTER IX

LAST DAYS

Tom Heriot lay on his sofa in his bedroom, the firelight flickering on his faded face. This was Monday, the third day since the attack spoken of by Lennard, and there had not been any return of it. His voice was stronger this evening; he seemed better altogether, and was jesting, as he loved to do. Leah had been to see him during the day, and he was recounting one or two of their passages-at-arms, with much glee.

"Charley, old fellow, you look as solemn as a judge."

Most likely I did. I sat on the other side the hearthrug, gazing as I listened to him; and I thought I saw in his face the grayness that frequently precedes death.

"Did you know that that giant of the force, Wren, had his eye upon me, Charley?"

"No! Why do you say so?"

"Well, I think he has—some suspicion, at any rate. He parades before the house like a walking apparition. I look at him from behind the curtains in the other room. He paraded in like manner, you know, before that house in Southwark and the other one in Lambeth."

"It may be only a coincidence, Tom. The police are moved about a good deal from beat to beat, I fancy."

"Perhaps so," assented Tom carelessly. "If he came in and took me, I don't think he could do much with me now. He accosted Purfleet to-day."

"Accosted Purfleet!"

Tom nodded. "After his morning visit to me, he went dashing out of the street-door in his usual quick way, and dashed against Wren. One might think a regiment of soldiers were always waiting to have their legs and arms cut off, and that Purfleet had to do it, by the way he rushes about," concluded Tom.

"Well?"

"'In a hurry this morning, doctor,' says old Wren, who is uncommonly fond of hearing himself talk. 'And who is it that's ill at Mr. Lennard's?' 'I generally am in a hurry,' says Purfleet, 'and so would you be if you had as many sick people on your hands. At Lennard's? Why, that poor suffering daughter of his has had another attack, and I don't know whether I shall save her.' And, with that, Purfleet got away. He related this to me when he came in at tea-time."

A thought struck me. "But, Tom, does Purfleet know that you are in concealment here? Or why should he have put his visits to you upon Maria Lennard?"

"Why, how could he be off knowing it? Lennard asked him at first, as a matter of precaution, not to speak of me in the neighbourhood. Mr. Brown was rather under a cloud just now, he said. I wouldn't mind betting a silver sixpence, Charley, that he knows I am Tom Heriot."

I wondered whether Tom was joking.

"Likely enough," went on Tom. "He knows that you come to see me, and that you are Mr. Strange, of Essex Street. And he has heard, I'll lay, that Mr. Strange had a wicked sort of half-brother, one Captain Heriot, who fell into the fetters of the law and escaped them, and—and may be the very Mr. Brown who's lying ill here. Purfleet can put two and two together as cleverly as other people, Charles."

"If so, it is frightfully hazardous—"

"Not at all," interrupted Tom with equanimity. "He'd no more betray me, Charley, than he'd betray himself. Doctors don't divulge the secrets of their patients; they keep them. It is a point of honour in the medical code: as well as of self-interest. What family would call in a man who was known to run about saying the Smiths next door had veal for dinner to-day, and they ought to have had mutton? If no more harm reaches me than any brought about by Purfleet, I am safe enough."

It might be as he said. And I saw that he would be incautious to the end.

At that moment Mrs. Lennard came in with something in a breakfast-cup. "You are a good lady," said Tom gratefully. "See how they feed me up, Charley!"

But for the hollow tones, the hectic flush and the brilliant eyes, it might almost have been thought he was getting better. The cough had nearly left him, and the weakness was not more apparent than it had been for a week past. But that faint, deep, far-away sounding voice, which had now come on, told the truth. The close was near at hand.

After Mrs. Lennard had left the room with the empty cup, Tom lay back on the sofa, put his head on the pillow, and in a minute or two seemed to be asleep. Presently I moved gently across the hearthrug to fold the warm, light quilt upon his knees. He opened his eyes.

"You need not creep, Charley. I am not asleep. I had a regular good sleep in the afternoon, and don't feel inclined for it now. I was thinking about the funeral."

"The funeral!" I echoed, taken back. "Whose funeral?"

"Mine. They won't care to lay me by my mother, will they?—I mean my own mother. The world might put its inquisitive word in, and say that must be Tom Heriot, the felon. Neither you nor Level would like that, nor old Carlen either."

I made no answer, uncertain what to say.

"Yet I should like to lie by her," he went on. "There was a large vault made, when she died, to hold the three of us—herself, my father and me. They are in it; I should like to be placed with them."

"Time enough to think of that, Tom, when—when—the time comes," I stammered.

"The time's not far off now, Charley."

"Two nights ago, when I was here, you assured me you were getting better."

"Well, I thought I might be; there are such ups and downs in a man's state. He will appear sick unto death to-day, and tomorrow be driving down to a whitebait dinner at Greenwich. I've changed my opinion, Charley; I've had my warning."

"Had your warning! What does that mean?"

"I should like to see Blanche," he whispered. "Dear little Blanche! How I used to tease her in our young days, and Leah would box my ears for it; and I teased you also, Charley. Could you not bring her here, if Level would let her come?"

"Tom, I hardly know. For one thing, she has not heard anything of the past trouble, as you are aware. She thinks you are in India with the regiment, and calls you a very undutiful brother for not writing to her. I suppose it might be managed."

"Dear little Blanche!" he repeated. "Yes, I teased her—and loved her all the time. Just one visit, Charley. It will be the last until we meet upon the eternal shores. Try and contrive it."

I sat thinking how it might be done—the revelation to Blanche, bringing her to the house, and obtaining the consent of Lord Level; for I should not care to stir in it without his consent. Tom appeared to be thinking also, and a silence ensued. It was he who broke it.

"Charles!"

"Yes?"

"Do you ever recall events that passed in our old life at White Littleham Rectory? do any of them lie in your memory?"

"I think all of them lie in it," I answered. "My memory is, you know, a remarkably good one."

"Ay," said Tom. And then he paused again. "Do you recollect that especial incident when your father told us of his dream?" he continued presently. "I picture the scene now; it has been present to my mind all day. A frosty winter morning, icicles on the trees and frosty devices on the window-panes. You and I and your father seated round the breakfast-table; Leah pouring out the coffee and cutting bread and butter for us. He appeared to be in deep thought, and when I remarked upon it, and you asked him what he was thinking of, he said his dream. D'you mind it, lad?"

"I do. The thing made an impression on me. The scene and what passed at it are as plain to me now as though it had happened yesterday. After saying he was thinking of his dream, he added, in a dubious tone, 'If it was a dream.' Mr. Penthorn came in whilst he was telling it.

"He was fast asleep; had gone to bed in the best of health, probably concocting matter for next Sunday's sermon," resumed Tom, recalling the facts. "Suddenly, he awoke at the sound of a voice. It was his late wife's voice; your mother, Charley. He was wide awake on the instant, and knew the voice for hers; she appeared to be standing at the bedside."

"But he did not see her," I put in.

"No; he never said he saw her," replied Tom Heriot. "But the impression was upon him that a figure stood there, and that after speaking it retreated towards the window. He got up and struck a light and found the room empty, no trace of anyone's having been in it. Nevertheless he could not get rid of the belief, though not a superstitious man, that it was his wife who came to him."

"In the spirit."

"In the spirit, of course. He knew her voice perfectly, he said. Mr. Penthorn rather ridiculed the matter; saying it was nothing but a vivid dream. I don't think it made much impression upon your father, except that it puzzled him."

"I don't think it did," I assented, my thoughts all in the past. "As you observe, Tom, he was not superstitious; he had no particular belief in the supernatural."

"No; it faded from all our minds with the day—Leah's perhaps excepted. But what was the result? On the fourth night afterwards he died. The dream occurred on the Friday morning a little before three o'clock; your father looked at his watch when he got out of bed and saw that it wanted a quarter to three. On Tuesday morning at a quarter to three he died in his study, into which he had been carried after his accident."

All true. The circumstances, to me, were painful even now.

"Well, what do you make of it, Charles?"

"Nothing. But I don't quite understand your question."

"Do you think his wife really came to him?—That she was permitted to come back to earth to warn him of his approaching death?"

"I have always believed that. I can hardly see how anyone could doubt it."

"Well, Charley, I did. I was a graceless, light-headed young wight, you know, and serious things made no impression on me. If I thought about it at all, it was to put it down to fancy; or a dream, as Mr. Penthorn said; and I don't believe I've ever had the thing in my mind from that time to this."

"And why should it come back to you now?" I asked.

"Because," answered Tom, "I think I have had a similar warning."

He spoke very calmly. I looked at him. He was sitting upright on the sofa now, his feet stretched out on a warm wool footstool, the quilt lying across his knees, and his hands resting upon it.

"What can you mean, Tom?"

"It was last night," he answered; "or, rather, this morning. I was in bed, and pretty soundly asleep, for me, and I began to dream. I thought I saw my father come in through the door, that one opening to the passage, cross the room and sit down by the bedside with his face turned to me. I mean my own father, Colonel Heriot. He looked just as he used to look; not a day older; his fine figure erect, his bright, wavy hair brushed off his brow as he always wore it, his blue eyes smiling and kindly. I was not in the least surprised to see him; his coming in seemed to be quite a matter of course. 'Well, Thomas,' he began, looking at me after he had sat down; 'we have been parted for some time, and I have much to say to you.' 'Say it now, papa,' I answered, going back in my dream to the language of childhood's days. 'There's not time now,' he replied; 'we must wait a little yet; it won't be long, Thomas.' Then I saw him rise from the chair, re-cross the room to the door, turn to look at me with a smile, and go out, leaving the door open. I awoke in a moment; at the very moment, I am certain; and for some little time I could not persuade myself that what had passed was not reality. The chair in which he had sat stood at the bedside, and the door was wide open."

"But I suppose the chair had been there all night, and that someone was sitting up with you? Whoever it was must have opened the door."

"The chair had been there all night," assented Tom. "But the door had not been opened by human hands, so far as I can learn. It was old Faith's turn to sit up last night—that worthy old soul of a servant who has clung to the Lennards through all their misfortunes. Finding that I slept comfortably, Faith had fallen asleep too in the big chair in that corner behind you. She declared that the door had been firmly shut—and I believe she thought it was I who had got up and opened it."

"It was a dream, Tom."

"Granted. But it was a warning. It came—nay, who can say it was not he who came?—to show me that I shall soon be with him. We shall have time, and to spare, to talk then. I have never had so vivid a dream in my life; or one that so left behind it the impression that it had been reality."

"Well—"

"Look here," he interrupted. "Your father said, if you remember, that the visit paid to him, whether real or imaginary, by his wife, and the words she spoke, had revived within him his recollections of her voice, which had in a slight degree begun to fade. Well, Charles, I give you my word that I had partly forgotten my father's appearance; I was only a little fellow when he died; but his visit to me in my dream last night has brought it back most vividly. Come, you wise old lawyer, what do you say to that?"

"I don't know, Tom. Such things are, I suppose."

"If I got well and lived to be a hundred years old, I should never laugh at them again."

"Did you tell Leah this when she was here to-day?"

"Ay; and of course she burst out crying. 'Take it as it's meant, Master Tom,' said she, 'and prepare yourself. It is your warning.' Just as she had told your father, Charles, that that other was his warning. She was right then; she is right now."

"You cannot know it. And you must not let this trouble you."

"It does not trouble me," he answered quickly. "Rather the contrary, for it sets my mind at rest. I have had little hope of myself for some time past; I have had none, so to say, since that sudden attack a few nights ago; nevertheless, I won't say but a grain of it may have still deluded me now and again. Hope is the last thing we part with in this world, you know, lad. But this dream-visit of my father has shown me the truth beyond all doubt; and now I have only to make my packet, as the French say, and wait for the signal to start."

We talked together a little longer, but my time was up. I left him for the night and apparently in the best of spirits.

Lennard was alone in his parlour when I got downstairs. I asked him whether he had heard of this fancy of Tom's about the dream.

"Yes," he answered. "He told me about it this evening, when I was sitting with him after tea; but he did not seem at all depressed by it. I don't think it matters much either way," added Lennard thoughtfully, "for the end cannot be far off now."

"He has an idea that Purfleet guesses who he really is."

"But he has no grounds for saying it," returned Lennard. "Purfleet heard when he was first called in that 'Mr. Brown' wished to be kept en cachette, if I may so put it; but that he should guess him to be Captain Heriot is quite improbable. Because Captain Heriot is aware of his own identity, he assumes that other people must needs be aware of it."

"One might trust Purfleet not to betray him, I fancy, if he does guess it?"

"That I am sure of," said Lennard warmly. "He is kind and benevolent. Most medical men are so from their frequent contact with the dark shades of life, whether of sickness or of sorrow. As to Purfleet, he is too hard-worked, poor man, to have much leisure for speculating upon the affairs of other people."

"Wren is still walking about here."

"Yes; but I think he has been put upon this beat in the ordinary way of things, not that he is looking after anyone in particular. Mr. Strange, if he had any suspicion of Captain Heriot in Lambeth, he would have taken him; he would have taken him again when in Southwark; and he would, ere this, have taken him here. Wren appears to be one of those gossiping men who must talk to everybody; and I believe that is all the mystery."

Wishing Lennard good-night, I went home to Essex Street, and sat down to write to Lord Level. He would not receive the letter at Marshdale until the following afternoon, but it would be in time for him to answer me by the evening post.

CHAPTER X

LAST WORDS

The next day, Tuesday, I was very busy, hurrying forward to get down to Clapham in time for dinner in the evening. Lennard's report in the morning had been that Captain Heriot was no worse, and that Mr. Purfleet, who had paid him an early visit, said there might be no change for a week or more.

In the afternoon I received a brief note from Mr. Serjeant Stillingfar, asking me to be in Russell Square the following morning by eight o'clock: he wished to see me very particularly.

Knowing that when he named any special hour he meant it, and that he expected everyone who had dealings with him to be as punctual as himself, I came up to town on the Wednesday morning, and was at his house a few minutes before eight o'clock. The Serjeant was just sitting down to breakfast.

"Will you take some, Charles?" he asked.

"No, thank you, uncle. I have just come up from Clapham, and breakfasted before starting."

"How is Mrs. Brightman going on?"

"Quite well. It will be a long job, the doctors say, from something unusual connected with the fracture, but nothing dangerous."

"Sit down, Charles," he said. "And tell me at once. Is Captain Heriot," lowering his voice, "in a state to be got away?"

The words did not surprise me. The whole night it had been in my mind that the Serjeant's mandate concerned Tom Heriot.

"No; it would be impossible," I answered. "He has to be moved gently, from bed to sofa, and can only walk, if he attempts it at all, by being helped on both sides. Three or four days ago, a vessel on the lungs broke; any undue exertion would at once be fatal."

"Then, do I understand you that he is actually dying?"

"Undoubtedly he is, sir. I was with him on Monday night, and saw in his face the gray hue which is the precursor of death. I am sure I was not mistaken—"

"That peculiar hue can never be mistaken by those who have learnt from sad experience," he interrupted dreamily.

"He may linger on a few days, even a week or so, I believe the doctor thinks, but death is certainly on its road; and he must die where he is, Uncle Stillingfar. He cannot be again moved."

The Serjeant sat silent for a few moments. "It is very unfortunate, Charles," he resumed. "Could he have been got away it would be better for him, better for you all. Though, in truth, it is not I who ought to suggest it, as you well know; but sometimes one's private and public duties oppose each other."

"Have you heard anything, uncle?"

"I have heard from a sure source that the authorities know that Captain Heriot is in London. They know it positively: but not, I think, where he is concealed. The search for him will now commence in earnest."

"It is, indeed, unfortunate. I have been hoping he would be left to die in peace. One thing is certain: if the police find him they can only let him remain where he is. They cannot remove him."

"Then nothing can be done: things must take their course," sighed the Serjeant. "You must take precautions yourself, Charles. Most probably the movements of those connected with him will now be watched, in the hope that they may afford a clue to his hiding-place."

"I cannot abandon him, Uncle Stillingfar. I must see him to the end. We have been as brothers, you know. He wants to see Blanche, and I have written about it to Lord Level."

"Well, well, I cannot advise; I wish I could," he replied. "But I thought it my duty to let you know this."

"A few days will, in any case, see the ending," I whispered as I bade him goodbye. "Thank you for all your sympathy, uncle."

"My boy, there is One above," raising his hand reverently, "who has more pity for us than we have for one another. He can keep him in peace yet. Don't forget that, Charles."

To my office, then, and the morning letters. Amidst them lay Lord Level's answer. Some of its contents surprised me.

"Marshdale House,

"Tuesday Evening.

"DEAR CHARLES,

"If you like to undertake the arrangement of the visit you propose, do so. I have no objection. For some little time now I have thought that it might be better that my wife should know the truth. You see she is, and has been, liable to hear it at any moment through some untoward revelation, for which she would not be prepared; and the care I have taken to avoid this has not only been sometimes inconvenient to myself, but misconstrued by Blanche. When we were moving about after our marriage, I kept her in unfrequented places, as far as I could, to spare her the chance of this; men's lips were full of it just then, as you know. Blanche resented that bitterly, putting it all down to some curious purposes of my own. Let her hear the truth now. I am not on the spot to impart it to her myself, and shall be glad if you will do so. Afterwards you can take her to see the invalid. I am sorry for what you say of his state. Tell him so: and that he has my sympathy and best wishes.

"Blanche has been favouring me lately with some letters written in anything but a complimentary strain. One that I received this morning coolly informs me that she is about to 'Take immediate steps to obtain a formal separation, if not a divorce.' I am not able to travel to London and settle things with her, and have written to her to tell her to come here to me. The fact is, I am ill. Strange to say, the same sort of low fever which attacked me when I was at Marshdale last autumn has returned upon me now. It is not as bad as it was then, but I am confined to bed. Spare the time to bring Blanche down, there's a good fellow. I have told her that you will do so. Come on Thursday if convenient to you, and remain the night. She shall hear what I have to say to her; after that, she can talk of a separation if she likes. You shall hear it also.

"Ever truly yours,

"LEVEL."

Whilst deliberating upon the contents of this letter, and how I could best carry out its requests, Lennard came in, as usual on his arrival for the day, to give me his report of Tom Heriot. There was not any apparent change in him, he said, either for the better or the worse. I informed Lennard of what I had just heard from the Serjeant.

Then I despatched a clerk to Gloucester Place with a note for Blanche, telling her I should be with her early in the evening, and that she must not fail to be at home, as my business was important.

Twilight was falling when I arrived. Blanche sat at one of the windows in the drawing-room, looking listlessly into the street in the fading light. Old Mrs. Guy, who was staying with her, was lying on the dining-room sofa, Blanche said, having retired to it and fallen asleep after dinner.

How lovely Blanche looked; but how cross! She wore a pale blue silk, her favourite colour, with a gold necklace and open bracelets, from which drooped a heart set with sapphires and diamonds; and her fair, silken hair looked as if she had been impatiently pushing it about.

"I know what you have come for, Charles," she said in fretful tones, as I sat down near her. "Lord Level prepared me in a letter I received from him this morning."

"Indeed!" I answered lightly. "What did the preparation consist of?"

"I wrote to him," said Blanche. "I have written to him more than once, telling him I am about to get a separation. In answer, my lord commands me down to Marshdale"—very resentfully—"and says you are to take me down."

"All quite right, Blanche; quite true, so far. But—"

"But I don't know that I shall go. I think I shall not go."

"A wife should obey her husband's commands."

"I do not intend to be his wife any longer. And you cannot wish me to be, Charles; you ought not to wish it. Lord Level's conduct is simply shameful. What right has he to stay at Marshdale—amusing himself down there?"

"I fancy he cannot help staying there at present. Has he told you he is ill?"

She glanced quickly round at me.

"Has he told you that he is so?"

"Yes, Blanche; he has. He is too ill to travel."

She paused for a moment, and then tossed back her pretty hair with a scornful hand.

"And you believed him! Anything for an excuse. He is no more ill than I am, Charles; rely upon that."

"But I am certain—"

"Don't go on," she interrupted, tapping her dainty black satin slipper on the carpet; a petulant movement to which Blanche was given, even as a child. "If you have come for the purpose of whitening my husband to me, as papa is always doing. I will not listen to you."

"You will not listen to any sort of reasoning whatever. I see that, my dear."

"Reasoning, indeed!" she retorted. "Say sophistry."

"Listen for an instant, Blanche; consider this one little item: I believe Lord Level to be ill, confined to his bed with low fever, as he tells me; you refuse to believe it; you say he is well. Now, considering that he expects us both to be at Marshdale to-morrow, can you not perceive how entirely, ridiculously void of purpose it would be for him to say he is seriously ill if he is not so?"

"I don't care," said my young lady. "He is deeper than any fox."

"Blanche, my opinion is, and you are aware of it, that you misjudge your husband. Upon one or two points I know you do. But I did not come here to discuss these unpleasant topics—you are in error there, you see. I came upon a widely different matter: to disclose something to you that will very greatly distress you, and I am grieved to be obliged to do it."

The words changed her mood. She looked half frightened.

"Oh!" she burst forth, before I had time to say another word. "Is it my husband? You say he is ill! He is not dead?"

"My dear, be calm. It is not about your husband at all. It is about some one else, though, who is very ill—Tom Heriot."

Grieved she no doubt was; but the relief that crept into her face, tone and attitude proved that the one man was little to her compared with the other, and that she loved her husband yet with an impassioned love.

By degrees, softening the facts as much as possible, I told the tale. Of Tom's apprehension about the time of her marriage; his trial which followed close upon it; his conviction, and departure for a penal settlement; his escape; his return to England; his concealments to evade detection; his illness; and his present state. Blanche shivered and cried as she listened, and finally fell upon her knees, and buried her face in the cushions of the chair.

"And is there no hope for him, Charles?" she said, looking up after a while.

"My dear, there is no hope. And, under the circumstances, it is happier for him to die than to continue to live. But he would like to see you, Blanche."

"Poor Tom! Poor Tom! Can we go to him now—this evening?"

"Yes; it is what I came to propose. It is the best time. He—"

"Shall I order the carriage?"

The interruption made me laugh. My Lord Level's state carriage and powdered servants at that poor fugitive's door!

"My dear, we must go in the quietest manner. We will take a cab as we walk along, and get out of it before turning into the street where he is lying. Change this blue silk for one of the plainest dresses that you have, and wear a close bonnet and a veil."

"Oh, of course; I see. Charles, I am too thoughtless."

"Wait an instant," I said, arresting her as she was crossing the room. "I must return for a moment to our controversy touching your husband. You complained bitterly of him last year for secluding you in dull, remote parts of the Continent, and especially for keeping you away from England. You took up the notion, and proclaimed it to those who would listen to you, that it was to serve his own purposes. Do you remember this?"

"Well?" said Blanche timidly, her colour coming and going as she stood with her hands on the table. "He did keep me away; he did seclude me."

"It was done out of love for you, Blanche. Whilst your heart felt nothing but reproach for him, his was filled with care and consideration for you; where to keep you, how to guard you from hearing of the disgrace and trouble that had overtaken your brother. We knew—I and Mr. Brightman—Lord Level's motive; and Major Carlen knew. I believe Level would have given years of his life to save you from the knowledge always and secure you peace. Now, Blanche, my dear, as you perceive that, at least in that one respect, you misjudged him then, do you not think you may be misjudging him still?"

She burst into tears. "No, I don't think so," she said. "I wish I could think so. You know that he maintains some dreadful secret at Marshdale; and that—that—wicked Italians are often staying there—singers perhaps; I shouldn't wonder; or ballet-dancers—anyway, people who can have no right and no business to be there. You know that one of them stabbed him—Oh yes, she did, and it was a woman with long hair."

"I do not know anything of the kind."

"Charles, you look at me reproachfully, as if the blame lay with me instead of him. Can't you see what a misery it all is for me, and that it is wearing my life away?" she cried passionately, the tears falling from her eyes. "I would rather die than separate from him, if I were not forced to it by the goings on at that wretched Marshdale. What will life be worth to me, parted from him? I look forward to it with a sick dread. Charles, I do indeed; and now, when I know—what—is perhaps—coming—"

Blanche suddenly crossed her arms upon the table, hid her face upon them, and sobbed bitterly.

"What is perhaps coming?"

"I'm afraid it is, Charles."

"But what is?"

"An heir, perhaps."

It was some moments before I took in the sense of the words. Then I laughed.

"Oh well, Blanche! Of course you ought to talk of separation with that in prospect! Go and put your things on, you silly child: the evening is wearing away."

And she left the room.

Side by side on the sofa, Blanche's fair head pillowed upon his breast, his arm thrown round her. She had taken off her bonnet and mantle, and was crying quietly.

"Be calm, my dear sister. It is all for the best."

"Tom, Tom, how came you to do it?"

"I didn't do it, my dear one. That's where they were mistaken. I should be no more capable of doing such a thing than you are."

"Then why did they condemn you—and say you were guilty?"

"They knew no better. The guilty man escaped, and I suffered."

"But why did you not tell the truth? Why did you not accuse him to the judge?"

"I told the judge I was innocent; but that is what most prisoners say, and it made no impression on him," replied Tom. "For the rest, I did not understand the affair as well as I did after the trial. All had been so hurried; there was no time for anything. Yes, Blanche, you may at least take this solitary bit of consolation to your heart—that I was not guilty."

"And that other man, who was?" she asked eagerly, lifting her face. "Where is he?"

"Flourishing," said Tom. "Driving about the world four-in-hand, no doubt, and taking someone else in as he took me."

Blanche turned to me, looking haughty enough.

"Charles, cannot anything be done to expose the man?" she cried. Tom spoke again before I could answer.

"It will not matter to me then, one way or the other. But, Charley, I do sometimes wish, as I lie thinking, that the truth might be made known and my memory cleared. I was reckless and foolish enough, heaven knows, but I never did that for which I was tried and sentenced."

Now, since we had been convinced of Tom Heriot's innocence, the question whether it would be possible to clear him before the world had often been in my mind. Lake and I had discussed it more than once. It would be difficult, no doubt, but it was just possible that time might place some advantage in our hands and open up a way to us. I mentioned this now.

"Ay, difficult enough, I dare say," commented Tom. "With a hundred barriers in the way—eh, Charley?"

"The chief difficulty would lie, I believe, in the fact you acknowledged just now, Tom—your own folly. People argue—they argued at the time—that a young man so reckless as you were would not stick at a trifle."

"Just so," replied Tom with equanimity. "I ought to have pulled up before, and—I did not. Well; you know my innocence, and now Blanche knows it, and Level knows it, and old Carlen knows it; you are about all that are near to me; and the public must be left to chance. There's one good man, though, I should like to know it, Charles, and that's Serjeant Stillingfar."

"He knows it already, Tom. Be at ease on that score."

"Does he think, I wonder, that my memory might ever be cleared?"

"He thinks it would be easier to clear you than it would be to trace the guilt to its proper quarter; but the one, you see, rests upon the other. There are no proofs, that we know of, to bring forward of that man's guilt; and—"

"He took precious good care there should be none," interrupted Tom. "Let Anstey alone for protecting himself."

"Just so. But—I was going to say—the Serjeant thinks you have one chance in your favour. It is this: The man, Anstey, being what he is, will probably fall into some worse crime which cannot be hidden or hushed up. When conviction overtakes him, he may be induced to confess that it was he, and not Captain Heriot, who bore the lion's share in that past exploit for which you suffered. Rely upon this, Tom—should any such chance of clearing your memory present itself, it will not be neglected. I shall be on the watch always."

There was silence for a time. Tom was leaning back, pale and exhausted, his breath was short, his face gray, wan and wasted.

"Has Leah been to see you?" Blanche asked him.

"Yes, twice; and she considers herself very hardly dealt by that she may not come here to nurse me," he replied.

"Could she not be here?"

I shook my head. "It would not be safe, Blanche. It would be running another risk. You see, trouble would fall upon others as well as Tom, were he discovered now: upon me, and more especially upon Lennard."

"They would be brought to trial for concealing me, just as I was brought to trial for a different crime," said Tom lightly. "Our English laws are comprehensive, I assure you, Blanche. Poor Leah says it is cruel not to let her see the end. I asked her what good she'd derive from it."

Blanche gave a sobbing sigh. "How can you talk so lightly, Tom?"

"Lightly!" he cried, in apparent astonishment. "I don't myself see very much that's light in that. When the end is at hand, Blanche, why ignore it?"

She turned her face again to him, burying it upon his arm, in utmost sorrow.

"Don't, Blanche!" he said, his voice trembling. "There's nothing to cry for; nothing. My darling sister, can't you see what a life mine has been for months past: pain of body, distress and apprehension of mind! Think what a glorious change it will be to leave all this for Heaven!"

"Are you sure of going there, dear?" she whispered. "Have you made your peace?"

Tom smiled at her. Tears were in his own eyes.

"I think so. Do you remember that wonderful answer to the petition of the thief on the cross? The promise came back to him at once, on the instant: 'Verily, I say unto thee, To-day shalt thou be with Me in Paradise.' He had been as much of a sinner as I, Blanche."

Blanche was crying softly. Tom held her to him.

"Imagine," he said, "how the change must have broken on that poor man. To pass from the sorrow and suffering of this life into the realms of Paradise! There was no question as to his fitness, you see, or whether he had been good or bad; all the sin of the past was condoned when he took his humble appeal to his Redeemer: 'Lord, remember me when Thou comest into Thy kingdom!' Blanche, my dear, I know that He will also remember me."

CHAPTER XI

DOWN AT MARSHDALE

It was Thursday morning, the day on which Blanche Level was to travel to Marshdale. She sat in her dining-room at Gloucester Place, her fingers busy over some delicate fancy-work, her thoughts divided between the sad interview she had held with Tom Heriot the previous night, and the forthcoming interview with her husband; whilst her attention was partially given to old Mrs. Guy, who sat in an easy-chair by the fire, a thick plaid shawl on her shoulders and her feet on the fender, recounting the history of an extraordinary pain which had attacked her in the night. But as Mrs. Guy rarely passed a night without experiencing some extraordinary pain or other, Blanche listened absently.

"It is the heart, my dear; I am becoming sure of that," said the old lady. "Last year, if you remember, the physician put it down to spleen; but when I go to him tomorrow and tell him of this dreadful oppression, he will change his opinion."

"Don't you think you keep yourself too warm?" said Blanche, who looked so cool and fresh in her pretty morning dress. "That shawl is heavy, and the fire is warm; yet it is still quite summer weather."

"Ah, child, you young people call it summer weather all the year round if the sun only shines. When you get to be my age, Blanche, you will know what cold means. I dare say you'll go flying off to Marshdale this afternoon in that gossamer dress you have on, or one as thin and flowing."

"No, I shan't," laughed Blanche; "it would be tumbled and spoilt by the time I got there. I shall go in that pretty new gray cashmere, trimmed with silk brocade."

"That's a lovely dress, child; too good to travel in. And you tell me you will be back to-morrow. I don't think that very likely, my dear—"

"But I intend to be," interrupted Blanche.

"You will see," nodded the old lady. "When your husband gets you there, he will keep you there. Give my love to him, Blanche, and say I hope he will be in town before I go back to Jersey. I should like to see him."

Blanche was not paying particular attention to this message. Her attention was attracted by a telegraph boy, who seemed to be approaching the door. The next moment there was a loud knock, which made Mrs. Guy start. Blanche explained that it was a telegram.

"Oh, dear," cried the old lady. "I don't like telegrams; they always give me a turn. Perhaps it's come from Jersey to say my house is burned down."

The telegram, however, had come from Marshdale. It was addressed to Lady Level, and proved to be from her husband.

"Do not come to Marshdale to-day. Put it off until next week. I am writing to you. Wait for letter. Let Charles know."

Now my Lady Level, staring at the message, and being in chronic resentment against her husband, all sorts of unorthodox suspicions rife within her, put the worst possible construction upon this mandate.

"I knew how much he would have me at Marshdale!" she exclaimed in anger, as she tossed the telegram on the table. "'Don't come down till next week! Wait for letter!' Yes, and next week there'll come another message, telling me I am not to go at all, or that he will be back here. It is a shame!"

"But what is it?" cried old Mrs. Guy, who did not understand, and knew nothing of any misunderstanding between Blanche and her husband. "Not to go, you say? Is his lordship ill?"

"Oh, of course; very ill, indeed," returned Blanche, suppressing the scorn she felt.

Putting the telegram into an envelope, she addressed it to me, called Sanders, and bade him take it at once to my office. He did so. But I had also received one to the same effect from Lord Level, who, I suppose, concluded it best to send to me direct. Telling Sanders I would call on Lady Level that evening, I thought no more about the matter, and was glad, rather than otherwise, that the journey to Marshdale was delayed. This chapter, however, has to do with Blanche, and not with me.

Now, whether the step that Lady Level took had its rise in an innocent remark made by Mrs. Guy, or whether it was the result of her own indignant feeling, cannot be told. "My dear," said the old lady, "if my husband were ill, I should go to him all the more." And that was just what Blanche Level resolved to do.

The previous arrangement had been that she should drive to my office, to save me time, pick me up, and so onwards to Victoria Station, to take the four o'clock train, which would land us at Marshdale in an hour.

"My dear, I thought I understood that you were not going to Marshdale; that the telegram stopped you," said Mrs. Guy, hearing Blanche give orders for the carriage to be at the door at a quarter past three to convey her to Victoria, and perceiving also that she was making preparations for a journey.

"But I intend to go all the same," replied Blanche. "And look here, dear Mrs. Guy, Charles has sent me word that he will call here this evening. When he comes, please give him this little note. You won't forget?"

"Not I, child. Major Carlen is always telling me I am silly; but I'm not silly enough to forget messages."

The barouche waited at the door at the appointed time, and Lady Level was driven to Victoria, where she took train for Marshdale. Five o'clock was striking out from Lower Marshdale Church when she arrived at Marshdale Station.

"Get out here, miss?" asked the porter, who saw Lady Level trying to open the door.

"Yes."

"Any luggage?"

"Only this bag," replied Lady Level.

The man took charge of it, and she alighted. Traversing the little roadside station, she looked to where the fly generally stood; but no fly was there. The station-master waited for her ticket.

"Is the fly not here?" she inquired.

"Seems not," answered the master indifferently. But as he spoke he recognised Lady Level.

"I beg your pardon, my lady. The fly went off with some passengers who alighted from the last up-train; it's not back yet."

"Will it be long, do you know?"

"Well—I— James," he called to the porter, "where did the fly go to?"

"Over to Dimsdale," replied the man.

"Then it won't be back for half an hour yet, my lady," said the station-master to Lady Level.

"Oh, I can't wait all that time," she returned, rather impatiently. "I will walk. Will you be good enough to send my bag after me?"

"I'll send it directly, my lady."

She was stepping from the little platform when a thought struck her, and she turned to ask a question of the station-master. "Is it safe to cross the fields now? I remember it was said not to be so when I was here last."

"On account of Farmer Piggot's bull," replied he. "The fields are quite safe now, my lady; the bull has been taken away."

Lady Level passed in at the little gate, which stood a few yards down the road, and was the entrance to the field-way which led to Marshdale House. It was a warm evening, calm and sunny; not a leaf stirred; all nature seemed at rest.

"What will Archibald say to me?" she wondered, her thoughts busy. "He will fly into a passion, perhaps. I can't help it if he does. I am determined now to find out why I am kept away from Marshdale and why he is for ever coming to it. This underhand work has been going on too long."

At this moment, a whistle behind her, loud and shrill, caused her to turn. She was then crossing the first field. In the distance she espied a boy striding towards her: and soon recognised him for the surly boy, Sam Doughty. He carried her bag, and vouchsafed her a short nod as he came up.

"How are you, Sam?" she asked pleasantly.

"Didn't think about its being you," was Sam's imperturbable answer, as he walked on beside her. "When they disturbs me at my tea and says I must go right off that there same moment with a passenger's bag for Marshdale House, I took it to be my lord's at least."

"Did they not let you finish your tea?" said Lady Level with a smile.

"Catch 'em," retorted Sam, in a tone of resentment. "Catch 'em a letting me stop for a bite or a sup when there's work to do; no, not if I was starving for 't. The master, he's a regular stinger for being down upon a fellow's work, and t'other's a—I say," broke off Mr. Sam, "did you ever know a rat?—one what keeps ferreting his nose into everything as don't concern him? Then you've knowed James Runn."

"James Runn is the porter, I suppose?" said Lady Level, much amused.

"Well, he is, and the biggest sneak as ever growed. What did he go and do last week? We had a lot o' passengers to get off by the down train to Dover, the people from the Grange it were, and a sight o' trunks. I'd been helping to stow the things in the luggage-van, and the footman, as he was getting into his second-class carriage, holds out a shilling, open handed. I'd got my fingers upon it, I had, when that there James Runn, that rascally porter, clutches hold of it and says it were meant for him, not for me. I wish he was gone, I do!"

"The bull is gone, I hear," remarked Lady Level.

"Oh, he have been gone this long time from here," replied the boy, shifting the bag from one shoulder to the other. "He took to run at folks reg'lar, he did; such fun it were to hear 'em squawk! One old woman in a red shawl he took and tossed. Mr. Drewitt up at the House interfered then, and told Farmer Piggot the bull must be moved; so the farmer put him over yonder on t'other side his farm into the two-acre meadow, which haven't got no right o' way through it. I wish he had tossed that there James Runn first and done for him!" deliberately avowed Sam, again shifting his burden.

"You appear to find that bag heavy," remarked Lady Level.

"It's not that heavy, so to say," acknowledged the surly boy; "it's that I be famishing for my tea. Oh, that there Runn's vicious, he is!—a sending me off when I'd hardly took a mouthful!"

"Well, I could not carry it myself," she said laughingly.

"He might ha' brought it; he had swallowed down his own tea, he had. It's not so much he does—just rushes up to the doors o' the trains when they comes in, on the look out for what may be give to him, making believe he's letting folks in and out o' the carriages. I see my lord give him a shilling t'other day; that I did."

"When my lord arrived here, do you mean?"

"No, 'twarn't that day, 'twere another. My lord comes on to the station asking about a parcel he were expecting of. Mr. Noakes, he were gone to his dinner, and that there Runn answered my lord that he had just took the parcel to Marshdale House and left it with Mr. Snow. Upon which my lord puts his hand in his pocket and gives him a shilling. I see it."

Lady Level laughed. It was impossible to help it. Sam's tone was so intensely wrathful.

"Do you see much of Lord Level?" she asked.

"I've not see'd him about for some days. It's said he's ill."

"What is the matter with him?"

"Don't know," said Sam. "It were Dr. Hill's young man, Mitcham, I heard say it. Mother sent me last night to Dr. Hill's for her physic, and Mr. Mitcham he said he had not been told naught about her physic, but he'd ask the doctor when he came back from attending upon my Lord Level."

"Is your mother ill?" inquired Sam's listener.

"She be that bad, she be, as to be more fit to be a-bed nor up," replied the boy: and his voice really took a softer tone as he spoke of his mother. "It were twins this last time, you see, and there's such a lot to do for 'em all, mother can't spare a minute in the day to lie by: and father's wages don't go so fur as they did when there was less mouths at home."

"How many brothers and sisters have you?"

"Five," said Sam, "not counting the twins, which makes seven. I be the eldest, and I makes eight. And, if ever I does get a shilling or a sixpence given me, I takes it right home to mother. I wish them there two twins had kept away," continued Sam spitefully; "mother had her hands full without them. Squalling things they both be."

Thus, listening to the boy's confidences, Lady Level came to the little green gate which opened to the side of the garden at Marshdale House. Sam carried the bag to the front door. No one was to be seen. All things, indoors and out, seemed intensely quiet.

"You can put it down here, Sam," said Lady Level, producing half-a-crown. "Will you give this to your mother if I give it to you?"

"I always gives her everything as is gived to me," returned Sam resentfully. "I telled ye so."

Slipping it into his pocket, the boy set off again across the fields. Lady Level rang the bell gently. Somehow she was not feeling so well satisfied with herself for having come as she felt when she started. Deborah opened the door.

"Oh, my lady!" she exclaimed in surprise, but speaking in a whisper.

"My bag is outside," said Lady Level, walking forward to the first sitting-room, the door of which stood open. Mrs. Edwards met her.

"Dear, dear!" exclaimed the old lady, lifting her hands. "Then Snow never sent those messages off properly after all! My lady, I am sorry you should have come."

"I thought I was expected, Mrs. Edwards, and Mr. Strange with me," returned Blanche coldly.

"True, my lady, so you were; but a telegram was sent off this morning to stop you. Two telegrams went, one to your ladyship and one to Mr. Strange. It was I gave the order from my lord to Snow, and I thought I might as well send one also to Mr. Strange, though his lordship said nothing about it."

"But why was I stopped?" questioned Blanche.

"On account of my lord's increased illness," replied Mrs. Edwards. "He grew much worse in the night; and when Mr. Hill saw how it was with him this morning, he said your ladyship's visit must be put off. Mr. Hill is with him now."

"Of what nature is his illness?"

"My lady, he has not been very well since he came down. When he got here we remarked that he seemed low-spirited. In a few days he began to be feverish, and asked me to get him some lemonade made. Quarts of it he drank: cook protested there'd be a failure of lemons in the village. 'It is last year's fever back again,' said his lordship to me, speaking in jest. But, strange to say, he might as well have spoken in earnest, for it turns out to be the same sort of fever precisely."

"Is he very ill?"

"He is very ill indeed to-day," answered Mrs. Edwards. "Until this morning it was thought to be a light attack, no danger attending it, nor any symptom of delirium. But that has all changed, and this afternoon he is slightly delirious."

"Is there—danger?" cried Blanche.

"Mr. Hill says not, my lady. Not yet, at all events. But—here he is," broke off Mrs. Edwards, as the doctor's step was heard. "He will be able to explain more of the illness to your ladyship than I can."

She left the room as Mr. Hill entered it. The same cheerful, hearty man that Blanche had known last year, with a fine brow and benevolent countenance. Blanche shook hands with him, and he sat down near her.

"So you did not get the telegram," he began, after greeting her.

"I did get it," answered Blanche, feeling rather ashamed to be obliged to confess it. "But I—I was ready, and I thought I would come all the same."

"It is a pity," said Mr. Hill. "You must not let your husband see you. Indeed, the best thing you can do will be to go back again."

"But why?" asked Blanche, turning obstinate. "What have I done to him that he may not see me?"

"You don't understand, child," said the surgeon, speaking in his fatherly way. "His lordship is in a critical state, the disease having manifested itself with alarming rapidity. If he can be kept perfectly calm and still, its progress may be arrested and danger averted. If not, it will assuredly turn to brain-fever and must run its course. Anything likely to rouse him in the smallest degree, no matter whether it be pleasure or pain, must be absolutely kept from him. Only the sight of you might bring on an excitement that might be—well, I was going to say fatal. That is why I suggested to his lordship to send off the telegram."

"You knew I was coming down, then?" said Blanche.

"My dear, I did know; and— But, bless me, I ought to apologize to your ladyship for my familiarity of speech," broke off the kindly doctor, with a smile.

Blanche answered by smiling too, and putting her hand into his.

"I lost a daughter when she was about your age, my dear; you put me in mind of her; I said so to Mrs. Edwards when you were here last autumn. She was my only child, and my wife was already gone. Well, well! But that's beside the present question," he added briskly. "Will you go back to town, Lady Level?"

"I would rather remain, now I am here," she answered. "At least, for a day or two. I will take care not to show myself to Lord Level."

"Very well," said the doctor, rising. "Do not let him either hear you or see you. I shall be in again at nine to-night."

"Who is nursing him?" asked Blanche.

"Mrs. Edwards. She is the best nurse in the world. Snow, the head gardener, helps occasionally; he will watch by him to-night; and Deborah fetches and carries."

Lady Level took contrition to herself as she sat alone. She had been mentally accusing her husband of all sorts of things, whilst he was really lying in peril of his life. Matters and mysteries pertaining to Marshdale were not cleared up; but—Blanche could not discern any particular mystery to wage war with just now.

Tea was served to her, and Blanche would not allow them to think of dinner. Mrs. Edwards had a room prepared for her in a different corridor from Lord Level's, so that he would not be in danger of hearing her voice or footsteps.

Very lonely felt Blanche when twilight fell, as she sat at the window. She thought she had never seen trees look so melancholy before, and she recalled what Charles Strange had always said—that the sight of trees in the gloaming caused him to be curiously depressed. Presently, wrapping a blue cloud about her head and shoulders, she strolled out of doors.

It was nearly dark now, and the overhanging trees made it darker. Blanche strolled to the front gate and looked up and down the road. Not a soul was about; not a sound broke the stillness. The house behind her was gloomy enough; no light to be seen save the faint one that burnt in Lord Level's chamber, whose windows faced this way; or a flash that now and then appeared in the passages from a lamp carried by someone moving about.

Blanche walked up and down, now in this path, now in that, now sitting on a bench to think, under the dark trees. By-and-by, she heard the front door open and someone come down the path, cross to the side path, unlock the small door that led into the garden of the East Wing and enter it. By the very faint light remaining, she thought she recognised John Snow, the gardener.

She distinctly heard his footsteps pass up the other garden; she distinctly heard the front door of the East Wing open to admit him, and close again. Prompted by idle curiosity, Blanche also approached the little door in the wall, found it shut, but not locked, opened it, went in, advanced to where she had full view of the wing, and stood gazing up at it. Like the other part of the house, it loomed out dark and gloomy: the upper windows appeared to have outer bars before them; at least, Blanche thought so. Only in one room was there any light.

It was in a lower room, a sitting-room, no doubt. The lamp, standing on the centre table, was bright; the window was thrown up. Beside it sat someone at work; crochet-work, or knitting, or tatting; something or other done with the fingers. Mrs. Snow amusing herself, thought Blanche at first; but in a moment she saw that it was not Mrs. Snow. The face was dark and handsome, and the black hair was adorned with black lace. With a sensation as of some mortal agony rushing and whirling through her veins, Lady Level recognised her. It was Nina, the Italian.

Nina, who had been the object of her suspicious jealousy; Nina, who was, beyond doubt, the attraction that drew her husband to Marshdale; and who, as she fully believed, had been the one to stab him a year ago!

Blanche crept back to her own garden. Finding instinctively the darkest seat it contained, she sat down upon it with a faint cry of despair.

CHAPTER XII

IN THE EAST WING

What will not a jealous and angry woman do? On the next morning (Friday) Blanche Level, believing herself to be more ignominiously treated than ever wife was yet, despatched a couple of telegrams to London, both of them slightly incomprehensible. One of the telegrams was to Charles Strange, the other to Arnold Ravensworth; and both were to the same effect—they must hasten down to Marshdale to her "protection" and "rescue." And Mr. Ravensworth was requested to bring his wife.

"She will be some little countenance for me; I'm sure I dare not think how I must be looked upon here," mentally spoke my Lady Level in her glowing indignation.

Lord Level was better. When Mr. Hill paid his early visit that Friday morning, he pronounced him to be very much better; and John Snow said his lordship had passed a quiet night. "If we can only keep him tranquil to-day and to-night again, there will be no further danger from the fever," Mr. Hill then observed to Lady Level.

The day went on, the reports from the sick-room continuing favourable: my lord was lying tranquil, his mind clear. My lady, down below, was anything but tranquil: rather she felt herself in a raging fever. In the evening, quite late, the two gentlemen arrived from London, not having been able to come earlier. Mrs. Ravensworth was not with them; she could not leave her delicate baby. Lady Level had given orders for chambers to be prepared.

After they had partaken of refreshments, which brought the time to ten o'clock, Lady Level opened upon her grievances—past and present. Modest and reticent though her language still was, she contrived to convey sundry truths to them. From the early days of her marriage she had unfortunately had cause to suspect Lord Level of disloyalty to herself and of barefaced loyalty to another. Her own eyes had seen him more than once with the girl called Nina at Pisa; had seen him at her house, sitting side by side with her in her garden smoking and talking—had heard him address her by her Christian name. This woman, as she positively knew, had followed Lord Level to England; this woman was harboured at Marshdale. She was in the house now, in its East Wing. She, Blanche, had seen her there the previous evening.

Mr. Ravensworth's severe countenance took a stern expression as he listened; he believed every word. Charles Strange (I am not speaking just here in my own person) still thought there might be a mistake somewhere. He could not readily take up so bad an opinion of Lord Level, although circumstances did appear to tell against him. His incredulity irritated Blanche.

"I will tell you, then, Charles, what I have never disclosed to mortal man," she flashed forth, in a passionate whisper, bending forward her pretty face, now growing whiter than death. "You remember that attack upon Lord Level last autumn. You came down at the time, Arnold—"

"Yes, yes. What about it?"

"It was that woman who stabbed him!"

Neither spoke for a moment. "Nonsense, Blanche!" said Mr. Strange.

"But I tell you that it was. She was in night-clothes, or something of that kind, and her black hair was falling about her; but I could not mistake her Italian face."

Mr. Ravensworth did not forget Lady Level's curious behaviour at the time; he had thought then she suspected someone in particular. "Are you sure?" he asked her now.

"I am sure. And you must both see the danger I may be in whilst here," she added, with a shiver. "That woman may try to stab me, as she stabbed him. She must have stabbed him out of jealousy, because I—her rival—was there."

"You had better quit the house the first thing in the morning, Lady Level, and return to London," said Mr. Ravensworth.

"That I will not do," she promptly answered. "I will not leave Marshdale until these shameful doings are investigated; and I have sent for you to act on my behalf and bring them to light. No longer shall the reproach be perpetually cast upon me by papa and Charles Strange, that I complain of my husband without cause. It is my turn now."

That something must be done, in justice to Lady Level, or at least attempted, they both saw. But what, or how to set about it, neither of them knew. They remained in consultation together long after Blanche had retired to rest.

"We will go out at daybreak and have a look at the windows of this East Wing," finally observed Mr. Ravensworth.

Perhaps that was easier said than done. With the gray light of early morning they were both out of doors; but they could not find any entrance to the East Wing. The door in the wall of the front garden was locked; the entrance gates from the road were locked also. In the garden at the back—it was more of a wilderness than a garden—they discovered a small gate in a corner. It was completely overgrown with trees and shrubs, and had evidently not been used for years and years. But the wood had become rotten, the fastenings loose; and by their united strength they opened it.

They found themselves in a very large space of ground indeed. Grass was in the middle, quite a field of it; and round it a broad gravel walk. Encompassing all on three sides rose a wide bank of shrubs and overhanging trees. Beyond these again was a very high wall. On the fourth side stood the East Wing, high and gloomy. Its windows were all encased with iron bars, and the lower windows were whitened.

Taking a survey of all this, one of them softly whispering in surprise, Mr. Ravensworth advanced to peer in at the windows. Of course, being whitened, he had his trouble for his pains.

"It puts me in mind of a prison," remarked Charles Strange.

"It puts me in mind of a madhouse," was the laconic rejoinder of Mr. Ravensworth.

They passed back through the gate again, Mr. Ravensworth turning to take a last look. In that minute his eye was attracted to one of the windows on the ground floor. It opened down the middle, like a French one, and was being shaken, apparently with a view to opening it—and if you are well acquainted with continental windows, or windows made after their fashion, you may remember how long it has taken you to shake a refractory window before it will obey. It was at length effected, and in the opening, gazing with a vacant, silly expression through the close bars, appeared a face. It remained in view but a moment; the window was immediately closed again, Mr. Ravensworth thought by another hand. What was the mystery?

That some mystery did exist at Marshdale, apart from any Italian ladies who might have no fair right to be there, was pretty evident. At breakfast the gentlemen related this little experience to Blanche.

Madame Blanche tossed her head in incredulity. "Don't be taken in," she answered. "Windows whitened and barred, indeed! It is all done with a view to misleading people. She was sitting at the open window at work on Thursday night."

After breakfast, resolved no longer to be played with, Blanche proceeded upstairs to Mr. Drewitt's rooms, her friends following her, all three of them creeping by Lord Level's chamber-door with noiseless steps. His lordship was getting better quite wonderfully, Mrs. Edwards had told them.

The old gentleman, in his quaint costume, was in his sitting-room, taking his breakfast alone. Mrs. Edwards took her meals anywhere, and at any time, during her lord's illness. Hearing strange footsteps in the corridor, he rose to see whose they were, and looked considerably astonished.

"Does your ladyship want me?" he asked, bowing.

"I—yes, I think I do," answered Lady Level. "Who keeps the key of that door, Mr. Drewitt?" pointing to the strong oaken door at the end of the passage.

"I keep it, my lady."

"Then will you be kind enough to unlock it for me? These gentlemen wish to examine the East Wing."

"The East Wing is private to his lordship," was the steward's reply, addressing them all conjointly. "Without his authority I cannot open it to anyone."

They stood contending a little while: it was like a repetition of the scene that had been enacted there once before; and, like that, was terminated by the same individual—the surgeon.

"It is all right, Mr. Drewitt." he said; "you can open the door of the East Wing; I bear you my lord's orders. I am going in there to see a patient," he added to the rest.

The steward produced a key from his pocket, and put it into the lock. It was surprising that so small a key should open so massive a door.

They passed, wonderingly, through three rooms en suite: a sitting-room, a bedroom, and a bath-room. All these rooms looked to the back of the house. Other rooms there were on the same floor, which the visitors did not touch upon. Descending the staircase, they entered three similar rooms below. In the smaller one lay some garden-tools, but of a less size than a grown man in his strength would use, and by their side were certain toys: tops, hoops, ninepins, and the like. The middle room was a sitting-room; the larger room beyond had no furniture, and in that, standing over a humming-top, which he had just set to spin on the floor, bent the singular figure of a youth. He had a dark, vacant face, wild black eyes, and a mass of thick black hair, cut short. This figure, a child's whip in his hand, was whipping the top, and making a noise with his mouth in imitation of its hum.

Half madman, half idiot, he stood out, in all his deep misfortune, raising himself up and staring about him with a vacant stare. The expression of Mr. Ravensworth's face changed to one of pity. "Who are you?" he exclaimed in kindly tones. "What is your name?"

"Arnie!" was the mechanical answer, for brains and sense seemed to have little to do with it; and, catching up his top, he backed against the wall, and burst into a distressing laugh. Distressing to a listener; not distressing to him, poor fellow.

"Who is he?" asked Mr. Ravensworth of the doctor.

"An imbecile."

"So I see. But what connection has he with Lord Level's family?"

"He is a connection, or he would not be here."

"Can he be—be—a son of Lord Level's?"

"A son!" interposed the steward, "and my lord but just married! No, sir, he is not a son, he is none so near as that; he is but a connection of the Level family."

The lad came forward from the wall where he was standing, and held out his top to his old friend the doctor. "Do, do," he cried, spluttering as he spoke.

"Nay, Arnie, you can set it up better than I: my back won't stoop well, Arnie."

"Do, do," was the persistent request, the top held out still.

Mr. Ravensworth took it and set it up again, he looking on in greedy eagerness, slobbering and making a noise with his mouth. Then his note changed to a hum, and he whipped away as before.

"Why is he not put away in an asylum?" asked Mr. Ravensworth.

"Put away in an asylum!" retorted the old steward indignantly. "Where could he be put to have the care and kindness that is bestowed upon him here? Imbecile though he is, madman though he may be, he is dear to me and my sister. We pass our lives tending him, in conjunction with Snow and his wife, doing for him, soothing him: where else could that be done? You don't know what you are saying, sir. My lord, who received the charge from his father, comes down to see him: my lord orders that everything should be done for his comfort. And do you suppose it is fitting that his condition should be made public? The fact of one being so afflicted is slur enough upon the race of Level, without its being proclaimed abroad."

"It was he who attacked Lord Level last year?

"Yes, it was; and how he could have escaped to our part of the house will be a marvel to me for ever. My sister says I could not have slipped the bolt of the passage door as usual, but I know I did bolt it. Arnie had been restless that day; he has restless fits; and I suppose he could not sleep, and must have risen from his bed and come to my sitting-room. On my table there I had left my pocket-knife, a new knife, the blades bright and sharp; and this he must have picked up and opened, and found his way with it to my lord's chamber. Why he should have attacked him, or anyone else, I know not; he never had a ferocious fit before."

"Never," assented Mr. Hill, in confirmation.

Mr. Drewitt continued: "He has been imbecile and harmless as you see him now, but he has never disturbed us at night; he has, as I say, fits of restlessness when he cannot sleep, but he is sufficiently sensible to ring a bell communicating with Snow's chamber if he wants anything. If ever he has rung, it has been to say he wants meat."

"Meat!"

The steward nodded. "But it has never been given to him. He is cunning as a fox; they all are; and were we to begin giving him food in the middle of the night we must continue to do it, or have no peace. Eating is his one enjoyment in life, and he devours everything set before him—meat especially. If we have any particular dainty upstairs for dinner or supper, I generally take him in some. Deborah, I believe, thinks I eat all that comes up, and sets me down for a cannibal. He has a hot supper every night. About a year ago we got to think it might be better for him to have a lighter one, and we tried it for a week; but he moaned and cried all night long for his hot meat, and we had to give it him again. The night this happened we had veal cutlets and bacon, and he had the same. He asked for more, but I would not give it; perhaps that angered him, and he mistook my lord for me. Mr. Hill thought it might be so. I shall never be able to account for it."

The doctor nodded assent; and the speaker went on:

"His hair was long then, and he must have looked just like a maniac when the fit of fury lay upon him. Little wonder that my lady was frightened at the sight of him. After he had done the deed he ran back to his own room; I, aroused by the commotion, found him in his bed. He burst out laughing when he saw me: 'I got your knife, I got your knife,' he called out, as if it were a feat to be proud of. His movements must have been silent and stealthy, for Snow had heard nothing."

At this moment there occurred an interruption. The Italian lady approached the room with timid, hesitating steps, and peeped in. "Ah, how do you do, doctor?" she said in a sweet, gentle voice, as she held out her hand to Mr. Hill. Her countenance was mild, open, and honest; and a conviction rushed on the instant into Blanche's mind that she had been misjudging that foreign lady.

"These good gentlepeople are come to see our poor patient?" she added, curtseying to them with native grace, her accent quite foreign. "The poor, poor boy," tears filling her eyes. "And I foretell that this must be my lord's wife!" addressing Blanche. "Will she permit a poor humble stranger to shake her by the hand for her lord's sake—her lord, who has been so good to us?"

"This lady is sister to the unfortunate boy's mother," said the doctor, in low tones to Blanche. "She is a good woman, and worthy to shake hands with you, my lady."

"But who was his father?" whispered Blanche.

"Mr. Francis Level; my lord's dead brother."

Her countenance radiant, Blanche took the lady's hand and warmly clasped it. "You live here to take care of the poor lad," she said.

"But no, madam. I do but come at intervals to see him, all the way from Pisa, in Italy. And also I have had to come to bring documents and news to my lord, respecting matters that concern him and the poor lad. But it is over now," she added. "The week after the one next to come, Arnie goes back with me to Italy, his native country, and my journeys to this country will be ended. His mother, who is always ill and not able to travel, wishes now to have her afflicted son with her."

Back in the other house again, after wishing Nina Sparlati good-day, the astonished visitors gathered in Mr. Drewitt's room to listen to the tale which had to be told them. Mrs. Edwards, who was awaiting them, and fonder of talking than her brother, was the principal narrator. Blanche went away, whispering to Charles Strange that she would hear it from him afterwards.

"We were abroad in Italy," Mrs. Edwards began: "it is many years ago. The late lord, our master then, went for his health, which was declining, though he was but a middle-aged man, and I and my brother were with him, his personal attendants, but treated more like friends. The present lord, Mr. Archibald, named after his father, was with us—he was the second son, not the heir; the eldest son, Mr. Level—Francis was his name—had been abroad for years, and was then in another part of Italy. He came to see his father when we first got out to Florence, but he soon left again. 'He'll die before my lord,' I said to Mr. Archibald; for if ever I saw consumption on a man's face, it was on Mr. Level's. And I remember Mr. Archibald's answer as if it was but yesterday: 'That's just one of your fancies, nurse: Frank tells me he has looked the last three years as he looks now.' But I was right, sir; for shortly after that we received news of the death of Mr. Level; and then Mr. Archibald was the heir. My lord, who had grown worse instead of better, was very ill then."

"Did the late lord die in Italy?" questioned Mr. Ravensworth.

"You shall hear, sir. He grew very ill, I say, and we thought he would be sure to move homewards, but he still stayed on. 'Archibald likes Florence,' he would say, 'and it's all the same to me where I am.' 'Young Level stops for the beaux yeux of the Tuscan women,' the world said—but you know, sir, the world always was censorious; and young men will be young men. However, we were at last on the move; everything was packed and prepared for leaving, when there arrived an ill-favoured young woman, with some papers and a little child, two years old. Its face frightened me when I saw it. It was, as a child, what it is now as a growing man; and you have seen it today," she added in a whisper. "'What is the matter with him?' I asked, for I could speak a little Italian. 'He's a born natural, as yet,' she answered, 'but the doctors think he may outgrow it in part.' 'But who is he? what does he do here?' I said. 'He's the son of Mr. Level,' she replied, 'and I have brought him to the family, for his mother, who was my sister, is also dead.' 'He the son of Mr. Level!' I uttered, knowing she must speak of Mr. Francis. 'Well, you need not bring him here: we English do not recognise chance children.' 'They were married three years ago,' she coolly answered, 'and I have brought the papers to prove it. Mr. Level was a gentleman and my sister not much above a peasant; but she was beautiful and good, and he married her, and this is their child. She has been dying by inches since her husband died; she is now dead, and I am come here to give up the child to his father's people."

"Was it true?" interrupted Mr. Strange.

"My lord thought so, sir, and took kindly to the child. He was brought home here, and the East Wing was made his nursery—"

"Then that—that—poor wretch down there is the true Lord Level!" interrupted Mr. Ravensworth.

"One day, when my lord was studying the documents the woman had left," resumed Mrs. Edwards, passing by the remark with a glance, "something curious struck him in the certificate of marriage; he thought it was forged. He showed it to Mr. Archibald, and they decided to go back to Italy, leaving the child here. All the inquiries they made there tended to prove that, though the child was indeed Mr. Francis Level's, there had been no marriage, or semblance of one. All the same, said my lord, the poor child shall be kindly reared and treated and provided for: and Mr. Archibald solemnly promised his father it should be so. My lord died at Florence, and Mr. Archibald came back Lord Level."

"And he never forgot his promise to his father," interposed the steward, "but has treated the child almost as though he were a true son, consistent with his imbecile state. That East Wing has been his happy home, as Mr. Hill can testify: he has toys to amuse him, the garden to dig in, which is his favourite pastime; and Snow draws him about the paths in his hand-carriage on fine days. It is a sad misfortune, for him and for the family; but my lord has done his best."

"It would have been a greater for my lord had the marriage been a legal one," remarked Mr. Ravensworth.

"I don't know that," sharply spoke up the doctor. "As an idiot I believe he could not inherit. However, the marriage was not a legal one, and my lord is my lord. The mother is not dead; that was a fabrication also; but she is ill, helpless, and is pining for her son; so now he is to be taken to her; my lord, in his generosity, securing him an ample income. It was not the mother who perpetrated the fraud, but the avaricious eldest sister. This sister, the one you have just seen, is the youngest; she is good and honourable, and has done her best to unravel the plot."

That was all the explanation given to Mr. Ravensworth. But the doctor put his arm within that of Charles Strange, and took him into the presence of Lord Level.

"Well," said his lordship, who was then sitting up in bed, and held out his hand, "have you been hearing all about the mysteries, Charles?"

"Yes," smiled Mr. Strange. "I felt sure that whatever the mystery might be, it was one you could safely explain away if you chose."

"Ay: though Blanche did take up the other view and want to cut my head off."

"She was your own wife, your loving wife, I am certain: why not have told her?"

"Because I wanted to be quite sure of certain things first," replied Lord Level. "Listen, Charles: you have my tale to hear yet. Sit down. Sit down, Hill. How am I to talk while you stand?" he asked, laughing.

"When we were in Paris after our marriage a year ago, I received two shocks on one and the same morning," began Lord Level. "The one told me of the trouble Tom Heriot had fallen into; the other, contained in a letter from Pisa, informed me that there had been a marriage after all between my brother and that girl, Bianca Sparlati. If so, of course, that imbecile lad stood between me and the title and estate; though I don't think he could legally inherit. But I did not believe the information. I felt sure that it was another invented artifice of Annetta, the wretched eldest sister, who is a grasping intriguante. I started at once for Pisa, where they live, to make inquiries in person: travelling by all sorts of routes, unfrequented by the English, that my wife might not hear of her brother's disgrace. At Pisa I found difficulties: statements met me that seemed to prove there had been a marriage, and I did not see my way to disprove them. Nina, a brave, honest girl, confessed to me that she doubted them, and I begged of her, for truth and right's sake, to help me as far as she could. I cannot enter into details now, Strange; I am not strong enough for it; enough to say that ever since, nearly a whole year, have I been trying to ferret out the truth: and I only got at it a week ago."

"And there was no marriage?"

"Tell him, Hill," said Lord Level, laughing.

"Well, a sort of ceremony did pass between Francis Level and that young woman, but both of them knew at the time it was not legal, or one that could ever stand good," said the doctor. "Now the real facts have come to light. It seems that Bianca had been married when very young to a sailor named Dromio; within a month of the wedding he sailed away again and did not return. She thought him dead, took up her own name again and went home to her family; and later became acquainted with Francis Level. Now, the sailor has turned up again, alive and well—"

"The first husband!" exclaimed Charles Strange.

"If you like to call him so," said Mr. Hill; "there was never a second. Well, the sailor has come to the fore again; and honest-hearted Nina travelled here from Pisa with the news, and we sent for his lordship to come down and hear it. He was also wanted for another matter. The boy had had a sort of fit, and I feared he would die. My lord heard what Nina had to tell him when he arrived; he did not return at once to London, for Arnie was still in danger, and he waited to see the issue. Very shortly he was taken ill himself, and could not get away. It was good news, though, about that resuscitated sailor!" laughed the doctor, after a pause. "All's well that ends well, and my Lord Level is his own man again."

Charles Strange sought an interview with his sister—as he often called her—and imparted to her these particulars. He then left at once for London with Mr. Ravensworth. Their mission at Marshdale was over.

Lord Level, up and dressed, lay on a sofa in his bedroom in the afternoon. Blanche sat on a footstool beside him. Her face was hidden upon her husband's knee and she was crying bitter tears.

"Shall you ever forgive me, Archibald?"

He was smiling quietly. "Some husbands might say no."

"You don't know how miserable I have been."

"Don't I! But how came you to fall into such notions at first, Blanche? To suspect me of ill at all?"

"It was that Mrs. Page Reid who was with us at Pisa. She said all sorts of things."

"Ah!"

"Won't you forgive me, Archibald?"

"Yes, upon condition that you trust me fully in future. Will you, love?" he softly whispered.

She could not speak for emotion.

"And the next time you have a private grievance against me, Blanche, tell it out plainly," he said, as he held her to him and gave her kiss for kiss.

"My darling, yes. But I shall never have another."

CHAPTER XIII

CONCLUSION

I, Charles Strange, took up this story at its commencement, and I take it up now at its close.

It was a lovely day at the end of summer, in the year following the events recorded in the last chapter, and we were again at Marshdale House.

The two individuals who had chiefly marred the peace of one or another of us in the past were both gone where disturbance is not. Poor Tom Heriot was mouldering in his grave near to that in which his father and mother lay, not having been discovered by the police or molested in any way; and the afflicted Italian lad had died soon after he was taken to his native land. Mr. Hill had warned Nina Sparlati that, in all probability, he would not live long. Mrs. Brightman, I may as well say it here, had recovered permanently; recovered in all ways, as we hoped and believed. The long restraint laid upon her by her illness had effected the cure that nothing else might have been able to effect, and re-established the good habits she had lost. But Miss Brightman was dead; she had not lived to come home from Madeira, and the whole of her fortune was left to Annabel. "So you can live where you please now and go in for grandeur," Arthur Lake said to me and my wife. "All in good time," laughed Annabel; "I am not yet tired of Essex Street."

And now we had come down in the sunny August weather when the courts were up, to stay at Marshdale.

You might be slow to recognise it, though. Recalling the picture of Marshdale House as it was, and looking at it now, many would have said it could not be the same.

The dreary old structure had been converted into a light and beautiful mansion. The whitened windows with their iron bars were no more. The disfiguring, unnaturally-high walls were gone, and the tangled shrubs and weeds, the overgrowth of trees that had made the surrounding land a wilderness, were now turned into lovely pleasure-grounds. The gloomy days had given place to sunny ones, said Lord Level, and the gloomy old structure, with its gloomy secrets, should be remembered no more.

Marshdale was now their chief home, his and his wife's, with their establishment of servants. Mr. Drewitt and Mrs. Edwards had moved into a pretty dwelling hard by; but they were welcomed whenever they liked to go to the house, and were treated as friends. The steward kept the accounts still, and Mrs. Edwards was appealed to by Blanche in all domestic difficulties. She rarely appeared before her lady but in her quaint gala attire.

We were taking tea out of doors at the back of the renovated East Wing. The air bore that Sabbath stillness which Sunday seems to bring: distant bells, ringing the congregation out of church, fell melodiously on the ear. We had been idle this afternoon and stayed at home, but all had attended service in the morning. Mr. Hill had called in and was sitting with us. Annabel presided at the rustic tea-table; Blanche was a great deal too much occupied with her baby-boy, whom she had chosen to have brought out: a lively young gentleman in a blue sash, whose face greatly resembled his father's. Next to Lord Level sat my uncle, who had come down for a week's rest. He was no longer Serjeant Stillingfar; but Sir Charles, and one of her Majesty's judges.

"Won't you have some tea, my dear?" he said to Blanche, who was parading the baby.

By the way, they had named him Charles. Charles Archibald; to be called by the former name: Lord Level protested he would not have people saying Young Archie and Old Archie.

"Yes, Blanche," said he, taking up the suggestion of the judge. "Do let that child go indoors: one might think he was a new toy. Here, I'll take him."

"Archibald need not talk," laughed Blanche, looking after her husband, who had taken the child from her and was tossing it as he went indoors. "He is just as fond of having the baby as I am. Neither need you laugh, Mr. Charles," turning upon me; "your turn will come soon, you know."

Leaving the child in its nursery in the East Wing, Lord Level came back to his place; and we sat on until evening approached. A peaceful evening, promising a glorious sunset. An hour after midday, when we had just got safely in from church, there had been a storm of thunder and lightning, and it had cleared the sultry air. The blue sky above, flecked with gold, was of a lovely rose colour towards the west.

"The day has been a type of life: or of what life ought to be," suddenly remarked Mr. Hill. "Storm and cloud succeeded by peace and sunshine."

"The end is not always peaceful," said Lord Level.

"It mostly is when we have worked on for it patiently," said the judge. "My friends, you may take the word of an old man for it—that a life of storm and trouble, through which we have struggled manfully to do our duty under God, ever bearing on in reliance upon Him, must of necessity end in peace. Perhaps not always perfect and entire peace in this world; but assuredly in that which is to come."

MRS HENRY WOOD (aka ELLEN WOOD) – A CONCISE BIBLIOGRAPHY

Danesbury House (1860)
East Lynne (1861)

The Elchester College Boys (1861)
A Life's Secret (1862)
Mrs. Halliburton's Troubles (1862)
The Channings (1862)
The Foggy Night at Offord: A Christmas Gift for the Lancashire Fund (1863)
The Shadow of Ashlydyat (1863)
Verner's Pride (1863)
Lord Oakburn's Daughters (1864)
Oswald Cray (1864)
Trevlyn Hold; or, Squire Trevlyn's Heir (1864)
William Allair; or, Running away to Sea (1864)
Mildred Arkell: A Novel (1865)
The Argosy (1865)
Elster's Folly: A Novel (1866)
St. Martin's Eve: A Novel (1866)
Lady Adelaide's Oath (1867)
Orville College: A Story (1867)
The Ghost of the Hollow Field (1867)
Anne Hereford: A Novel (1868)
Castle Wafer; or, The Plain Gold Ring (1868)
The Red Court Farm: A Novel (1868)
Roland Yorke: A Novel (1869)
Bessy Rane: A Novel (1870)
George Canterbury's Will (1870)
Dene Hollow (1871)
Within the Maze: A Novel (1872)
The Master of Greylands (1872)
Johnny Ludlow (1874)
Bessy Wells (1875)
Told in the Twilight: Containing 'Parkwater' and nine short stories (1875)
Adam Grainger: A Tale (1876)
Edina (1876)
Our Children (1876)
Parkwater: With four other tales (1876)
Pomeroy Abbey (1878)
Lady Adelaide (1879)
Johnny Ludlow, Second Series (1880)
A Tale of Sin and Other Tales (1881)
Court Netherleigh: A Novel (1881)
About Ourselves (1883)
Johnny Ludlow. Third Series (1885)
Lady Grace and Other Stories (1887)
The Story of Charles Strange (1888)
Featherston's Story. A Tale by Johnny Ludlow (1889)
The Unholy Wish and Other Stories (1890)
The House of Halliwell. A Novel (1890)
Ashley and Other Stories (1897)
Victor Serenus (1898)

Johnny Ludlow. Fifth series (1899)
Johnny Ludlow. Sixth series (1899)

Translations

Les Channing. Traduit de l'Anglais par Mme Abric-Encontre (1864)
Les Filles de Lord Oakburn: Roman traduit de l'anglais par L. Bochet (1876)
La Gloire des Verner: Roman traduit de l'anglais par L. de L'Estrive (1878)
Le Serment de Lady Adelaïde: Roman traduit de l'anglais par Léon Bochet (1878)